Shadows and Lies

a&b

Shadows and Lies

MARJORIE ECCLES

This edition first published in Great Britain in 2006 by
Allison & Busby Limited
13 Charlotte Mews
London W1T 4EJ

A catalogue record for this book is available from
the British Library.

10 9 8 7 6 5 4 3 2 1
ISBN 0 7490 8239 9
ISBN 978-0-7490-8239-0

Printed and bound in Great Britain by
Bookmarque Ltd, Croydon, Surrey

MARJORIE ECCLES was born in Yorkshire and spent much of her childhood there and on the Northumbrian coast. The author of over twenty books, serials and short stories, she is the recipient of the Agatha Christie Short Story Styles Award. Living on the edge of the Black Country, where she taught creative writing, inspired the acclaimed Gil Mayo series. A keen gardener, she now lives with her husband in Hertfordshire.

Also by Marjorie Eccles

Novels
The Shape of Sand
Killing a Unicorn
Pandora's Box
Echoes of Silence

Gil Mayo series
Cast a Cold Eye
Death of a Good Woman
Requiem for a Dove
More Deaths Than One
Late of This Parish
The Company She Kept
An Accidental Shroud
A Death of Distinction
A Species of Revenge
Killing Me Softly
The Superintendent's Daughter
A Sunset Touch
Untimely Graves

Collected Short Stories
Account Rendered

1909

MARCH

The exercise book stares accusingly back at me, its pages as blank as when I first opened the book. After half an hour, I don't yet have the faintest idea how to start.

There they stay, the lost years, tantalisingly beyond my reach, and for perhaps the hundredth time, I ask myself why I am able to remember nearly everything about my life up to a certain point, but not the time between then and my present situation? What fate has decreed my life should be split in two – and that I should simply have no recollection about what happened in that gap? Nine years have been effectively erased from my consciousness, so successfully that I might never have lived through them. The dark suspicion that I might well never know what happened to me during that time doesn't bear thinking about.

Dr Harvill has suggested that if I start at the beginning and focus all my concentration on writing down that part of my life I do remember, the missing years may follow quite naturally. Well, he is a professional mind doctor, he should know. Myself, I am sceptical. But since I have nothing to lose – and nothing much else to do, either, and perhaps everything to gain – I suppose it cannot do any harm to do as he suggests.

So here I am, in my house in St John's Wood, sitting at my desk, a small walnut davenport with drawers at the side and a sloping top; an elegant piece of furniture, like the chairs and the coromandel wood table, the upright piano with the tasselled runner across its top, and the cushioned sofa. Did I choose any of these pieces myself? Did I decide on the narrow, elegant vases on the mantelpiece? The pictures? Occasionally, I have lightning stabs of near-memory about little things: I can almost believe I see myself stitching that silk cushion over there, buying the sheet music for The Merry Widow *that I found in the piano stool, but perhaps not. I am more inclined to believe that it is wishful thinking, since I cannot even remember how many years I've lived in this house, when I first came, or if indeed I've always been alone here, except for someone like Rosa – though this seems unlikely. There are, after all, those presences, sometimes glimpsed, sometimes just sensed, which must mean something.*

So what, precisely, do I know? Almost everything about my early life, at any rate. I know that I was born in 1876, which makes me thirty-three years old. I know that my name was Hannah Jackson, and yet the money in the bank is in the name of Smith, which is a great mystery in itself, since I never had any money. I wear a wedding ring, so I am presumably Mrs Smith, and however that came about I still haven't fathomed. The name seems as improbable as the title of Mrs, since I have no recollection of any husband. Although...

Yes, if I am honest, that is one thing I do not need to question; I have known what it is to be married. How else would I have these unsatisfied longings, that memory of passion, and love?

I apparently own this house and have a small but adequate income from investments. I have learned that I was injured in an accident when I was riding on the top of a London omnibus, one blowy morning last autumn. And now it's March, and I still remember nothing of it, except for that one last, blinding moment, that piercingly clear picture which flashed across my eyes before I lost consciousness: the runaway brewer's dray colliding with the motor omnibus in the milling traffic on Ludgate Hill; the shouts and cries of the passengers; the barrels rolling all over the road; the screams of the horses... 'Trauma' (which is what Dr Harvill calls the state occasioned by that blow to the head which I received in the accident) has effectively erased what went before it.

This sitting-room of mine is a comfortable, even luxurious room; not ostentatious, but certainly not the room of someone who has ever had to watch the pennies. The bright fire has been lit by my maid, Rosa. She is the one who cooks and keeps everything spotless, with the help of a woman to do the rough. The household consists only of Rosa and myself, so the work is undemanding.

She has become something more than a servant, Rosa Tartaryan, though not yet someone I can regard as a friend. A dark, intense woman, she has her own friends, whom I've yet to meet; she is part of a small circle of Balkan émigrés, who seem to exist in a shadowy half-world, meeting in gloomy cafés and plotting ways in which they can return to their own country. Revenge is what they want, for the bloodshed and misery inflicted on their people by the Turks who have occupied their land. She came to England in a roundabout way, exactly how I've never been able to discover, for no one can be more tight-lipped than Rosa when she wishes to keep her own

counsel. She says she came to work for me in answer to an advertisement I had inserted in The Gentlewoman, just before the accident. In the absence of any evidence to the contrary, I must believe
her.

Though she dislikes talking about her own past – I have the feeling that terrible things may have happened to her before she reached
England – she is forever trying to get me to talk about the old days,
in an effort to help me remember my lost years. She never presses me
too much, which is not like fierce Rosa – so that I occasionally have
the feeling she knows more than she pretends, despite her assurances
that she wasn't with me in what I always think of as The Time
Before: those lost years. She is much the same age as me; she looks
after me well, cooking nourishing, tasty meals to which I fail to do
justice. The clothes in my wardrobe, from my previous existence,
don't fit. Rosa tut-tuts over me and says I'm nothing but skin and
bone, and will become ill again, but I don't care. There is nothing,
as far as I am aware, for me to live for. Inside, I feel dead.

I am apathetic about this trying to remember: in fact, I am sure
Dr Harvill believes me downright perverse, though this, I think, is
rather than admit his methods are not working. But why should I
even try? Knowledge of those lost years, I feel sure, will bring me
nothing but pain. But in the dream last night, I again saw the boy,
and though I haven't today glimpsed his shadow-self, his mischievous, faun-like face, as I've always done previously after dreaming
of him, I feel the pain even more than usual; and something small
and hard and stubborn inside me is insisting that for his sake I
should do as Dr Harvill suggests and make some effort.

Very well, then, I will. But not until it is finished will I show it
to the doctor. It's not exactly that I don't trust him, though he is a
little too smooth for my liking; his answers come too quickly, his
solutions sound too pat. Yet who am I to question his methods?
Perhaps they will work, after all.

I stare out over the small, pleasant garden. I can see other gardens
along the quiet street, several of them with forsythia bushes making
a great show, and suddenly, I see the forsythias Mrs Crowther
ordered to be planted at Bridge End House.

They'll do well enough for a beginning.

Chapter One

He hadn't let them know he was coming, but that was Sebastian all over.

He and Louisa had driven all the way down into Shropshire through intermittent, heavy rain, arriving in the village in the middle of a thunderstorm. He drew up to her father's house and she made a quick dash to the door, throwing a cheerful goodbye over her shoulder and disappearing inside with a shake of her umbrella and a wave of her hand. Having driven circumspectly enough until then, Sebastian put his foot down, at last able to give his new Austin Ascot the full reign of its fifteen horse-power, taking the next two miles at a reckless thirty miles an hour along the narrow lanes towards the lodge gates of Belmonde.

Thunder continued to roll over the distant hills, the skies wept and draughts insinuated themselves round his ankles. As the vehicle sluiced up the long, rising drive, winding through the mixed conifers and huge banks of dripping rhododendrons, so magnificent in spring, so ineffably dreary in the wet, his cheerfulness began to evaporate. The motorcar hood had given little protection from the rain which drove in at the sides and without Louisa, small as she was, beside him, he felt cold, damp, and acutely conscious of her absence. The depressing thought came to him that it always rained when he came home these days, perhaps echoing his mood. The pathetic fallacy, as Louisa might say: nature possessing human feelings.

It was nothing of the kind, of course – the truth was, he was simply annoyed with himself for having declined to go across the Channel to Longchamps for the racing with Inky Winthrop, a decision that had left him twiddling his thumbs in a London tiresomely bereft of friends and acquaintances. The weather hadn't helped, of course. The exhausted end of summer had turned wet and cold, with London permanently wrapped in rain, umbrella spokes catching you in the eye whenever you went out, and everyone splashing duck-footed about the pavements. The theatres had nothing new to offer and with the House in recession, there were none of the usual hullabaloos issuing from Westminster to cause a bit of excitement: even the Irish were quiet. Most of his other friends were up in Scotland, shooting grouse, and moreover, every amusing young woman he knew seemed to have taken herself off abroad to capture the last few weeks of sun in Biarritz or Monte Carlo or some such place. Pretty little Violet Clerihugh was in San Remo with her mother, and Sebastian, having just emerged, blinking like a mole, from the concerns which had occupied him exclusively for weeks, and feeling he needed a respite to refresh himself, was left disconsolate for many reasons, and short of cash. In a nutshell, he was thoroughly put out.

Though nothing like as much as Louisa, tossing her bright brown hair, incandescent with fury about the arrest and imprisonment of one of those dangerous women's rights persons she so admired, declaring that the treatment being meted out to this woman in prison – confinement and the appalling threat of being fed by force if she persisted in her hunger strike – was nothing short of inhuman. If anything was needed to sway Louisa from an admiring but reluctant hesitation on the brink of the women's suffrage cause, that was it. After having begun to think her enthusiasm had at last begun to wane, Sebastian was now very much afraid she might be poised to plunge right in. He hoped that her father, over the next few days, would make her see sense. He was the only one who might.

Louisa was very good at advising other people, not so good at listening to what was best for herself. She'd neatly turned the tables when Sebastian had tried to steer her away from such dangerous involvement: "Oh, stuff! Involvement's what being alive is all about, isn't it?" When he hadn't replied, she'd added abruptly, giving him a very direct look, "You'll have face up to the facts some time, you know, stop fooling around and start taking things seriously. It's been nearly a year, after all."

"Dearest Louisa, you should know by now I'm not cut out for taking life seriously."

"Oh, Seb!" Then, sighing softly, "All right, sorry. Sorry." She said no more, and he'd been grateful that she hadn't pressed this particular, emotionally fraught point.

After all, she wasn't to know (though he thought she might suspect) that it wasn't the fact of his brother's death he couldn't face – it was the consequences resulting from it that weighed him down. When Harry, after resigning his commission in the regiment had, more for the devilment of it than anything, got himself taken on as a war correspondent for the *Daily Bugle* during the struggle against the Boers more than a decade ago now, it had forced them all to accept that the golden boy, Harry, everyone's darling, might not, after all, be invulnerable. Wholly admiring, and envious of his brother, but prepared for grave news at any time, Sebastian, then still a schoolboy, had first become aware of what would inevitably follow if the inconceivable were to happen, and Harry should be killed: that the mantle of heir to Belmonde, which his elder brother wore with such debonair ease, would then fall upon his own shoulders. Harry, however, had continued to lead his usual charmed life, showing incredible bravery in getting his despatches through and emerging from the war with barely a scratch – only to die last year in that shockingly inglorious way. Leaving Sebastian back where he started, seeing no possibility of doing anything more exciting with his life than fulfilling the role of a country gentleman, when what he wanted was...well, he hadn't known what – until now. But, afraid of tempting fate, aware of battles ahead, so far he'd mentioned nothing of that to anyone, not even Louisa.

In the dark afternoon, a sudden sharp curve appeared in the long winding drive. Although he knew every inch of the road and that particular bend was very familiar to him, the speed at which he was travelling had made him take it faster than he ought (though he was unlikely to encounter anything other than a pheasant from the game preserves either side) so that when he saw the – the *apparition*, was how he afterwards thought of it – he wasn't able to stop immediately. As soon as he could, he slowed and reversed back round the curve to the same spot, but now he could see nothing. It must have been some trick of the light, he told himself, that had made him think he'd seen the figure of a woman, wrapped in a heavy coat and with a hat pulled low over her eyes, standing a few yards back from the drive in the shadow of a dripping larch. Almost as if she'd heard the approach of the motor car and hoped not to be seen.

Yet still unwilling to believe she'd been a figment of his imagination, for Sebastian was not given to fancies, and was gallant enough not to wish to leave any woman alone in such conditions (despite the hat and coat, she must have been soaked to the skin, for she hadn't appeared to have even an umbrella to protect her) he stayed for a while until his eyes should become accustomed to the gloom under the trees, trying to convince himself that they hadn't been playing him tricks. Another lightning flash, however, lit up the scene and showed it to be quite devoid of any human presence – unless the woman was unaccountably hiding behind some tree or, more likely, had turned and hurried back the way she had come. The lightning was followed very soon by a great clap of thunder and another torrential cloudburst. More unnerved than he should have been by the occurrence, he drove forward again, this time more circumspectly, dismissing it from his mind.

The drive opened out presently and there appeared in front of him Belmonde Abbey; an abbey no longer, not for nigh on four centuries, but a sprawling pink brick-and-sandstone house which had grown in a haphazard manner on the original site. Nothing to speak of architecturally...parts had been added, and others demolished at the whim of subsequent owners, with scant regard for aesthetics, and its manifold crenellations and turrets were an affront to Sebastian's sense of style – but he'd grown up with it and regarded it with an exasperated affection. Unprepossessing under the lashing rain, creeper covered, it was anchored to the earth by surrounding trees on three sides and on its front by a parterre of four circular and four ogee flower beds. These were placed with geometric precision within a smooth grass square, which itself was weighted at strategic points by the solidity of yew topiary clipped into perfect spheres and cones. A design much approved of by his father.

Ignoring this horrid sight, Sebastian drew up to the front door in a scatter of wet gravel and stopped the engine. Leaving the motor where it was, he dashed up the front steps through the pelting rain and burst into the hall before the footman could get to the door to open it.

"Mr Sebastian! How very good to see you."

This was Blythe, arriving hard on the heels of the footman, only a little breathless, quickly regaining his composure at being thus outflanked, mortified to think the famed hospitality at Belmonde was lacking in welcome, even by the unexpected arrival of the young master.

"It's OK, Mr Blythe," said Sebastian, disregarding the old butler's pained expression at the use of the Americanism, and allowing himself to be divested of his waterproof coat, and his cap. "Anyone at home?"

An unaccustomed air of quietness hung about the house, making him wonder belatedly if he hadn't been too hasty in his decision to come down without first ensuring that his mother would actually be here, or whether she was away on a Saturday-to-Monday at some friend's country house. There were no mandatory events in the social calendar she might be attending, at this dead end of the season, but it did occur to him that he hadn't come across her for some time at any of these sort of occasions, which was where he most often met his mother. For the last few years, Sebastian had had his own bachelor rooms in Albemarle Street.

Blythe, however, informed him that all the family were at home. "A quiet weekend has been planned. Her Ladyship has been slightly indisposed, and she and Sir Henry – and your grandmother – are all here. The only guests are Mrs and Miss Cashmore. Fortunately, no others were expected."

Thank God for that, thought Sebastian, suppressing a groan at the thought of the Cashmores. An empty house, without his mother's support in his approach to his father, would have meant a wasted journey. It would have been even worse to have arrived to find the place full of the same set forever encountered in one country house or another – but he frowned. "My mother, ill? And no one let me know, Mr Blythe – why was that, I wonder?"

"It was nothing serious, I understand. She is much improved."

"I'm relieved to hear it."

"Yes, quite well again, though I believe she is resting at the moment. Sir Henry is in the business room."

"In that case," said Sebastian hastily, "I won't disturb him. Have my bags seen to, there's a good fellow. I'll just have a wash and then I'll go and see my grandmother."

"You will not be regarding this – attachment – with any seriousness, of course, Sebastian," stated his grandmother, Lady Emily Chetwynd, approaching her subject at once, but smiling. "Dalliance with a village maiden is all very well, dear boy, almost a rite of passage, one might say, but you have enough good sense to be aware that one – especially you – must always have regard to the future."

Sebastian automatically returned her smile – a reflection of his own, a sideways smile and one that showed great charm. He wasn't particularly handsome, or not quite so obviously so as Harry had been, but he had an open, pleasingly mobile face showing a quick intelligence, and a readiness to smile that quickly endeared him to people. Folding his long legs and perching on the stool near to where his grandmother sat, very upright on the edge of her chair, declining the use of the backrest for support, he reached out and took her hand, bending his head over it to avoid her quick old eyes. Gently he adjusted her rings, which had recently been enlarged to fit over the swollen knuckles and which consequently slipped about loosely above them. The softness of her hands was eloquent testimony to the fact that she'd never had need to do a day's work in her life, but even Lady Emily was mortal, and arthritis was no respecter of persons. Apart from a stick to help her rise from her seat more gracefully, however, she allowed no concessions to painful joints.

Sebastian, though exceedingly fond of his grandmother, was in fact surprised by how angry her words had made him – in so far as he ever was angry, for he was too easy-going to let such emotions trouble him overmuch. But Louisa, to whom Lady Emily was referring jocularly (though not by any means as jocularly as a stranger might suppose) was not in any circumstances to be regarded as a subject for jest.

"Dash it, I only gave her a lift from Town. You've got it all wrong, Grandmama. There's no question at all of any – attachment, as you put it. Louisa's a jolly girl, but there's nothing remotely like that between us. Too clever for me, for one thing."

"Yes, I'm quite aware of Louisa's intelligence – and my admiration for her knows no bounds," she returned drily, "but being a clever young woman with strong opinions does not preclude the possibility of falling in love with the wrong person. On the contrary, I've often observed that people of high intelligence do not always possess much common sense."

"Well then, since I don't know anybody with much *more* common sense than Louisa, you needn't be afraid she's in the least in love with me," returned Sebastian, with a laugh that was not quite as light as he might have hoped. "And besides —"

"Besides what, my dear boy?"

"Oh, nothing."

He knew this was an infuriating reply. His grandmother, much as he loved her and admired her indomitable courage, invariably had the effect of reducing him to the language and attitudes of the schoolroom, though he hoped she didn't mean to. But devil take it – Louisa! She was coming down a bit hard on someone he'd known all his life, someone he'd always thought she liked. Not good enough in her eyes for a Chetwynd, of course (Lady Emily was herself the daughter of an earl), especially not the heir. As children, the Chetwynd and Fox families had played together without any of the stuffy social distinctions so many people thought fit to perpetuate. To his mother indeed, with her transatlantic tolerance, such nuances – or so she declared – were absurd, they could have played with the under-gardeners' children for all she cared. Besides, the Fox's were so charming, all of them, with their easy manners and good looks. Even Sir Henry hadn't objected to friendship with them, and was civil enough with their father when he invited him to dine at Belmonde, as he ritually did, once or twice a year, in the interests of good neighbourly relations. Eccentric as Augustus Fox was, his was a decent family, after all. Not the same class as the Chetwynds, but respectable. Louisa's maternal grandfather had been an archdeacon, and Augustus himself had been a much esteemed Oxford scholar in his day.

The only problem, as far as Sebastian was concerned, was: who would be good enough for Louisa? A question which had recently begun to occur to him with surprising and troubling regularity.

Lady Emily picked up her tapestry, destined for a fire screen, in which game birds and other fauna gambolled wantonly together amongst autumn foliage, and dexterously threaded her needle with scarlet wool. Despite her painful fingers, she did a little work on her project each day, as a discipline. "Well, it's good to see you," she said, changing the subject. "How long is it since you've been down, you disgraceful boy?"

"Too long, perhaps, Grandmama," Sebastian admitted. "But I'm forever bumping into Mama in London, you know – and Father, too, sometimes, though he's always so dashed busy, seeing to his affairs. When he's there, that is."

Lady Emily did not immediately reply. Sebastian, too, thought he had better not elaborate this point. It was becoming all too increasingly obvious that his father was inclined to spend less and less time away from Belmonde, that Adèle was often left to attend social functions alone in Town and elsewhere; though this left her free, of course, to entertain and be entertained, to attend concerts, theatre and the opera, all of which were anathema to her husband; to shop or to slip across to Paris to visit her dressmaker. To do as she wished, in fact.

The silence lengthened between them as Lady Emily stitched on, and thought about Sebastian. It was all very well to say let the boy sow his wild oats, as his mother did – he was a young man, and young men needed their diversions; a gay life was only to be expected – but that sort of thing could not go on forever. He had been through the requisite wild, reckless period but she was optimistic that it was now over, though she did not care for some of the young bloods he called his friends, such as George (Inky) Winthrop, his old schoolfellow, who spent too much time at the races, or so she heard through the grapevine. And he still showed more inclination to gallivant around Greece and Italy with a sketchbook than to find himself a useful occupation which might be the making of him: the Army, perhaps, or even politics, like her second son Monty, though not, she thought, the Church. He was in no hurry either, it seemed, to look for a suitable wife who would provide him with a son and heir, and she was afraid of that independent streak in him that might at any time make him marry someone unsuitable: Louisa Fox, for example.

He said abruptly, in the way he often had of picking up her thoughts, "It's all a nonsense, isn't it? I've never wanted – all this, you know, Grandmama." He had no need to elaborate his meaning, but he added, "Harry would have done it so much better than I."

"Do you really think so?"

For a moment darkness lay between them: things which could not be said. Not for the first time, Sebastian wondered how much his grandmother knew – or guessed – about Harry's private concerns. Then she rallied. "It cannot be helped, the way life turns around. Don't sulk over it, Sebastian dear. It's not in your nature. And the sooner you accept the inevitable, that you are now the heir and there is nothing you can do about it – and a great deal more you should be doing – the happier we shall all be."

It was briskly said, though Lady Emily had not meant the advice unkindly. It was what her grandson needed to hear, little as he wished to. At the moment, his mind was as stubbornly set as his father's.

"There's no hurry. You know Father wouldn't thank me for pushing my nose in. He must do everything himself, doesn't trust anyone else."

Lady Emily sighed. Indeed. She must speak to Henry. It was high time her eldest son came to his senses and realised that he and Sebastian had both taken up a stance from which it was difficult to back down, though one of them had better do so. It might seem to her grandson that there was no hurry, but Lady Emily was no stranger to the sudden vicissitudes of fortune and knew it was dangerous to discount them – look at what had happened to Harry. And Henry did have an alarmingly high colour at times, just like his father, who'd died of an apoplexy when he was fifty, leaving Henry with a mass of debts, enormous death duties, a run-down estate and not much idea how to go about setting things right. Given his nature, however, Henry had immediately buckled down and learned how to do so. Since then, he'd become more and more wrapped up in Belmonde, giving little thought to anything other than the conviction that his heir should never be left to pick up the pieces as he had been – in itself an undoubtedly laudable ambition. The irony of it was that Henry and his son were at loggerheads not, Lady Emily was sure, because Sebastian was unwilling to learn how to shoulder his future responsibilities but rather that he was convinced – with some justification – that his father couldn't accept that everything would not run away out of control should he let go of the reins for one single moment. While Henry chose to believe his son was congenitally bone idle. She often felt she would like to knock their heads together.

It was Sebastian's turn to change the subject. "What's all this about my mother being ill?"

"Not ill, my dear, just a trifle under the weather. I don't think it's anything much, though I do believe she's worried about Sylvia – which, of course, is the last thing she would admit. Your sister has apparently taken up with this frightful woman from India who has persuaded her to join some peculiar sect."

"Annie Besant," returned Sebastian gloomily. "I have heard rumours."

"That's the name, Annie Besant." Lady Emily's lips pressed together. The woman was dangerous, a radical. A person who took up with one cause after another. To be sure, her championship of those poor little girls who worked with phosphorous in the match factories had caused some improvement in their terrible working conditions. But she was also outspoken on taboo subjects such as birth control, and had indeed – quite rightly – been prosecuted for publishing material on the same subject as likely to deprave or corrupt those whose minds were open to immoral influences. Well, at least Lady Emily couldn't see Sylvia being caught up in anything like that...though one had hardly thought her inclined to religion, either. Perhaps it was her childless state, after seven years of marriage, which was, contrary to appearances, worrying her and causing her to turn to whatever might bring her hope.

"I am right in assuming, am I not," she enquired with a dangerous inflection, "that this Besant woman now calls herself a Theologist?" She drove her needle through the red eye of a particularly haughty-looking pheasant.

"Theosophist."

"Theosophist, then. Let us not split hairs."

Sebastian, knowing her views on the subject, thought that he had better not add that Annie Besant was also a sympathiser with the women's suffrage movement. One dangerous thing at a time.

"No wonder your poor mother is worried. It's worse than I thought. I believe those people believe in Buddha and reincarnation and no red meat – and free love to boot, I have no doubt," Lady Emily stated with ill-informed exaggeration.

Sebastian shrugged. "Algy should put his foot down."

"Algy? Oh, my dear!"

Well, no, perhaps not.

Sylvia had married well, but Algy Eustace-Bragge was – in Sebastian's words – an awful muff, despite being able to give Sylvia every material thing a woman could want. Her grandmother, however, suspected Sylvia did not have it all her own way, something which she understood and rather approved of: a man should be master in his own house, while at the same time, a woman should be capable of getting what she wanted, without resorting to outright dominance. She herself had never had any difficulty in bringing Chetwynd around to doing exactly as she wished. It was something upon which she and her daughter-in-law were at one. Henry was putty in Adèle's hands, though she was clever enough not to let him know this. Which was just as well, because Henry, ever since he was a child, could only be pushed so far. Since his marriage, his mother had learned that applied to his wife, too.

Despite herself, she had become quite fond of Adèle, able to overlook the fact that her father had made his fortune in meat-packing in Chicago, and not only because she had most certainly saved the fortunes of the Chetwynd family – if only temporarily. From the fastness of her own unmodernised wing at Belmonde, where nothing, not a stick of furniture or a piece of wallpaper, had been changed for half a century, Lady Emily observed with a keen eye the changes Adèle had brought to Belmonde, and while she certainly did not approve of everything, she had found it expedient, on the whole, not to interfere. Adèle was not, as she had expected a daughter-in-law to be, biddable. She knew how to charm, but she had an iron will and was unscrupulous in getting what she wanted, despite being deceptively softly-spoken, and entirely agreeable. Indeed, she quite often got the better of her mother-in-law, which few people did.

There was no denying Adèle was hopelessly extravagant, renowned for her hospitality and the lavish parties she loved to give, never mind that Henry thought them – and most of that circle of those so-called clever people she liked to call her friends, come to that – largely a waste of time and money; he was terrified of being cajoled into joining them in their after-dinner pencil and paper games; he could not have composed an epigram if his life had depended upon it.

"Speaking of your mother," said Lady Emily, glancing at the gold fob watch pinned to the armour-plated elegance of her splendid bosom, and putting an end to disagreeable thoughts for the time being, "I told her I would join her for tea. Shall we go along?"

Chapter Two

"Don't light the lamps, Margaret. It's so pleasant here in the fire-light, with the rain outside."

Louisa, now warm and dry, leaned back and settled her head against the comfortably cushioned inglenook seat and stretched her legs to the great fireplace, heaped with blazing oak logs. Her father and her sister Margaret, a fair-haired woman of mild disposition, sat on a similar seat, opposite. Between them was a laden tea-table, and behind them the large, shadowy room that stretched across the width of the house. The firelight winked on shining brass and copper and polished floors, throwing long, leaping shadows on to the low ceiling and into hidden corners, and Louisa thought how lovely it was to be home. Yet for all that, she would not permanently exchange it for her freedom, her frugal little room in London.

This need for independence (she was studying at the London School of Medicine for Women in Bloomsbury) was something Margaret would never completely understand. Louisa caught the anxious glance cast in her direction before her sister turned to spear a crumpet on the two-foot long toasting fork and hold it to the fire. She ought not worry so much, it made her look every one of her thirty-five years, though she probably couldn't help that by now; it had become a habit.

Margaret's next words reproached Louisa with their sweet concern. "You look tired, Louisa, are you sure you're not at your books too much?"

Louisa smiled and shrugged, though if the truth be told, she did feel a trifle listless, an unusual state for her. She might be small, but she made up for it in energy.

"Fiddle-faddle!" their father intervened robustly, taking another scone. "Since when did studying ever hurt anyone?"

"Not you, at any rate." Louisa smiled affectionately. "What are you working on now, Father?"

"I must show it to you." He became loquacious, explaining his latest enthusiasm, a contraption he'd made, involving two revolving glass plates and a thin metal wiper, a machine designed by a fellow called Wimshurst to demonstrate the workings of electricity. Now that he'd finished it, in time to show his small grandsons when they came to visit, he could get back to The Book. For as long as Louisa could remember, Gus had been engaged in compiling a tome (which no one, not even himself, realistically ever expected to be finished), comprehensively and ambitiously entitled "The Complete Lepidoptera of the British Isles." Now retired from his practice as a doctor, he spent most of his time scratching at his manuscript – when some new experiment or idea wasn't catching his fancy – poring over his butterflies and insects or venturing out to catch them with his net. His disinclination to kill other wild animals did not endear him to the local hunting fraternity, but this worried him not one whit.

"There's too much flame on the logs, you'll burn that crumpet, Meg," said Louisa. "I'm only tired because I was up late last night after attending a meeting."

"Your suffragettes?" Margaret nearly lost her crumpet in the fire as she turned to gaze at her sister. "Oh, my dear, I do hope you're not going to become too involved!"

"Of course not, you know I can't afford to let anything get in the way until I've qualified. I've no time for anything else," answered Louisa impatiently.

"At least that's something to be thankful for. How can these women submit themselves to the prospect of such degradation? How can they be so unladylike? Disgracing themselves. Screaming, being carried off kicking by the police! And as for hunger striking...I've read that there's talk of actually feeding them by force." Margaret's indignant face was vividly flushed, perhaps from being too near the fire. She herself would never dream of being associated with anything of the sort, but one could never be sure with Louisa. The twelve years' difference in their ages might have been thirty, so differently did they view life.

"More than talk – there's at least one of my friends, at this very moment, who is refusing to eat and is being force fed."

"What?" Two shocked faces were towards her.

"I daresay she feels the cause is worth it," Louisa said. "But as a doctor – an embryo one, at least – it horrifies me. As a woman, it enrages me. It's an utter abomination, whichever way you look at it. Now they've started, they will carry on. One day, some woman will die, and then perhaps they'll take some notice."

"Then they shouldn't refuse to eat. But oh, Louie, it would surely never come to that?"

"It could, Margaret," came from their father. A doctor himself, he could not but be in full agreement with Louisa's views on this unspeakable practice. At the same time, though he had a certain sympathy for the cause she espoused, he agreed with Margaret; it was self-inflicted, and in any case, such extreme methods were unlikely to have the desired effect, he was sure. These women were right in their aims and ideas, but the way in which they were trying to forward them could only be counter-productive. Putting people's backs up, throwing bricks and stones like street urchins, damaging property. The last time he'd seen Louisa, she'd been on fire with an idea which was being mooted, that of organising a regiment of women to descend on the West End of London, mingle with the homegoing workers and then shatter as many shop windows as they could. Deliberately get themselves arrested and sent to prison, in order to make an open stand for their rights, no doubt to achieve the same end result as this mistaken young woman Louisa had spoken about – a flamboyant gesture which had unpleasant undertones of martyrdom. But his fears for Louisa's safety forbade him to voice such thoughts, aware that his younger daughter needed little encouragement. Despite her denial of any participation, the words 'not yet' had hung in the air, and he was only too afraid that when she had gained her qualifications, she would instantly become more active in support of this franchise business. Louisa had been a tomboy and could throw a cricket ball with the best of them. Hurling a stone through Swan & Edgar's window wasn't that much different, after all. He sighed. Out of all his seven children, he had a special bond with Louisa, which was why she worried him most – even he, easy-going, eternal optimist that he was.

"I would have thought, Louisa," Margaret ventured, "that you'd seen enough of fighting for causes to know what damage can ensue."

Gus threw her an affectionately exasperated glance. Margaret had no tact, though she was good as gold. When his dear Ellen had died in late childbirth this eldest daughter of his had self-lessly assumed her mother's role, thereby missing her chances of marriage. She appeared quite content to remain here, seemingly forever, satisfied to be nothing more than a homemaker in the same tradition as her dead mother. Her self-effacement had not rubbed off on to Alice; the baby she'd brought up had become a blithe and confident child, though she, too, lacked Louisa's vehe-mence. Louisa, of course, had enough of that for all three.

"Oh, I don't forget that, Margaret," she was saying now, "how could I? My one and only adventure."

"No doubt there will be others."

Louisa threw her a quick glance, but her sister's profile remained as serene as ever, her eyes innocent of guile. Sometimes, Louisa wanted to shake her composure with true stories of what had really happened to her during that legendary escapade but mostly, she wanted nothing more than to forget it. She was sick and tired of having to remember, and to recount for people's entertainment tales of what had happened to her when she was still a child. It was not, and never had been, in her opin-ion, a subject for entertainment – in fact, the whole episode, despite its heroism, had been so much talked about that it was in danger of becoming a tremendous bore. Over and done with, it should be relegated to the past, where it belonged. As far as she was concerned, the best thing to come out of that experience was that it had decided her future. From that time on, she had known that the only thing she wanted to do was to study medicine and become a lady doctor – regardless of the fact that the title was still regarded as being a contradiction in terms by many people.

Margaret's voice broke into her thoughts. "What a pity Sebastian couldn't spare the time to have tea with us," she mur-mured, accepting her father's cup for another refill.

"I asked him, but he wanted to get home."

"Only natural, I suppose – I scarcely remember the last time he was at Belmonde."

"Since he only gets a lecture from his father every time he does come down, one can scarcely blame him for that."

There was a short silence, and Gus added pacifically, "Sir Henry's naturally hoping for a great deal from Sebastian now. He suffered a hard blow in losing Harry."

"So have they all suffered, Papa," Louisa said sharply, trying to banish from her mind the worry she'd had quite often lately, that one of these days Sir Henry's patent disapproval might cause Sebastian to do something quite stupid and irrational, which he would certainly later regret.

"Quite so," Gus agreed, as neutrally as he was able. To lose a son so young – and one so attractive, so full of life and charm and promise as Harry had been – and still to be alive oneself…the old left behind, the young taken…Gus had seen this many times in the course of his working life, and had never come to terms with the sadness of it. He did not like Sir Henry – or not very much – but he could sympathise with the views of a man in his position. Harry had had his faults, of course, but they had been forgotten; he was remembered – and perhaps should be – for his quickness of spirit, the smiles that could charm the birds off the trees, and his jokes. But Gus suspected that his brother's elevation to sainthood since his death must be an added burden for Sebastian to bear.

Well, no doubt everything would take care of itself, given time. Every family coped with grief in its own way. What worried him more was the growing intimacy between this, his dearest girl, and Sebastian. Louisa was well able to take care of herself, of that he had no doubts, but the two young people had been thrown together in London, and from what he could gather, they were now very thick and spent more time together than he would have thought mere friendship dictated, when of course anything closer than that was doomed. Gus was extremely fond of the young man, but…Louisa and Sebastian, no, it simply wouldn't do. Their upbringing, their destinies, were too far apart. Marriage between them wasn't to be thought of. It wasn't only their different stations in life, or that Gus was afraid his dearest daughter wouldn't acquit herself properly among these people (he was proud that Louisa could hold her own anywhere) but that the aimless, pleasure-loving existence of Sebastian and his acquaintances would very soon get on her nerves. Work, to her, and a purpose in life, was the very backbone of existence, it made you what you were, a principle she had inherited from him.

Chapter Three

Sebastian's arrival at Belmonde had made no difference to his father's routine. Sir Henry took his tea in his business room, as he invariably did, excusing himself from joining Adèle on the grounds that he had no time to waste. In fact, he was addicted to tea, which he had brought in to him in a giant teapot at intervals throughout the day, and which it pleased him to drink from a workman's pint mug, an eccentricity which would not have been appreciated in his wife's drawing room. The truth was he felt out of place there: the potted palms and the heavy scent of the tuberoses, gardenias and other exotic flowers she loved, and ordered to be brought in from the hot-houses in opulent profusion, made him feel claustrophobic. The room's delicate colours, the watercolours in gilt frames, the draped ivory silk shades over the lamps, the white fur rugs, made him uneasy, as though he might have brought something in on the sole of his shoe – a not improbable supposition, given the amount of time he spent in the stables and on his farms.

He would, in fact, have liked nothing better than to spend every day of his life at Belmonde, and signified this by donning Norfolk jacket and knickerbockers immediately he came down, only changing into anything else under protest. Begrudging any time spent elsewhere, he kept up with the demands of the social season only when necessary, to appease his wife, for he did not, like the rest of his family, or so he repeatedly said, need the constant stimulus of the outside world.

So, on this miserable, wet afternoon, following an unprecedented series of events which had shaken him to the core of his being, he lit one of the Egyptian cigarettes he always smoked, and took a welcome swig of the extra-strong Indian tea he preferred. A naturally dark and gloomy place, the business room was made even darker by oak panelling and high bookshelves in the fireplace alcoves which contained mouldering, leather-bound volumes rarely, if ever, taken down. The light from the single, green-shaded lamp on the desk threw the corners of the room into deep shadow and glanced off a series of steel engravings over the mantelpiece. A rubbed and buttoned velveteen sofa, once a fine Victorian peacock colour but now faded to a patchy and indeterminate greyish green, provided a repository for half a dozen amorphous cushions and a crotcheted and fringed Afghan shawl. This room, and the gun room which led off it, comprised the heart of his own little kingdom. Now, while the dogs, after their walk, snored and steamed damply on the moth-eaten zebra skin spread in front of the fire, Sir Henry sat in his fat brown leather chair which had, over the years, sagged in the seat, split on the arms, and accommodated itself comfortably to his form, while his land agent sat opposite.

"Well, now, Seton," he began, forcing his attention on to the serious business of replenishing the yew hedges along the park boundary, by the Seven Oak Field, which had caught some sort of disease and were apparently dying off.

"Must come out, all of them."

Although the fifth baronet had every last detail of the management of the estate at his fingertips, he was undoubtedly helped by having such a competent agent as Alexander Seton, a cultivated and amiable man with whom Henry had been at school. He had taken up estate management after suffering a severe reversal of his fortunes when his father died, leaving him with a mountain of debts to pay off and no alternative but to sell his family home in Northumberland. That this, a situation similar to, but so much worse than Henry's own, could happen to Seton (whose wife had been a Percy) had so shocked Henry that he'd agreed to employ his friend as his agent. He was cautious, however, about letting him have his head, and Seton might have resented this had he been temperamentally less amiable, but as it was, Henry's controlling and overriding need to be in on every last detail suited them both, and had ultimately resulted in a long and mutually rewarding partnership.

Henry pushed back his chair, walked restlessly over to the fire and stirred it with the brass poker, then added another large lump of coal from the scuttle with the tongs. "By the way, you were right, Seton. Had a look at Jordan's cottage when I was up there with the dogs this afternoon – time we did it up and let him move back. Suit us better, of course, for him to live permanently in the lodge if he had a wife to see to the gates during the day, but since he hasn't...bad policy to leave them unattended, with all these malcontents around. Tell him he can move back to the cottage as soon as we've had the roof seen to and found another lodge-keeper, will you? Married, this time."

"He'll be over the moon. He hates living in the lodge – can't bear to be more than a few yards from his pheasant chicks."

Seton tactfully forbore to remind Henry that he'd been told this situation might arise – in fact, he'd warned him only last week that he was in danger of losing one of the best and most experienced keepers he would ever have. Jordan was seething with resentment at having had to move into the vacant lodge when his original cottage further in the woods had been judged unfit to live in and too expensive to repair. It was one of the niggling, sometimes counter-productive, economies that Henry was introducing all the time – but at least he'd been man enough to acknowledge his mistake this time. The amount of money needed to make the keeper's cottage sound was relatively small, and the repairs would be little trouble compared with losing Jordan. He wondered what had made Henry change his mind and see sense – though on second thoughts it was fairly obvious: up there in the woods today with the dogs, in this weather, he must have seen how quickly the cottage was disintegrating, left entirely as it was to the elements.

"And there's also the question of Ensor's farm," Seton added, pressing the advantage. "No doubt you'll wish to discuss that with Sebastian, if you're going to sell?"

"When he condescends to come down." Henry's black brows came together.

"He's here. Arrived about an half an hour ago."

"What?"

"I understand he didn't wish to disturb you."

Henry said nothing to this, uneasily aware of the usual mixture of feelings aroused in him whenever his son and heir paid them a visit, or even when they met by chance. He was never as comfortable with Sebastian as he should have been. It had fallen to Sir Henry's lot to be a gentleman landowner and he saw it as a privilege, but one which entailed many responsibilities, to his tenants, to the land; duties which he fulfilled conscientiously. As he saw it, it was necessary to devote the whole of one's time to the business. One couldn't pick it up and discard it whenever one felt like it, and Sebastian should realise this. He ought to be learning to manage the estate economically (which God knew was in deep enough waters), being ready, when the time came, to step into his father's shoes, though Henry didn't consider himself in his dotage yet, and tried not to remember he was fifty-six and that time might be running out. Not leading, as Sebastian did, what seemed to Sir Henry to be an aimless way of life: when the boy wasn't at the races or chasing some pretty young woman, he was wandering around Europe, messing about with pencil and paper, when at his age he ought more properly to be thinking about getting himself settled in life. By that Henry meant the absolute necessity of finding a wife with money and providing an heir. If Sebastian didn't watch it, Sylvia might even yet upstage him with a son and heir. He'd have to look to his laurels then, or Belmonde could go to a Eustace-Bragge, God forbid.

Adèle, as was to be expected, excused the boy, said he was simply lively and impetuous, but Henry called this attitude bumptiousness. He didn't want to listen to Lady Emily, either, when she said it was a defect time would cure, especially if he was allowed more rope.

More rope? What the devil did she mean by that?

Encouragement, perhaps, rather than disapproval, she replied.

Encouragement? Good God. The boy would get above himself – he'd want to make changes. Besides which, Henry feared his son might have inherited his mother's extravagance, though to give him his due, he rarely asked for money to augment the small legacy left him by his grandfather, as Harry, regrettably, had often done. "Which goes nowhere nowadays," Adèle had recently exclaimed. "Henry, can't you allow him a little extra?" No, he'd replied flatly. With the new government land taxes he found so deeply offensive, income tax up to one-and-two in the pound, plus supertax, he was not disposed to fling money around.

And now there was this other, unbelievable, damnable business.

When Seton had gone, Henry poured himself a Scotch and to the devil with whether the sun was over the yard arm. His nerves were shot to pieces – and he knew Seton had noticed. He reached out across his desk, and after selecting another cigarette from the heavy Britannia metal box with a picture of the Taj Mahal in enamel on the lid, and lighting it, he slid the box aside and picked up the sheet of paper it had concealed. For the tenth time he read the words written on it, and for the tenth time he didn't believe them.

Adèle, at least, in the scented and modish luxury of her pretty drawing room, was delighted to see her son. "Sebastian, how lovely. And how well you look. London must indeed suit you, to keep you away from us for so long."

"Don't tease, Mama. But I'm sorry I haven't been down to Belmonde lately – and to hear you haven't been so well."

She waved a deprecating hand. "It was nothing. Not the tiniest need to worry, dearest."

Standing facing her with his back to the fire, he searched her face as she rang the bell for tea. Despite her denial, she did not seem quite up to the mark – not as soignée as usual, and she was having difficulty with her breathing, which usually happened only when she was agitated or upset. His searching glance also revealed a grey hair or two that he'd never before noticed (but wouldn't dream of mentioning) in her luxuriant, wavy dark hair; she was unusually fidgety with it, patting and smoothing it into place, evidently having been out riding or walking so that the damp had frizzed up its usual silky smoothness. It was not beauty (Adèle was not beautiful, though her sudden, illuminating smile sometimes made her seem so), but her intriguing, somewhat elusive personality that had charmed all London when she first appeared on the scene and still, wherever she went, made her the centre of attraction. There were rumours, never substantiated, of numerous men who – despite the glowering Chetwynd – had offered themselves as her lover. Half Sebastian's friends declared themselves devoted to her. Nevertheless, to have all London at your feet, to flirt and be a little naughty was as far as she would permit herself to go, of that he was certain. Yet he was always aware that behind the outward extroversion was an enigma, hiding secrets she chose not to reveal. Not being possessed of a devious mind himself, Sebastian didn't allow himself to dwell on what they might be. Of one thing he was quite certain: he had never come within a mile of understanding the complex and subtle woman his mother was.

Outwardly so agreeable and accommodating, there was, in fact, very little Adèle wanted that she didn't get. On her arrival here as a bride, for instance, she had seen the state of Belmonde and promptly put it in order, so that now it was exactly as she wished it to be. She'd installed a heating system to combat the chesty coughs brought on by the English winters. She had been ruthless in disposing of whatever furniture she took a dislike to, and greedy in the acquisition of treasure from other parts of the house to furnish the flower-filled rooms she had made quintessentially her own. The glossy white paint and fashionable pale mauve walls of this particular room made for a modish background that nevertheless went well with the Chippendale furniture, the upright walnut piano with its brass sconces, and the Georgian mirrors. Sebastian was amused to see that her elegant, narrow silk tea-gown with its split skirt, revealing slim ankles in pale silk stockings and elegantly strapped shoes, although faintly striped with turquoise, was of the same delicate mauve as the walls, and wondered whether it was deliberate. Knowing his mother, he thought perhaps it was.

A scatter of rain flung itself against the windows, causing him to glance out over the drenched garden, and without warning the eerie feeling that had made such an impression on him when he had seen – and then not seen – that female figure in the woods, came back sharply. What had she been doing there – and why had her vanishing affected him in that way? Very likely she had simply been up to the house to leave a message for one of the servants and was hurrying away out of the rain. Yet the hairs on the back of his neck stood up, and it needed a conscious effort of will to walk across the room and deliberately choose a seat with its back to the window.

As he made to sit down, he almost tripped over some worthy-looking knitting in a repellent shade of dark green, destined for the poor, no doubt, which had fallen on to the floor by the side of this, the most uncomfortable chair in the room – right next to the French window, where there was a draught. "Where are the Cashmores?" he asked, looking around as if he might find them lurking behind a potted palm, and very glad indeed that he did not.

"I let them have Dombey and the Daimler to pay a visit to that aged aunt of theirs at Much Wenlock. She really can't last much longer and Dora's mother is desperate that she shouldn't leave her money to the missionaries. They had to go and see her – never mind that poor Dora has another of her colds."

"She's left her knitting on the floor." He put the unlovely work aside, revealing a gout of dried mud which a careless house-maid had missed, defiling the white carpet. "It couldn't have been her I saw, then, in the park as I drove through," he remarked, crumbling the mud into a nearby pot plant. "I fancied I saw a woman there, wearing the same sort of hat Dora wears."

"My dear, *no one* wears hats like Dora!" She added quickly, in the very British clipped delivery she'd cultivated to perfection to cover her American drawl, "Besides, she won't put a toe outside if there's the slightest chance of a shower."

Dora Cashmore and her aged mother were poor relations, who spent long periods staying with one or other of their extensive family connections in order to save on their household expenses. One would not have minded this so much had they not been so very dreary, mother and daughter alike. Nevertheless, Adèle was always carelessly charming to them. Even to Dora, who was a tiresome little creature, very nearly the wrong side of thirty, wearing a permanent look of martyrdom and forever snuffling and mopping her eyes. "Oh dear, I'm afraid such quantities of flowers do have this effect on her sinuses," her mother would apologise, above the sneezing. "If we might just sit over there, or perhaps, dear Adèle, have this vase moved to one side?"

The misery inflicted on Dora by all those flowers massed in every room at Belmonde always made Sebastian wonder how she and her mother ever endured to stay here. Perhaps he knew why, but he had become adept at being unaware of the languishing looks Dora cast upon him.

Tea was brought in, tiny sandwiches and hot scones under

silver covers, all of which Sebastian demolished with speed, wishing they were more substantial. "I missed lunch."

"Then let me give you some of this cake, darling," his mother suggested. "It looks quite delicious and they'll be too upset if we send it back uncut." She took no heed of the raised eyebrows of her mother-in-law, which said that she'd never namby-pambied *her* boys that way. But Harry, now dead, was proof that one should follow the dictates of one's own heart; there was but one bite at the cherry. It was fast becoming a philosophy with Adèle.

As soon as Sebastian had finished the last of the sandwiches and had eaten two slices of the airy lemon sponge, iced and decorated with sugared violets, drunk another cup of tea and sat back, satisfied at last, she rose and went to the piano. "What would you like me to play? Schubert – or Chopin?" When down here at Belmonde, restlessness devoured her; she always needed to be occupied with something. Outdoors it was tennis and sometimes croquet; she enjoyed fly-fishing, had a splendid seat on a horse, and rode to hounds with flair and courage; she was also an excellent shot and could walk for miles over the hills. Indoors, when it was not cards, or conversation, Adèle was usually found at the piano. Now, without waiting for answer, she chose a melancholy Chopin étude...she had none of the domestic arts, had never been known to pick up a needle and thread, but she played the piano beautifully, with almost professional skill, and as her fingers strayed over the keys, her tense shoulders seemed to relax. When the last notes had died away, she twirled the piano stool around. "Come, sit over here, Sebastian, where I can talk to you," she commanded, waving to an ivory brocaded sofa. "Tell me the latest gossip."

"My dear Mama, London's so empty at the moment, there's no chance of even the smallest titbit."

"Have you seen Monty lately? I haven't seen him in an age." She reached out and took a black Russian cigarette from an enamel box, fitted it into a jade and gold holder. "I wonder how he is?"

"Oh, much as usual, I suppose." Sebastian struck a match and lit the cigarette for her. "Haven't seen him since I lunched with him at his club – but that was weeks ago."

"Have you not? He was to have come down this weekend, you know, but he telephoned to excuse himself. The Irish question again, I suppose, or something equally tiresome."

Adèle finished her cigarette. She should not have been smoking. It hurt her chest, but her nerves needed soothing more. She turned back to the piano, striving to regain the rigid control over herself which she could almost always summon at will, but it was impossible to rid her mind of Monty. A well liked man, personable, cool and debonair, with smooth, sandy hair, light eyelashes and brows, his skin didn't tan easily, but had a summer sun-flush from riding every morning in the Row; by means of regular visits to the gymnasium and the Turkish baths, games of tennis in the Members' courts, he kept himself fit and trim. He liked the good things in life, collected fine porcelain and works of art, and never raised his voice, but had an air of good humoured authority that engendered respect. In almost every way, the antithesis of his brother. She forced a tight smile and played a nervous little arpeggio, echoing the frisson which tingled its way all the length of her spine.

A couple of hours later Montague Chetwynd, MP, the honourable member for East Lyndon, drew up his motorcar outside the house. Upon entering and being helped to divest himself of his waterproof (despite which, like Sebastian and Louisa, he was exceedingly wet) he waved aside the information that he had of course missed tea in Lady Chetwynd's drawing room, but if he wished, some would be brought to him. He had driven himself down through the rain, he said, and declared himself in need of something stronger than Adèle's Lapsang Souchong. "Thanks, Mr Blythe, but I'll go and see my brother. Where is he?"

"In the business room, Mr Montague. Er – will you be staying, sir?"

"I daresay you have a room ready, since you were expecting me until yesterday? Good. Changed my mind about not coming down after all."

"Indeed sir. I'll have your bags taken up to your usual room."

"Well, Henry," said Monty, entering the business room and managing to avoid wafting away the fug of tobacco that hung there like a miasma. "A pretty kettle of fish, this, and no mistake, hmm?"

Chapter Four

"The trouble with Sebastian," remarked Adèle, preparing for bed, being helped out of the black and white striped satin she had worn that evening and feeling some comment from her was expected in answer to her husband's rather sour remark on their son's unscheduled arrival, "is that he doesn't know what he wants at the moment, poor boy."

Her maid took the pins out of her hair and began brushing it. It crackled with electricity under the long, rhythmic strokes, and the maid tutted and poured a drop or two of bergamot-scented oil into her palms, which she proceeded to smooth into the thick, dark waves.

"At twenty-four, that's an indulgence he can't afford," replied his father sourly. "You've spoilt him, allowed him to get away with too much."

Whereas you have never spoiled Sylvia? Or, come to that, showed Sebastian how much you really care for him? thought Adèle, who knew her husband better than to voice such thoughts, however.

She sighed and went behind the screen, followed by her maid. Her stays loosened, she let herself sigh with relief. "Thank you, Lily, that'll do nicely, you can get off to bed now." She went back to her dressing table and looked at her reflection, dissatisfied. She must get rid of this peignoir – give it to Lily, who admired the fashionable but rather washed out pink colour known as ashes of roses. It took away what little colour she had in her face today.

The maid left the room and Henry went on, "What's he doing down here, I'd like to know."

"Sebastian? My dear, it is his home."

"Pity he doesn't remember that more often."

Adèle wisely ignored this. "He behaved very well at dinner, I thought – so kind to Dora Cashmore, poor dear. She's really upset at having to leave us for the Falconfields, but since you feel we're being eaten out of house and home – I can't think why, Dora simply pecks at her food, though her mother makes up for it, I suppose – perhaps it's just as well."

She wasn't sure whether Henry had heard her or not. He was wandering in and out through the door to the bathroom that connected their rooms, as was his habit while undressing and preparing for bed, while interjecting sporadic remarks.

"What's been the matter with you tonight?" he asked suddenly. "Like a cat on hot bricks all evening. I'm surprised at you not having more control. Everyone must have noticed."

Her heart skipped a beat. Here it came, what had been resolutely avoided all evening. She rose and went to the window, stretching out a slim hand to draw aside the edge of the plum-coloured velvet curtains which contained her bedroom so safely within their thick, deep folds, and stood looking out over the not quite dark garden. "I'm sorry."

"Sorry?" he repeated, coming up behind her and placing his dark, hairy paw on her soft, rounded shoulder, spinning her around. "Dammit, Adèle, I don't want you to be sorry. Not to me, anyway. Monty upset you or something, coming unannounced like that? That – and everything else," he added sombrely.

His hand fell as she moved away from him slightly, still feeling the heat of his body through the thin satin. "*Upset?* Oh no, why should a little thing like that upset me?" She laughed bitterly.

Unsettling was not the word for Monty's unscheduled arrival at Belmonde. Although, since Lady Emily had arranged to partake of a meal in her own rooms, he had dined with her in order not to upset either the arrangements or his mother, only afterwards joining the rest of them in the drawing room. He'd offered no general explanation for his change of plan about spending the weekend here, other than that of finding himself suddenly free and deciding that London was intolerable without congenial company. It was a pity he hadn't joined them for dinner, she thought. Had he done so, Henry would have had to find some topic of conversation, rather than sit there brooding. His mother would probably have joined them. Sebastian would have responded to his godfather's quick wit and urbane presence and would not have been left alone to charm the Cashmores. And she would not have had to struggle to suppress everything that was churning around inside her.

As it was, she had found it an intolerable effort to keep the conversation moving at all, wondering if there was ever going to be an end to a day which had become interminable. She'd looked across her dining table, where a benign light from the lamps fell on to the crystal and silver, the gleaming mahogany, where all was pleasant and civilised, and wondered if she were the only one to discern the undercurrents that felt to be drawing her down into unknown depths. She thought not: an almost tangible tension had twanged between them all: Henry especially was on edge; only Monty, joining them later, was as much in control as he normally was. Even Sebastian, for his own unexplained reasons, had been distrait: she played down his restlessness to Henry but she was acutely aware of it. Occasionally, especially tonight, she felt him hovering on the brink of some decision he might later regret. Once it had been Harry, of her two boys, Harry whom she had loved to distraction, who had worried her. Now there was just Sebastian...

And Sylvia, of course. But Adèle really preferred not to think about Sylvia, who was a disappointment to her. So quick and amusing, so popular and attractive, that no one ever thought of her as much more than a social butterfly, which was a mistake. She was sharp and critical of her mother, she knew too much about her and when they were in society together, she outshone Adèle with her sparkling conversation. She had married that fool, Algy. Above all, she was twenty-eight and had not yet done her duty by Algy and given him a son. One who might, failing all else, continue the Chetwynd line.

It had been borne upon Adèle more and more lately that it was up to her to keep a steady hand on the tiller or the family might founder. They were Chetwynds, they must stand together, come what may. She felt, deep down, perhaps even more than Henry and his mother, the importance of family: to her it was not only tradition, it was blood. Her quick, American blood mingled with the thicker, slower blood of old England. She had succeeded, without eschewing any long-held traditions, in moulding her life as wife of the fifth baronet to exactly the shape she felt it ought to be – and nothing, if she could help it, was going to interfere with that.

The rain outside seemed to have finally stopped. Moonlight was pouring in a silver wash over the garden, lighting up those absurd statues of Henry's under the Wellingtonia. An oblong of golden light fell on to the lawn from the smoking room window, where Monty and Sebastian had adjourned to smoke a cigar. Henry had declined to join them, and escaped by saying he had things to see to before bed and besides, had to be up betimes tomorrow. She had, in fact, been relieved to see the back of him, his brooding presence was so unnerving, although it meant she'd been left alone to play bezique with Dora Cashmore, until at long last Dora declared she must go and get her beauty sleep, and Adèle almost fell on her knees with gratitude. Her nerves had reached screaming point. She could bear no more of what had happened between them all today. All she wanted was oblivion.

She felt Henry's eyes on her back now as she gazed out into the darkness, but he wandered disconsolately away from her before she could turn and see his expression. Even now, they avoided bigger issues, as they always did. "What's this?" he asked suddenly from behind her.

She turned round. He had picked up the ornament Lily had just removed from her hair, which she'd been wearing all night but which he typically hadn't noticed until now, a somewhat decadent-looking thing with a woman's naked body in the sinuous shape of a mermaid with butterfly wings, made from gold, iridescent green-and-blue enamel and black opals.

"Oh, just some trifle I fell in love with when I saw it in Liberty's," she lied. "You've seen it before, many times."

"Have I?" He never noticed what she wore, or forgot if he did. "How much did it cost?"

"I don't remember," she answered lightly, looking away, and not because she was inclined to laugh, as she usually was when he stood there looking ridiculous in nothing but his shirt and his dark socks pulled up over his long underwear, and with his gloomy face, fussing over nothing, as usual. She had better be careful: Henry was not nearly so obtuse as people thought him. He adopted a blinkered approach to anything outside Belmonde, apparently uninterested in whatever was happening around him;

and then suddenly he would come up with some astute comment, which showed he had been listening after all, and was all the more disconcerting because quite often it was very much to the point. It never did to push Henry too far. No one had more reason than she to fear the dark, deep moods that could come upon him, like this one which had hung over him all day.

Henry tossed the ornament back on to the dressing table with a disapproving frown. Dammit, money meant nothing to her, undoubtedly because she had never known the lack of it. She had attracted him and he'd begun to court her immediately she'd been launched into London society, though the fact that she was heiress to a reasonable fortune, at a time when the affairs of Belmonde were in a parlous state, was not entirely absent from the equation: she had captured a title and a historic family background which meant a great deal to her, and he had gained the wherewithal to put Belmonde back into shape which, as far as he was concerned, was a fair bargain. He hadn't known then that it was a temporary respite – or that money ran through her fingers like water. She'd no idea of its value, and spent a fortune on clothes and trifles, on long white kid evening gloves, for instance, which could only be worn once. She would give handfuls of coins, florins, half-crowns or even a sovereign if she felt like it, to a beggar. Anything which took her fancy she bought without a moment's hesitation, like this jewelled gee-gaw. And would tire of it in a moment, too – or more likely, for she was generous to a fault, give it away to anyone who admired it. Probably to Dora Cashmore.

"Are you feeling better?" he asked, looking at her shadowed reflection in the looking glass.

"Yes," she said, but her breathing gave her away. All her fears were rushing back.

"You look as though you could do with a good night's rest."

She doubted whether she would sleep at all. "You too, Henry."

"I still have things to do, don't forget. Try to get some sleep," he added, with such unexpected gentleness that tears rushed to her eyes. As always, Henry could wrong-foot her when she least expected it. And as always, he spoiled it. He put his heavy hand upon her shoulder again as she reached for the small bottle of drops, saying harshly, "That's no answer. Get a grip on yourself. You'll do no one any good, that way. What's done's done, and you'd better get used to it."

The smoking room with the lighted windows that gave out on to the lawn was a gentlemen's retreat: a tantalus on a sideboard, deep armchairs, some rather racy prints hanging on the dark green walls, and fringed lamps hanging low over the green baize of a billiard table in the background. The old house settling itself for the night around them. Monty, extolling the virtues of holidaying in Italy, Sebastian half-listening, thinking of other things.

Sebastian roused himself to say, "I believe congratulations are in order?"

"What? Oh, my speech in the House. Water under the bridge by now." Monty smiled slightly.

His uncle's ability to keep cool and unruffled in the face of whatever happened was something Sebastian admired and envied. But he surely didn't really believe that the fuss which had arisen would be so easily forgotten? When, just before the recession, he had spoken pertinently to a crowded House against the question of women's suffrage, and had in particular condemned the growing tendency to make violent attacks against property. The speech had been printed in full in *The Times* and caused quite a sensation. There had been a derisory cartoon in *Punch*. Give these women the vote, he had demanded, and what will they want next? Sexual equality in everything? It had been very popularly received in certain quarters.

"Under the bridge for some, but not everyone," said Sebastian. "It's made enemies for you. These women don't forget."

Monty busied himself with trimming the end of a cigar. "I don't doubt – but with the franchise must go a certain amount of responsibility. I've seen little evidence of that in these women so far. They're acquiring a taste for violence for its own sake – damaging property is only a short step from further outrage, and alienates any sympathies one might have had for their cause. It simply confirms what most men know to be true – that women are too hysterical to make rational decisions and be given the vote."

Sebastian laughed. "You'd better not let Louisa hear you say that."

"Louisa?" Monty's brows rose enquiringly. "Ah, yes. Louisa – Fox?"

Sebastian always forgot that Monty, living as he had in London ever since coming down from Oxford, didn't know the Fox's in the same way the rest of the family did. "Yes, the same Louisa."

"Are you seriously interested in this young woman?"

Sebastian, who had come dangerously close to denying Louisa once already that day in the conversation with his grandmother, would not do it again. He was more and more beginning to ask himself why, when he'd known Louisa all his life and only now, now that she'd become so irrevocably wrapped up in her desire for a career, had he woken up to the knowledge that all the Pamelas and Cecilys and Idas – and even Violet Clerihugh – meant so little to him as to be nothing. Yet he still hesitated.

Anything one said to Monty, however, wouldn't be repeated. The circumspection so necessary in his professional life had spilled over into his private concerns; he was as trustworthy as the Bank of England. He had come to politics fairly late, after failing to live up to what had once promised to be a brilliantly successful career at the Bar. He had not attained the very highest office in his parliamentary career either, which he might well have done had he not preferred to work behind the scenes and influence policy and events from the sidelines. Having been at Balliol with Asquith, when Asquith became Prime Minister a year ago he had been appointed a junior minister at the Foreign Office. Since then he had come to be regarded as something of an expert in the continuing turbulent affairs of the Balkans and the Ottoman empire. He was regarded as very sound. Yet there was that astonishing anti-feminist speech, not only considered rash and ill-advised in some quarters, but out of character. It had made a few people look at him twice.

"Louisa?" repeated Sebastian, not without a trace of bitterness, "I'm afraid she's not interested in me. Only one thing really concerns Louisa – her future career as a doctor."

"Then you'd do well to keep it that way, dear boy. Wouldn't

do, you know. Wouldn't do at all." He regarded Sebastian over the edge of his glass. "Nevertheless, you should be thinking about getting married."

"From a confirmed bachelor, that's pretty rich – if I might be so bold."

"But I am not the heir to Belmonde."

Sebastian had always been curious as to why Monty had remained unmarried, but his personal life was not open to discussion. A suave and subtle man, it was often remarked that Montague Chetwynd was a dark horse. He was liked by almost everyone, attractive to women, at ease with men. His name had been linked several times with various eligible – and sometimes not so eligible – women. A prudent marriage could have done much to further his career. But he'd remained single, the despair of many a mama with marriageable daughters on the look out for a catch. And one somehow couldn't imagine Monty encumbered with a wife and children, thought Sebastian.

"I met Violet Clerihugh and her mother when I was in San Remo," he remarked a moment or two later, taking up a billiard cue and chalking the end. "Pretty young woman."

Violet was one of those girls to whom Sebastian had been introduced by Sylvia, who lost no opportunity of contriving an introduction to some girl or other whom she thought of as a suitable – and sufficiently rich – future chatelaine of Belmonde. "When are you going to find yourself a suitable wife?" she demanded constantly. "It's not a question of inclination, you know – you have a duty, now that Harry – now that Harry's no longer here." Which was one reason why he had taken to keeping out of his sister's way as much as possible.

But Violet was pretty; more than that, she was an only daughter, who would bring wealth to her marriage. She was downy as a peach, short and plump, but she knew how to dress well, and he'd come to see she was not as empty-headed (nor as docile) as she liked to appear. One hot afternoon last summer, when a group of young men and girls had been fooling about as they punted on the Thames near Richmond, she'd pretended to fall in at the edge. It had – Sebastian had seen quite clearly – been no accident. The water was shallow and she'd only got her feet a little wet; he knew she'd only done it to attract attention to herself, as silly girls will, but he'd rushed to her rescue, and she'd allowed him to remove her shoes and rub her feet dry with a cloth from the picnic hamper (through her silk stockings, of course) while watching him steadily through a pair of large brown eyes. Being married to Violet would probably not be the milk-and-water affair one might imagine. For a moment there, looking at the carnation flush on her cheeks, the soft gold of her hair, holding her pretty foot in his hand, he had felt an electric charge pass between them and had very nearly proposed to her there and then, but had drawn back in time, without knowing why himself.

Violet, however, remained hopeful. He knew for a fact that she had since refused at least one offer, one which would have ultimately resulted in her becoming a duchess.

"You could do worse," remarked Monty.

Sebastian shrugged, taking up his cue.

"Just remember," went on his uncle, smiling but giving Sebastian the full benefit of his curiously penetrating look, "when we're talking of Belmonde, personal wishes don't enter into this at all. Neither yours, nor mine, nor anyone's." He glanced at his pocket watch. "Come, then, if we're to have a game. It's been a long day and I for one am more than ready for bed."

'Bread-and-butter before cake,' was one of the many aphorisms of his old nanny which had lodged permanently in Sebastian's consciousness – and which he still sometimes felt a compulsion to obey. Accordingly, after breakfast on the day following his late night session in the smoking room with Monty, his uncle's strictures on his obligations still ringing in his ears, he dutifully spent part of the morning in the business room with his father, in consequence of which, after an hour had passed, both were feeling the strain. Sir Henry, smoking ferociously, and with his mind for some reason untypically unfocused, had been even more intractable than usual and at last, relieved by having done his duty, mightily in need of fresh air to cool his temper, Sebastian took himself and the dogs out for some mind-clearing exercise.

The church bells were ringing across the fields. Lady Emily

would have been driven to church in the stately Daimler, as she always was on Sundays, perhaps accompanied by his mother, and the Cashmores, no doubt. His father went only when it was his turn to read the lesson. Today Sebastian did not feel at all in the right frame of mind for divine service, either – mainly because he hadn't yet mentioned the purpose of his visit: neither to his mother, nor to his father. The time with Sir Henry certainly hadn't been propitious this morning – but still, he was infuriated with himself for his lack of moral fibre in failing to take the bull by the horns.

A tentative sun gave promise that today might eventually turn out to be an improvement on the previous day, though moisture still dripped from the tree branches, heavy in the full leaf of late summer, and the formal bedding that blazed around the house, already tired with the end of the season, had a bedraggled and beaten look from the recent heavy rains. As he strode along the wide, paved paths running between dark yew hedges, Sebastian wondered sardonically what new thing might have arrived in the garden to surprise him.

Several years ago Adèle, unbeknownst to Sir Henry, had ordered in at great expense a dozen classical statues to line the path that ran in a descending prospect from the terrace outside the drawing room, with the purpose, she said, of leading the eye down to the focal point of the lake. Sebastian would not easily forget the ensuing uproar.

"But the gardens are so dull, Henry," she'd remonstrated, watching him from under her lids. "Surely you don't begrudge a few guineas to make them a little more attractive?"

"A few guineas! Dull? How can you possibly say that? My father had them redone at unbelievable expense when I was a boy."

"Yes, darling, I know. All that Victorian shrubbery. Too, too dreary."

Enraged, Henry had stumped off. Had he suspected she might be laughing at him? It was possible, but at last, after months of wrangling, he'd conceded the point to the extent of promising that he would see what he could do. Or perhaps he'd only agreed in case Adèle should ever take it upon herself to do such a thing again. After which, never one to do things by halves, he had astonished everyone by getting caught up in the project himself: not only did he commission the parterre in front of the house that Sebastian found so particularly nasty, but on every visit to Belmonde, there were all manner of unexpected – mostly not altogether felicitous – pieces of statuary, obelisks, follies and goodness knows what else to be found popping up in unexpected places. What Sir Henry had initially reluctantly agreed to in order to please his wife had grown into a dotty obsession of his own. A fountain and a lily pond with a grotesque grouping of mythological figures in the centre now graced the lower terrace, and a monstrous folly had been constructed from what remained of the stone walls that had once been part of the original abbey. Better than either were the replanted rose gardens, with a cascade behind them that tumbled from the rocky upper reaches of the grounds outside the garden proper. But also, alas, a laburnum walk (which led nowhere) had appeared on one of the lawns. Sebastian doubted whether much of this was what his mother had had in mind.

Nothing new appeared this time, however, at which to marvel or grimace. He strode through to the copse which marked the end of the formal gardens, leaving behind the nine marble Greek Muses Henry had unhappily grouped beneath old Sir George's two hundred foot Wellingtonia. The tree had become the roosting place for generations of pigeons, and the statues had consequently acquired a patina not originally intended, and were not now a pretty sight, his mother's *bête noire*.

Belmonde was set on a southward-facing hill that sloped up gradually from the river towards the house, and then more steeply behind it; beyond the trees and behind the house rose a series of thickly wooded hills. Sebastian whistled up the frisky young springer spaniel, Dizzy, and the more sedate Sophie, a curly-coated black retriever bitch, and went through a ruined, ivy-clad arch that was a remnant of the old cloisters and was indeed the only part of the abbey left standing, then he took a familiar pathway, steep and rocky, his still angry strides leading him to his objective, a bosky, rowan-shaded clearing halfway up the hill.

Entering the clearing, there appeared before him a small, silent pool surrounded by huge outcrops of red rocks and clumps of ferns, fed by a spring which never dried up, where the sun rarely reached. At the back of the pool was a big, upended sandstone slab with a hole which the water had worn through the soft stone, around which a head surrounded by leaves had been carved, the hole serving as the mouth. This was not a carving done at his father's behest, but by some much older, unknown directive...it was an object of speculation, said to have existed long before the arrival of the monks at Belmonde, a strange, pagan symbol to be found in the grounds of an abbey. There was a similar head carved on the lintel of the Green Man in the village. In the way the open mouth curved, as if in a laugh, in the pointed ears, the curling hair, Sebastian was always, irresistibly, reminded of Harry.

Leaving the dogs to a seventh heaven of hopeful rabbiting, and turning his back on the pool, he sat on the grass looking over the view, which from here extended well beyond the Abbey grounds and over the fields. The Bonhommes, a small religious order, had chosen well when, in the fourteenth century, they had picked the site where their little community could settle, and where it had quietly flourished for two hundred years until Henry the Eighth's troopers had arrived, sacked the abbey and dispersed its holy inhabitants to find shelter and sustenance wherever they could. And there it had lain in ruins until the first Chetwynd, an enterprising wool merchant, had purchased the land from Queen Elizabeth and built a modest manor house with the scattered stones, thereby beginning two hundred years of habitation by the same family. On the whole the Chetwynds had been fair-minded, responsible landlords and employers, and the tenor of life had remained peaceful and undisturbed. Somehow, the goodness of the Bonhommes seemed to have filtered down the centuries so that it lay like a benevolence over the estate, running through it like a length of silk.

Sebastian, the last of the line, loved Belmonde deeply, but he had long come to realise that theirs was increasingly regarded as a life of privilege, and the radical in him wasn't sure whether such privilege was right, or whether, in the long run, it could last.

More than that, he was terrified, not of possessing, but of becoming possessed by Belmonde, as it possessed his father. Trying to come to terms with the mixture of emotions his inheritance always aroused in him – his family and his love for the place, the spell it exerted, his obligations against his inclinations – Sebastian could only pray he would one day be worthy to face up to it. But, like St Augustine, not yet.

Certainly not now.

Very recently, a young man he'd been at school with had, in Sebastian's rooms, come across one of his sketchbooks, leafed through it with interest and asked casually why he'd never thought of becoming an architect.

"What?"

And there it was, flashed upon his consciousness in an instant like a lightning bolt, seared upon his soul for ever – the realisation that this was always where his life had been leading. Since childhood he'd carried a sketchbook with him wherever he went. Natural scenes didn't leave him cold: the loved, familiar view of the gardens now spread below him where he sat, the abbey ruins, the silver snake of the Severn winding on the flat plain below, the series of hills on the other side rising to a melting blue on the horizon, the church steeple and the roofs of the village just visible through the trees could hardly do that. But it had always been buildings that caught his imagination more. Fascinated by the way they were constructed, his sketchbooks became filled with details of the line of a roof, the ornamentation of a corbel, the proportions of a house. Even as a child in church on Sundays in the shelter of the big family box pew he would furtively draw and try to understand the construction of the springing vaulting of the stone roof or the exact proportions of the pillars which supported it – that is, when he wasn't wickedly caricaturing the droning parson, or Miss Phillimore, the organist, nodding on her bench.

Later, especially in Greece and Italy, he'd been ravished by the relics of classical antiquity and the splendours of the Renaissance. And later still, escorting his mother on a visit to her family in Chicago, where he was left breathless by both the modern skyscrapers of Sullivan, and the low-pitched prairie houses with their flowing interior spaces of Frank Lloyd Wright.

"I can get you an introduction to a man I know," said his friend, and from then on, it had been a settled thing in his mind, inconceivable that anything else should be open to him. Somehow he would do it, even the long, daunting period of training required by the Royal Institute of British Architects. As it turned out, this now looked unnecessary. The man his friend knew was an architect with a growing reputation, who himself was largely self-taught, having dropped out of architectural school after two years. Jones introduced Sebastian to Arthur Wagstaffe, a big, shambling, pragmatic man who was gaining a name for himself for sensible, no-nonsense, value-for-money buildings. Plainer than the usual Baroque revival which was the thing of the moment, but beautiful because they were so honest.

He had listened to what Sebastian had to say, looked carefully at the exquisite drawings in his portfolio – and laughed. "Don't let yourself get carried away with funny ideas about concert halls and cathedrals. Don't forget, architecture's about drains as well. What are your mathematics like?"

Not his strong point, Sebastian had been forced to admit, abashed.

"Well, they were never mine either, but you'll learn as you go."

Sebastian had gone away with his heart on fire, his head full of talk of draughtsmanship, the need to gain knowledge of practical applications, calculations – and the offer of a job as a paying pupil in the New Year, when the man he was due to replace had left. He sometimes had the feeling that it had been too easy, but as yet he'd managed to tell no one, not even Louisa, since he believed his family had the right to be the first to know. Sylvia he could envisage having hysterics at the very idea, though his mother might well accept it as simply one of the crazes young men were apt to take up and then abandon. His grandmother, on the other hand, would certainly be seriously displeased, and would no doubt see it as a betrayal of his obligations. Without exception, they would all be astonished. Not one of them, he thought, would entirely believe he was serious.

As for his father – the decision was sure to raise a furore, notwithstanding that architecture was a perfectly respectable profession, and there was nothing about it to be ashamed of. It wasn't as though he would be condemned to scraping a miserable living in a garret as an artist, dammit – but he knew his father would never be persuaded to see it like that, much less to stump up the money he would need to pay for his pupillage. Sebastian certainly didn't have the money to fund himself. He just about got by as it was – and he still owed a hundred pounds on his new car.

He smoked a cigarette, buried his head in his hands, and it wasn't until the sun was high in the sky above the brow of the hill that he realised it was nearly lunch time. Calling the dogs to heel, he made his way back to the house.

He turned into the stable yard just in time to encounter a very small boy pedalling up towards the back entrance on a bicycle much too large for him. Red-faced and panting with the effort, the lad clutched a letter in one hand, which proved to be for Sebastian himself, from Louisa, with 'Urgent' scribbled across the corner.

Having read it, he turned to the waiting boy, whose fascinated eyes were now glued to the Ascot in front of the stables in the yard, at present being cleaned of the previous day's mud by one of the grooms, wielding a shammy leather and hissing under his breath as if he were grooming a horse. "Well, Davey – it is Davey, from the smithy, isn't it? – this letter demands my presence in the village urgently, and as you see, I've no means of transport at the moment. What do you say to lending me your bicycle, hm?"

"T'ain't mine, sir. 'Tis Miss Louisa's. 'Er borrered it me, to get here quick."

"Right, then, I can return it to her."

Barty considered. "'Er give me a thrupenny bit."

"I believe I could make that sixpence."

A tanner? A predatory gleam appeared in the boy's eye. "It be a long walk into they village."

"It's all downhill," Sebastian replied heartlessly. Relenting, he added, "I dare say Timmins will let you sit in the driving seat of my motor and show you how things go if you behave yourself."

"Cor!"

Sebastian felt in his pocket for a sixpence and the bicycle was handed over with no further argument from the budding extortionist.

Chapter Five

Flying down the village street towards the Fox's house on Louisa's bicycle, sending the would-be intimidating flock of hissing geese on the green about their business, waving to Lister's youngest little girl who was sitting on the cottage doorstep blissfully blowing bubbles from a clay pipe dipped in soapy water, Sebastian scarcely registered the knot of excited people gathered outside the village school, the bicycle propped up against its wall, or the horse and covered cart drawn up outside.

He did, however, become aware of the unusual silence among the crowd as he approached. He raised a hand in salute and this was returned, but without the usual cheeriness. He felt the stares on his back and prudently lessened his speed until he came suddenly on the house, sitting like a surprise in the bend of the road.

It always brought a smile to his face, the old manor house that Augustus Fox had purchased from the Scot who had bought it sixty years ago, added to it and sentimentally renamed it 'Aynholme' – although it was still known to everyone in the locality, and the family, too, for that matter, as the manor. On the outside, the best thing that could be said about it was that it was decidedly individual: to the original Jacobean buildings had been added fancy Victorian extensions and a Scottish baronial tower to one side, in questionable but exuberant taste, which nevertheless had appealed to Gus's quirky sense of humour when he first saw it. Whatever it looked like outside, inside it was spacious, pleasant and comfortable, an ideal house in which to bring up a large, widely-spaced and energetic brood. Children could be noisy here, slide down banisters, roast chestnuts in its huge, old-fashioned fireplaces, play hide and seek in its many secret corners (though once Barty had been tied up as an enemy Red Indian, left in the pepper-pot tower and been forgotten). There was a field where you could play French cricket without being fearful of spoiling the lawns. Robert, now married with children of his own, had been Sebastian's greatest hero, and it was here that the boys – and Louisa – had fished and climbed trees, where

Louisa had beaten Sebastian at conkers and let him teach her how to skate on the pond behind the house. He still missed Gus's wife, Ellen, an endless source of comfortable common sense, who had always made sure there were cups of cocoa, cake and glasses of milk available for hungry children. Or better still, crusty bread, still warm from the oven, plastered with sweet butter and raspberry jam – ambrosia! Having known this untidy house with its threadbare carpets and scuffed, well-worn furniture so intimately from childhood, Sebastian often felt more of a sense of homecoming here than he did at Belmonde.

The door was opened, almost before he'd lifted the knocker, by Louisa, who had strategically placed herself in her father's study, where she had a good view of anyone coming round the bend in the road. He saw at once by her flushed face and bright eyes that something was up, but before he could enquire, Gus had called a greeting to him from behind his open door.

The old man looked up with a smile when he saw Sebastian in the doorway. His manuscript was on the desk; Louisa had evidently been writing down notes for her father, at his dictation, a task all his girls were roped in to do from time to time, since his deteriorating eyesight was not up to the manuscript pages of his 'Lepidoptera'. He was wearing, as he invariably did, a black jacket and pepper-and-salt tweed trousers of exactly the same pattern as always. Whether it was the same outfit, or whether he'd taken a liking to the style and simply gave his tailor a repeat order when necessary, Sebastian had never had the temerity to ask. Or why he chose to wear such a formal jacket when its line was invariably spoiled by bulging pockets which were the receptacle for a magnifying glass, pencils and India rubber, a small sketchpad and a bag of the striped humbugs of which he was inordinately fond.

They exchanged small talk, and after a few minutes the paper bag came out. The sweets having been offered and declined, Gus popped one into his own mouth. "Well, Louisa," he said indistinctly, "You've been very helpful, as usual. Run along now. You're like a cat on hot bricks. I can see there are things you want to talk to Sebastian about."

She led the way to a seat in the inglenook in the big main room, where the fire was still a heap of warm pink ash from the previous day, and threw on another huge log. Today didn't have the same chill of a damp summer's day as yesterday, but it was a big, draughty room that demanded a fire, and except in the deepest heat of summer, one was usually kept lit. The scent of woodsmoke and beeswax was one Sebastian always felt was inseparable from this house. He took the bellows from her and gave the embers a go. When the log had caught flame he sat down, and only then did he ask her whether anything was wrong.

"This letter came this morning." Louisa picked up the sheet of thick, inlaid cream paper lying on the settle beside her and handed it to Sebastian. On it was written a declaration in a forceful but unmistakably feminine hand: "Freed, this morning! Mary, at 11 a.m!" It was signed with a single initial: A.

He handed it back. "Who is Mary? And who's A?" Though he had little doubt they were more of the brave, foolish women who were always getting themselves locked up on one pretext or another in order to bring their grievances to the attention of the public.

"Friends in the movement. Mary Leigh – oh, Seb, she's been so brave —"

"What has she done?"

Climbed on to a roof in Birmingham, apparently, and bombarded the police protecting the Prime Minister with tiles and slates. Then been taken to Winson Green prison. As must have been her intention, thought Sebastian.

"Then she went on hunger strike and those monsters fed her by force. But it's all right, she's out now, she'll be looked after."

"Force feeding. Good God." He couldn't begin to understand the depth of passion and feeling that could drive a woman so far. "But – what is it – is that why you wanted to see me so urgently?" he asked, though he couldn't see that it could be.

"No, it wasn't that – at least, not entirely." She looked confused, and flushed slightly. "Oh, I don't know…I had a little spat with Meg that upset me, and – well, I just felt I wanted to see you. There's no one else I can talk to about these things. I know you're sympathetic, underneath, only you won't commit yourself. I'm sorry, I shouldn't have bothered you."

"Of course you should. I'm always good for a shoulder to cry on, if nothing else, you know that," he replied, trying to hide how inordinately pleased he was that she'd turned to him for support. In fact, she was right: he had a good deal of sympathy with what the women were striving for, and he'd often thought it might be rather jolly to join those male medical students, friends of Louisa's, who were always ready to interrupt meetings with their rowdy songs and bags of flour and rotten eggs, only he'd never quite got around to it. If her fellow sympathisers had all been like Louisa, now...but the truth was, some of them acted more like harridans than ladies and, like this Mary Leigh, whoever she was, frightened him to death with their intensity. "But why have you and Margaret quarrelled?"

"Oh, it was nothing, really. This letter. I dare say she would soon have dismissed the unwarranted joy it caused me as the usual feminist hysterics," she said drily, "and we'd have made it up and that would have been that, if this other business in the village hadn't come up and made it worse."

He recalled the unusual stir as he rode down the street. "I noticed Perkins' cart outside the village hall as I passed, and the crowd. What's happened?"

"You haven't heard? I would have thought they'd have been up to see you all at the house before now."

"I've been out all morning. I met young Davey with your message in the stable yard and came down here immediately. Who are 'they', pray?"

"The police. Apparently a woman's body has been found in the Abbey grounds in mysterious circumstances."

"What? One of the village women?"

She shook her head. "No one knows who she is. She's a stranger, no one from here, or seemingly from anywhere round about."

"In the Abbey grounds, did you say? When was she found?"

"This morning – by the gamekeeper who lives at the lodge —"

"Jordan."

"Tom Jordan, yes. But they seem to think she died yesterday. Poor woman, she must have been taken ill and then died from exposure, out there in all that rain. What's the matter? Is anything wrong?"

"What? Oh no, no. Do go on."

But of course, something was very wrong indeed. That woman he had seen had been real enough, after all. But why had she not left the grounds by the main gates as he'd surmised? If she'd had no right to be there at Belmonde, could she have somehow lost her way, looking for some way out, other than by way of the main drive, along which she must have entered? The gates weren't kept locked nowadays, and were left unattended, except at night. Due to his father's economies, there was no one at the lodge to open and shut them during the day when Jordan was about his gamekeeping business. But the woman wasn't to have known this, and might have slipped in, thinking them left temporarily open.

He became aware that Louisa, after a curious glance, was speaking again, an unusual edge to her tone. "According to Margaret, she must have been one of 'my' suffragettes. Why else would a lone woman be lurking in the Abbey grounds, if not to throw a brick through a window, or to cause some other mischief?"

"So that's why you quarrelled?" he asked, temporarily distracted from thinking about that poor woman's fate. "Hmm. Well, I have to say it seems a perfectly sensible viewpoint, especially given that my Uncle Monty was expected down here this weekend. After that speech he made last month, he might well be regarded as a target —"

"And the fact that there are simply no grounds for such suspicion isn't sensible?"

The colour had risen in her face, and for once he said what he had been thinking for a long time. "Dear Louisa, you simply can't let these hysterical women who are running this campaign and making martyrs out of themselves take you over and jeopardise your chances of a career with all their nonsense."

"Nonsense?" The colour receded, leaving her face unusually tight-lipped and angry. Then she took a deep breath. "Don't let this become an argument between us." She stood up abruptly and rested her forehead on the great stone lintel than ran ten feet across the fireplace. She was wearing a fashionably narrow, russet coloured dress that came a little above her ankles, with a high waist and an inset of patterned silk filling in the V-neckline; a long necklace of dark amber beads hung nearly to her waist, almost the colour of her bright chestnut hair, which at the moment was flying round her face where she'd run her fingers through it. But when she turned round to face him and spoke, it was rather sadly.

"You needn't be afraid I shall turn into one these 'hysterical women' – though I wouldn't have the chance of a career at all had it not been for one or two of them. But Seb, I'm a medical student. If you'd seen the terrible things I've seen, you'd feel the same...women knocked about by their husbands...often abandoned by them and then forced to work on starvation wages to keep their children fed...marriage and divorce laws that keep them tied down. Wasn't it Rousseau who said, 'Man is born free but everywhere is in chains'? If he'd said women he would have been nearer the mark. Can't you see how hopeless they must feel with no one to turn to? Can't you see how it's turning them to violence, too? One can hardly blame them for it."

He was humbled by her passion and sincerity, though he was more afraid than ever for her safety. "Yes, I do see that, but I'm very sorry indeed you and Margaret should have quarrelled over it."

"It'll blow over – and I dare say," she sighed, "it was more my fault than hers. I take offence too easily on these subjects. And there's always the faint possibility," she added honestly, swallowing hard, "that she – and you – may be right, to some extent. There are some women in the movement who must go to physical and emotional extremes."

"Which only makes everyone think they are motivated by nothing more than a desire for notoriety."

"I'm afraid that may be true in some cases – though they'd say they had no more desire than to put the Cause in the public eye. But really," she went on, "Meg's such an old sobersides. I believe she thinks women who have the nerve to protest deserve everything they get! No, perhaps that's unkind —"

"Who deserves everything they get?"

This was Alice, who had just come through the door, pulling off her tam-o'-shanter, cheeks glowing with riding her bicycle from Sunday confirmation classes at the rectory, where she also shared lessons during the week with the rector's children. Sebastian stood up, ready to give her a big-brotherly hug, as he usually did when they met, before realising it wouldn't do, not this time. Though her hair wasn't yet up, she had taken another step towards young womanhood since the last time he'd seen her. Receiving no answer to her question, she went on with obvious excitement, "Have you heard the news?"

"I've just told him, Alice."

"I don't mean about your friend, though that's really good, isn't it, Seb? I meant the woman who's been found."

"Yes, Alice, Louisa's told me."

"What you can't have heard – nor you, Louisa, since it's just come from Joe Simmons – is that they don't think she died from exposure."

"Then what?" Louisa sounded a little nonplussed.

"Joe Simmons says there's a police inspector come from Bridgnorth, and he thinks she was killed! Old Perkins says she might have been trespassing and was shot."

"What!"

There followed a taut silence before Louisa and Sebastian spoke simultaneously: "Then Old Perkins has been at the bottle again, take no notice," came from Louisa, and from Sebastian, "My dear Alice, you'd better inform Tom Perkins that we haven't yet started shooting trespassers at Belmonde."

In any case, it was inconceivable that anyone would have been out shooting in that weather yesterday – or even if they had, that the woman had been shot, accidentally or otherwise.

"Well," said Alice with relish, "they're taking her away to cut her open and find out more."

As a young child Sebastian had been subject to nightmares, and he could not now rid himself of the feeling that he was again in the middle of one. The bad feelings he'd had about this woman, right from the first moment he'd seen her, were reinforced tenfold. He was aware of shadows closing in, of a scent of evil.

As he left the Fox's house and began to walk home to Belmonde, taking the short cut behind the house which avoided the longer way through the village, he tried to reassure himself he couldn't realistically have been expected to go searching through the sodden woods yesterday for a woman he might or might not have seen. But his conscience gave him a wretched feeling that had he done so, and offered help, she might have been alive now, and not have died from exposure – or, unlikely as it seemed, from being shot.

That being said, on the premise that sooner or later the police would want to see him, and the feeling that it would look better if he were to approach them rather than the other way round, after hesitating for only a moment, he made a firm decision and turned back. Outside the village school, the crowd had thinned, though some with nothing better to do were still hanging around. Sebastian had been known to them all from childhood, and though he was Sir Henry's son, he was well-liked; they exchanged greetings as he made his way to the door, but he was aware of curious glances, people wondering what connection the folk from the big house might have with this business.

"What's going on, Joe?" he asked the village policeman who was standing on guard, arms folded.

"Haven't you heard, Mr Sebastian? There's been a dead woman found in the Abbey woods."

"Yes, I do know that, and I'm sorry to hear it. Who is she?"

"Don't ask me. But we got the big guns out," Simmonds said, rolling his eyes. "Chief Constable's been here from Shrewsbury and the inspector from Bridgnorth's come over, so I dare say we shall find out just now. Want to see him, then, the inspector?"

"It might be as well."

When Sebastian was taken inside, he found himself alone with a policeman who was engaged in a struggle with a long hooked pole, trying to open the top of one of the high windows. As well he might wish to, for the room was stifling, with the peculiarly distinctive school smell of chalk-dust, ink, the dry wood of the planked floor and generations of children. All Miss Edith Swanson's pupils, from five years old until they left at thirteen, were housed together in the one room, where the older ones (those who were bright enough) were expected to help the younger to learn their letters and do their sums. But now, with the harvest holidays still on so that the children could help in the fields, and Miss Swanson on a walking tour in the Dolomites with her old college friend, the room was presently out of use. The big blackboard on its easel had been rubbed clean and all the child-sized double desks, each with its built-in bench and its desktop scarred with generations of inkblots and scratched-on initials, had been pushed to the sides of the room, as they were when the schoolroom doubled as the village hall.

The inspector acknowledged Sebastian's arrival with a nod, and valiantly carried on with his task, while Sebastian, wondering whether to offer to help and deciding it wouldn't be appreciated by one of the stalwarts of the police force, perched on one of the desks, prepared to wait.

Having finally succeeded in letting some air into the room, the other man, mopping his perspiring face and rubbing his hands with a handkerchief, came to sit at Miss Swanson's desk which, with the blackboard, was set on a dais, and was now covered with official looking papers. "That's a bit better," he announced. "Can't work without breathing, eh?" He still looked mightily as though he'd have liked to open the neck of his thick navy blue serge tunic, were it not for holding on to his dignity; as it was, he made do with passing a finger between the inside of the high collar and the roll of damp red flesh it had pushed up.

After ascertaining Sebastian's name, the inspector offered his own. A Welshman by the name of Meredith, he was stockily built, short for a policeman. Settling himself down, he regarded Sebastian steadily. "You got something to tell me, sir?"

Before answering that, Sebastian asked a question of his own, the one he'd asked of Joe Simmonds. "Who is she, this woman who's been found?"

"Haven't been able to identify her yet. Seems she's a stranger to these parts."

"Is it true she's been shot? If so, we'd better find out which tomfool was out there at Belmonde with a gun – without permission, and on a day like yesterday."

"Oh, and where did you get the idea, then, that she'd been shot? And at Belmonde?" Meredith asked, very Welsh, giving an appraising glance to this assured young sprig of the landed gentry perched against a child's desk, one leg thrown negligently over the other knee; polished but mud-stained gaiters, well-cut tweeds, high round stiff collar, thick dark-brown hair neatly side-parted.

"Well, she was found in the grounds, after all, wasn't she?" Sebastian was disconcerted by the keen glance, but rather relieved at the implications of the inspector's words. "Do you mean she *did* die from natural causes?"

"As to that no, I'm afraid she did not. And as to dying at Belmonde – she could have been killed elsewhere and brought in – dumped, like."

"But I saw her there – alive. That's what I came to tell you. At least, I thought I got a glimpse of her before she disappeared," Sebastian added lamely, slightly less assured. "Disappeared from sight, I mean."

Meredith's interest sharpened. "Saw her, did you? And what time was this, then?"

"Thought I saw. I couldn't really swear to it, you know. I only saw her in a flash, as I was driving up to the house. It was bucketing down and she wasn't equipped for the rain. I thought to give her a lift, but when I reversed to where I'd seen her, I could see no one. Perhaps it wasn't the same woman."

"No, I think we might reasonably assume there was only one." Meredith spoke quietly, slowly, but Sebastian had the sense that his intelligence was as sharp as the polished silver buttons on his tunic. "And the time?" he repeated.

"About half past three it would have been. But Mr Blythe – the butler – could probably tell you more precisely. I arrived at the house a few minutes later."

Butlers, was it? Didn't have butlers in the Rhonda, where Daffyd Meredith came from, and sometimes wished he could return to, pleasant as the quiet town of Bridgnorth was. The reason he lived there at all was that he'd married a girl whom he'd met on a bicycling holiday when he'd strayed over the border, and she wouldn't move away from her native town. "Quite so. Sheltering under the trees, was she? No umbrella – only a hat and coat?"

"As far as I could see."

"And you've no idea who she might be?"

"No," said Sebastian, in the face of the sinking feeling that he might now be able to make a guess, at least in a general direction.

Meredith heaved himself out of his chair and went across to the group of desks behind Sebastian. When he came back, he was holding out a sodden bundle. "Would these be the garments?"

The cloth of the coat and skirt was heavy brown tweed, the hat was one that would be deemed serviceable rather than fashionable, a stiff brown felt with a deep crown, the brim turned up at one side and held in place by a modest brooch of some pewterlike metal set around an insignificant chip of amber – the sort of hat his mother or his sister probably wouldn't acknowledge as existing. The smell of wet wool rose up as Meredith held up the articles. Sebastian shrugged, aware of the feelings of pity and anger the pathetic belongings aroused in him. "Something like that, I suppose, but it's impossible to say. I tell you, I wasn't anywhere near her."

"She was also wearing strong boots, recently resoled and heeled. The costume's not expensive, but it's of decent quality. Apart from the pin in her hat, she wasn't wearing jewellery of any kind, not even a wedding ring. And her gloves – grey cotton, darned at the tips of one forefinger and the thumb, look you. I'd put her down as a respectable, working class woman – not, at any rate, a woman able to indulge in expensive tastes. But...take a look at this."

'This' was a silk scarf which Meredith now brought to the table, watching Sebastian's frown as he looked at the delicate thing, its rich, iridescent peacock colours catching the light. "Anything strike you as odd, sir?"

Odd, no. But it was faintly recognisable. Then he remembered he had bought a similar scarf in Regent Street for Louisa's last birthday. It hadn't come cheap. "Compared with the other clothes...well, it's a pretty incongruous combination."

"Very good." The inspector nodded approvingly. "I see you follow my meaning."

"Not entirely..."

Instead of explaining himself, the inspector said obliquely, "She wasn't shot, as you assumed, Mr Chetwynd, accidentally or otherwise. She was found in the stream."

"You mean she fell in?"

Meredith weighed him up before answering. "There is reason to believe she was dead *before* that. When a person drowns, you see, there are signs – froth from the mouth or nose, that sort of thing. There was none in this case. There will be a post mortem, of course, and if there is no water found in her lungs, which the doctor believes there will not be, then she was not breathing when she entered the water."

"She died and *then* fell in?"

"Or died and was *put* in." He paused. "There were also marks on her throat."

"Good God!" The impossible conclusion hung almost tangibly on the air. *Murder.* At Belmonde. Where violence had been virtually unknown since the Dissolution, when the abbey had been sacked by the troopers of Henry the Eighth. Sebastian felt a kind of anger: what right had this woman to have the temerity to walk into Belmonde and disturb its serenity by getting killed? Then he saw how absurd this was, not to say unfeeling, and laughed at himself shamefacedly.

"With – the scarf?"

The inspector shook his head. "The marks were not the mark of a ligature. Someone had his hands around her throat while she was still alive. If that was how she died, why she was left in the stream afterwards is still a puzzle." Leaving it at that, he walked to the table where the clothes had lain and, like a conjuror producing rabbits out of a hat, he brought forth a small pasteboard oblong, which he put on the desk.

"Return ticket to London. Looks as though she intended to go back the same day. Slipped inside the palm of her glove, see, for safe-keeping. She didn't have a bag with her, which I find interesting. Never known a woman happy without a bag of some sort for long – no money, no comb, not even a handkerchief."

The inspector sat down and there was silence for a while. "Where exactly was she found?"

"Where the stream goes by that derelict gamekeeper's cottage, near what seems to be called the bothy and the pheasant pens."

"The devil she was!"

"It was the gamekeeper, Jordan, who found her."

Jordan was a black-browed, sour individual, taciturn of speech but, according to Sir Henry, the best gamekeeper in Shropshire. Unmarried, wary of women. Not, one would have thought, the type to get near enough to any female to strangle her, much less with an expensive silk scarf. And for what reason? He might knock a man down, or break his head with a stick, when his black temper was up; he had big, coarse hands that would certainly be capable of strangling anyone, but Sebastian had seen him free a dog caught in a rabbit-snare with a touch as gentle as a woman's. "He wouldn't have done anything like that, not Tom Jordan."

"Maybe not, but pending further enquiries, we have him in custody. The person who 'finds' the body is naturally suspect – and Jordan's known to have a temper, I gather – and to drink – and no one seems to have seen him at any time yesterday."

"But look here – murder!"

The inspector raised an expressive eyebrow, but remained silent.

"Well," Sebastian said awkwardly, at last, preparing to leave. "You've heard what I came to tell you…"

"Thank you. I appreciate that, sir. I take it you'll be staying here for the present." This did not sound like a question. "You may have been the last person to see her alive, see. Apart from her murderer, of course."

Sebastian felt a sense of unreality sweep over him. Was the inspector, simply because both he and the victim had arrived from London on the same day, suspecting some connection between them? Did he believe a word of Sebastian's story? Did he think he had murdered the woman? "Sorry, I can't stay. I'm due to drive Miss Fox back to London on Monday. She came down with me."

"Miss Fox? Who's she? Did she see the woman under the trees, as well?"

"No." Sebastian explained who Louisa was, and where she lived. "She has lectures to attend in London next week. It's important she gets back."

"I'm sorry, but unless we get this cleared up before then, you may have to ask Miss Fox to find some other means of getting back – she shouldn't have much trouble getting a train from Bridgnorth." Meredith had seemed to have the business so very much at his fingertips, with little doubt as to the identity of the murderer, that Sebastian was surprised when he added, "It's a puzzle, this one. Unknown woman, not obviously a vagrant, no obvious motive for her being killed, unless it was the theft of her handbag. Not the sort of thing that happens in these parts, at all – it looks very much as though we're going to have to borrow a detective from London to help us out on this. We've telegraphed for one, and with luck he might be here by Monday, Tuesday at the latest. That's why I have to ask you to stay – until he's had a word with you." He stood up and extended a hand. "Thank you for coming in, sir. That's all I have to say for now."

It occurred to Sebastian that the inspector was by no means as confident as he had sounded, that perhaps he didn't believe Jordan was undoubtedly guilty; he had, after all, just admitted that this was being regarded as no ordinary, common or garden murder – if any murder could ever be called that. He began to have the impression that there was also a great deal more that the man might have said, had he so chosen, about who this woman might be, and why she was here. And again he thought that perhaps it was no coincidence she had been found in the Belmonde woods, and that, having been found there, it might well turn out to be nothing short of a catastrophe for the hitherto unassailable Chetwynd family.

Chapter Six

The news that a body had been discovered on the estate was brought to Sir Henry by Seton, via one of the estate men who had come upon an almost incoherent Jordan in the woods, mumbling and ranting about dead bodies. Having first made sure, by demanding to see the body in question himself, that Jordan had not been drunk or taken leave of his senses, and that the woman was certainly dead, Will Shefford had guided him into the little bothy where the gamekeeper kept his tools and his fencing and the feed for his pheasant chicks, and where he'd been sleeping the previous night on a rough truckle bed, keeping watch for poachers. His chicks, which he'd hand-reared since spring, were almost ready to be released into the wild, and he'd slept with one ear open and his shotgun at his side, ready to scare off any intruders.

"I suppose I mun leave you, Tom," said Shefford, "while I go tell Mr Seton." He looked doubtfully at the keeper, and then around the bothy. An empty bottle told its own story. "You got coffee or summat up here, then?"

No answer came from Jordan, and Shefford filled the keeper's blackened tinkers' kettle from the stream and set it to boil, after feeding the dying fire with dry wood. He found tea, but no milk, laced the brew with plenty of sugar and thrust a mug into Jordan's hand in the hopes that he would drink it.

"Don't you go doing anything daft, Tom – we'll be back just now."

With this further injunction, Shefford had hurried to the house on the edge of the park where Seton and his wife lived, to find them still at breakfast. After that the matter was taken out of his hands by the agent, who first saw to it that the police were informed and then went up to the bothy, and Jordan, to await the arrival of PC Simmonds, after which he felt it was more than time to inform Sir Henry, who couldn't be found for some time.

Eventually the search led to the little room off the long gallery where Henry kept his coin collection. Seton saw immediately that something was troubling him; he could spend hours poring over the collection which he'd begun when he was a boy, and which included a louis d'or of exceptional value to him because it had reputedly been given to a Chetwynd by Louis XIII himself. He resorted to examination of his precious collection in times of stress as other men might seek solace in drink, or women, and to find him there when he should have been at church reading the lesson was indeed an indication that something was deeply troubling him.

After the news was broken to him, he returned with Seton to the clearing where the body had been found, only to be told by Will Shefford that both body and gamekeeper had already been taken away by the police.

"The police!" growled Henry. "I suppose by that you mean Joe Simmonds? What the devil does he mean by taking away my gamekeeper?"

"Begging your pardon, Sir Henry, it were the Bridgnorth inspector as took him away."

Seton intervened to say, "They'll need to get the straight facts from him, and they could hardly keep him here." He added, "I think it might go very badly for him. The woman seems to have been strangled, you know – and though he says he found her —"

"If Jordan says that, he's telling no more than the truth. Whatever his faults, he's no liar."

Shefford nodded. "That's right. Never knowed Tom Jordan tell a lie."

Seton also was inclined to be of the same opinion, but he thought any man might be a liar if he found himself faced with a murder charge. He kept his counsel, however. Sir Henry had been in a strange mood for the past week, and he seemed very shocked at what had happened – though possibly, Seton felt, more at the impropriety of such an event occurring on his land than of a woman having cruelly died there. But then, such a woman could be nothing to him, after all, a stranger with whom he had never had any contact.

"What was the woman doing up here in the first place?" Henry said brusquely, confirming Seton's belief. "Getting herself killed, what's more?"

* * *

Detective Chief Inspector Crockett, from Scotland Yard, arrived at Wolverhampton High Level station the morning of the following day, which he considered nothing less than miraculous in the light of the short time he'd had to prepare himself. It had been an annoyance hard to swallow when the summons had come from Shropshire. He'd had to make hasty arrangements for someone else to take over the case he'd been engaged on for the last six weeks, and was just nearing completion, but he wasn't anxious to displease the Assistant Commissioner, who had stressed the importance of an immediate response. Moreover, the Chief Constable in Shrewsbury had said he wanted the best man available, and Crockett couldn't deny he was that man, and that his superiors had agreed enough with his estimation to send him.

He had been advised to take a train to Wolverhampton, where someone would be waiting with some form of transport for the rest of the journey, rather than take the other line to Bridgnorth with the number of changes which would be necessary. Quicker this way, perhaps, he told himself, but hardly could it have been less unpleasant. For the last half hour or so, the train had been thundering through a dismal landscape of factories, filthy canals and chimney stacks belching forth black smoke. Out of the carriage windows for mile upon mile he'd been regaled with the spectacle of chain-making shops, foundries and heavy metal works wedged huggermugger in between narrow streets of terraced red brick houses. He'd caught glimpses of fiery infernos through the open doors of great sheds, peopled with teams of men sweating at the forges and furnaces. "Like the god Vulcan and his myrmidons," had murmured the talkative old gentleman who was his companion in the compartment, to an uncomprehending Crockett: there was nothing godlike about the scene to him, as the train roared on and the clang of metal and the screech of grinding machinery sounded even above the noise of the carriage wheels. The roar of industry, the heart of England – ye Gods, no wonder they called it the Black Country!

Never mind, he told himself, it should prove an incentive for him to crack the case as soon as possible so that he could get back to the Smoke – which he'd once believed to be the dirtiest place on God's earth. And well it might be, but at least it was civilised.

Inspector Daffyd Meredith was there on the platform to meet him. They exchanged a brief handshake on introducing themselves, but Crockett said nothing more, just gave Meredith a curt, unpromising nod. Meredith showed no indication that he'd expected anything else, and led the way out.

As they emerged from the station, the London man coughed ostentatiously, looking around with unconcealed distaste at the pall of smoke and grime hanging over the town. He was somewhat mollified to see a gleaming motorcar waiting for them, impressed despite himself. Even the Metropolitan police were still making do with bicycles and public transport. He was beginning to feel quite affable by the time they were seated in the red leather interior behind the driver, with the hood thrown back to the bright sunny day and the town left behind.

Meredith had decided that the journey from Wolverhampton to Belmonde would provide the opportunity, not only to give the London detective the facts of the situation, but also for them to get each other's measure, and he was rather glad, in view of Chief Inspector Crockett's demeanour so far, that he'd asked for a motor rather than a pony and trap – and that he'd chosen to meet the detective personally. His wife was always telling him not to judge a person's character by their taste in clothes: she liked a man to be as smart and up-to-date as his circumstances would allow, whereas Meredith tended to feel that any red-blooded male who showed too much interest in how he dressed wasn't to be trusted. He therefore held his peace for the time being and tried not to look too obviously sideways at Crockett.

A bit of a dandy, this DCI had turned out to be – a check suit and a well-brushed brown bowler, grey suede spats and a silk handkerchief in his top pocket, at the moment being employed to flick away imaginary smuts from the pristine cuffs of his immaculate shirt and – God save us! – a pink carnation in his buttonhole. Meredith couldn't resist an inward chuckle – he hoped that in the large travelling bag he'd offered to carry for the detective were a pair of stout boots, at least. Prancing about the woods at Belmonde wouldn't do his spats or his shiny shoes much good. Some sort of waterproof could doubtless be found for him, if necessary, but a man's boots needed to fit his own feet. He might have been surprised had he seen Crockett, who liked to think of himself as a master of disguise, dressed up when necessary with a beard and a spotted handkerchief around his neck, his hands filthy and thick grime under his nails.

But as their journey proceeded, Meredith saw that Crockett might do, after all, for within a mile or so of the big town, the scenery had improved, and with it his temper. As they bowled along from Staffordshire and into Shropshire, through villages and leafy lanes, with wooded hills rising in the distance, Crockett almost visibly thawed. He began to speak of the case, and to ask for the facts.

"So she was from London, then, the victim?"

"Well," Meredith replied in his considering way, "we know she came on the train from London. But whether she lived there, of course, is a different matter." He went on to say that, unlike Crockett himself, she had chosen to arrive at Bridgnorth. Passengers arriving there with a London ticket were few and far between, and a woman answering her description had been remembered by the ticket collector. She'd made enquiries as to what means she should employ to get to Belmonde village, and had been directed towards the local carrier, who was picking up deliveries of goods which had been brought in the guard's van of the very same train she had arrived on. The carrier, Timothy Childe, had been spoken to and said he'd dropped her off at the gates of the Abbey. He also said she'd had some sort of fancy way of talking when she asked him for the ride – London or some such, he couldn't rightly say- at any rate it wasn't Welsh, that being the only foreign accent he'd have recognised. By that criterion, both detectives were 'foreigners'.

Apparently, Childe had claimed he and his passenger had no more conversation after that; Constable Simmonds had added that this was very likely the truth. Unless he'd completely broken with the tradition of a lifetime, Childe would have been, if not actually drunk, at least well away by that time in the afternoon. His horse knew its own way home, and he usually slept with the reins slack in his hands, in the way of carters the world over. He'd reckoned the lady had paid him a shilling, but couldn't recall whether she'd taken it from a purse or handbag, or simply from her pocket. She certainly didn't have any baskets or bundles with her. "So, she's a complete mystery," finished Meredith.

"I suppose you know," said Crockett, after a pause, "that Mr Montague Chetwynd, MP is the brother of your Sir Henry Chetwynd?"

Meredith inclined his head. "That's so. And he was staying at Belmonde last night."

"Was he, by Jupiter?"

Crockett said no more, for they were now approaching Bridgnorth, which looked worth more than a second glance. He'd felt a great pity as he'd passed through the Black Country for all the people who were forced by circumstances to live there, and was pleasantly surprised to find something far different here. The picturesque little town rose high above the Severn on sandstone cliffs, tier upon tier, so steeply that access to the High Town, Meredith informed him, was only by way of a punishingly steep and tortuous road, or by several equally demanding sets of steps which had been carved over the years into the soft red sandstone – or nowadays by the new cliff railway, of which the inhabitants were very proud. "Won't need to bother about that, though, Mr Crockett, you'll be served very well at the Falcon in the Low Town where we've put you up."

Crockett nodded and instantly resumed the conversation where he'd left off, before they should be interrupted by arrival at the inn, where they must stop to leave his bag. "You'll be aware also, I suppose, that Mr Montague Chetwynd is one of those in the Houses of Parliament who is strong against these viragos who are clamouring for the vote?"

"Thinking of that speech of his in the Commons last month?"

Meredith's response showed that he'd got there before him; he wasn't such a bumpkin as he'd at first seemed to Crockett, misled by his slow speech and deliberate responses, and accustomed as he was to the Cockney sharpness of his underlings, and the general pace of things at Scotland Yard. "Yes. We have been wondering if the victim might have been one of them...had she known he was to be there." He added drily, "Up to all sorts of mischief, these women in London, we hear – though of course, we're not of enough importance here to attract that sort of attention."

Crockett saw that Meredith's tongue was firmly in his cheek, and warmed further to him. He appreciated a man with a sense of irony. And he had to allow that it was, so far, the only explanation which seemed to fit: that the victim could be one of these so called suffragettes, who would go to any length to publicise their cause; who actually seemed to relish imprisonment. Crockett sighed. He definitely did not want this case to have anything to do with these pesky females, who unfortunately included in their number a certain young lady who had declined as yet to become Mrs Crockett in favour of casting in her lot with them, and for whom he had a very soft spot. In his opinion the Prime Minister, Mr Asquith, had got it right when he refused to listen to them. But even if this woman had been a suffragette, the most rabid anti-franchiser could scarcely have thought that grounds enough to kill her?

Come to that, it didn't sound, from what Meredith had told him, as though Jordan, the gamekeeper, the one who claimed he'd found her and was therefore the prime suspect, had a motive, either. Or indeed anyone else who had been at Belmonde that night, though he would reserve judgement on that point until he'd interviewed all of them himself.

"The question is, of course, if she was a suffragette and came here with some deliberately evil intention, would she have been alone?" asked Meredith.

"That's unusual, I'll admit, they normally work in pairs at least, but perhaps she was just spying out the lie of the land." Or just out to perpetrate one of their usual tricks: throwing through a window a brick wrapped in a paper with 'Votes for Women!' written on it? "They're up to anything, you know." His sigh was fetched up from the bottom of his heart. Only a couple of weeks ago, his Agnes had been involved with heckling ministers arriving for a meeting at Westminster, and been dragged away by the heels, taken to Bow Street and had been lucky to be charged only with breaching the peace. Sweet Agnes – who until now had spent her life peaceably looking after her father – Agnes, with her peaches and cream complexion, her lovely golden hair, and the lightest hand with a sponge-cake than anyone else he knew. It was unbelievable, the people this dratted cause was drawing in. "Whoever would have dreamt these ideas have been going on for years at the back of so many decent women's minds?" he asked with another deep sigh.

"Don't know about that," said Meredith. "Put there, more like. By that Mrs Pankhurst and her brood. Nothing they're not up to." Mrs Pankhurt's daughter Christabel had actually had the effrontery to subpoena Lloyd George – the Chancellor of the Exchequer, no less – the Welsh Wizard, on some trumped up charge. That had really shocked Meredith. What was the world coming to? But he was for some reason unhappy with the suffragette theory about this murder, and he went on to explain why. Those clothes of hers, for one thing, had shown that the victim was unlikely to have been a woman of means – unless she'd been down on her luck – which in itself went against her being a suffragette, who were invariably ladies, recruited from the upper or middle classes. The rest, though perhaps more in need of suffrage, were normally too busy looking after their families or earning a living to have the time or the means to indulge themselves in such a way.

Meredith, working as a quiet country policeman, hadn't come across much in the way of murder during his career, but when he had, the explanation for it had usually been much simpler – a fit of jealous rage by a husband, drunkenness, a fight gone wrong. In this case, the motive might just turn out to be the simple theft of the victim's handbag. Maybe. The larger question of why she'd been killed and dumped in the stream remained.

"So she never reached the house, if that was her purpose," he said, "and if young Mr Chetwynd is to be believed, she was last seen at just before half past three – and found dead at ten o'clock the next morning. The doctor wouldn't commit himself to saying anything any more than that she had been dead for probably fifteen to eighteen hours, according to the state of rigor the body was in."

"Then it's the hours between three-thirty and about seven

o'clock we're concerned with. Narrows the possibilities."

"Probably nearer three-thirty than seven, unless she was wandering around the woods in the rain for three or four hours. The servants say no one called at the house all day."

"Hmm. I'd like to go and see them all at the big house for myself, before I do anything else. Just a matter of satisfying myself," Crockett added pacifically. "Tell me what's been done so far."

He immediately appreciated the difficulties Meredith had outlined when it came to interviewing the Chetwynd family. It wasn't only that they were local gentry, though this did make things delicate. No treading on toes, here, or the Chief Constable could descend like a ton of bricks on the Assistant Commissioner in London, with a consequent domino effect, ending up with Crockett at the bottom of the pile. No, it was more a matter of the Chetwynds themselves, who presented what appeared to be an unassailable front and made it clear they didn't see what they had to do with the matter.

He was given a small room in which to do his interviews with the servants, but afterwards, when he asked to speak to Lady Chetwynd, was summoned into her presence. Whether this was a policy of intimidation or not, Crockett wasn't sure, but to a certain extent, it succeeded, despite his own opinion that he was well able to be at ease anywhere, and with anyone.

For one thing, it was not only Lady Chetwynd herself, smiling and gracious, but somehow aloof, beautifully dressed in a high-necked blouse of violet colour, her dark hair puffed out in a fashionably wide style, but also the pastel-coloured room which put him at a disadvantage. Opulently luxurious, feminine, smelling of flowers. Even in his best suit and his spats, with his patent leather shoes gleaming and fresh pomade on his hair, he felt as out of place as a Pearly King at a funeral, as gauche as he had when he'd done his first interview as a young constable. Moreover, the room was too hot. He had to resist the urge to run a finger inside his collar.

For another, Lady Chetwynd sat at the piano all the time, with the chair he had been offered some distance away and at right angles to it. The lid of the piano was up and the fingertips of one hand rested on the framework of the keyboard, while the other hand remained in her lap. The position gave him the disconcerting impression she was only waiting for him to leave before she could carry on playing – or that, indeed, she might start at any moment. It was difficult for him to determine her expression except when she chose to turn her head to face him. A charming profile, but profiles didn't give much away. Not that Adèle Chetwynd had anything to conceal, or so it appeared. She had been a little ill lately, she confessed, and had spent most of the previous day in her room. Later, she had been with the family at tea and, except when she was changing for dinner, in their company for the rest of the evening, she told him in a very English drawl which yet had a faint overtone that told him she might have come from across the Atlantic.

"It's all too simply dreadful, of course, though what in the world all this has to do with any of us, I simply cannot imagine. I realise we're obliged to answer your questions, and if it leads to finding who killed this woman, I for one am only too pleased to do so...but what *do* you suppose this woman could have been doing, wandering around our woods?"

She sounded very relaxed, but he noticed the quick rise and fall of her breast, the way her breath caught a little as she spoke, making him wonder if she had difficulty with her breathing. Just at that moment, the door was opened and Lady Emily stood in the aperture. Her daughter-in-law started, and her hand moved in an involuntary gesture on the keys, striking a discordant note.

"My dear Adèle – you're a bundle of nerves. Have they told you the police are here?"

Lady Chetwynd smiled, her composure quite restored. "*Belle-mère*, this is Inspector Crockett, of Scotland Yard. My husband's mother, Lady Emily Chetwynd."

Chief Inspector, thought Crockett, rising to his feet. He didn't correct the mistake.

The dowager was what he thought of as a grand old dame. Her be-ringed hands rested on the silver knob of an ebony cane, but she had the upright posture all Victorian young ladies learned in the schoolroom to see them through life, and an imperious lift of the head. "What's all this nonsense about Tom Jordan?" she asked, eyeing Crockett, choosing an upright chair for herself and motioning him peremptorily to resume his seat.

"I wish we could say it was nonsense, but we don't know yet."

Unexpectedly, she smiled. She had been a beauty, in her day, he saw, and then thought, she still is. Her eyes were perhaps a little faded, a forget-me-not blue rather than the sapphire they had probably once been. Her face was wrinkled, but that slightly crooked smile was irresistible, the sort that may have once driven many a rejected young man into contemplating suicide. Crockett was under her spell in less than a couple of minutes.

She said forthrightly, "Tom Jordan's a hothead, always was, but if you imagine he would strangle anyone with a silk scarf, you're wrong. I doubt whether he's ever seen a Liberty scarf in his life."

This was what happened in a place like this, where the big house and the village had been socially interdependent for generations. Rumour ran through their hitherto peaceful lives like a hot knife through butter – rumour, speculation, gossip and guesswork mixed with fact. Like everyone else, Lady Emily apparently knew the suspect well; but she did not appear to know the precise nature of the crime. Yet she knew about the scarf: Perkins, the village constable, doubtless. He made a note to speak to him. Was it a guess that it came from Liberty?

"We have to take everyone into account. And the circumstances are very suspicious, my lady."

"No doubt. But things are not always what they seem, are they?" Her eyes flickered. For all her composure, he felt that she was shaken by the events. He suspected she was not easily shaken, that life had held more sorrow for her than this death of a stranger, which had taken others besides herself by surprise, but she was an old lady.

He left them both in what he privately thought of as Lady Chetwynd's boudoir, and went to question Sir Henry – a mere matter of form, but it had to be done. He wasn't by any means satisfied with the outcome there, either. Sir Henry's land agent, Alexander Seton, and later, the gamekeeper Jordan's own statement had confirmed that he had been out in the woods the previous day until just before his son's arrival. "And why not?" he asked belligerently, his black brows coming together. "I'm out and around the estate every day of my life, when I'm here at Belmonde. No reason why yesterday should have been any different."

If his son had been telling the truth about seeing the woman in the woods – and there seemed to be no reason why he should have mentioned it, if not – then Sir Henry could hardly have strangled the woman and been back in time to be taking tea when Sebastian arrived at the house – unless he had gone out again afterwards, which was of course quite possible. Yet where was the motive – indeed, where was the motive for anyone having committed such a murder? But Sir Henry was a man inclined to bluster, and moreover, not adept at lying, and to Crockett, experienced as he was in dealing with those who were strangers to the truth, it was pretty obvious he hadn't been told the whole story.

As for Montague Chetwynd: The Honourable Member for East Lyndon had already gone back to London. He was a busy and important man. He could not afford to let the unexplained death of an unknown woman on his brother's estate – however unfortunate it was – interefere with his Parliamentary duties. But in any case, according to the butler, he had not arrived until about seven on Saturday, having driven up from London.

The suffragette theory, in any case, seemed increasingly pointless to Crockett – if any form of attack were to have been made on him, then it would surely have been on his own property, in London, where it would have attracted the maximum amount of attention. These women rarely did anything on the quiet – publicity for their demands was what they thrived on. Moreover, as Meredith had been quick to point out, since Chetwynd did not come all that often down to Belmonde, there was the implication that someone in the organisation must have known him well enough to have the information that he had indeed planned to be there that particular weekend. This was quite possible, of course. Women in the Movement were quite apt to circulate in political spheres as well as in the upper echelons of society. Crockett could have named quite a few families who would have done a great deal to have the names of their daughters – and sometimes their wives – erased from the police records and therefore from public consciousness, shameless as they were.

He was told there had also been present at Belmonde over the weekend a Mrs Cashmore and her daughter, Miss Dora Cashmore, but Meredith had not deemed it necessary to prevent them from leaving as they had planned on the Monday morning. They had on Saturday been out visiting an elderly relative in Much Wenlock and hadn't returned until late afternoon, when they had gone straight to their rooms to rest before dinner. Apart from the fact that they could not add anything to what had already been said, Meredith had thought it unlikely either was capable of committing such a crime.

In theory, everyone in the house, including the servants, could account for their movements from three-thirty onwards. In practice, it seemed to Crockett, any one of them, in a house this size, could have slipped out and murdered the woman – though as yet there seemed no cogent reason why there should have arisen a need to do something so drastic.

Chapter Seven

"Look here," announced the young woman with flushed cheeks and bright brown hair escaping in tendrils from under her woolly hat, marching into the schoolroom the following morning , followed by a helplessly protesting Constable Simmonds. Crockett was in sole possession of the schoolroom for the time being, having left Meredith in Bridgnorth arranging, amongst other things, for the post-mortem to be held as soon as possible. "I hear I'm going to have to find my own way back to London tomorrow. It's most inconvenient, you know. I especially arranged to come down with Sebastian – Mr Chetwynd – because I've a large box of books I must take back with me and he was going to drive me back. I am Louisa Fox, by the way."

"Sorry, sir," put in the mortified constable, "but I couldn't say her nay —"

"That's all right, Simmonds. Leave this to me. Very pleased to meet you, Miss Fox. I —"

"I suppose I can arrange for someone to take me to the station and have the books conveyed by taxi at the other end, but it's not very convenient. Can't you question Sebastian now and let him go for the time being? Oh Lord, that sounds as though you might suspect him, which is quite ridiculous. You surely can't believe he had anything to do with this murder?"

"I'm sure such a resourceful young lady as you appear to be could indeed have managed very well about your books," answered Crockett, smiling in spite of himself, "but as a matter of fact, there shouldn't be any difficulty."

"Oh."

"I'm Detective Chief Inspector Crockett, from Scotland Yard. I don't doubt Mr Chetwynd can drive you back after I've seen him later today. From what I've already gathered, it will only be a formality and then he'll be quite free to go when he wishes – so long as he tells me where I can get in touch, if necessary. Won't you take a seat, miss?" He gestured to the only one available, one of the pushed-back desks.

"That's all right, then." She hitched herself on to it. Her feet didn't reach the floor, but she didn't appear to be self-conscious about the fact. "Look, I'm sorry about bursting in on you. I'm not usually so ill-mannered – though I must confess I am inclined to be a bit impetuous at times. Is there any way I can help?"

"I'm not sure. Er – what time did Mr Chetwynd leave you at your house on Saturday?"

"Just after three, about ten past, I think."

And Blythe had confirmed to Meredith that he had arrived at Belmonde at three twenty-five. There was no chance that between then and the time he had left Louisa that he could have found the time to get to the clearing, only accessible on foot, strangle the woman, throw her into the stream, and then get back to the house.

"Mr Crockett —" began Louisa, then stopped.

"Yes, Miss Fox?"

"There are a lot of rumours flying around the village, as I suppose you're aware. We're a very small community, and this has caused quite a stir. I know you've arrested Tom Jordan —"

"Not yet. We are merely questioning him."

She dismissed this quibble with a wave of her hand. "Nobody believes he did it. He's not a violent person, really. Besides, he never has anything to do with women – he'd run a mile if one appeared up there in the woods. He's —" She stopped, as if uncertain, then went on in a rush. "People seem to think the woman was a suffragette, bent on some sort of mischief, but that can't really be feasible, you know. It's not our policy to work alone, for one thing —"

So, she too was one of them! Oh, Lord. Crockett would never cease to be amazed at the diversity of the women who joined that unholy band.

She seemed belatedly to realise what she'd said, and smiled wryly. "I shouldn't be saying this to a policeman, should I? You're not exactly the best of friends to us."

"There's a remedy for that, but I don't want to get into an argument about it, Miss Fox."

"I wouldn't dream of arguing with you, we women never get the best of it with men like you. But in any case, I'm afraid I wouldn't be entirely convincing." She sighed. "I'm not whole-hearted enough to get involved in the militant side of things – and besides, my medical studies take up all the spare time I have. But that can't be wrong, can it? Being a doctor is the best way I know of helping women." She fiddled with her gloves. "But I'm afraid some of the members are inclined to think I'm not active enough."

"Take my advice and stay inactive, Miss Fox. You stick to your doctoring."

She looked as though he'd said something amusing, and after a moment, he saw that maybe he had. Most people, especially men, thought a woman wanting to be a doctor was as outrageous as women wanting the vote, and more degrading than the things they were willing to do to get it.

Sebastian was still kicking his heels, impatient to be told he was off the hook and could take himself back to London, but before he did, he knew he must find some opportunity to talk with his father about the real purpose for this visit home. So much had been going on that it had seemed highly inappropriate to raise what was all too likely to cause another furore. But now, both had risen early and were alone together and, suddenly wanting to get the business over before he should lose his courage, he at last blurted out what he had intended to present as a reasoned argument.

He could not have chosen a worse moment if he'd tried. Everyone knew Sir Henry regarded breakfast as the most important meal of the day, which he took early and in silence, reading the newspaper as he tackled his porridge and the devilled kidneys, bacon and eggs while they were still fresh from the kitchen. He'd looked up from his newspaper and nodded a good morning, even more taciturn than usual, unfocused and with his mind obviously elsewhere, while Sebastian helped himself to some cold ham and toyed with it for a while before suddenly bringing up the subject uppermost in his mind. There had not been the blazing row he had expected. His father had not erupted like Vesuvius. Instead, there had been cold disbelief etched on his face, and an ensuing silence which Sebastian had steeled himself not to interrupt, holding on to his temper in case he said something for which he would later be sorry. After which, Sir Henry had departed abruptly. Presently, there had come the bang of the business room door.

The air in the dining room seemed all used up. Why had he spoken so impulsively? Sebastian cursed his own folly. He should have known better than to broach such a touchy subject at such a time, when his father was so preoccupied over this terrible business of murder being committed on the estate. But he had suddenly despised himself for being so weak-kneed as to need his mother's support, and had seized the opportunity without thinking. Too late, he saw his mistake. Had he waited until his mother was present, she might at least have helped to smooth the path.

Like many normally easy-going people, when he did lose his temper, Sebastian could lose it royally; but it was a rare occurrence which never lasted long and he bore no grudge afterwards – nor, usually, did the recipients of it when they had got over the shock, for it was only ever provoked by unfairness or a threat to his independence. It was both which rankled now. He couldn't see why the simple wish to take up a profession, the desire to be useful in the world, should be in any way worse than Harry's quixotic adventure to South Africa – and certainly better than the idle life he'd led subsequently. But Harry had been astute enough to show an interest in his inheritance, to hide his boredom with Sir Henry's endless preoccupation with Belmonde. He seethed for half an hour under the injustice of it, disregarding his breakfast and letting his coffee go cold, by which time, though still simmering, he was beginning to go off the boil. Anyone would think I were the heir to a dukedom, rather than a piffling baronetcy, he fumed – but he was damned if he was going to give up his only chance of doing what he had set his whole heart upon. Refusal of monetary help was the worst that could happen. Sebastian decided he could face that prospect – sell his car as a last resort, pay his pupillage with the money left to him by his grandfather, and live off dripping toast, a delicacy to which Louisa had introduced him.

Louisa! With a jolt, he remembered the reason he'd risen early. He wanted to see and confer with her before she set off to catch the London train, as she must if he was to be kept here by the police. He poured himself another cup of hot coffee and burnt his mouth in the process of drinking it, before leaving the dining room in haste and making his way outside.

There existed, in a deep corner between two of the twin towers of the house, a dark and gloomy Victorian grotto, or fernery, where the sun never shone, lit only by a sort of skylight, and which no one ever visited except as a short cut to the stable yard. Because of the damp, its door tended to stick, sometimes immovably for days at a time, and always had to be opened with force. Sebastian attacked it with his usual shove, helping it with his knee. This time, perversely, it gave easily and he fell inside, almost to his knees, and knocked his funny-bone with excruciating pain. Cursing under his breath, he picked himself up, just as Blythe, hearing the fall, reached the door. "You all right, Mr Sebastian?"

"I expected the door to be sticking, as usual. I see you've had it attended to."

"I got the joiner round first thing this morning to shave some wood off. Time it was done, after all these years. Couldn't get it open nohow yesterday."

"Well, he's made a good job of it. I shall have to remember in future, unless I want to break my neck."

The fernery was dark and had a sinister aspect, a place that would cool anyone's temper. A cave-like space with a low roof, dominated by a grotesque, greenish statue of Poseidon, god of the sea and earthquakes, wearing nothing but a look of thunder and a strand of seaweed, and wielding a trident which seemed poised to be plunged into whatever creatures might lurk in the depths of the fern-ringed pool beneath. The mossy walls, from which more ferns sprouted here and there, ran with damp and were encrusted with shells and fossils. By the time he set foot in this grotto Sebastian had realised it was still too early to burst in on them at the manor – and besides, he realised there was still need to collect himself before seeing Louisa. Despite the penetrating cold, he paused, nursing his still-tingling elbow, leaning against Poseidon's leg, one foot on the flints that formed the rim of the basin, thinking about what he had to say to her.

As he stared down into the murkiness of the water, a gleam of gold between the fronds of a fern that grew among the flints caught his eye. He bent to extract whatever it was and found it to be a cuff-link. There it lay on his palm for several seconds, gold and black onyx, while he wondered where he'd seen it before, until the dank, chill air of the place sent a sudden shiver of ice down his spine. He thrust the cuff-link into his pocket and turned abruptly to leave; here – this darkly-shadowed place, which had something inescapably secret and corrupt about it – was not a place to linger.

Once he had stepped out of the darkness and into the sun-shine, he took a deep breath of the warm air and walked more circumspectly towards the stable yard. Early as it still was, there were Monty and his mother, having just come back from an early morning ride. They made a striking pair: Monty, tall and athletic, the sun shining on his fair hair; his mother, who was not tall but whose graceful deportment and the way she carried her head made her seem taller, and who always looked well in riding habit. Her colour was heightened and they stood as they had dis-mounted, facing each other while the horses were led away. They had not seen him and Sebastian hesitated to interrupt what was obviously a private moment. Monty was holding his mother's arm, their eyes held with an intensity he could almost feel. He saw her try to pull away. Monty would not let her go, but kept his hand clamped tightly around her wrist. She gave a small excla-mation and for one incredulous moment, Sebastian thought he had been hurting her. Before he could step forward, however, he heard his uncle ask quickly, "Did I hurt you?"

Adèle's chin lifted. "Not in the least," she said tightly.

"I'm afraid I did. Forgive me, I did not mean it. You know how I get carried away by the force of my arguments." He still held her wrist, however.

At that, she turned her head angrily aside and when she saw Sebastian, she drew in an involuntary breath, whereupon Monty, following her glance, immediately let go of her. She came towards Sebastian, smiling, and enquired in an ordinary voice whether he was going to ride, though the heightened colour had fled from her face. Her riding crop was in her right hand, her left dangled, the fingers red where the blood had coursed back. "I would have asked you to come with us, had I known."

"No – I'm going to take a walk. Just need a breath of air."

Adèle nodded and went into the house, while Monty stayed chatting pleasantly, yet Sebastian could not rid himself of the picture of his uncle's face as he had gripped Adèle's hand. What had they been arguing about? A vein still throbbed near Monty's temple, a sure, inherited giveaway of the Chetwynd temper – even in someone as normally controlled as Monty.

The idea that he had deliberately hurt Adèle was unthinkable, but something disturbing had certainly occurred between them. A thought passed through Sebastian's mind which he could not yet put a name to.

This shocking thing which had disturbed the propriety of life at Belmonde was making everyone out of temper and on edge, he thought as he walked on between the yew hedges, followed by the dogs who, sensing a walk, had bounded round the side of the house as he set off. Yet logic dictated there was no compulsion to be unduly upset about the death – even the murder – of a woman none of them had ever set eyes on. Shocked, yes, sad, even, as anyone must be at such a thing. But anything else was surely hypocrisy – even if they found out she had indeed been one of those suffragettes, come to badger Monty, which was quite possible, of course. Inky Winthrop's father, also in Parliament, had lately had a stone thrown through the window of his motor. Fortunately – although it broke the window – it had missed Lord Winthrop and merely knocked off his chauffeur's hat.

Or unless the victim was who Sebastian feared she might be.

Walking down the sloping avenue between the statues, averting his eyes from the dismal collection beneath the Wellingtonia, he found himself by the lake. The sun was out in earnest now and the stretch of water, serene and untroubled, was dappled by coins of sunlight under the trees that shaded the far end, and sparkled brilliantly in the middle, looking fresh and almost irresistibly inviting. He was a good swimmer and knew the lake from boyhood: where it went deep, where the treacherous underwater reeds were, where one could climb out easily on to the bank. He knew how long it took to swim the lake end to end, or to circle the little islet in the centre, where the mallards nested, and where the old punt, which no one had used for years, lay half-submerged at the edge.

But he was too old to undress and plunge in without thought, to roll himself dry on the grass like a puppy as he and Harry had done as boys. He hesitated, not for long, but long enough, for in the next moment he looked up and saw Louisa on the far bank.

"You came by the back way," he said, hurrying round to join her. "Another few minutes and I might have missed you – I was on my way to see you."

"I came that way because I went by the school to see the policeman who's arrived from London."

"What's he like – the great detective?"

She laughed. "Not quite what you'd expect. He had a flower in his buttonhole. Quite the swell. He says wants to see you later today and then apparently you'll be free to go, so I'll wait and return with you. Another day will make no difference in the circumstances." She sat on a rustic seat by the lake edge. "Tell me why you wanted to see me?"

"If it's all the same with you, I'd rather walk. I can tell you as we go."

She took one look at his face and agreed. They set off to follow the dogs, who of their own accord had chosen to lope up the hill behind the house, a path which would eventually join the one he'd taken the previous day. Sebastian let them go where they would, and they seemed to know when they reached the clearing and the Green Man pool that he would pause as he usually did, and ran off on their own pursuits.

He and Louisa found a rock and sat facing the sun. "Well, Seb, what is it you're bursting to tell me?"

He grimaced. "Is it that obvious?"

"To anyone who knows you, yes."

He told her then what he had told his father, except that he did not feel constrained this time to get it out in a few bald sentences and be done with it. Her reception of his news was more than he could have expected or desired: her eyes glowed, impulsively she kissed him on the cheek, though it was only as a sister might.

"I can't tell you how glad I am. I've been hoping for so long

that you'd find something worthy of you, someday. I must confess I never thought of you as an architect, though now I can't
imagine why not. It's so exactly right in every respect. Do tell –
what happened, what made you decide." When she'd had every
little detail from him, still smiling, she added, "The mood you
were in earlier this summer, I should have guessed. I knew something was up."

"Such as what? Did you imagine I was preparing to join the
Foreign Legion?"

"I was prepared to think anything. You've seemed
almost...desperate...at times. I'm so glad it's nothing like that."
She paused. "But what about your father?"

He grimaced. "What would you expect?" She had received his
news with such obvious delight that it made him feel no other
person's opinion in the matter counted a jot. He looked down
into her glowing eyes. She did not instantly look away, and he
felt he could fall into them forever, but he found no encouragement of the sort he looked for there. He almost groaned.
"Louisa —" he began.

She stopped him before he could go any further with a quick
look that seemed to say to him in more than words: Take care.
Don't say anything we might both regret. He obeyed the unspoken injunction. What was the use? Like a fool, he'd ignored the
dictates of his own heart, and failed to grasp the best thing in his
life, his shining star, and now it was too late. Louisa was set on
her chosen career, which certainly wouldn't include marriage,
and nothing would deflect her from it. He had heard her say too
often that she would never marry, and when Louisa said something, she meant it – did she not?

The silence lengthened. At last she said, "I wish you and Sir
Henry were on better terms – but you know...I wonder if I dare
say? It's hard for you to have lost Harry – but think how hard it
is for him to have lost one son, and now, as he sees it —"

"Harry. Oh yes, Harry," he said, not liking the bitterness he
heard in his own voice.

He was going to have to tell her what had been going through
his mind. It was what he had intended to do all along, yet he hesitated to elaborate, not from delicacy, for he knew he could be as

straightforward as he wished with Louisa and she would not be shocked, but because in the cold light of day, what he had begun to imagine seemed outrageous. In the end, he said simply, "Harry had a mistress."

"Hmm. Well, that's hardly the most astonishing thing I've ever heard. I might have been surprised if he had not," she said drily. "Who was she?"

"That's just the point. I have no idea. Some married woman, most probably, I thought at first."

It was the most likely explanation for what Harry had confessed to him, since unmarried girls were, of course, strictly off limits for anything but the most chaste of encounters – and then only in the presence of someone else. Chaperoned within an inch of their lives, even a snatched kiss was enough to ruin their reputation and leave them on the shelf for ever. All the world knew that a young man expected his wife to come to him pure and unsullied, though no such strictures applied to the opposite sex, quite the contrary: it was almost *de rigeur*, within a certain set, for a young man, while searching for a suitable wife, to take a lover, quite possibly from among the young married women of his acquaintance, a situation made possible by the women's husbands turning a blind eye, lest their own extra-marital activities should become suspect.

Such liaisons were an open secret, and yet...Sebastian had never heard the slightest whisper – even after Harry's death – of his name being linked with anyone. "I've asked around, but no one knew of any mistress – and Harry was hardly the most discreet of men, was he? I had the fact from his own lips, otherwise I might never have believed there was any such woman, disregarding the fact that he was drunk at the time he told me. Unless —"

"Unless she was not a woman known to his friends."

"Exactly. You read my mind, Louisa. Though even so, I would have thought someone would have known. An actress, or a dancer, perhaps? He wouldn't tell me her name."

Not that it had been a matter of any importance at the time – just an *amour* which he hadn't deemed it any business of his to pry into. And afterwards – well, it was over and done with and any woman who indulged in these sort of affairs would be well able to take care of herself. If she were indeed a married woman, she would not welcome intrusions from him – and if she were an actress, or a Gaiety girl, or anything like that, as he was inclined to suppose must be the case, then she would soon find someone else to be her protector. One suitor more or less could hardly make much difference.

"But supposing she was neither, Sebastian. Or had no husband to support her? Supposing Harry had been keeping her and she was left destitute when he died?" With her quick intuition Louisa had precisely followed his line of thought. "If she were in want – and came to seek assistance from his family? If, in fact, she was the woman who was killed?"

A silence fell. "If Harry had been keeping a woman like that, he would have left provision for her."

"Would he? He was still young, he hadn't expected to die."

More than that – would he have allied himself in the first place with a woman such as the one who had been killed here? There had been a distinct whiff of prayer meetings and good works about those clothes. Try as he might, Sebastian couldn't make the leap of imagination required to see Harry taking a mistress who wore a hat like that. In any case, if he had, what could she have hoped to gain from presenting herself to his family? What proof was there that anything between her and Harry had ever existed? What right did she have to claim support from them?

"Do you suppose I should tell the police? It's nothing more than the vaguest of suppositions, after all."

"I think we should try to find this woman ourselves. Then if we do succeed, there'll be no need to tell the police because she can't be the woman who's been killed."

"We?"

"You don't think I'd leave you to do it on your own?"

"Louisa. No," he said firmly. "It's not to be thought of. I believe she must be found before we alert the police, but finding her is up to me."

"How are we to start?" she asked, ignoring this.

"I'll think of something. But you are not to be involved." He was very much afraid he might be going to turn over stones and reveal things which might better remain concealed, yet at the same time, a bitterness which he did not like had entered into his memories of Harry, which he desperately needed to have cleared away. Exorcised might be a better word.

He was suddenly on fire, with a violent urge to set about the search with the same enthusiasm he had lately been giving to his studies. Harry's mistress must be found, and the idea that the strangled woman had anything to do with his brother put paid to once and for all. And then perhaps he could give undivided attention to his personal life. As to how finding the woman was to be accomplished, he was hanged if he could think how, at the moment. Monty, perhaps, might help. Monty knew everything. But then, the obvious occurred to him. The first person to talk to must, of course, be Sylvia, Harry's twin.

At this same moment, he became aware of the dogs making an unusual fuss around the pool. Dizzy was snuffling and barking, nosing around the rock on which the head of the Green Man was carved. Unnoticed before, he saw that the water had almost ceased to pour through the hole, had in fact dwindled to a mere trickle either side of the big rock. The spaniel was excitedly tugging at something from behind.

"Something's wedged in the mouth," Louisa said.

Whatever it was, Sebastian realised he could not reach it without plunging into the stream above and getting his feet soaked, which he wasn't about to do. "All right, fetch!" Both dogs immediately began to attack the wedged object enthusiastically, and Sophie eventually had it out.

Long before that, Sebastian sensed what it would be. When it finally came loose, with a gush of water through the hole, Sophie, wet through, dropped it obediently at Sebastian's feet, shaking water all over his polished leggings.

"Good gracious!" said Louisa, "how on earth did that get there?"

Before picking it up, they stood looking down at the stout, tough-looking object, its chunky, serviceable shape, with its rough-surfaced leather, water-soaked but impenetrable, which appeared to have suffered not at all from the attentions of the dogs' teeth. A small-sized Gladstone-type bag, about fifteen inches long, just big enough for carrying a few papers, or such as a woman might have used. Sebastian was well aware that he probably should not open it, but hand it to the police intact. His curiosity overcame his scruples. He took it and placed it on the rock upon which he and Louisa had been sitting and opened the clasp.

The bag was old, its lining torn in places, but the water had not penetrated the tough leather to the inside, where there were two hinged compartments containing very little: nothing more, in fact, than a shabby cloth purse with coins in it that did not quite add up to a guinea. A folded handkerchief, plain white hem stitched cotton with no embroidery, monogram or laundry mark. A tortoiseshell comb and a few hairpins in a pocket. A small oblong card, painted with roses, pathetically scuffed.

"A scent card," explained Louisa, sniffing at what was now only a faint memory of the attar-of-roses with which it had originally been impregnated. "To slip into a drawer to perfume lingerie, or rub on your wrists for the fragrance. They're given away as samples. Poor woman," she added softly. The card, indeed seemed to say more about the woman than her plain and serviceable clothes had done.

Sebastian put the card back into the little pocket where it had come from, almost pushing it by mistake behind the torn lining, which had become detached from the frame. As he smoothed the shabby cotton back, he felt something behind it. Cautiously, he drew it out: a blank envelope, sealed but bearing no address or information to indicate what it contained – he could well have in his hands the means, perhaps, of identifying the dead woman, the proof of whether she was or was not the person he had almost come to believe was certainly Harry's erstwhile mistress. At any rate, once the police had opened it they might be in a better position to discover who could have had a motive for killing her, and that would be that. Belmonde would be rid of this business, once and for all. Suspicion must hang over them all until the murderer was caught, until the police either found the person responsible, or decided that no one in the house had either the opportunity, or indeed a reason to murder.

He sat fingering the envelope, while Louisa watched him

quizzically. A letter? If so, it must be a short one, since there was no thickness to it. "Shall we?" he asked, then shook his head in answer to his own question. His lack of scruple did not extend to letting him open it, though he sat staring at it for some time before replacing it, with the other articles, back in the bag, still puzzling over the questions to which neither he nor Louisa, nor anyone else, it seemed, had any answers.

Of one thing Sebastian could be quite certain, however. The bag had not been wedged into the mouth of the Green Man when he had visited this spot the previous day.

Chapter Eight

"What have we here, then?"

Crockett studied the bag and its contents carefully, before at last slitting the envelope open. Inside was nothing but a single sheet of cheap paper, seemingly torn from an exercise book, on which was written in a cramped, odd-looking writing, the name and address of a Mr & Mrs Alfred Crowther, Bridge End House, at Bridge End, in the West Riding of Yorkshire.

"We'll telegraph the police up there, ask them to see these Crowthers and find out if they can throw any light on it," he announced at last. He did not relish the prospect of a journey up to Yorkshire, having been there once before and having no desire to repeat the experience. He hadn't been warm from the moment he'd stepped from the train. Those damned winds, whistling down the Pennines! Siberia could be no worse. Admittedly, it had been winter then, but still the prospect of a visit did not fill him with joy.

Enquiries conducted by the electric telegraph, however, elicited no more useful information from the West Riding Constabulary than the fact that Alderman Alfred Crowther of Bridge End House was a respected and well-to-do woollen manufacturer of that town, and that neither he nor his wife, when questioned, could conceive of any reason why their address should be in the possession of a woman apparently quite unknown to them. At this, Meredith suggested sending on to them by post the pencil sketch Sergeant Palmer (who fancied himself as an artist) had made of the dead woman. He had produced a very creditable effort that gave a good impression of what she might have looked like in life, and the idea bolstered Crockett's hope that he might yet avoid a visit to that benighted part of the world. All the same, he hesitated...a dead face was a dead face; it wasn't possible to convey a typical glance, to know whether her features had usually been animated by laughter, frowns, fears or hopes. Miss X had not been possessed of any distinguishing or outstanding features. Just an ordinary woman, with brown hair and dark eyes – but if you had known a person when they were alive, you would surely recognise the contours of their face, the shape of their nose, the way the mouth was set.

"Capital idea, Meredith," he said. "Ask Sergeant Palmer to copy it, and we'll have it posted immediately."

He did not feel hopeful of success. And indeed, word came by return of post that the Crowthers had carefully examined the sketch, had shown it to the rest of their family, but all of them were prepared to swear she was a woman they had never seen before in their lives. No arguing with that, the answer was unequivocal. Nor could the Crowthers, though intrigued and slightly alarmed, put forward any suggestion as to why a stranger to them should be in possession of their name and their address.

It was raining again in London, as Sylvia Eustace-Bragge emerged from the black-painted door with the shining brass plate in Harley Street and hurried down the steps to where a motor-cab was waiting. Her heels tapped smartly and her voice, which she did not normally allow to betray her, was sharp as she rapped out a peremptory order for the driver to take her straight home. Once inside the cab, she threw back her veil over the confection of tulle and feathers which surmounted the huge, fashionable hat perched on her hair, and sat rigidly straight-backed on the cushioned seat, her thin, heavily-ringed hands, white to the knuckles, clenched on her small kid pochette.

She had long ago decided she did not like Dr Mortimer; now, after this last humiliating examination, she knew she detested him – personally, and for the contribution he made to her general misery. The thread of her life felt to be unspooling from the bobbin on which had been tightly wound, there was nothing she could do to stop it, and Dr Mortimer's unequivocal remarks had emphasised this. Nothing physically wrong, he had told her, yet again, eyeing her as she extracted the necessary twenty-pound banknote from her purse to pay what she considered the exorbitant fee. (She dare not write a cheque, for Algy would find the stub when he went through her cheque-book, and demand an explanation.) When the doctor took the note from her, he patted her hand. His own hand was large and white, revoltingly freckled, like the first signs of mould on a piece of cheese. No reason why you shouldn't yet have half a dozen babies. Nothing wrong with you, m'dear.

M'dear. How dare he take such a liberty!

Besides, anyone who really knew the fashionable, much-admired, ironic, amusingly malicious Sylvia Eustace-Bragge knew that, whatever else, she wasn't anyone's dear.

The carriage rolled on. Autumn would be early this year; the rain had already brought down leaves from the plane trees and glued them on to the damply glistening pavements. A fitful sun, struggling against an overcast sky for several hours, had now given up the attempt, and it was dark and miserable as only a drizzly, late summer afternoon in London could be. Much too early for the gas-lamps to be lit yet. Not wet enough for an umbrella, which was nothing but an encumbrance in the busy streets, anyway, but damp enough to be thoroughly unpleasant. Motor traffic – that ever increasing problem in the already over-crowded and noisy thoroughfares of the city – was as usual fight-ing for position with horse-drawn carts and vans; a packed motor omnibus dangerously overtook them, and her driver swerved, throwing her to one side. Sylvia righted herself and placed her small, elegantly-shod feet more firmly together; but she did allow herself to press into the corner of the cab to find more pur-chase – at least as far as the sweeping brim of her hat would allow.

Perhaps there was something wrong with Algy.

Well, hardly. Not if the rumours of the little love nest in St John's Wood which had reached her were true. The love nest with the fledgling sparrow in it. But that was something she did not intend to dwell upon.

Sylvia had inherited from her mother that facility of closing her mind to whatever she didn't wish to think about, and rarely dwelt on the dissatisfactions of her marriage, though sometimes, in moments of despair, she owned that it had been a mistake to marry Algy; occasionally, she even admitted that the fault had been entirely hers. She could acknowledge that now, when it was too late, when she was saddled with him. It had never been exactly a love match, at least on her part, and Harry had warned her against it, though it was he who had teased her into consid-ering Algy in the first place, because of his money, and then been appalled when she had not only considered but accepted him.

But Algy, although he appeared to be such an ass, had not seemed such a bad proposition. His family had been in trade, admittedly, but this could be disregarded since a great deal of new money had come to him through his terrible old father. Old Enoch Bragg had been one of the Chetwynds' Shropshire neighbours with whom Sir Henry had sat on the bench and who was now thankfully deceased; who had left his son tens of thousands a year, made from the manufacture of decorative iron railings in his native Birmingham. But although Algy might be a lightweight in the opinion of many, the truth was that his rather vacuous, good-looking face concealed the fact that he was more intelligent than he was given credit for, at least in one respect, for it was certainly true that he had inherited his father's astuteness where money was concerned. After passing uneventfully through Eton, where it was not expected, after all, that one should necessarily distinguish oneself, and having come into his inheritance, he had removed himself as far as possible from the scene of the family business, selling it at a respectable profit but retaining shares in it, while investing the rest of his fortune shrewdly. He had left behind the great pile his father had built in Shropshire on his retirement and come to live in London, inserted a hyphen between his middle and his surnames, added an 'e' to elevate the plebeian Bragg, and become a gentleman of leisure.

To be fair, Algy was not parsimonious, in fact rather the opposite. He bought her expensive presents and jewellery, and the household was lavishly run; he liked to see his wife well-dressed, her clothes to be in the forefront of sophistication, and he paid her extravagant dressmaker's and milliner's bills without the flicker of an eyelid. However, he kept a close eye on expenses and – apart from her pin money that she could spend as she wished – insisted that she must account for every penny; having been subjected to this regime himself with his father, he saw no reason why the same situation shouldn't exist between himself and his wife. Original ideas did not come easily to Algy. He couldn't – or didn't – see that being beholden to him in this way was anathema to Sylvia. Too utterly humiliating.

So she had been forced to resort to a hundred small deceptions and subterfuges each quarter to put together the money she so desperately needed, that money he must never know about. So far, she had managed it by pinching and scraping a few pounds here and there, by selling off discarded trifles she might otherwise have given to her maid, and by being mean about tips, but all of it was as a drop in the ocean.

Her natural inclination had been to try and boost her finances at cards, an idea which she might have known was doomed to failure from the start. The set she moved in were notorious gamblers, and the stakes high...she was an inveterate loser, yet she could not stop, nor forego the excitement the gamble engendered. Algy had several times been forced to pay off her debts, but with that quiver of his rather long nose which told her she had better be wary. It was soon obvious she was not going to make the money she needed in the card room. In despair, last quarter, she had daringly sold a sapphire ring Algy had given her in the early years of their marriage, and had since been in a fever of anxiety lest he should find out, for he kept a sharp eye on her possessions, and though she hadn't worn the ring for years, he might at any time notice its absence.

For the moment, however, her appointment with Dr Mortimer was obscuring even her money worries. Life was unfair, so grossly unfair! It was no thwarted maternal instinct that was the driving force behind Sylvia's frantic desire to have a child, however. She had not been blessed with a particularly maternal streak – in fact, she rather disliked the idea of children and, if the truth be told, had never been very interested in the means of getting them. It was simply that she could not countenance the possibility that the day might come when the Chetwynd line might die out, leaving Belmonde with no heir to carry on its traditions.

For Sylvia had a strong suspicion that Sebastian, like Monty, might very well never marry, and for the same reasons. There was an unexpected streak of romanticism running through the Chetwynd family; Monty had subdued his desires with politics, and it was not be to supposed that, having reached the age of forty-eight, he would suddenly decide to marry – and it was obvious to Sylvia, who had a quick instinct for these things, that

Sebastian was head over heels in love with Louisa Fox, whether he knew it yet or not, when of course it was absolutely out of the question that he should make a fool of himself and marry her. (Though Louisa herself might well be a stumbling block to that, one of these new women who wanted nothing more out of life than to set themselves up as equals with men, with careers of their own. The functions of a career as a doctor and that of a future Lady Chetwynd Sylvia saw as wholly incompatible.) It was obvious to her that her brother must marry someone who would in every way be more suitable as a wife and mother to the future heir of Belmonde, but Sebastian was so odd, so difficult about things like that. It was more than likely he would decide never to marry at all, to remain single, like his uncle, through simple cussedness, rather than not marry Louisa. He laughed off the idea that his only importance in life was simply to look after Belmonde, find money through marriage, and produce an heir for it; he had always been half American, not only by birth but in his attitude towards family.

But if – she had drawn in her breath when she thought about it – if she herself should have a son, there was a chance, and quite possibly one that was not all that remote, that this son might come into an inheritance which, but for an accident of birth – (if she had been the son and Harry the daughter) – might have been hers anyway. All her life, Belmonde had meant more to her than anyone could ever know. She loved it deeply, uncritically, without reservation. As for the name of Chetwynd, Algy, she was perfectly certain, would not be averse to changing his name if it was put to him in the right way.

But...here she was, thirty years old and no sign. She had tried everything: quack medicines, the most expensive doctors, old wives' tales...even her flirtation with Mrs Besant and her quirky religion, only to find that Mrs Besant was more concerned with preventing, rather than encouraging, children being born. Nothing had availed.

Dr Mortimer, that detestable man, had dared to suggest that she might try to entice her husband more often into her bed as a means of getting a child. She thought of the love-nest in St John's Wood, and was repelled. Perhaps she too, then, should take a lover in the hope that she might be more successful with him...but where was she to find one who would excite her any more than Algy did in their statutory once-a-week lovemaking? All the same, what Sylvia wanted was invariably what she got. She had been outrageously spoiled by her father, aiding a nature that could not bear to be thwarted. This need for a child was fast becoming an obsession; her whole life revolved round schemes and plans whereby it might become fact – no, not might – must.

The world outside passed like the blurred images of a magic lantern as the cab bumped round the corner into Knightsbridge and passed Harvey Nichols' department store, light blazing from its windows on to the damply greasy pavements. She might just have time, before they closed at four, to order the taxicab round to Harrods, that great shrine of fashion where anything could be bought, and slip in to buy something – even if it were only a lace collar or a pair of gloves, to cheer herself up. But she decided the experience she had just undergone had been too exhausting, too shaming to be dismissed like that. She would go home, get her maid to make her a hot cup of tea, unpin and unlace her, let down her hair and rest until it was time to get ready for the ballet, where she and Algy were to join the Cranstons in their box to see Nijinsky and afterwards to make up a supper party at the Ritz. I shall wear my new velvet, thought Sylvia, and instantly felt better. She was absolutely in love with it, it was simply divine, and so becoming, with an elegance of line that accentuated her tiny waist. Deep rose colour, warming her pale skin, its soft lustre adding a sparkle to her eyes. And my pearls, she thought, already feeling their heavy, milky opalescence trickling sensuously through her fingers. Perhaps Algy might again find her as beautiful as he once had, and perhaps there was a chance she might feel more warmly towards him, too.

Half an hour later, sitting at her desk in her small, pretty house off Sloane Street (Algy saw no reason for a larger establishment), Sylvia took out her cheque book. She must go through her accounts, pay off a few pressing bills, small things she had asked to be charged, in order not to pay cash. Algy would want explanations but she would think of something. More importantly, she must get hold of more ready money. Even her father, always persuadable where she was concerned, had begun to show concern at the number of requests she was making. She pulled her writing case towards her. 'Dear Mama,' she began, then stopped.

She couldn't ask her mother for money, either. Adèle had reasons for not enquiring too closely into the necessity for any request from Sylvia, but the fact that her daughter needed money for which she couldn't ask her husband might alert her suspicions. She wouldn't speak of it to Sir Henry, but she might well mention it to Monty. And Sylvia did not want Monty to know that she was in danger of failing to keep her part of the bargain.

She crumpled the thick, cream-laid paper and threw it into the fire before rising to consider once more what was in her jewel-case, pressing her lips together in frustration as she examined the contents. Most of her better jewellery was kept in the safe in Algy's study, while the most expensive of all was in the bank, only to be taken out when needed for a special occasion. Much of that, of course, was quite hideous, passed on to her by her late mother-in-law, pieces with which she would gladly have parted had she dared, unlike the marvellous modern things from Cartier in Paris and Tiffany in New York. Algy, whatever his other faults, had exquisite taste. Her thin fingers scrabbled through the pretty but inconsequential bits and pieces in the box with increasing despair. What she had here were mere trifles, bagatelle.

Oh, Harry, Harry! she groaned. No one could understand the unendurable agony of losing a twin, one's other self, so close, so perfect a companion. And yet, she was still angry with him – for dying and leaving her, for the manner of his death, and for the secrets and the mess of the unfinished business he had left behind him. Why, why had he been taken so cruelly, so untimely?

The post-mortem confirmed that the still-unidentified woman had died from manual strangulation. Medical evidence had also shown that the victim's body had lain undisturbed several hours after death before being moved to where she was found. Which meant she had either left the grounds after Sebastian had seen her, been killed and then been brought back, which Crockett considered unlikely. Or, before being put in the stream, she had been killed elsewhere on the estate and left until it was convenient to dispose of her. But where on the estate? And why had she been placed in the stream?

Since no new evidence had turned up, Tom Jordan was cleared of suspicion and an inquest passed a verdict of murder by person or persons unknown. The victim had been unknown, of no direct consequence to anyone in the village, and the talk would soon die down. The murder would become a nine days' wonder, all set to go down as the stuff of legend in the annals of Belmonde Abbey, on a par with the story of the second earl's wife who had eloped with her groom, or the day when the soldiers of Henry VIII had ridden up and sacked the Abbey, or the tale of the Roman Catholic priest who had, or had not, been walled up.

Crockett meanwhile received orders summoning him back to London and a more important investigation.

"Well, there we are," said Meredith with resignation, "I'm not satisfied, but I suppose we must consider the case closed."

"It may be in abeyance, but it isn't yet finished." These questions posed by the PM were the sort of picky problem which called for a good deal of ferreting and nosing around, much better suited to Meredith's painstaking approach than Crockett's more wide-ranging style. "I'd take it kindly if you'd keep your eyes and ears open and keep me informed of any developments, Mr Meredith."

JUNE

Last night I had another of those dreams which left me, as usual, as limp as a rag, in which the child came to me again. His features were not precise and distinct – they never are – and I longed to draw him to me so that I could look into his face, but as usual, he was beyond my reach. Quick to – well, to dematerialise.

Dr Harvill explained that dreams are to be welcomed, and I take his point, which is why I cannot understand the almost superstitious dread which has so far prevented me from telling him about this particular, recurrent one. He is still so convinced that by gradually moving through my life, recording as much as I can possibly remember, I may yet discover in what ways fate has led me to this point where I now am. I must be patient, he says, I haven't yet given myself enough time. Well, he is an expert, trained in Heidelberg. Perhaps they see things differently there.

I am sure the good doctor would say this beautiful child of my dreams is simply a manifestation of my subconscious, perhaps a wish-fulfilment, and I most definitely do not want to be told this. But last night, the boy felt so real, as if he were trying to communicate with me, to urge me to wake up and live again. I reached out to him and his name was almost on the tip of my tongue.

As it always does after I've dreamt of him, the pattern will re-establish itself. I know that throughout the next few days I shall see him again when I least expect it. A fleeting glimpse, perhaps sitting, improbably, cross-legged on the birdbath, or even more implausibly, perched on a high shelf of the bookcase, hands clasped around one knee, the other leg dangling. Or I might look up from my writing and see his head peeping mischievously around the edge of the door. If I try to approach him, he is gone, but even if I don't, he soon becomes blurred, until he is nothing more than a grey shape that eventually disappears altogether; and until the next dream, I'm left with this dull, aching void where my heart should be.

How can an emptiness ache? Yet I can assure you it does, like those amputated limbs of the wounded men I helped to nurse. I could do no more for those brave soldiers than hold their hands, bathe their brows until the chloroform and drugs did their work. Did it ever disappear, that phantom pain, that agony? I cannot say, for I never saw any of them again, after the war had ended.

1894

Mrs Crowther's forsythias…those great arching fountains of gold that emerged from their bare winter stems every spring to challenge the bitter cold and the pall of smoke that always lay over Bridge End, the small town in the Calder valley. The black smoke from the mill chimneys, blown on the wind that whipped across the Yorkshire moors, down the bleak Pennine slopes and into the valley, constitutes one of my abiding memories of the place where I was born, along with the buzzers from the mills signalling the starting and finishing times and the dinner hour for the weavers and machine-minders; the acrid smell of wool grease that permeated the whole town, and the creak of the wagons and the clopping hooves of the horses drawing the carts piled high with great, square, sacking-wrapped bales of raw wool.

I was Hannah Mary Jackson then, a child of the vicarage, an only child, and the blackened stone church where my good and gentle father was vicar lay at the junction with the main road and the end of a steep, narrow street of back-to-back houses. I used to love to watch the billowing, snow-white washing strung from house to house across the street – very few of them had gardens – and to hear the wind cracking the sheets, though no doubt the women who'd laboured over washtub and copper until their fingers were raw didn't feel the same about the grime and smuts that were blown into them. Most of the houses in the town gave out directly on to the pavement, though if it were one of the better streets, they might be able to boast a small, sour plot of earth by the door, roughly the shape and size of a grave, where the hopeful planted sunflowers or even grew a cabbage or two, and the feckless left their rubbish and trod the black earth down flat. Where Mary Mellor, the verger's wife, planted her favourite wallflowers, and her husband 'Lijah grew a bush of lad's love for sprigs to put in his buttonhole, and both cried shame on the feckless. Not that there were many of that ilk. Respectability was all to those hard-working women in their clogs and shawls. They even scrubbed the grime off the flagstones on the pavement outside their door, donkey-stoned their doorsteps white, and polished their windows until they shone. And blew the smuts off the washing and started again.

My mother, never very strong, died in 1891, when I was fourteen. My father, the Rev. Aldous Jackson, followed her to the grave within six months, allegedly dying from a stroke, though they'd been such a devoted couple it didn't seem inconceivable to me that he'd died of a broken heart. A good Christian man, he hadn't, alas, been a provident one. I wasn't quite destitute, however; he'd made provisions for me in the way of my future education, and a tiny allowance was to be paid to me when I reached the age of eighteen.

Mrs Crowther had been a good friend of my mother, and after the funeral, she took me to Wakefield, to what was to be my new home: a school for the orphaned daughters of the clergy with which my father had had some connections. We went by train and when we arrived, Mrs Crowther sniffed the carbolic-scented air and cast a searching look at the room where we were received: varnished pitch pine seats and one picture, The Light of the World. She listened with me to the strictures of the pious, though no doubt well-intentioned, woman who met us, as to how I should continue to receive a Christian education as long as I conducted myself properly. She said, "Hannah, wouldn't you rather come and live with us at Bridge End House?"

What a question! If she'd asked me if I would rather live in Paradise, the answer could have been no more joyful.

Mrs Crowther briskly dealt with the formalities, brushing aside any difficulties, and after some discussion we returned to Bridge End, where it was arranged that I would live with the Crowthers as one of the family and continue to share lessons with their daughter, Lyddie (which I had in any case been doing for some time), until I was old enough to earn my living, or perhaps to act as companion to Mrs Crowther, though I couldn't see how she could ever need a companion, so full and busy was her life with her family and all manner of occupations and social and charitable duties, not to mention the entertaining of countless friends. Alfred Crowther was one of the town's most respected alderman, and a JP, the head of Abraham Crowther & Sons Ltd, prosperous woollen manufacturers, makers of blankets, and very well regarded both locally and throughout the West Riding. A 'warm' man (which in Yorkshire stood for wealthy) but, though his family lacked for nothing, he kept a modest household.

From the very first, I was welcomed into their happy family. I remained closest to Lyddie, the only girl, already the dearest friend I had in the world, though her nature, as well as her appearance, was very different from mine. I was a little, black-haired thing, my olive-green eyes too big for my pale face, and 'thin as a match wi' t'wood scraped off', as 'Lijah Mellor used to say, and the cold winds were apt to give me chills and chest infections. I was also inclined to be shy and retiring, while Lyddie, having grown up with boisterous brothers, was lively, brimming with energy and full of fun, with a smile that lit up the day. Her mass of soft, light brown hair, which began the day smoothly brushed and tidy, by midday usually reverted to its natural curls, and was the bane of her life. Her hastily tucked-in blouses soon became untucked, her collars askew. But her smile never varied.

For a while, we continued to share her governess, a small, sour-looking woman from Alsace, who was supposed to improve our French but instead, since her mother came from Strasbourg and her sympathies were with those who lived on the other side of the Rhine, spoke mostly German to us. Alderman Crowther was deeply patriotic and not fond of Germans – or foreigners of any kind, for that matter – and when he found out, he issued Mam'selle with her marching orders and thereafter we were put in the charge of a young woman called Rhoda Rouncewell, uncompromisingly English, but also well-educated, sympathetic and of an open and enquiring mind.

Not only did Rouncey, as we affectionately called her, improve our education and our knowledge of the wider world: as we grew up, she taught Lyddie to be less impatient when dressing, so that her clothes and her unruly hair remained more or less in place throughout the day, and myself how to make the most of what figure I had. I might still have grown up in Lyddie's shadow, given her bonny good looks and my drab appearance, but that would be to deny her sweet good nature, which meant she never set herself above anyone. As I grew older I began to fill out a little and gradually began to outgrow my tendency to take cold so easily, albeit I was prone to troublesome coughs on occasions and still looked deceptively fragile. I use the word deceptive advisedly, for the truth was, I had become energetic both in actions and opinions, entirely due to Rouncey's bolstering of my self-confidence. I was in fact in danger of becoming too outspoken, so I took refuge in becoming known for my common sense.

In the evenings, Rouncey would drop her role of governess and we'd sit and listen while she talked to us about the paintings and sculpture in the great art galleries and churches of Florence and Paris and Venice, all cities she had visited. I, in particular, hung on her words, seeing in my mind the pictures she drew, though sadly aware that I was never likely to have the opportunity to travel to such exotic locations. But above all she taught me, at least, to love books and reading, something which even my meagre means would always allow.

She'd been educated at Girton College, Cambridge, though she had, of course, been denied a degree, since women couldn't be admitted to full membership of the university, but her education had given her an emancipated outlook and a strong belief in her own abilities to make her way in the world: we were left in no doubt that she was only working as a governess until something more suitable to her talents turned up. On winter evenings we curled up on the rug before the fire as it burned frostily, our hands around cups of cocoa, and talked endlessly about women's situation in the world, the good they could do if only they had equality with men. She encouraged us to believe that a woman's role consisted of more than being easy on the eye, domesticated, charming and obedient to either husband or father, as most men believed they should be.

Mrs Crowther, however, saw no reason why all this high-flown thinking should prevent Lyddie and me from being taught how to cook and keep a house running properly. At Bridge End, come what may, the washing blew on the line every Monday; the ironing was done on Tuesday; Wednesday was baking day, and every single day the sweeping, polishing and dusting was attended to, the doors and windows flung open to let the fresh, moorland breezes blow in to air the rooms. She was determined that exercising our brains shouldn't make us ashamed of being good Yorkshire housewives.

It was inevitable that our lives seemed less colourful when eventually Rouncey decided to leave us, having stayed much longer than she had originally intended. Now that she'd lain down the foundations of our education, and we were both seventeen and young women, she really couldn't lay any claim to stay with us. She was leaving with regret, she said, but it had been obvious for some time that she was growing restless to be off again. So it came as no surprise when she told us that she'd succeeded in obtaining a position in America, no less, doing some kind of confidential work for an official in the British Embassy in Washington. The news caused such a stir! We girls thought it unbelievably exotic, but after we'd seen her off on the first stage of the journey that was to lead her to the other side of the world, I was left with an empty feeling I didn't seem able to fill, wishing for the impossible, that I might have gone with her, and a longing which I knew could never be satisfied, to experience a world that was wider than the proscribed circle in which we moved.

Lyddie missed Rouncey too, of course, but not, I think, with the same intensity as I did. She wasn't in the least bookish, her only contribution to culture being to thump out tunes from the latest operettas on the piano and enthusiastically sing the words; but she too longed for adventure, though of a different kind to me. Her heroines were those intrepid ladies who climbed the Matterhorn, lived alone and undaunted amongst Arab tribes in the desert, sailed as far as Australia, or travelled the golden road to Samarkand. "We'll see the world, too, someday, you and I, Hannah," she often declared, forgetting that her situation was, after all, entirely different from mine. The possibility of foreign travel wasn't excluded from her future by lack of money or anything else. Her life was predictably laid out – she would in all probability marry someone with means, and even if by some quirk she didn't, she would at some time have money of her own. Within limits she would be able to do exactly as she pleased.

But for the moment, at any rate, she was quite happy and content to be with her family and friends, in the place where she'd been born.

Whereas I...

I really didn't in the least wish to contemplate my future, when I should, at some time, be forced to find work, possibly – horrid thought! – as a governess, like mam'selle from Alsace. Or remain here, growing plain and middle-aged, as Mrs Crowther's companion. The allowance my father had left me would scarcely be enough to keep body and soul together. Meanwhile, our life went on pretty much as before. But not for long. It was to be less than a year before Lyddie left us, too.

Chapter Ten

Life changed for all of us when Lyddie became engaged to Lyall Armitage.

He was Yorkshire born and bred, the youngest son of a solid family in the wool trade. Amos Armitage, Sons & CO Ltd, Spinners & Dyers, were a long-established firm, and its present head, Frederick Armitage, was well-known to Lyddie's father through their dealings at the Wool Exchange in Bradford. The two men were on the best of terms, both inside and outside business; the families moved in the same social circles and the Armitages' eldest son, Lyall's brother, had married a cousin of Lyddie's, so it appeared to be a suitable match from almost every point of view.

Nothing is perfect, however, and there was one big flaw in the arrangement, which was that Lyall, unlike his brothers, had declined to enter the family concern, much to the aggravation of his father, who totally failed to understand his lack of interest in the wool trade. At seventeen, he'd sailed out to Africa, the land of limitless opportunities, where fortunes were being made overnight in diamonds or gold. But it was in the wild and rich game country north of the Limpopo where he had settled and lived an active and adventurous life, often on the edge of danger, working as a big-game hunter, and later also as an interior trader. He led hunting expeditions and exported ivory and ebony, ostrich feathers, and the tobacco, coffee and cotton planted by the pioneers who'd flocked there and established towns such as Salisbury and Bulawayo. Operating from this last place, Lyall's eventual success had by now justified himself in the eyes of his father.

On this first visit home to England for several years, he had arrived laden with trophies: an hour ago he'd come up to Bridge End House for tea, bearing an elephant's foot made into a stand, now standing in the bay window of the dining room, holding an aspidistra in a brass pot.

There were five of us in the dining room that day: myself and Lyddie; Lyall Armitage; Mrs Crowther; and Ned, who was the youngest of the family, grounded from his boarding school in Harrogate through a mumps epidemic, and though he was sixteen and fairly grown up on the whole, as impatient for his tea as though he hadn't eaten for months. But we wouldn't start until the head of the house came in. Meanwhile, Mrs Crowther, whose hands were rarely idle, made pleasant conversation while stabbing a fine steel crotchet hook into white cotton, creating a froth of fine lace destined to be a doyley for the Girls' Friendly Society sale of work. In front of the fireplace stood Lyall, in characteristic attitude, arms folded across his chest, one leg thrust forward. Lyddie sat nearby, intent on hearing more of the exploits, already legendary from his letters to his family who now, in the light of his success, relayed them to anyone who would listen, embellishing them in the process. Tales were being passed around of hunting expeditions into the bush, and his many dangerous encounters with wild beasts: how he'd shot his first lion when he was seventeen; escaped from a charging rhino; killed crocodiles; of his experiences confronting equally wild, unknown tribes with strange names. Lyall only smiled faintly and did his best to play down these tales of desperate adventure, but his far-seeing gaze, even as he spoke, seemed to be looking out over the dramatic wide views and the untrammelled far horizons of the veld's wide open spaces.

"I think it's that which makes Africa so special to you, Lyall. Being free," murmured Lyddie, with a barely discernible sigh. I knew she was afraid that even now, in view of the difficulties ahead, he might change his mind about taking her back with him as his wife.

His eyes on her bent head, he took a deep breath and said quietly, "It's more than that. Being there is – being alive." It was clear that he loved Africa with all his heart and soul, and from every word he spoke it was very obvious he hoped she would learn to love it, too. The last time she and Lyall had met, Lyddie had still been a schoolgirl, but now she'd matured into a lovely and lively young woman. He was lean and dark and burnt brown as a nut, an attractive if rather serious man, one who knew his own mind, and no doubt could have made his choice of a wife from any of a dozen women. But from the moment he'd looked into Lyddie's laughing eyes it was obvious to everyone he was lost. She was, in any case, a blueprint for the sort of wife he needed – courageous and spirited, unafraid of the distance which would separate her from her parents and family and the safe and settled life she had been brought up to expect; and with enough British grit to face the edge of danger associated with the unknown and the hardships she would inevitably be exposed to. Indeed, she was afraid of nothing. Had she been a man, she might well have chosen for herself the life that Lyall had followed.

She, too, had fallen in love with her whole impetuous nature. She didn't always consider the consequences of her actions, but this time she had, and was prepared, if Lyall asked her, to follow wherever his interests dictated, ready to brush aside every objection. Lyall wasn't quite so sanguine about the outcome of his proposal as she was. He was afraid, she told me, that her father might think he didn't have the right to ask for her hand in the circumstances.

"But if that turns out to be the case, then he and I must beg to differ. He won't think that, though, will he, Hannah? Not my father? He'd never stand in the way of my happiness. I won't let him!"

It was true that Alfred Crowther could deny his only daughter nothing, but of course, as Lyall – and Lyddie, too, for that matter – well knew, he had good reason to be worried that this young man proposed to take her off to Africa after they were married. He could have forbidden her to marry Lyall, of course, but he was wise enough to see opposition would only strengthen Lyddie's determination – this daughter who could twist him round her little finger, but who he knew to his cost could be stubborn as a mule when she'd set her mind on anything. It was not perversity or heavy-handedness on his part which prompted his reluctance, however, nor even the thought of losing his daughter to another man, whom he in any case liked, it was simply his fears for her safety.

"What's going to happen out there in South Africa, hm?" he demanded of Lyall, as we drew up to the table and addressed ourselves to what was before us. Nothing was ever allowed to interfere with mealtimes in the Crowther household. Dinner we ate at half past twelve, and high tea we always had at six, after work was done. Today it was pork pie, cold meat and tomatoes, followed by buttered currant teacake, slabs of parkin, seed cake and the apple pie left over from dinner, should anyone still be hungry. "Are we going to let old Kruger and his Boers get away with it, then?"

Anyone who read the newspapers couldn't fail to be aware of the present troubles in South Africa – most of it stemming from the scramble for land there between the Boers, the native black peoples and the whites who had settled there; land rich in diamonds, gold and other precious minerals. We all knew by now, since the *Daily Mail* had told us so often, that the Afrikaans-speaking Boers were a stiff-necked, pigheaded, intensely religious people who believed they were the elect of God. Following the lead of their intransigent old leader, Kruger, the President of the Transvaal, they regarded the black Kaffirs on whose land they'd settled as ignorant savages, another species of being, while using them as slaves to perform the manual labour and menial tasks that were beneath a white man. More than that, however, the Boers, who were predominantly farmers cultivating their isolated tracts of farmlands out on the veld, considered themselves to be superior to other white men who'd settled there, most of them British – *Uitlanders,* they were called, foreigners, aliens – especially the British: Godless foreigners, who tended towards a dangerous liberality with the blacks and had actually abolished slavery.

"I don't believe there's any intention of letting them get away with anything, sir. But the situation is tense, and above all we need to be moderate. Our government could easily do something they might later regret."

"That means we continue to sit back and do nothing, I suppose?" Alderman Crowther was a man softly spoken and comfortably built, with a long, melancholy face and old-fashioned Dundreary whiskers, but he had a pair of shrewd eyes that belied any tendency to self-indulgence, in himself or in others. "Rather than giving the Uitlanders some support against these beggars?"

"Nothing of the sort, I hope! Things have been allowed to

come to a disgraceful pass, that I'll grant you, but one day the Home Government might begin to see the sense of sending out a force to put them in order. Let's pray their shilly-shallying won't mean the decision comes too late."

"Well, that remains to be seen," opined Mr Crowther, who could never be described as an optimistic man. "One thing's absolutely certain – we can't let go of our suzerainty."

Suzerainty, another unfamiliar word that had entered our vocabulary lately. Translated, it meant that we had first seized power from the Boer republics and then, in return for their help against the Zulus, had given them concessions to rule themselves independently – with the proviso that they were still under British sovereignty. This conditional restriction had rankled for years. The Afrikaners had never really accepted the loss of their full independence.

"Why can't we let them have their freedom?" I heard myself ask suddenly. "They founded the republics, after all. Those Uitlanders have no need to stay, if they don't like it – but I suppose they're making too much money to get out."

They were all used to my sharpness and knew it meant very little – it was just the way Hannah was: outspoken, the same way Lyddie was headstrong and impulsive. I did, on the whole, try to curb my tongue, though. I must not lose my reputation for common sense in return for being seen as a vinegary old maid, like Miss Lumb, who made our dresses.

"A bargain's a bargain," said Lyddie's father. "When I give my word to a man and put my name to a document, I don't renege on it the moment it suits me. Why should we allow them to do so?"

"At one time I was of your mind, Hannah," added Lyall. "Independence for the Boers – until I found that license was all they wanted and understood by the word." He became eloquent on the subject: these Uitlanders had made their money, right enough – some of them counted their fortunes in millions, and included amongst them was the prime minister of Cape Colony, a man called Cecil Rhodes, an ambitious Englishman who'd reached that office before he was forty, after buying up other men's diamond claims and forming the vast de Beers mining company, besides having an enormous stake in the country's gold mines. The Boer rule in the Transvaal, however, was incredibly harsh in every way, but the Uitlanders' biggest grievance of all seemed to be that, despite all this and the exorbitant taxes they were subject to, they were not yet enfranchised. When it came to being unable to vote, on top of having to dig so deep into their pockets, they were understandably in a fighting mood – and demanding intervention by the Home Government.

"Opinion's fast gaining ground," said Lyall, "that it's time to show the burghers they can't do just as they like – that if Kruger's overthrown, that'll be the end of the troubles...but Kruger's stubborn as an old goat and he and his Boers aren't so easily dismissed as all that."

"That's what our history master, Mr Temple, thinks," put in Ned, pausing long enough in the serious business of eating to interject a remark. "He says it's high time we kicked Brother Boer all around the Transvaal and booted him out. Pass the bread and butter, please, Lyddie."

Lyall smiled rather grimly. "Your Mr Temple might find we'd bitten off rather more than we could chew if we did – I've had many years of dealings with 'Brother Boer' and it's easy to underestimate his obstinacy, not to mention his ability to fight. They're an uncouth lot, only half civilised, for all their bible-punching – hang me, if I wouldn't sooner have a Kaffir than a Boer – but make no mistake, they'd be a hard nut to crack."

"Well, it seems to me one side's as bad the other, and I call this 'intervention' nothing more than meddling in their affairs," I said. "Their independence seems a little price to pay to avert a war."

There was a small silence. "Hannah Mary, quite contrary," murmured Ned, under his breath but loud enough that his mother heard him, so he said no more, only winked at me to show me he meant no malice. I knew he was just ribbing. Ned and I were the best of friends and although he was a couple of years younger than me, he always took my part.

The family were used to Lyddie and me expressing our opinions on topics of the day, though I sometimes wondered if Mr Crowther had regretted leaving the care of his young ladies to a graduate of Newnham college with views that were not always meek and womanly. On the other hand, Yorkshire folk were plain spoken and women were no exception to that.

"War, Hannah?" he asked now. "Who's talking of it coming to war? That would cost the country a pretty penny, and no mistake!"

He seemed less upset at the thought than might have been imagined, the alarming prospect being somewhat modified, I supposed, by thoughts of the millions of yards of khaki cloth and army blankets that would be needed in such an event.

"You're right," said Lyall, "I don't subscribe to the idea that war's inevitable, either, but if – *if* it should come, I believe it would in any case be confined to the Transvaal and the Free State."

A look passed between Mrs Crowther and her husband, for from all we heard, north of the British Bechuanaland border, across the Limpopo, was not the safest of places, either. Cecil Rhodes, among his other ambitions, had grandiose plans for the expansion of white supremacy in South Africa and beyond; a strong desire to see the British flag planted, in fact, right over the African continent, but this did not seem to be a view universally shared by the black people in those countries he had annexed. The previous year, a war had broken out, when some tribes thought Rhodes had cheated them over an agreement to mine gold on their land. White people had been massacred and pioneer settlers in outlying farms had been murdered in their beds. The rebellion had eventually been put down, their leader, Lobengula was dead, but if one was to believe all one read, that would not be the end of it. The battle was over but the war was not yet won.

So, between the warring black tribes in the north, and Kruger and his Boers further south, Africa was not the most tranquil place on earth at the moment, and in view of all this, Lyall was wise enough to see that he could make no rash promises for Lyddie's absolute safety. In all honesty, he was forced to admit that the situation remained volatile, but swore that Lyddie's welfare would always be his prime concern.

I saw that this attitude had met with Mrs Crowther's approval. She sighed and looked from one to the other and though she said nothing just then, I sensed that Lyddie's battle was won. Anyone who had Edith Crowther's approval also had her husband's. Lyall was showing himself to be an honourable and right-think-ing, far-sighted man, much more than the dashing adventurer his family made him out to be. She quite clearly believed that, what-ever turned out, they could entrust their daughter to him, and that Lyddie's feelings in the matter should be respected. Though younger than Lyall by a decade, she wasn't a young woman to give her affections lightly.

All this talk of sweeping Lyddie away to an exotic, unknown country sounded to me very fine and romantic, despite the dan-ger, and I was very happy for her that she'd found such a man whom she could love and marry, but I had my doubts about the civilised aspect of the sort of life she would be forced to lead (which in my ignorance and insularity, I then equated only with the availability of as many books as I could get hold of; with cul-tivated people and the museums and art galleries and such-like of which Rouncey had spoken so warmly) and I could scarcely con-ceal my dismay that their marriage would necessitate her going back with him to the other ends of the earth, to lead such an iso-lated and perilous existence.

But Lyddie swept aside all objections and declared blithely that there were surely many worse places to settle, set up home and raise a family, she would soon make friends with the other expatriates in Bulawayo. I was sure she would. Everybody liked Lyddie, because she liked most people, and she was always so good-natured, she'd do anything for anybody, as her Aunt Lydia, for whom she'd been named, was fond of saying. But I looked at the vastness of Africa on the map and found that large areas of it, like the rest of the world, were indeed reassuringly pink. But oh! there were sure to be wild animals, mosquitoes and snakes and other unmentionable terrors. She might die of some unknown tropical disease. She could be killed in a way too hor-rible to contemplate by some black heathen. How could she sur-vive? I realised on due reflection that this last was an unnecessary question. Lyddie was born to survive anything.

* * *

I would have hated her to think me jealous, and so as the preparations for her wedding went ahead, we had a great deal of fun shopping for her trousseau. Apart from the sensible brown holland outfits of the sort Lyall had advised, and Miss Lumb ran up for her, Lyddie also managed to acquire quantities of pretty underclothes, shady hats and dresses in light silky materials with the new, narrow silhouette, drawn smooth and tight across the hips to fall in graceful folds behind — "Not an old-fashioned bustle in sight, Hallelujah!" she declared happily. Her mother tutted a little, but as Lyddie pointed out, the heavy coats and skirts with their leg-of-mutton sleeved jackets, the sensible shirt-waists and ties which were fast becoming almost a uniform here at the moment would surely be insupportable in all that heat.

Mrs Crowther confessed to me privately that she was sure she was never going to see her only daughter again. But having weighed up the situation in her sensible, down-to-earth way, and come to the conclusion that denying her would cause only more unhappiness all round, she forbore to say this to her starry-eyed girl. Having come to terms with the idea that it was inevitable, she carefully packed up a thin china tea service, delicately painted with roses, that had been her own mother's most cherished possession. She saw to it that Lyddie was equipped with a good supply of Carter's Little Liver Pills, several tins of Benger's Food, carron oil in blue bottles for sunburn, and several pounds of Lipton's tea. Then she told Lyddie, "Go, and make a good man happy."

"And never forget you are a daughter of Empire," advised Alderman Crowther, which made us giggle.

For my part, I couldn't help adding, "Oh, but how I shall miss you."

"But you have Willie, Hannah dear," Lyddie reminded me.

It was true enough that I, too, by now, had the interest of a young man – well, not so young, but young enough. He was called Willie Dyson and had already attained the coveted position of manager at the Crowther blanket mill. He still lived with his mother, and was good to her; he sang in the church choir, and he wished for an understanding between us. I knew I was very lucky, for he was a dear, good-living man, who always showed me great respect, and I reproached myself for wishing he were, sometimes, maybe rather more exciting, just a little less sensible, and that if I cast my lot in with him, my future life would not be so predictable.

"Or there's always Walter Beaumont," she added wickedly.

"Not even in jest, Lyddie!"

For I might have looked higher than Willie Dyson, had I not been so choosy. I might have accepted the proposal of the new curate, who had a substantial private income and his sights set on a bishopric. He thought I should make a good wife for a clergyman – I was, after all, the daughter of one. But Walter Beaumont looked like a frog, and spittle collected at the corners of his mouth when he spoke, adding to the impression. And even his most ordinary utterances sounded like a sermon. No, I shuddered, if wedded bliss meant marrying the Reverend Beaumont, then single I would remain for the rest of my life. Even though, above all things in the world, I could imagine nothing worse than the fate of being an old maid, known as Poor Hannah to all the family.

For more than anything, I wanted to know what it was like to love and be loved. To explore those mysterious, melting feelings that made me long to know how it would be to surrender oneself completely to another, to submit with a reckless intensity to the passion I dreamed of when I lost myself in my books and read of women like Madame Bovary or Anna Karenina.

I did not somehow think that would happen with Willie Dyson.

Chapter Eleven

Lyddie was married to Lyall Armitage in November, and they sailed for South Africa immediately afterwards. The household seemed unbelievably quiet. Flat and empty. January was a particularly bad month, with a bitterly cold wind and, what with thick snow lying on the moors and nine-foot high drifts blocking the roads over the tops, we were confined to the house for much of the time. I wrote letters to Lyddie. I read anything I could get hold of. I wound up the gramophone and put on her favourite records, but there seemed no point to it, when there was no one there to sing the songs with me, or to practice dance steps with. I took up sewing, an occupation hitherto despised, and found that if I put my mind to it, I was quite good with my needle, and was able to copy some of those new modern dress styles Lyddie had bought, though they were hardly the sort of clothes Willie would consider suitable for his wife to wear, especially the one of beautiful, heavy peacock-blue silk made over from Mrs Crowther's best frock, which she declared she would never fit into again. It was beyond my imagining, as I fingered the soft sensuousness of the material under my fingers, when I would ever have the chance to wear it. However, the dressmaking kept me occupied. I was rudderless, and longed for something to happen, yet I was wary of praying for it. God answered prayers, that I had never doubted, but not always in the way you wanted.

Then came letters from Lyddie, full of excited accounts of their journey to Cape Town: concerts on board ship, dancing and entertainments every evening, dining at the captain's table – there seemed no end to it. They had stopped en route at Madeira, a volcanic island rising straight from the sea, a miracle island of flowers and sunshine, where Lyddie had ridden up the steep paths to the very top on an ancient, but very steady and patient old cob, before thrillingly tobogganing down in a sort of basket sledge. Life so far had been nothing but fun, and she was making the most of it. As a new bride, she was fêted and spoiled a little. Everyone was so kind. Her new dresses were much admired.

At the end of February, a whole bundle of letters arrived at once, again full of amusing incidents and the surprises and excitements of her new life. Cape Town was a very fashionable place, modern and full of wealthy Uitlanders with mining interests in Kimberley and Johannesburg, with their big new houses and imported new-fangled motorcars, and the newly-weds had stayed there to enjoy a giddy few weeks of social life before embarking on the long, tiring journey by train up-country, to the terminus of the great railway line which Cecil Rhodes was determined to drive right through the African continent, from Cape Town to Cairo.

'The train journey was not exactly comfortable, but it was luxury compared to what we were about to endure. The railway is still not within five hundred odd miles of Bulawayo, and I was horrified that after leaving the train on the Bechuanaland border, we would have to make the rest of our journey by nothing less than a stage coach! Fancy, it was a great, heavy, lumbering thing that shakes you from side to side like anything, drawn by ten mules, which were very sorry-looking creatures, but better than an ox-cart, I suppose. When I saw the state of the roads (if such you can call the deeply rutted, sandy tracks, up the mountain and down again) I was forced to admit that anything else would have been impossible. You can see I have a lot to learn!! We stopped at night in primitive roadside inns, and saw much wildlife on the way, lions and giraffes, a leopard once, and game birds there for the shooting. At one point, we came across at least twenty ostriches sitting down in the road and blocking the way, terrifying the mules who refused to budge an inch further until the native coachmen jumped down and chased the birds off. You should have seen them run! Such queer things, hardly a bird at all, it seems, since they're taller than a man and have bald heads and big popping eyes, long thin necks and a very disagreeable expression. For all the world like Councillor Greenwood.' We all laughed when we read this, and within the family, the manager of the local Co-op stores was forever afterwards known to us all as Councillor Ostrich. 'It was very hot,' she went on, 'but oh, what a beautiful land this is, north of the border. Lyall promises even more beauty when he takes me on what he calls a "safari", further into the interior, where all is lush and green and teeming with wildlife, and there are spectacular views. As for my house here –

well, it's a dear little place, never mind its tin roof, and I'm deter-
mined to make it homelike. I've hung lace curtains and we ordered
a piano and several other things in Cape Town, which are to be sent
up to us and will make it more comfortable – though what condi-
tion they will be in when they arrive is hard to imagine – better than
I was, I hope. My insides felt stirred up like Christmas pudding.

  'There *was a snake in the garden yesterday. I hit it on the head*
with a spade that Jacob, our boy, had left against the wall, and killed
it stone dead, though I am told I must never try to do this again, as
it was just a matter of luck.'

  I put the letter down and poked my finger through the bars of
the canary's cage that hung in the window overlooking the same
old view of the town spread below, the descending grey stone
roofs against the dull green Pennine slopes, the grey skies and
the tall mills shadowing the road through the valley, their even
taller chimneys billowing out smoke. I stroked the bright yellow
feathers of the little bird. He sounded happy enough in his cage,
singing his heart out, year after year, but perhaps it was despair.

For the next twelve months, Lyddie's letters continued in the
same cheerful, optimistic vein, full of her new experiences. My
own went on in the same old predictable, routine way. I couldn't
yet bring myself to give my hand in marriage to Willie.

  And then, out of the blue, came horrifying news. The thing we
had all dreaded had happened: a further rebellion, out there in
the country which we were now told we must call Rhodesia, after
Cecil Rhodes. Now, in a new outbreak by the concerted native
tribes, the citizens of Bulawayo had escaped being massacred
only by a strategic miracle. Lyddie and Lyall had lost their home
and practically everything they possessed – but they had, thank
God, escaped unharmed, by fleeing southwards, to the frontier
town of Mafeking, on the Transvaal-Bechuanaland border, the
big railway depot on the line from Cape Town, and consequently
an important trading post.

  It was there that they were now to make their home, at least
until the present troubles should be over. Lyddie typically made
light of the danger they'd been in during the weeks of their
escape and wrote that the small town promised well; it was an
expanding and prosperous place, with a sizeable British expatriate

community already living there, plus all the amenities of banks, hotels, and even a racecourse, and, naturally, a cricket ground. It was not only the administrative centre of British Bechuanaland but also the headquarters of the Bechuanaland Protectorate Regiment and the British South Africa Police – and things were always lively with uniforms around, weren't they?

Mrs Crowther was only too happy that they were safe, never mind the details, and comforted to hear that there would be other Englishwomen with whom Lyddie could become acquainted, and that indeed, there were actually people living there who came from Dewsbury, already known to the Crowthers as friends of friends.

However…reading anxiously between the lines of subsequent letters, it seemed that the move was not suiting Lyddie as well as she'd imagined it would. Whereas her previous letters had made it reassuringly obvious to us that she was exceedingly happy with her new life and her new husband, the ones from Mafeking had become disquieting. For the first time she complained of homesickness; she wrote that it was, after all, nothing of a place, the climate was unbearable; she felt very low in spirits. All this was contrary to everything we knew of Lyddie and worried Mrs Crowther very much, until another letter came to say she was expecting a child. "There. I knew there had to be some reason why she wasn't herself – this explains a good deal. I'm so very relieved." She was wreathed in smiles, but all the same, I could see she still had something on her mind.

In the end, when we were alone in the drawing room one evening after dinner, she came and sat down beside me and took hold of my hand. It was some time before she said anything, and when at last she came to the point, it was about Lyddie she spoke. At a time like this a young woman needed her mother, she began. Things did not always go as smoothly as they ought, and particularly with a first child. Women were inclined to have strange fancies, especially during the first few months, and in view of what Lyddie had been through, Mrs Crowther was afraid that she might be finding the prospect of motherhood a little alarming, coupled with the loneliness she must be feeling in Lyall's enforced absences, due to his business commitments.

Had it not been for her wretched hip, which had been giving her a great deal of pain lately and was even forcing her to use a stick, Mrs Crowther would have gone out there herself to be with Lyddie, but in the circumstances, that was scarcely possible. She hesitated before going on tentatively, quite unlike her usual brisk self...would I, she asked, consider going out to Africa – just until Lyddie's child was born, and maybe, perhaps, staying for a little while afterwards, to see her settled? At the Crowthers' expense, of course. If the idea did not appeal to me I was to feel under no obligation to accept. "Though it would ease my mind so wonderfully...on the other hand, everything sounds so dreadful out there, I don't know that we've any right to ask it of you, so think it over carefully, Hannah dear – and before making any decision, will you go and listen to what Mr Crowther has to say?"

It was highly unlikely that whatever Alderman Crowther would have to say on the subject would make any difference. Excitement pulsed through my whole body at this glorious opportunity, which I had no intentions of allowing to pass me by. But I went to see him in his study, because in his rather bluff way he'd always shown me affection, and since Lyddie had left I'd become quite a favourite of his. I knew he had my welfare at heart and would give me good advice.

He watched me gravely where I sat on the low fender stool, packing his pipe for him, as I did every night. "I wonder if you quite appreciate how dangerous the situation is out there, Hannah?" he began.

"I can hardly fail to understand, after what's happened to Lyddie and Lyall —"

"Aye, they've had a lucky escape, for which we must thank God."

"But now they're in a place of safety —" I began.

"For the time being."

I said nothing, busying myself with finishing the pipe, putting the lid on the Chinese tobacco jar and taking the pipe across to him. He patted my hand and smiled sadly. I suppose he knew my mind was already made up, but he waited patiently while I resumed my seat by the fire and tried to find an answer. I didn't wish to appear rebellious or ungrateful after everything he'd done for me, but I was finding it difficult to know what to say.

"It's not simply the situation up there in Rhodesia, of course, not by any means," he said at last, perhaps trying to make it easy for me, though I suspect he knew, at the back of his mind, just how I felt. "Lyall once remarked that if war with the Boers came about, he believed it would be confined to the Transvaal and the Orange Free State. I don't think anybody seriously believes that any more."

"If there is going to be a war, that's all the more reason —" I began.

He held up his hand. "I wouldn't willingly send you into such a situation. My dear, headstrong daughter declined to listen to her parents' advice; she stepped into the unknown without so much as a backward glance, but at least she'd chosen to go with the man she loves, whereas yours is a slightly different case. I believe you're level-headed enough to see this, lass."

I drew myself up. "Send? If I go, it'll be entirely of my own free will, Mr Crowther."

He made one last attempt. "You're an intelligent young woman, Hannah, and I know no one who could benefit more from this chance to see something of the world, but I wouldn't want you to blind yourself to what you might be facing."

Lyddie's departure had left me feeling very much at odds with myself, try as I might to combat the not very commendable feeling that life had dealt me a wretched hand. I should never cease to be grateful for the love and kindness shown to me by these dear people, who'd always encouraged me to regard myself as one of their own. But I knew I wasn't one of them, nor could I ever expect to be. My circumstances were entirely different, and I was wretched at being condemned to a grey and uneventful future, never to know anything outside the narrow confines of the West Riding, my world circumscribed by Sunday School teaching and the thrill of a weekly shopping expedition to Dewsbury, which was larger than Bridge End, though that wasn't saying much. But now, here I was, being offered a positive chance to do something about it – nothing less, in fact, than escape. My life, which had been drab and forlorn, was suddenly filled with colour and hope. The cage door had opened and I could at last spread my wings and fly towards the sun.

"If Lyddie's in danger – and in her condition, too – I wish for nothing more than to be with her. I think I shall have to go, Mr Crowther."

In fairness to myself, I have to say that I believe I would have gone, anyway, however bleak the prospect had been. Not only for myself, but also for the Crowthers, as much as for Lyddie. Because I loved them, as I knew they, out of their goodness, had found it in their hearts to love me.

Alfred Crowther gave a resigned sigh. "That's what I thought you'd say, Hannah. So be it then. So be it."

"What a spree," said Willie Dyson mildly, admirably concealing his true feelings.

"Well, I don't know about that. It won't all be a bed of roses."

That wasn't in any way how I really thought of the prospect that was opening before me, of course, but I'd always tried, in fairness to him, to conceal my restless nature. My sharpness didn't fool him, however, and he had the sense to see it was no use trying to stop me. The wide world beckoned and he couldn't deprive me of my chance to see some of it. "I'll come back, Willie," I promised. He smiled a little wryly, but made the best of a bad job. Perhaps he knew me better than I knew myself. Every time he'd urged me to name a date for our wedding, I'd always responded by telling him there was plenty of time.

The evening before I left, we set out for the last time on our favourite walk up on to the moors, our destination being the Old Pack Horse right on the top, where we would stop for refreshments before the walk back. Not inside the inn, of course, for Willie was a staunch teetotaller and had signed the Pledge. Touch, taste nor handle, for strong drink was the temptation of the devil. Instead, we would find a grassy bank outside to sit and rest and drink the ginger beer from a stone bottle he had brought for us in his pocket.

As we walked, he put whatever he was feeling behind him, took my hand and sang softly. He was a happy, contented man, and he loved to sing. I think this capacity he had for taking joy from the moment was the thing I liked most about him. He was studying to be a lay reader at the church, which was as near a substitute for being ordained as he could get. The possibility of theological college, with all its attendant expenses, even had he been able to gain admission, was denied him. Where would he have got the money, who would then have supported his mother? It never entered his head to be resentful of his fate, as it entered mine. He was a much better person than I was.

After we'd walked for about a mile, and left behind the last huddle of old, stone-roofed weavers' cottages, the road became rougher under our feet, and the little pebbles rolling on the thin layer of soil over the rocks beneath made the going harder. We paused for a breather and Willie spread his jacket to enable us to sit on some craggy outcrop near the path. It was a lovely early summer evening, with a beautiful sky, and the wide, free moors spread all around us. From up here, the dirt and drabness were obscured, and the view, perversely now that my departure was near, made me realise that in many ways I was going to miss my familiar life very much. Dull as it was, I still loved Bridge End, and the warmth of the people who lived there; it was all I'd ever known. Below us was spread the unremarkable little town, where presently the lights would prick the dusk, and where the foursquare mills rose by the river, their tall chimney-stacks reaching to the sky. At the head of the valley the brickworks loomed, now closed for the night, with a telpher-span for carrying clay from a pit at the far side. The winding gear stood quiet, and the wheel and the trucks, suspended in midair, hung dramatically black against the pale green and rose evening sky.

Presently, Willie put his arm around my waist, and as if sensing my thoughts, he said, "You won't get all this in Africa, Hannah. You'll miss it."

"Of course I shall, but I won't mind. Not for the short time I shall be there. At least there won't be ten-foot snowdrifts like we had here last winter."

"Indeed no, I'm told it's a thirsty land, hot and dusty. It can be harsh and cruel, too."

"Don't forget how I like the sun. And think how much better it will be for my cough."

"Will you miss *me*?"

"Of course I shall." I was truly sorry I couldn't put more

conviction into my voice. He was so *nice* – and sensitive, too, not to have mentioned the danger I was sailing into. I'd really become quite fed up with people warning me of that, as if I was too stupid to be aware of it.

The rough, tussocky grass around us was all bent in one direction by the strong breeze that even now came down from the tops, though it wasn't cold. A clattering beck beside us tumbled downwards to join the shallow river in the valley bottom, and all around were gorse and cotton grass and delicate, nodding harebells. Nearby, a pair of laverocks sang a courting duet, liquid and sweet. Never had an evening seemed more poignant.

Willie had been casting glances at me for a long time. Then suddenly, he pulled me to him and began to kiss me in a way he'd never done before. He became more urgent, and I drew back in a sort of panic, though I ought to have known I needn't worry. Being Willie, he released me at once, sensing my reluctance, and didn't force himself on me, but when he spoke, his voice was hoarse, and he put his finger under my chin to make me look at him. "Why not, Hannah? You know what they say, when the gorse is out, it's kissing time."

It wasn't the kissing in itself I objected to. I tried to laugh it off. "That's just an excuse. There aren't many months when the gorse isn't out, somewhere."

"Exactly. So why have we waited so long to get married?"

I did, then, begin to be a little afraid of what I heard in his voice. "This isn't the time to talk of that, when I'm going away." I pulled myself away, stood up and smoothed my skirt. "We'll never get to the Pack Horse at this rate."

"To the deuce with the Pack Horse!" he said, quite roughly for Willie. "Sit down again, Hannah." His hand, as he pulled me back down, was hard and strong and for the first time in my life, I felt a stir of excitement as his skin touched mine. But what he saw in my face softened his voice as he went on, with a sigh, "Don't be frightened of me, lass, there's no cause."

After that we sat for a while in silence, until he stood up and held out his hand to help me to my feet. We resumed our walk.

I knew that he'd mastered himself when presently he began to sing softly again, under his breath, in his lovely baritone voice.

The tune was vaguely familiar.

"What's that you're singing, Willie?"

He smiled and raised his voice a little and repeated the chorus:

"When the fields are white with daisies,

I'll be coming back to you...

When the fields are white with daisies, I'll return..."

"I remember it now," I said. "And I promise I will. Before the daisies and buttercups are out again, I'll be home."

1909

November came, and with it fog that blanketed most of England. Here in the capital, the added fumes of London's million smoking, belching chimneys brewed it up into a real pea-souper; gaslights became yellow glimmers in the gloom, making the roads and streets death-traps for the unwary, and into every building a noxious yellow reek filtered, laying a film of grime over everything. Yet the fog seemed no denser to Detective Chief Inspector Crockett than the doubts, uncertainties and silences still surrounding the case of the dead woman found two months ago at Belmonde.

It was unheard of for Crockett to feel at a loss, yet today, free for the moment after being under constant pressure for the last few weeks, at liberty for once to reflect on the Belmonde case and the short time he'd spent working there, he felt distinctly unsettled. Though the murder was still officially the business of the police in Shropshire, he couldn't escape the mortified feeling, always at the back of his mind, that he, the man from the Yard, had failed to provide the experienced help they'd needed, and that the mystery had never been as fully investigated as it should have been. His summons back to London had been to a case considered by the powers-that-be more important than an investigation out in the back of beyond which was already losing its steam, and he'd had no choice but to return.

Since then, the enquiry had, to all intents and purposes, been unofficially abandoned, though not in Crockett's mind. As far as he was concerned, failure was never a condition to be contemplated, and a morose conviction that he ought to do something about it had grown. The investigation he'd returned to deal with – a series of rapes and murder in the docklands area – had been successfully concluded with the capture and arrest of the killer. Relief that it had not after all turned out to be another unsolved Jack the Ripper case had resulted in much appreciation from high places for Crockett's part in apprehending him, but the initial euphoria of that was wearing off: he knew it wouldn't be long before another job landed on his desk, in which he might not be so lucky. That there were murders which never would be solved was one of the facts of life every police officer was bound to accept. Mercifully few with which he'd been called to deal had fallen into this category; all the same, he was always dogged by the feeling that next time could turn out very differently.

Inaction of any sort was anathema to him; moreover, he had his reputation to consider here at the Yard, where he was able to bear the nickname of Dandy Crockett with equanimity because he knew that his reputation stood high enough to overcome it – so far. But I'll be hanged if I know what to do about Belmonde, he'd said to himself. Then this morning he'd received an unexpected communication from Meredith, still apparently chasing shadows out there at the back end of nowhere. Not that he seemed to be getting any further, Crockett thought as he rubbed his eyes, smarting from the fog, put on his spectacles and made another attempt to re-read the notes. Meredith's writing was difficult to decipher in the dim room. He swore under his breath at the dratted day and found a wax taper to light the gas, merely to discover with increased irritation that not only had the incandescent mantle burnt out, but so had the one in the other bracket on the opposite wall; no one had bothered to change them, and without a mantle the blue flame when the gas was lit was useless. Nor could he find replacements in the cupboard where they were supposedly kept.

He swore again, and for a while, continued the losing struggle to read what seemed to be a mere treading over the same old ground – until the name of Louisa Fox – that young woman who'd marched in on him in the schoolroom – caught his eye. Meredith had also talked to her and made the point that she knew the family well: there was, he felt, something she and young Chetwynd had up their sleeves, though he didn't go so far as to believe either were involved in the murder. Some family secret, he had surmised, which could have a bearing on the present case?

Well, that was nothing new. It was something Crockett himself had sensed. Murder inevitably brought skeletons out of cupboards, where most families would have preferred them to remain hidden. It would be odd indeed if, in their long history, the Chetwynds possessed none – and to say the least, not one of them had been forthcoming when they were first questioned. But the particular mention of Sebastian Chetwynd and Louisa Fox interested him. He gave up his attempt to read, sat thinking for a while, then went across to the telephone.

Propping his buttocks on a desk, he reached for the wall-mounted instrument and asked for the number of the police station at Bridgnorth. After some time, he was connected to a far-away voice on the other end of the line which informed him that the inspector was at that very moment driving out to Belmonde.

Meredith's methods might be slower than Crockett's, but he had not been idle since the departure of his colleague. He had, early on, been forced to let his prime suspect, Tom Jordan, go, through lack of any evidence, or indeed any motive. But far from consigning the mystery of the murdered woman to the unsolved annals of police history, he had kept it in his mind ever since the London man had been called back to the Yard. Meredith's was a slow and patient nature; he believed in giving time for the initial excitement and perhaps panic to subside, when, lulled into a sense of false security, the culprit might give himself away. After Crockett's initial questioning, and the apparent abandonment of the case, whoever had done the murder must by now believe himself in the clear. It was perhaps time for Meredith to do a little questioning on his own account, even if it meant disturbing once more the apparently smooth relationships and comfortable lives of those fortunate beings living at the Abbey.

The pony-trap's wheels grated on the stony road surface in the eerie silence engendered by the fog – not the obnoxious yellow reek that it was in the capital – but all the same, progress was slow as it swirled around, thick as curdled cream. Trees loomed spectrally along the sides of the road, familiar landmarks were non-existent. The pony trotted on, blinkered and unaware of anything but the small section of road ahead visible to him. Meredith reflected that he was rather glad he had not elected to arrive at Belmonde by one of the new-fangled motors (though it might have been more appropriate perhaps, given the status of this enquiry). As the hollow clop of a big horse's hooves and the rumble of heavy wheels signalled a cart approaching in the other direction, which then loomed up through the fog with alarming suddenness, he was glad that he had, after all, elected to drive himself in the pony trap. As far as he knew, it had never yet killed anyone.

It seemed his first interview would have to be postponed, since the man he wanted to see, Joseph Blythe, the butler, was busy elsewhere at the moment. "Tell him I'd be obliged if he would spare me a few minutes later, then," Meredith said to the young footman who'd opened the door, and asked for Lady Chetwynd's maid meanwhile.

Lily Chater received him in a small room that was strewn with bits of sewing and feminine garments of all kinds, evidently devoted to the mending, pressing and repairing of her mistress's clothes. A flat iron stood on its end on an ironing table and a smell of warm linen pervaded the room. An elegant tweed walking costume on a hanger depended from the picture rail. The maid had been busy treadling a sewing machine when he was shown in, and rattled along to the end of a long seam in some grey, silky material, then took her time to snip off the thread with scissors and fasten it off before looking up. "What is it?" she asked coolly, raising her eyebrows.

Meredith gave his name and sat himself on a chair inside the door. He hadn't been invited to take a seat but he was not going to stand in front of this young madam. She had a pursy little mouth and it hadn't taken him a minute to see that he couldn't expect much from her, certainly nothing in the way of tittle-tattle or gossip which might turn out to be useful. However, his first question, as to how long she had been with Lady Chetwynd and whether she was happy in her position as lady's maid, elicited a sharp response.

"Happy? Of course I am. Nobody could wish for a better mistress." Lily was quick and alert, slim and personable, dressed in a tailored serge skirt and a modestly patterned blouse tucked into a neat waist, but she had knowing eyes and had cultivated a painfully genteel accent that grated on him. "When she heard that my previous lady had dismissed me – without a character, I might say, and only because she found I was walking out with my young man and hadn't seen fit to tell her about him – Lady

Chetwynd took me on and I've been with her ever since – that's five years." Unlike most of the other servants, he recalled, nearly all of whom had been with the family all their working lives. Which was, of course, part of the trouble. So far they could not be induced, through loyalty – or maybe fear of losing their positions – to say anything remotely damaging to their employers. "She's that kind and considerate," went on Lily Chater, in her affected voice, "I'd do anything for her Ladyship...I won't have a word said against her, nor would I leave her for all the tea in China."

"Not even for your young man?"

"Oh, him," Lily said, tossing her head. "He's long gone. Wanted me to marry him straight away and give up being in service, but he wasn't worth losing the opportunity of being with her Ladyship."

When it came to the day in question, Lily said in a rather bored voice that she didn't remember much about it, and implied, picking a stray thread off her dark blue skirt, and beginning to thread a needle, that it was unreasonable to expect her to remember details after two months. "Oh come," said Meredith, "a bright young woman like you must have a better memory than that."

Oh. Well, not really, but she did remember that her mistress hadn't been so well that day. She sometimes had trouble with her chest, and her breathing had been quite bad. She'd retired to her room after lunch and stayed there until she called Lily to redo her hair and help her dress before going down for tea. "Wet weather frizzes one's hair up no end, you know," added Lily, who evidently remembered the essentials, if little else, patting her own. "The dampness gets everywhere when it's as wet as it was those last few weeks."

"I see." Meredith absorbed this hitherto unsuspected piece of information on the feminine toilette while thinking of what the young woman had just said. Her mistress could evidently do no wrong in Lily Chater's eyes. *I'd do anything for her.* Did that include lying for her mistress? Meredith decided the question was, for the moment at any rate, irrelevant, since he couldn't see what Lady Chetwynd could have to conceal. He could hardly envisage her white, be-ringed hands round anyone's throat, throttling the life out of them.

* * *

"Sorry to keep you waiting," apologised Blythe. "We can use Mrs Fosset's room, where we can be undisturbed. No doubt she will send us some refreshment presently."

The housekeeper's room was a cosy, old-fashioned sanctuary, with a bright fire blazing, dark green and red crotcheted woollen antimacassars smoothed over the back of each of the horsehair chairs drawn up to the hearth, a small polished table already laid with cups and saucers and a lace-trimmed cloth. The walls were covered with a fruit-patterned wallpaper from the last century, in colours predominantly plum, grey and brown; framed photographs of the family stood on every available surface, and on the sideboard, a pair of glass domes covered arrangements of wax fruit and flowers. It was a comfortable Victorian haven in which Blythe was evidently accustomed to making himself at home.

Coffee was brought in by a maid who remained to pour it before departing with a bob. Despite his affability, Meredith saw from the first that old Blythe would be a hard nut to crack. He was very old indeed, but spry and by no means slow-witted. He had ruled below-stairs for more years than Meredith had been alive, and loyalty to the family above stairs was the paramount thing in his life. Service with the Chetwynds must have something to recommend it, the inspector mused, to be able to inspire devotion in two such different personalities as Lily Chater and Joseph Blythe.

"What's all this about, Inspector? I thought it was all over. I've been here fifty-eight years, man and boy, and we have never had such a thing happen before at Belmonde."

It seemed to Meredith that the old butler was affronted at the indignity of what had occurred rather than the tragedy. "Oh dear me, no, Mr Blythe. We police are like the British bulldog, you know. Never let go," he said portentously, swallowing the last mouthful of an excellent slice of Madeira cake. "But now and then we do miss the odd little thing that might just turn out to be important. So let's go over your original statement again, if you don't mind. Let's see, what time did you say Mr Sebastian got here?"

"Three-thirty. In the middle of a thunderstorm."

"Three-thirty. So he said, too. Precisely?"

"Perhaps a few minutes before."

"I believe in your original statement you said no one else had called at the house that day. That would be at the front door, of course?" Blythe inclined his head. "Good. Before I go, I'll confirm with those in the kitchen that no one came to the back, either."

"That won't be necessary. I can speak for the rest of the staff," Blythe said stiffly. "I questioned them myself, and there was no one except for the usual delivery people and so on – all of them known to us."

"And Sir Henry? He was out that afternoon until – what time?"

"I couldn't say – you must ask one of the maids – or Mr Seton, who was there with him. He'd have rung for his tea as he always does, at whatever time he wants it, and one of them would have taken it in, seeing that it was the day for the large silver, and I was in the dining room supervising most of the afternoon. Some ornate items there, too big to move and must be polished in situ. Can't always trust these young footmen to do that sort of job properly nowadays, I'm sorry to say."

"He wasn't expecting anyone, then?"

"If you mean the woman who was murdered, certainly not." The old butler's voice took on a noticeable edge. "As I said, he went out as usual after lunch, to walk the dogs. Mornings are for estate business, sometimes with Mr Seton, sometimes alone, but if he had been expecting anyone in the afternoon, he wouldn't have gone out at all, not Sir Henry. In any case, a woman of that sort would hardly be the type to call on him."

"Remarkably well informed as to what sort of woman she was, eh, Mr Blythe?"

Blythe looked down his nose. "It was soon a matter of common knowledge, Mr Meredith."

"Hmm, I suppose that's so." Meredith fumbled with his notebook. "And her Ladyship? Miss Chater says her mistress was resting in her room all afternoon."

"Don't believe anything that girl says. She gives herself airs and she's a flighty piece, what's more – set her sights on Albert, the footman, she has, though much good may that do her, for he's turning out to be a trouble-maker. I have my eye on the pair of them." Blythe would have no jurisdiction over Lily Chater, but a footman was another matter. It was evident Albert's days were numbered. "Not that I have any reason to believe her Ladyship wasn't in her room that afternoon," the butler went on. "Indeed, she looked most unwell at lunch, so I dare say Miss Chater is right."

The strapping young footman who had let him in knocked on the door, saying, when he entered, "If you please, Mr Blythe, Lady Emily sends her compliments and asks the inspector if he'd be so good as to see her before he leaves."

"Lady Emily, Albert?" Blythe regarded the young man over his spectacles. Clearly this was not a request he was prepared to accede to without question.

"Yes, Mr Blythe. She said to take your time, sir," the footman told Meredith. "She'll be in her sitting room until eleven o'clock, which is the time she goes out for her drive."

Meredith looked a his watch. If he went now, that would give him twenty minutes in which to speak to Lady Emily. "I'll come along now."

He thanked Blythe for his time and the footman led him through a series of rooms filled with mirrors and scented, flowering, hothouse plants, up staircases where generations of Chetwynds regarded each other gloomily from one wall to another, along a confusion of corridors, until even Meredith, who had a good sense of direction, doubted whether he would ever find his way back through the maze.

The journey led to the west wing, and the house as it had presumably been before the advent of the present Lady Chetwynd – possibly, judging by the age of some of the pieces – before the advent of the dowager.

They turned the corner of a staircase, and there the footman came to a halt.

"Lady Emily's sitting room is just along there," he said, indicating a wide oak door further along the corridor. "But first, can I have a word, sir?"

"You've something to tell me?"

Albert shuffled his feet. "Well, sir, it's like this. I feel I have a duty." Oh yes, thought Meredith sceptically. Duty. Telling tales out of school, more like, rather than anything which might be useful. "This murder you're looking into, see...well, there's something I think you ought rightly to know."

"Go on." Meredith didn't like the sound of this. If it came to that, he didn't much like the look of Albert himself. Eyes too close together, and a look of self-righteousness.

"Well, see, it's my job to sort the post when it comes of a morning, and it strikes me there's been something funny going on. Some letters for Sir Henry. The first one I noticed came second post one day, on its own like, which was how I noticed it particular, I reckon. When I took it into him in the business room, he changed colour. I thought nothing of it, except that maybe it was likely to be a nasty bill, but they went on coming. Regular as clockwork, they were. London postmark. Always the same envelopes, same sort of funny writing, see..."

"Funny, how?"

"Spiky looking, like."

"Hmm," said Meredith. "I'm wondering why you think it's necessary for me to know about the personal correspondence Sir Henry had from his friends."

"It might have been personal, but I don't reckon it was any friend sent them letters. Not the way they upset Sir Henry. And they was addressed to 'Sir Chetwynd'." Albert sniggered, his lip curling at the idea that any friend would have the ignorance to address him so mistakenly. "Nor have there been any more since that woman was found dead," he added.

He was a handsome, sulky fellow with a high colour and deep-set eyes, very smart, his broad shoulders straining his frogged and braided jacket, the brass buttons on his waistcoat winking. Meredith could recognise an attitude that spelled trouble, a face that wanted revenge. What had Sir Henry done to this fellow?

The door along the corridor which the footman said led to Lady Emily's apartments opened, and there she stood in the doorway, leaning a little on her silver-knobbed cane. "Come in, Inspector Meredith, out of this draughty corridor. Thank you, Albert, that will do."

* * *

She indicated a chair he should take and sat herself in an upright one on the opposite side of the fireplace, where a bright coal fire burned, and raised her feet on to a velvet footstool. Immediately, she took up a tapestry that lay on a table by her side and began stabbing her needle into it.

After the preliminaries were over, she wasted no time in coming to the point. "I see you are wondering why I have sent for you. The nub of it is, Inspector Meredith, that I am not of the opinion that lies should be told in an enquiry of this nature."

He could not forbear a smile. "A lady after my own heart."

"That's as may be, but it has never been my opinion that any good comes from hiding the truth. I shall be greatly relieved if you can get to the bottom of what has been happening, for Henry's sake, as well as for everyone else's, and if he won't help you, then I will." She paused and put aside her sewing. "What was Albert saying to you?"

"I don't know that I should —"

"You will not, I assure you, tell me anything I don't already suspect about that young man. May I speak to you in the strictest confidence?"

"Well, of course, I —"

"Good." She lifted the tapestry, but then let it drop into her lap. "There is a great deal of unrest about these days, as I'm sure you're aware. Dangerous people about, inciting the lower classes to all sorts of unruly behaviour. Here at Belmonde we pride ourselves on our good relations with the servants. That young man, Albert, for instance...his family has served the Chetwynds for generations, with unswerving loyalty. His father was coachman here for thirty years – and now there is a rumour that he has been upsetting the other servants, inciting them to demand higher wages, better conditions. I am happy to say that they are every one of them well aware they would get no better treatment anywhere in the land than at Belmonde, and are quite content with conditions as they are. Albert's trouble-making has come to Sir Henry's ears, however, and he has been put under notice to leave. My son is being most lenient with him in letting him stay until he has found another situation." She paused to let that sink in. "I see you understand me."

Indeed, thought Meredith, that was a leniency so unprecedented he immediately suspected pressure from Albert on Sir Henry about those letters, and he suspected this was what Lady Emily wished to convey, without saying it in so many words. Immediate dismissal for stirring up dissension would have been more usual. "So if he has said anything to you – and if he has not already done so, I am sure he will – I would advise you to take very little notice of anything he says."

"About what, my lady?"

"About the letters my son has been receiving," she answered without prevarication, meeting his glance fair and square. "Never mind how I know about them – or what I suspect he has said to you. I may be old, but I know human nature, and there is not much goes on at Belmonde that I don't make it my business to be acquainted with. It would avail you nothing to pursue that matter – they were letters of a delicate nature. From – a lady. Need I say more?"

Ah, but what lady, Meredith asked himself, and wondered why Lady Emily was lying.

"I'll do my best to see they cause no embarrassment," he said, with which she had to be content.

After making the abortive telephone call to Shropshire, Crockett went back to his desk. He rocked his chair on its back legs. Through the already murky window, made even murkier by the fog, he thought he dimly discerned a faint lightening of the atmosphere, a distant gleam of sun. He flipped through Meredith's report again. He smoked a cigarette. At last, throwing caution to the winds, he poured a slug of whisky from the hidden bottle in his locked bottom drawer, then stood in the shadowy room, lit only by the popping gas fire, sipping his drink with his back to it, one thumb in the armhole of his waistcoat, debating his choices. He could let the matter take its own time and direction, or he could make things happen.

Tipping the rest of the whisky down his throat, almost without conscious decision, he knew his mind was made up to take the latter course, one much more to his taste. There were too many loose ends, which had never been pursued, or tidied up to his satisfaction. He began to have a little idea. It wasn't very professional, and he couldn't be sure if it would pay off, or whether, in the end, there would be nothing for it but to seek permission to take up the investigation again, though he had doubts that his superintendent would support such an application.

In the absence of any female detectives in the CID, he would normally employ the wife or sister of one of his constables for any job needing a woman's touch, but in this case something more was needed. He decided to make an approach to Agnes Crawford, the lady who stood highest of any in his regard, and enlist her help. Although having refused to become engaged to him until the question of women's suffrage was settled and her work for the Cause would be over – which as far as Crockett could see, would be never – he was still hopeful that she might, one day, be induced to change her mind. And since she was, for the most part, of a naturally sweet and helpful disposition, he was almost certain she could be persuaded to assist him on this occasion.

Agnes lived with her father, a schoolmaster from whom she had absorbed radical inclinations from an early age, and who tolerated – nay, encouraged – such unwomanly activities as she was presently engaged in. These days, Crockett could never be sure of when he might catch her at home – she always seemed to be out when he called, doing God knows what for this dratted Women's Political and Social Union (though as to the precise nature of this work, and in view of the opinions she'd recently been expressing, he preferred to remain in ignorance). To his sorrow, she'd once more taken part with other women in a rowdy disturbance; this time in harassing the Prime Minister while he was on holiday at Lympne Castle in Kent, following him everywhere he went, even to church, throwing stones through the window when he was having his dinner, yelling their slogans. She and others had been dragged away kicking and screaming by the police and once again taken before the magistrates. That the women arrested were so obviously ladies had influenced the magistrate to be lenient with them, which had not been their intention at all and had infuriated Agnes. Next time, she would certainly do something they could not ignore, so that they would be forced to send her to prison – she might even take it into her head to go on hunger strike. Sweet and angelic-looking Agnes! He lived in constant fear that one day it might fall to his unenviable lot to have to arrest her in the course of his duty.

Rather than make a fruitless journey to her father's house in Ealing to find her not there, he sent a note round, asking if they might meet at a time and place convenient to her. She must have been at home, after all, for she was prompt in her reply, and asked him to meet her at the Lyons' Corner House in Piccadilly at four that afternoon.

Half an hour before he was due to set off, there was an interruption. He very nearly persuaded himself to refuse to admit the callers; afterwards, he was very glad indeed that he had not succumbed to the temptation.

Chapter Thirteen

The two men were patently foreigners: the one big and shambling, with a sallow complexion, a drooping moustache and sad,
dark eyes which also drooped at the corners; the other a thinner,
sharper and younger version of him. Their names were Saroyan:
Gevorg and Stepanos. They were brothers and they said they
were Armenian. Both were bundled up against the onset of an
English winter in long, shabby dark overcoats and thick scarves
and hats which they kept on, and the big one, Gevorg, was
already exuding sweat by the time they were shown in to see
Crockett. Perhaps it was the sweat of fear. Armenian exiles who
had fled their country had plenty of reasons to be afraid of offi-
cialdom. Driven from their homes at the whim of the Turkish
janissaries who were tools of those who presently ruled then,
they were accustomed to equating any form of authority with
violence. The two men had been passed on to Crockett as a person who'd had some little experience in dealing with their compatriots when he'd worked in the East End some years ago,
where the immigrants were constantly being brought to the
attention of the authorities: Londoners were automatically suspicious of anyone with a foreign accent, and particularly of those
who lived together in tight little enclaves, kept to their own language and customs, were always in debt, and regularly drunk;
they were suspected of being anarchists, of making bombs with
which to blow up the Houses of Parliament. And indeed, they
were a fierce lot, bridling at any imagined insult and ready to
fight with any who dared challenge them. Not infrequently they
fought among themselves.

Crockett did not at that moment want to see them. He had a
good deal of sympathy with these shipwrecked survivors of
humanity, but they always spelled trouble; he wished to the devil
the desk sergeant who had sent them in to him, but his antennae
began to quiver when he learned they'd come to the police asking for help in tracing a fellow countryman of theirs – or rather,
fellow countrywoman. Her name was Rosa Tartaryan and she
hadn't been seen for two months. That 'two months' was what

made him sit up and take notice. The exact date was even more significant, for it was the day before the murder at Belmonde Abbey.

Many women – amongst the sad stream who constantly disappeared in London – had been reported missing at that time, but none, for one reason and another, could have been the one the police had been seeking. Could this really be the break in the case he'd been hoping for? Crockett told himself this would probably be just another false trail, without really believing it.

It was too late to ask the men to identify the body; she'd been buried long ago – just another unexplained death among the hundreds regularly coming to the attention of the police: mostly poor people without hope, down on their luck, homeless or dying of disease or starvation. The rich were rich but the lives of the poor were indeed 'nasty, brutish and short.'

But he did still have the sketches PC Barton had made of the corpse – and there were, of course, the clothes.

The elder Saroyan rested his melancholy gaze on the sketch for a long time. It was a worthy attempt, a truthful enough representation of the dead woman's features, but Crockett wondered yet again how anyone would be capable of recognising a breathing, sentient human being whom they had known, and perhaps loved, from it, though certainly the couple in Yorkshire, the Crowthers, had been adamant she was *not* anyone they had ever known. The man fingered the heavy woollen coat and skirt, nodded when he saw the Gladstone bag. But it was when he saw the hat that he broke down. Tears brimmed in his sad, dark eyes as he touched the cheap metal brooch, with its pathetic little chip of amber. "She is dead."

"Yes, I'm afraid so. I am very sorry." And so Crockett was, beneath the elation he felt that the identity of the murdered woman was no longer a mystery. He explained where she'd been found, and the circumstances of her death, and was met by stares of grief and bewilderment.

"Rosa?" They exchanged uncomprehending glances. Gevorg was the first to recover himself. He dashed the tears away. "Tell me who did this. I will cut out his heart, I will —"

His brother laid a restraining hand on his knee.

"Tell me about her," said Crockett.

He had to concentrate hard to penetrate the guttural accent, which grew thicker the more excited Gevorg became, the further the narrative progressed. The men were members of a cell of the Armenian Liberation Movement, exiles based here in London. In their own country, they had been working subversively for the liberation of their people, who were groaning under the yoke of Turkish tyranny. Forced to flee, lucky to escape with their lives, they continued their work here, by setting up printing presses and issuing pamphlets which they distributed whenever they could in an endeavour to stir up British interest (doomed to failure, thought Crockett cynically) in the plight of native Armenians. However, they were sometimes successful in smuggling some of their literature into the homeland and indeed had become a thorn in the flesh of the authorities there. "We are not peasants, we can read and write, we are teachers. In our own country, my brother was a lecturer at the university in Yerevan," Gevorg stated with pride, and went on to say that they feared worse oppression was still to come. "Our oppressors are only waiting to deal our nation a mortal blow. More Armenian blood will be spilt at the dictates from Constantinople! I spit on the Turks! But we shall never, never stop crying Liberty!" The sad eyes lit with a fanatical fervour.

"All that is true," put in the younger brother, Stepanos, silent until then. "It is difficult for you, here in Britain, to believe, but our tormentors are intent on nothing less than genocide, nothing will content the Turkish butchers but to wipe our nation from the face of the earth, to drown the Armenian liberation movement in a blood bath. All we have is a dream of creating a free and peaceful Armenia." He was not as choleric as his brother; his voice held barely an inflexion, yet looking at them, Crockett knew which one he would rather take on. He knew, of course, that most of the Armenians gathered in London were dissidents, exiles from their country because they had lived in fear of imprisonment, or of losing their lives. No conquered people love their rulers – especially when they suffer terrible atrocities such as those he had read of in the newspapers, committed by those who called themselves the Young Turks, but it had all been happening a long way off, to an unknown people in a distant country that was only a name, a pinprick on the map of the world. Now, suddenly, it was in the room with him.

"It is our enemies who have tracked her down," declared Gevorg. "They must pay."

Crockett was not without sympathy for him. He could understand that as far as they were concerned, enemies lurked around every corner, every footstep behind them in a dark street might herald the approach of someone determined on revenge, or retribution, and he felt he couldn't rule out the possibility, unlikely as it seemed, that Rosa Tartaryan had indeed been subjected to this fate, perhaps by someone who'd followed her and strangled her as an act of revenge, or as a warning to her friends. She had led a dark, secret and potentially dangerous life. But he was reluctant to accept this too easy explanation without reservations. Whether what Gevorg propounded was so or not, what had she been doing out in the woods at Belmonde in the first place?

"She's been missing for two months. Why did you not come to us before this?"

There had quite often been times when they had not seen her for several weeks, Gevorg shrugged, taking up the tale again. It appeared that Rosa, though an exceedingly zealous member of the organisation, had found a position which had taken her away from them, but it paid such an excellent salary that it had justified her temporarily giving up active work for the movement; the exiles were always in dire need of money, and she contributed almost everything she earned to the common fund. She had gone to live in with her employer, although she had returned as often as possible to the house where most of her friends lodged, or to one of the cafés where they met. In between her visits, they had not kept in touch; it was safer that way.

"Safer? Was there some reason her employer shouldn't know about her private life?"

"It is always safer, my friend, that the left hand should not know what the right is doing," said Stepanos.

Crockett appreciated that secrecy and caution must by now be ingrained, while thinking at the same time that the occupation

Rosa had taken up was a very innocent one, that of companion-housekeeper to a widow. Her English, according to the brothers at any rate, was very good, and she was also a fine cook, so she'd had no difficulty in being accepted for the position. She lived well and comfortably and best of all, she was able to put extra money into the exiles' kitty from time to time, since she was often given presents of money by the woman for whom she worked.

"What was the name of this generous employer?"

She was a Mrs Hannah Smith, and she lived, they believed, in north London. More than that, they had never been told. Rosa, it seemed, had carried the code of secrecy to extremes, though her compatriots didn't appear to find anything unusual in this.

"Did she ever go to Yorkshire?"

They looked blank, perhaps never having heard of Yorkshire.

"Maybe with her employer? To the West Riding?" he pressed, able by now to quote the name and address found on the slip of paper by heart. But he drew blank. The brothers were evidently as nonplussed as he was as to why Rosa should have had this in her bag.

As they prepared to leave, Gevorg asked if he might have the brooch. "I gave it to her," he said, looking at the cheap little trinket as he might have looked at the Kohinoor diamond. "She wore it always – for me."

"I'll make arrangements for you to have all her things, as soon as possible. Just leave me your address."

When they had gone, Crockett sat down to think, hardly able to believe that things were at last beginning to move. Perhaps he would not now need to ask Agnes to help him. But a moment's thought showed him that it still might be desirable. And why should he deny himself the opportunity of seeing his beloved?

Accordingly, he had set off at the appointed time, having had an interesting conversation with Inspector Daffyd Meredith in between. The morning's fog had indeed lifted by this time, a pale sun had emerged to reveal a hazy autumn day, and now here he was, having smoothed his hair with brilliantine and combed his moustache carefully, made sure that his high collar was spotless, and bought a fresh carnation for his buttonhole and a bunch of

Parma violets for Agnes from a flower-girl outside the underground station in the Circus. Why she had chosen this particular place, he couldn't imagine, except that it was clean and convenient for a hot cup of tea and a nicely toasted and buttered teacake such as he had just consumed, and the presence of ladies was not frowned upon, even without a male escort.

A waitress approached and asked if there was anything else they wanted.

"Agnes?"

Agnes, who had not eaten anything – she was one of those people who seemed to live on air – said no thank you, and pushed her teacake across to Crockett. "Another pot of tea, perhaps," Crockett said to the waitress, and when she had gone, and the string trio in the corner by the palms was playing the Indian Love Lyrics, which he knew Agnes was very fond of, and which might soften her to agree to what he was about to ask, he reached across the table and took his young lady's hand.

"I want to ask you to do something for me, Agnes."

"Anything – within reason," she answered cheerfully, but with a wary gleam in her eye.

"Do you know a young woman called Louisa Fox, a member of your WPSU? She's studying to become a doctor."

"Yes, of course I know Louisa – quite well, as a matter of fact. She's not a committed member – yet. But I'm working on her. She does come to meetings occasionally, and addresses envelopes sometimes, that sort of thing. I like her very much, but I have to say she's one of those who only gives the Movement half-hearted support."

Crockett let go her hand. Miss Fox had not struck him as being half-hearted; she had in fact impressed him with her sense and sensibility when she had marched in to see him. "I don't suppose it's a case with her of not having anything else to do with her time," he said stiffly. "She is committed to her studies." He realised too late that his choice of words had scarcely been tactful, but he did not like to hear the censoriousness of her tone.

And Agnes did not like the implied criticism. "Now, John, I won't have you talking to me like that. I know she has her plate full – but she's not the only one."

Crockett drummed his fingers on the green tile top of the table and looked dark.

Agnes was exceedingly pretty when she was angry, with her face above the grey fur collar flushed, her chin lifted and her pretty dark blue eyes sparkling and matching the colour of her costume exactly. She wore an extremely becoming hat. He sighed and determined to try to repair the damage of his unthinking remark. But she was not one to hold on to a grievance, and before he could speak, she was smiling again and saying, "What is it you want me to do then, John?"

His face cleared. He took her hand again, thinking how well the little pearl and garnet ring he had already bought for her would look on her slender fourth finger – or better still, the plain gold band he'd been waiting for nearly two years to slide on. Those pretty hands should be embroidering tablecloths and pillow cases for her bottom drawer, not sewing banners or throwing bags of flour or even worse, bricks. Patience was not one of his virtues and all this unnecessary waiting for their marriage exasperated him. He was by no means wealthy, and could never expect to be, but he earned a good wage and had put by enough to set them up when they were married. He had the sense, however, to know when he was banging his head against a brick wall.

"Well, Agnes," he said, forcing his mind from profitless thoughts. "It's like this…"

"Let's get this straight," said Agnes, who was a woman of direct speech, "you want me to spy on Louisa Fox."

Crockett looked pained. "You have a hard way of putting it. I simply want you to get her to talk, and to keep your ears open."

"Because you think she had something to do with this murder?" She buried her face in the cool, sweet-smelling violets he had brought her and breathed deeply, as if for calm.

"Not in the least, Agnes. Not so fast. But she knows the family well, and since there seems no reason that we can discover for the dead woman to have been in the grounds at Belmonde, and since you swear there was nothing planned by your suffragettes —"

Agnes looked up from the velvety flowers. "Nothing scheduled, and no one has been reported missing. There are all sorts of women on the fringes of the Movement, but none of them, I should think, would have decided to act on their own initiative in that way."

"Exactly. So if we rule out suffragette involvement for the time being – which was only considered because of Montague Chetwynd visiting there – then we are back to the family. The officer in charge there has had to let Jordan, the gamekeeper, go – not a shred of evidence against him."

"You suspect one of the family of murdering this woman?" Her eyes grew wide.

"Not – precisely. But that place – Belmonde Abbey. Something indicates all isn't as it should be there. The Chetwynds have closed ranks – we didn't get a straight answer from anybody, and why that should be, I'd very much like to know. I'm not fond of unsolved puzzles, as you know – and then, today…"

He then told her of the visit of the Armenians. "So we know that the name of the murdered woman was almost certainly Rosa Tartaryan. Why she went to Belmonde is still as mysterious as ever." But he remembered the conversation with Meredith about the letters Sir Henry had been receiving and the word blackmail, which had lodged in his mind. "We also know that she'd been working as a sort of companion-housekeeper to a Mrs Hannah Smith."

"So you must find this Mrs Smith?" She grimaced. "Smith. That's not going to be easy."

"I've already set wheels in motion."

"There's something else, John?"

"Yes. The name Hannah Smith rang a bell. After the two Saroyans, the Armenians, had left…" He hesitated. "It's a long story, too long, perhaps?"

"Never mind that. You can't leave me on tenterhooks."

"Well, then. It came back to me that earlier this year, the eldest son – Henry Chetwynd like his father, but known as Harry – was killed in an omnibus accident, which was in itself a little puzzle. Why should a man like him be riding on the top deck of a London omnibus – a young man of means who reportedly never went anywhere except by cab? You might say there was no reason why he shouldn't have decided to do so on a sudden whim, but there were several more questions about that incident, which is why I remember it particularly. I wasn't on the case, but I followed it, and I recall that one of the questions concerned a young woman and a child who were also on the omnibus. The woman suffered a blow to the head and she lay in hospital, insensible, for a long time. When she eventually came to, she could remember nothing of the accident – nor even who she was, poor lady. But by that time the case had come to the ears of her maid, who eventually took her home. I don't remember the maid's name, but if it turns out to be Rosa Tartaryan, then we have a connection. The injured woman's name, you see, was Hannah Smith."

"Oh. And the child?" asked Agnes, now very much interested.

"A little boy of about two or three years old. He suffered a slight concussion, and a broken collar bone, but he soon recovered. However, he was either a latecomer in learning to speak, or too upset by the accident to utter. At any rate, he was unable to tell us his name. He was taken to see Mrs Smith while she was still in the coma and asked if she was his mother, but he screamed and refused to look at her."

"Presumably, if her head was injured, she was swathed in bandages," Agnes said drily. "Enough to make any child scream. I suppose they're reunited now."

"She wasn't his mother. When she was able to talk, she denied ever having had a child. There were several people injured in the accident, and three other people died besides Harry Chetwynd, including a woman who was thrown right out on to the street and killed as she hit the pavement."

"Of course, I remember now – I read about it at the time – the accident caused quite a sensation, didn't it? But surely someone remembered who the child was with?"

Crockett spread his hands. "It was a very breezy day, though bright and sunny, I believe, and the ladies on the omnibus – who in my experience are usually the ones to notice such things, are they not? – were more concerned with keeping their hats in place than looking about them on the 'bus."

"And I suppose the gentlemen were occupied with their newspapers – or looking at the ladies."

"No doubt. At any rate, no one remembered seeing anyone

with a child on their lap, or with one seated next to them: he was only a very small child, remember, not easily noticed. And since no one else claimed him, it was assumed he must have been with the woman who'd been thrown out – and who remains unidentified to this day. From her ragged clothing and general appearance, she seemed to have come from the poorest of the poor. Nobody ever came to us, looking for a woman of her description – but then, women like that, as you know, leading a hand-to-mouth, rootless existence, come and go."

"With no one to know or care if they're never seen again," agreed Agnes with a sigh. "But tell me, was the child poor and ragged, too?"

"No. He was well-dressed and cared for. She may, of course, have been looking after him for someone."

Agnes wryly acknowledged this. "Some women are not always particular about who they entrust their children to, that's true enough. But if so, why did no one come forward to claim him? And what's happened to him since?"

"A home was found for him with the childless widow of one of our policemen. She's become devoted to him – but nearly a year later, he still doesn't speak."

"Poor mite." Agnes poured them both another cup of tea. The string trio had retired from behind their palms and there was silence except for the clatter of teacups and cutlery, the quiet murmur of ladies talking over their tea and cakes, the ceaseless sound of motor traffic passing on Piccadilly, the clop of hooves, a jingle of harness and the cries of a news vendor. "But you still think that Harry Chetwynd might have had something to do with Mrs Smith and the little boy?"

"I can't rid myself of the notion that he had."

"In that case, is it possible the murdered woman at Belmonde could have been this Mrs Smith, and not Rosa Tartaryan?"

"No. I'm convinced Gevorg Saroyan wasn't mistaken in his identification of the sketch of her – nor of her clothing. But something else has cropped up." He then told her of the conversation he'd had with Meredith, just before leaving his office. "It's quite possible Rosa might have been putting pressure on Sir Henry."

"Because she knew Mrs Smith and Harry Chetwynd were – connected, in some way?"

"That's it. And supposing – regardless of the fact that she vehemently denied ever having a child – the child on the 'bus *should* turn out to have been hers —"

"— and Harry Chetwynd's? Oh, goodness. I see. The rightful heir? That could put the cat among the pigeons, for all sorts of reasons." Agnes stirred her tea and Crockett finished off her tea-cake (excellent, plenty of currants, not mean with the butter, toasted just right) and wiped his mouth.

"Going back to where we started," Agnes said, "why should Louisa Fox know anything about this, or indeed, be any more willing to talk than the Chetwynds, especially if she's friendly with the son, Sebastian?"

"I shall be following my own line of enquiry – see if I can trace Mrs Smith through the hospital where she was treated. But meanwhile, it cannot do any harm to find if anyone at Belmonde knows anything about her. It needs tact and diplomacy and I know of no one who has more than you, my dear. Louisa Fox might unwittingly say something, if you can gain her confidence. But I'll admit it's a very long shot."

"And a very tall order." Then she smiled. "But for the sake of the little boy, one that's worth trying, hmm? You have a very tender heart under that tough exterior, Chief Inspector Crockett. Not to say a silver tongue."

"I don't like unfinished business," he answered, brusquely, to cover his confusion, and added, "It's you who have a tender heart. I knew you wouldn't fail me, Agnes. You never do."

Her colour rose as she played with the sugar tongs. "In the circumstances, John, that's a very handsome thing to say, though it isn't quite true, is it? I'm afraid I'm very tiresome to you at times."

But his breath caught in his throat as he looked at her and thought he saw a promise in her eyes.

AUGUST

Two months have gone by since I last wrote.

I have been ill. Not physically, but living with such confusion that I thought I was going mad...which I had certainly not expected to happen, if or when my past at last began to make sense. It was remembering Hugh, of course, which triggered everything else. How naturally that came back to me, all the details of our first meeting. But everything has its price: afterwards, sliding into my mind like a snake, came the memory of that night: a dark night with the great yellow moon out, the figures of the men sharp against the curve of the kopje as they went to take their turn at watch. And after that came the rest of it, like a dam bursting, carrying all before it, like the Malopo River when the rains came, like the time I fell into the sluit.

I could not stem the flood as it eddied around me, day after day. Pictures of that other, distant life, all the bright fragments and the dark, rushed by – in no sort of order, but sometimes with such clarity I felt myself actually, physically back there. At others, they were vague and undefined, impossible to pin down. I wanted to grab every precious insight and hold it, before it escaped me forever, but if I attempted to arrange these epiphanies into some sort of sequence, they slipped away and I was in terror they would never come back. I began to feel ill, as though I were burning up; over-stimulated, I suppose, but at least not empty, as I had been before.

Nothing lasts, however, even despair. It gradually became apparent that I must do as I did before, and go forward, step by careful step, in my building up of this picture of my past. I should go truly mad, otherwise. One's mind cannot hold everything at once, it's too much to expect the brain to sort out all the accumulated dross of a forgotten half-lifetime. I didn't need Dr Harvill to tell me that, though he did. I have not been back to see him since. I don't know why, but I cannot feel it is quite so easy as he makes out. He has an answer for everything, but the world is not quite so simple.

So, I must return to that momentous turning-point in my life: my arrival in South Africa.

1896

The train steamed and rattled over the vast, seemingly endless, elevated grasslands which in South Africa are called the veld. It was nearly six o'clock in the morning and I'd been travelling for three nights and two days in this bone-shaking monster, but thankfully, at last, I would soon have reached my journey's end.

We had left Cape Town at nightfall, in a train crowded with British soldiers travelling north, but seats had been reserved for me, and for Mrs Winstanley, who was to travel with me as far as Kimberley. There our ways would part, after nearly three weeks spent together.

The travelling companion who had been found for me had proved to be a stout, imposing lady, but despite her dogmatic opinions and formidable manner, she sheltered me under her wing like a large mother hen with a precious chick, yet encouraged me to join in whatever new experiences and pleasures were on offer – and there were many, both on board the *Norham Castle* and in the places where we stopped, such as beautiful Madeira, where I saw and enjoyed some of the same diversions Lyddie had described. Life on board was every bit as delightful as I had hoped and expected. I was outward bound for adventure, determined to enjoy every minute. Flying fish and dolphins followed in the ship's wake, under stars thick and bright as never at home. There were games on deck and musical evenings. We were served with delicious meals, and I learned to play bridge.

Mrs Winstanley's biggest fault was that she was an inveterate match-maker. She was delighted to see that I was never short of dancing partners among the army officers who were journeying out to join their regiments, but warned me not to be too hopeful of this as a prelude to any romantic attachment. I hadn't deemed it necessary to tell her that I was – almost – promised to a man called Willie Dyson – nor could she have known that I was not the sort to cherish any illusions as to my chances in life. Indeed, I often thought, can this really be me, Hannah Jackson? And had to remind myself that it was highly unlikely this delightful state of affairs would carry on once I left the ship.

It seemed that it could, for a little while longer at any rate, for when we reached Cape Town, Mrs Winstanley wouldn't hear of me staying anywhere but with her at the Mount Nelson, which I soon discovered to be the most luxurious in a city noted for its excellent hotels.

Mrs Winstanley's husband was in diamonds. She was travelling back to join him after attending the wedding of their son in England.

Shall I ever forget my first sight of Cape Town and Table Mountain, with its long flat top rising up to the brilliantly starlit sky? We steamed into port in the dark and there it was, an electrically-lit city vying with the stars' brilliance, lying under the shadow of the mountain and reflected in the sea. It still seemed magical the following day, even when I viewed the city through a haze of dust. Wide streets, lined with palms; gardens filled with tropical flowers; well-stocked stores – and, too, the palatial offices and clubs of the *nouveau riche* Uitlanders from Kimberley and Johannesburg. I noticed that although they drove the motorcars imported from Europe and America, those same people often sat back in rickshaws drawn by Kaffirs, whose tin shanties lay alongside their patrons' conspicuous homes, designed to show off their enormous wealth. I had been brought up by my father from an early age to believe in the equality of all human beings, and it was a disconcerting mixture I found there, a cosmopolitan but unequal society, where the natives performed all the hard, menial and distasteful tasks while the rich white people, whatever their dissatisfactions with one another, enjoyed a lavishly ostentatious style of living.

"And luxury's just what these Boers can't stomach," announced Mrs Winstanley, pointing out the burghers to me: burly, bearded men with wide brimmed hats and inflexible expressions. Bible thumpers, she called them, farmers who lived a hard and solitary life on their isolated farms, but who were here in Cape Town to put the Boer side of the interminable disputatious questions of the day.

In the matter of manners and customs, Mrs Winstanley proved invaluable. She had a kinder and – from what I saw from other white people – novel way of dealing with the native servants, such as the black maids in the hotel and the porters who carried our luggage on to the station: believe them to be honest unless proved otherwise, give them a smile, respect their different way of life, my dear, but never forget they are still uncivilised. She used much less tortuous diplomacy with the white troopers we encountered on the station platform, who hindered our progress on to the train by their heavy kit-bags, and on whom she bestowed a Look, expecting nothing less than for them to get out of her way. I was amused to see how instantly they obeyed her.

But then, Ada Winstanley was not a woman to be trifled with. As we settled in the train, she took the opportunity to prepare me for my arrival in Mafeking. "Don't expect too much of it," she'd warned. "It was only properly established a few years ago by white settlers...prospectors and so on. You're likely find it very raw and uncivilised, my dear – such places are a magnet for the undesirable element. I speak with authority. I've seen what happened in Kimberley."

I don't think she'd ever been to Mafeking, but she made the frontier town sound as though it was the last outpost of the Empire (and maybe I should find that she wasn't far wrong, though I hoped not). She harped on the same theme several times, but conceded that it should be a good place to find a husband. "Just think of all those officers quartered there, Hannah."

I replied, much nettled, that I wasn't looking to marry anyone just yet, and as for soldiers – individuals who were expected to obey orders without question were not my cup of tea.

"I should keep remarks like that to myself, if I were you."

"By that you mean I mustn't speak my mind?"

"It would probably be more circumspect. Though I wouldn't," she added after a moment's thought, "expect they set overmuch store by manners and conventions up in Mafeking."

I steered the conversation towards other, less controversial subjects, things that I hoped to see and experience: the sunshine, the wildlife – and what about the strange and delicious tropical fruits Lyddie had written about that we'd certainly never seen in Bridge End?

"Overrated, my dear. Decidedly overrated, all of it."

It was a somewhat dampening view of my much anticipated visit and depressed me a little. But then I decided I was sorry she felt that way and hoped I wouldn't become so blasé.

Rarely have I spent such an unrestful night as that first night, on a hard bed which made me painfully aware of every bump and jolt of the train. I was not comforted to remember it was to be a three-day train ride, with but a few stations en route. The next morning, I woke to find we were bucking along the high, arid plateau of the Great Karoo, its stony plains and illimitable veld, where in the shimmering heat, under the pale, almost colourless sky, occasional groups of twisted thorn trees rose above the endless miles of light-coloured, waving grasses, the height of a man – so endless in fact that it acquired a sameness that was no rest for the eyes. Eventually, we left it behind and passed through country that was wild and sometimes splendid, the crystal clear, limpid air allowing glimpses from time to time of distant bare hills and mountains. There was very little sign of life anywhere other than long, ox-drawn wagon-trains, or when we stopped at wayside stations to walk about and stretch our legs, to buy drinks or something to eat.

The only other occupants of the compartment, besides myself and Mrs Winstanley, were two children and their mother, a large Dutch lady who regarded me and my attempts to make friends with her children with undisguised hostility. In the end Mrs Winstanley advised me in a low voice to have nothing more to do with her. "She's the wife of a Boer, she'll speak nothing but Afrikaans. Take no notice of her," my friend advised. "Their old Kruger states quite openly that Kaffirs are mere creatures, with no more soul than a monkey, and I dare say she thinks the same of us."

After that we and the family travelled without further communication. The Boers, thankfully, disembarked at Kimberley, where Mrs Winstanley was also to leave me.

A long stop was scheduled there to allow many of the passengers to leave the train and for the rest of us, those who were to continue, to seek refreshment – bodily refreshment that is. There was certainly nothing there for the soul, as far as I could see. Nothing but the depressing sight of yellow mine-dumps, mile after mile of huge mounds of residue from the diamond-quarrying or open-pit excavations which had made millionaires of men like Rhodes. Spoiled earth that was the real cost of extracting diamonds from what was being called the biggest hole in the world.

Gritty dust hung like a miasma in the air when we alighted from the train. It was hot. I went to stretch my legs and to look for a drink, while Mrs Winstanley left her luggage with me and went in search of her husband, who had a motorcar waiting for her. Making my way through the crowds, I found a shack that called itself a refreshment room.

"Excuse me, ma'am, but I shouldn't risk eating any of that if I were you."

I turned to see a uniformed officer indicating the assortment of unappetising food laid out on the counter. "I assure you I've no intention of doing so," I told him, averting my eyes from the obscene cloud of flies buzzing around it.

"Very wise. The tea should be all right, though. May I order you some?"

I hesitated, looking around the shanty – it was nothing more – that served as a refreshment room. I was very thirsty, but the idea of sitting at one of those filthy tables was abhorrent, the thought of drinking tea out of cups which looked as though they hadn't been washed since the last person had used them even more so. Well, there was water to be had on the train, though it was always tepid.

"Perhaps you're right," he remarked, following my glance at the array of cups. "I say, why don't we get back on to the train? If there happens to be a spare seat in your compartment, I'd appreciate the honour of sharing my breakfast with you. My mother always sees that I'm supplied with enough for twenty. I've some bottles of tea, too. Cold, but very refreshing."

His *mother*?

I'd already had what passed for breakfast on the train, and I was none too sure about being in the company for the next five hundred miles of a strange young man, no matter how charming he might appear. He had thick fair hair bleached even fairer by the sun, and blue eyes in a tanned face, a clipped moustache and pleasing manners, altogether a very attractive combination, but that could be very deceptive. He might turn out to be the world's most tedious bore.

"I'm afraid my seat's in a Ladies Only compartment."

"My own compartment's confoundedly full, or I'd ask you to join me there." He looked disappointed.

"We-ell..." Ladies Only compartments were designated as such in order to protect the said ladies from cigarette or pipe smoke, or from gentlemen who might become too familiar. But the train was equipped with side corridors and after all, it would be simple enough to leave the door open while we chatted. He smiled as if he'd known what I was thinking, and said he was well known to all the railway people on this line, and that no difficulty would arise, and in the event none did. We'd barely introduced ourselves on the platform – he was Captain Hugh Osborne, of the Bechuanaland Rifles, an armed force which policed the borders and endeavoured to keep the peace, and he was travelling from here to re-join his unit which was garrisoned in Mafeking – when Mrs Winstanley came sailing towards us.

She seemed delighted to see me talking to the young officer I'd just met and they shook hands warmly. "You know Captain Osborne?" I asked, somewhat taken aback.

"Hugh? Why, I've known him from the cradle. Have I not, Hugh?"

Before the train left again, under the guise of saying a final few private words of goodbye, she took the opportunity of telling me how pleased she was that Hugh Osborne and I had met. What a fine young man he was, from one of the best families in Kimberley. (Thus was his mother and his breakfast explained.) Though it was a pity, she added, he'd been so foolish as to join the army and not the family business – diamonds, of course – one of the richest in Kimberley, now part of Cecil Rhodes' big de Beers company.

Little as I'd known her, I had a sense of leaving part of the past behind me as I waved farewell to my companion of the last few weeks, but I soon settled down. When Captain Osborne and I had shared the bottled tea (he was quite right, it was deliciously refreshing) he didn't impose his company on me further, although he came back along the corridor several times during the rest of the journey to make sure I wasn't bored, or suffering any undue discomfort, a concern which I found both amusing and endearing. The further we journeyed from civilisation, the less I wanted to dwell on what lay before me. With Mrs Winstanley's warnings ringing in my ears, at every turn of the wheels I was beginning to wonder if this enterprise might turn out to be not the adventure I had hoped for, but a folly – yet what was the point of an adventure if it wasn't spiced with a little apprehension?

It soon became apparent, however, that such thoughts were not possible in the company of Hugh Osborne. One would have been a chilly mortal indeed not to have been warmed by his obviously good intentions. He was amiable and willing to talk, and by the time we'd covered not many more miles, we were very well informed about each other.

When he learned that the purpose of my journey to Mafeking was to visit Lyddie and her husband, he looked decidedly pleased. Yes, of course he knew Lyall Armitage, who had worked as a Scout for his unit many times...not much he didn't know about the territory north of the Limpopo. Best of fellows. And Mrs Lyall is safe in Mafeking? Good. Not the best spot for women over the border at the moment. Still fighting all over the place and no organised opposition as yet in position. However, it seemed General Carrington's chief staff officer was expected any day from England to lead a campaign against the rebels. That was the purpose of the troops on this train, who were being sent on ahead of his arrival.

I sat opposite him and watched the sunlight through the train window on his smooth hair, bleached fair as the grasses of the veld outside, and decided I liked very much what I saw of this tall, well-brushed young officer. Despite what I'd said to Mrs Winstanley, my experience of military men had been extremely limited, based on one particular soldier, a friend of George Crowther's whom I'd particularly detested. Captain Osborne could scarcely have been more different. Born in South Africa, he'd been sent away to school in England, where he seemed to have acquired all the upright attributes necessary for his chosen career: the determination to live an honourable and courageous life – prepared, if need be, to face death in the service of his country. He much admired Cecil Rhodes' declared intention to extend the British Empire in Africa. I didn't feel disposed to argue with him over this; he would, I felt, always be utterly loyal, once he had given his heart and mind to anything, to any cause. I didn't see then, or even later, how deeply conventional, even rigid, this streak in him was.

Naturally, I didn't form all these opinions during our journey, but over the course of the next few months, by which time we were quite at ease with each other, although, right from the first, it was evident to me at least that we were destined to become friends.

His father had come out to South Africa as a British mining engineer before succumbing to diamond-fever, buying up as many claims as he could and becoming rich in the process. He had died fairly recently, and left his mining interests to his children. The others were anxious to continue working in the business, but Hugh had no such ambitions. "Oh Lord, no. Not with two brothers already in it – and a sister. Very managing sort, Amelia. I don't somehow see myself as an office boy." The reason, in fact, that he'd obtained leave to go down to Kimberley had been to sign overall control of the management of the business to his siblings. He'd always been the restless sort, he added with his self-deprecating smile, cursed with a streak of adventure hitherto undetected in a family more inclined to the tendency of making money.

I guessed this was a tongue-in-cheek way of saying that it wasn't in his nature to be idle, that he craved action. He had joined a fighting force because he believed in British justice, even if – or perhaps especially – upholding it meant a good scrap now and then. "The fighting over the border has actually been very sharp lately. The Kaffirs' god – witch-doctor, high-priest, whatever you like to call him – has been stirring them up and they've decided they don't care for being ruled by foreigners after all."

"Fancy." I was taken back to the discussions in the schoolroom at home, when Rouncey had often pointed out that simply marching in and raising the flag of sovereignty did not obligate the natives to accept it, "Didn't we just move in and declare their land henceforth belonged to Britain?"

"Not at all! There were agreements, after all." I seemed to have unwittingly touched a nerve. "Trouble is, don't you see, the natives can't quite see it like that. They've been accustomed all their lives to raiding and killing and stealing their neighbour's land and cattle, and having theirs stolen. They think they can go to war with us and get their land back just as if we were another tribe who'd wrested it from them."

"How very unsporting of them!"

To give him his due, he laughed. "Miss Jackson, it's hardly a question of that. British policy, you know, is always to preserve the tribal system – and what the Kaffirs don't realise is what being under our influence can do for them. If you saw the conditions in which they live, you'd see how much they need the benefits civilisation can bring."

My father had once brought home as a guest a missionary who had worked in Africa. He, too, had spoken of improving the lot of the heathen by the civilising influence of the British, especially in the matter of making them Christians. My father had been doubtful about this justification for imposing on the 'heathen' a religion they perhaps did not want or need. I supposed that the truth, as it usually does, lay somewhere between the two.

"I'm afraid there's going to be more bloodshed before it's over. But at the moment, it looks as though we have the rebels nicely pincered between the columns we already have up there. Rhodes thinks the neck of the rebellion is broken."

"And what do you think, Captain Osborne?"

"Oh, I'm just a soldier, doing what I'm told." He smiled. "But you, Miss Jackson, I see you have a certain propensity for argument."

"Debate." I smiled back, but thought perhaps it was time the conversation was steered in another direction. "Tell me about these black people. They sound very fierce."

"The Matabele? I should say so! They're originally Zulus, you know, quite formidable warriors." He laughed. "Which they've every need to be. If they return home after a failed attack, their womenfolk have an unfortunate tradition of breaking their necks."

"My goodness. Aren't you afraid of them?"

"Pretty damn scared, actually, begging your pardon. Anyone who said he wasn't would be a fool or a liar. It's a sight to put the fear of God in anyone, to see one of those coming at you, I can tell you. Barefoot, wearing nothing but a leopard skin and feathers and a big shield, armed to the teeth with spears and all that." He broke off suddenly. "I say, I'm frightening you, and that's unforgivable —"

"You wouldn't say that if you knew what a family of boys I've grown up with."

"You, Miss Jackson? Do tell me about it."

And so, in my turn, I sketched the details of my own life, and though dull indeed in comparison with his, we went on from there. Whatever else, at that time we were never, Hugh Osborne and I, short of things to say to each other.

On the last morning of the train journey, Mafeking appeared suddenly out of the blue. At first sight, it seemed that Mrs Winstanley's gloomy predictions might prove to be correct. This couldn't possibly be my destination, could it? This insignificant huddle on a baking plain in the middle of nowhere? A little, tin-roofed town set saucer-like in the midst of the great undulating veld, its rusty-red roofs and low, mud-brick buildings predominantly echoing the colours of the earth: the reddish sandy soil, the boulders, the dust, and the bare ochre rocks? But yes, there was the sign, boldly painted on a board on the platform: MAFEKING.

Surrounding the station were corrugated iron railway sheds and workshops, freight wagons and a great locomotive in the sidings, piles of track and sleepers stacked in preparation for when the next leg of the line was laid. Not a very prepossessing sight.

I felt dirty and gritty-eyed but, tired as I was, I stepped off the train with a smile in my heart, overjoyed at the prospect of reunion with Lyddie, and was quite disconcerted to find no one there to greet me. I stood amid the sea of khaki uniforms as the troopers poured out of the train and on to the platform, feeling very forlorn, craning my neck and hoping but failing to see

Lyddie, with her cheerful smile and her arms wide, ready to throw around me. Perhaps it had been too much to expect her to stand about waiting for trains when she was expecting a child in less than four months.

I tried to collect my wits and began to thread my way through the milling crowd of men, ducking only just in time to avoid being hit in the face by a kitbag which a large trooper was shouldering. Unaware of what he'd done, it was only when he heard my involuntary exclamation that he spun round. "Oh heck, sorry, miss! Didn't see you standing there, like. You all right, love?"

The soldier, a big strapping lad of no more than eighteen or nineteen, was looking down at me with concern. I heard the broad accents of the West Riding, of home. The men on the train were the mounted infantry of the West Riding, York and Lancaster Regiments, and I felt suddenly overcome with a feeling of homesickness, something I hadn't experienced since leaving Bridge End. It must have been because I was very travel-weary that the familiar tones nearly brought tears to my eyes.

"Yes, I thought someone would be here to meet me…"

"Long way from home, aren't you, then?" He smiled, pushing his hat to the back of his head and mopping his brow. My own accent was obviously as recognisable as his.

"This is going to be my home for some time." I blinked and hoped my dismay at the prospect wasn't too apparent.

"Oh? Well, mine an' all, till they send us up-country, but I've seen worse places." A whistle indicated that the commanding officer was endeavouring to bring some semblance of military order to the milling troops before marching them off to their quarters. "Best of luck, lass!" A cheerful grin and a smart salute, and he was gone.

And all at once, there was Lyall, a little unfamiliar in his khaki bush jacket and a wide, slouch-brimmed hat. Browner than ever, his teeth very white under his bushy moustache. I noticed immediately that he looked tired, with a crease of worry between his brows, and older, but the warmth of his welcome almost made up for Lyddie's absence. He apologised for not being there to help me from the train – he'd come on his bicycle and hadn't been able to find anywhere to leave it, since army transport, waiting to unload supplies from the train, had blocked the station entrance. "Come, we must get you settled in, Hannah dear. Lyddie's simply longing to see you."

Hardly had he spoken but we were hailed by Captain Osborne, threading his way along the platform between the marshalled troops. The two men smiled and shook hands, and on learning from me how kindly I'd been taken care of, Lyall thanked the captain warmly.

"Always a pleasure to assist a charming lady."

We spoke a little more before Hugh Osborne took his farewell and departed to report back to his headquarters. "May I come and visit you some time, Miss Jackson?"

"Of course. That is —?" I gave Lyall an enquiring glance.

"Our home is yours now, Hannah. You'd be very welcome, Osborne."

Lyall watched him go with a smile. "I see you've already made a conquest. Capital fellow!" He hesitated. "Shall we walk? The house isn't far – not above a couple of hundred yards, and it'll give you an opportunity to see something of the town, and to stretch your legs."

"Lyall, how is Lyddie?"

He didn't answer immediately, looking around for a native boy who could take my luggage and his bicycle to the house, nor did he afterwards, when he had found one. I felt the first small stab of unease.

The morning was still cool and fresh, the air sharp and clear, and the small town was busy and purposeful, conducting its business before the sun reached its zenith. As we left the station and walked through the market square, we passed white women carrying homely shopping baskets, and black women gracefully walking with bundles balanced on their heads. Native children, mother-naked except for a small leather apron, ran about or played in the dust. A pack of thin and unnervingly silent yellow dogs followed us at a distance. There were bicycles everywhere. I breathed in wood smoke and metallic dust and the sweet, heavy perfume from some unidentified plant in a garden we passed, a combination that was to become so familiar to me: the smell of

Africa. And everywhere, overpoweringly at times, was the sharp reek of horse.

"There's the native town – their stadt." Lyall pointed to a large but scattered accumulation of thatched, round huts standing at some distance from the town proper, each with an outer wall encircling it, where smoke rose into the air from cooking fires. Beyond it, a streak of silver at the bottom of a slope showed the river, the Malopo, in its deep creek. "The location's actually much bigger than the white town – in fact, about six thousand natives live there, mainly Barolong and a few others, to our sixteen hundred or so."

"So all the natives are not hostile?" I asked, mindful of that conversation in the train about the fearsome Matabele warriors.

He smiled. "We live amicably." Apparently the Barolong, who counted their wealth in cattle and raised crops to support themselves, were a people who had been settled on the banks of the Malopo long before the white settlers arrived, and were peaceful enough, though they could fight when they had to. "And look," he added, scarcely pausing for breath, "here's the new Catholic church, just erected, and St John's, where we worship." Mudbrick again. We continued on our way, puffs of red dust rising at every step, with Lyall pointing out such sophistications as Riesle's, the best hotel in town which, despite such an accolade, appeared dismayingly primitive, as did the clothing store and the fishmonger's, and the haberdashery shop.

This, then, was the end of my great adventure. I'd hoped to broaden my horizons and though I hadn't been so foolish as to imagine I would be coming within striking distance of the sort of culture I'd once dreamed of experiencing, I hadn't expected quite such a God-forgotten sort of place. I pulled myself up short...how silly I was. It was surely the people who lived here, thrown together for whatever reason, who were the community, not these chancy-looking buildings of mud brick and corrugated iron – and I had to admit that attempts had been made, within limits, to turn the little town into somewhere tolerably smart. Shade trees had been planted at intervals along the streets and the houses had gardens. There were several churches and chapels, a school, a racecourse, and even a Masonic Hall. The townspeople were obviously fostering a community spirit, making the best of it. I was sharply reminded that I'd better do the same for the time I was here.

I could hardly wait to see Lyddie, but Lyall was walking slowly, almost dawdling, one might say, raising his hat every few yards to some acquaintance, pausing to show me some new sight. Once or twice he'd seemed about to say something to me, and then changed his mind. I quickened my pace. "Take it easy, Hannah. You'll soon learn not to rush about in this country. Look around you and get your bearings."

"Lyall, I shall have plenty of time for that later," I said, swatting flies. "What is it you want to say?"

After some initial hesitation, he answered, "I'm afraid you might think you've been brought out here under false pretences."

And then he went on to tell me that Lyddie had lost the child she was carrying, the doctor giving it as his opinion that this was entirely due to the arduousness of their escape. "She's taken it badly," he said abruptly, "hasn't shed a tear, but she's so listless, and depressed, she takes no interest in anything – all quite unlike Lyddie, as you well know. She wasn't like this last time. She was even riding again within a few weeks."

"Last time?"

It seemed that there had been another premature baby the previous year. "She didn't want to worry you people at home by telling you, especially since she was very soon well again. This time, however..." He shook his head. "I'm forced to leave her from time to time, out of necessity, and now – well, it's something I can't do anything about. I don't mind telling you, I'm hanged if I know what to do."

Lyall, strong and independent when it came to coping with the big things was, like most men it seemed, helpless in the face of life's eternal verities.

Not that I felt much less helpless. "I suppose," I said lamely, "you must give her time." Admittedly, no one could be less of an authority on this sort of thing than I, but women having miscarriages weren't exactly an uncommon occurrence, even in Bridge End, and I'd picked up enough to know that the experience could be mentally demoralising as well as physically enervating, perhaps for quite some time.

Lyall stopped and turned to face me, his hands on my arms. "Your coming here is a godsend, Hannah," he said quietly. For a moment he looked as though he'd like to say more but, like me, found nothing to say.

Chapter Fifteen

She was browner and had lost her plump bounciness. In fact, she looked 'nesh', as we used to say, pinched and peaky; her cheekbones had sculpted hollows beneath. Her smile was still the same, but her eyes were empty.

When the first emotional greetings were over, Lyall tactfully stated he had business to attend to, and wobbled off down the stony street on the bicycle the boy had brought back from the station, leaving Lyddie and me to begin the business of catching up with the news.

At last, we broke off to enjoy a lunch she'd prepared with her own hands. "It's no good leaving this to the boys, they're all alike, no idea," she said impatiently. Though the meal comprised unfamiliar ingredients, I enjoyed it and did it full justice. Lyddie ate little, but talked non-stop, her hands restless. Suddenly, she paused in the middle of what she was saying, then went on in a rush. "Ought I to have telegraphed you, Hannah, when I lost the baby, and stopped you from coming? Perhaps I should have done, but I – oh dear, I so wanted you here – Lyall, dear man, doesn't know how to begin to deal with me, now I'm being so difficult." And with that she burst into tears.

"Lyddie."

In the short space of time since I'd arrived, I'd already asked myself countless times how I might to be able to help her, and each time my heart had failed me when I thought how little I knew of what it must be like to lose a little scrap of humanity, before it was even a real baby. I knew of course that there wasn't anything I *could* do, save hold her hand and let her have her cry out, as her mother would have said. Lyall had said that up to now she'd shed no tears, so perhaps this storm of weeping was what she needed.

Presently she dried her eyes and became calmer. Although she was dry-eyed now, she'd visibly drooped, and I was about to suggest she took a nap when she did so herself. "I'm supposed to rest – and you must be exhausted – I know what that journey's like."

I was quite glad of the opportunity to snatch some rest, after my sleep-deprived nights on the train, and in fact after I'd undressed and laid down, I slept deeply for several hours. I woke hot and sticky, to find the dusk gathering and to hear music being played on the gramophone Lyall had managed to pick up from somewhere – a thin, scratchy sound which presently, after some difficulty, I identified as the Jewel Song from Faust. How very odd it sounded, Nellie Melba singing in the swiftly gathering dusk of an African night.

I found water in a jug on the wash stand, and by the time I'd dressed, splashed my hands and face and tidied my hair, shaken my shoes before putting them on as I'd been warned to do, in case of scorpions lurking inside, the darkness was almost complete, the clouds of flies had settled, and outside the insect noises of the night were rising to a crescendo. I picked up my lamp and made my way towards the source of the music.

The house had a corrugated iron roof and as far as I could judge was little different from any other that I'd so far seen in Mafeking, a one storey building of sunbaked clay bricks, but it was quite comfortable. It wasn't very big, to be sure, but the roof had wide eaves for coolness, a striped awning at the front and a veranda out at the back overlooking a garden shaded by a paw-paw tree and a jacaranda. Sweet-smelling jasmine grew by the door. Doves cooed and an exuberant purple-flowered bougainvillea draped itself over the walls and veranda.

Inside the house, the walls were papered and the red concrete floor was polished – under the layers of dirt and grit that had piled up, that is. There were family photographs on every wall and surface, but their frames were tarnished. Lyddie had attempted homeliness by hanging lace curtains at the windows, but they hung crookedly and it was obvious they needed a wash. She had never been much addicted to housework, but she was Edith Crowther's daughter. That she hadn't noticed – or didn't care – about the general disorder told me more about Lyddie's state of mind than anything else could have done.

Later, that night, I heard the story of their escape.

When disturbing rumours had begun to circulate that the native tribes in Matabeleland and Mashonaland were said to be again raising impi, or groups of warriors, Lyall had immediately despatched some of their personal belongings to Mafeking, where he had established a depot for his stores some time before. He made hasty preparations for himself and Lyddie to follow as soon as they were able. They had almost left it too late and were forced to escape into the bush on foot, with but a few provisions and the clothes they stood up in, the Kaffirs in pursuit and the house behind them looted and in flames. The story of how they'd eventually been able to make their way to a wayside staging post, a rudimentary place where the proprietor had sheltered them until they could board the next coach for Mafeking, was a story of desperate adventure. At one time, as they lay concealed, they could hear their pursuers within a few yards searching for them.

It had cost Lyddie the life of her baby – but at least they themselves had survived. Someone had been doing sums recently and had estimated that at least ten per cent of the white population had been butchered.

Now, once again, the tribes were said to be on the move in a concerted onslaught to wipe out the remaining white settlers entirely. "Who are determined to sit tight and see this thing out," added Lyddie, with a glance at Lyall, "which we should have done, too, had Lyall not been so concerned for my safety. The whole place is in turmoil – the women are terrified of venturing out and being cut up into little pieces, yet terrified of staying put and being burnt to death in their beds."

"It's what the tribes call a chimurenga," Lyall explained to me, "a war of liberation. Liberation from the white usurpers, as they see us. So it goes without saying that every available man will be needed to fight them."

No one said anything. The breathless, thrumming night was filled with the endless chirruping accompaniment of the cicadas. Lyddie said at last, her colour high, "But this new commander from Britain will be here any day. He's going to waste no time when he arrives in sending up his reinforcements to deal with the situation."

"I have no doubt, my dear, but meanwhile, the horror goes on, as you know. The only thing to do is to take this thing by the scruff of the neck immediately and deal with it."

"That need not mean you."

"Every man has his duty in a case like this."

"And are there not duties at home?" she murmured, looking down at the table.

Lyall stretched out his hand and held hers, forcing her to look at him. "I must. And I can go with a lighter heart now that you won't be alone. Hannah will stay here and take care of you for as long as you need her, will you not, Hannah?"

I watched as the lamp flickered, and huge winged insects immolated themselves in the flame. I thought of the trooper I had met on the station and what might be in store for him. I thought of Captain Osborne, exhilarated at the prospect of a good scrap. And what of myself? Lyddie was dearer to me than a sister; I was bound to her with ties stronger than blood or family. But had I not walked from one trap into another?

Lyddie didn't rise with her old, accustomed alacrity the next morning, and I was left alone after Lyall had gone to his company stores near the railway. I waited for some time and then made a cup of tea. Mrs Crowther's heart would have rejoiced to see that her rose-patterned service was still intact, having survived all the vicissitudes its owner had been through – apparently one of those precious possessions Lyddie had fortunately been able to send on ahead.

I thought she was asleep when I took the tray into her bedroom, but as I tiptoed back to the door, she stirred and spoke. "Goodness, you're up early, Hannah." She sat up as I handed her a cup of tea. The soft, dense mass of hair, no longer quite so bright, fell over her shoulders like a cloak. "You'll have to learn to sleep as late as you can – that way the day doesn't seem so long."

I poured tea for myself. "What does one do, all day?" I asked, after a while.

"Do?" She grimaced and then laughed shortly. "Oh, there's ever so many things to *do* in Mafeking. We have bazaars and Sales of Work. There are tea parties and tennis parties, when it isn't too hot – though when isn't it? The men have their cricket matches, and the racing up at the racecourse, and there's the

Masonic lodge. And when the officers aren't away up there over the border, fighting, there are polo matches. Last week, the operatic society put on *The Mikado* – oh, there's no end to the fun." She laughed, a brittle sound; the teacup rattled on the saucer and for a moment I thought she was going to burst into tears again. But instead she blinked and after a while said, in a queer, blank sort of voice, "I've made a mistake, Hannah. I'm simply not equipped with the constitution to endure this sort of life."

Maybe this wasn't the bold adventure she'd set out upon, what she had come out to Africa for – not being able to share Lyall's adventurous pursuits as she had done at first, and forced into what I could see for her was the much more difficult and dull path of enforced domesticity in an unsympathetic environment. Last night, even when she was recalling that desperate escape, the awful consequences, she'd been animated and her eyes had shone with remembered excitement. But, as Lyall had stressed, their mode of life at the moment was only temporary – and as for Lyddie not having the constitution to endure any kind of hardship…I simply did not believe that.

I sat on the bed and held her hand. "Life in Mafeking doesn't sound so very different from Bridge End to me. Come on, buck up! Whatever happened to that daughter of Empire?"

Perhaps reminding her of how we'd giggled at her father's injunction was not the most tactful thing to have done, but it brought the ghost of a smile. "I'm sorry, I should be ashamed of myself. Don't scold me, Hannah, though you've every right. But I shall be better directly, now that you're here, you'll see. Poor Lyall, he's been so patient with me…" She gazed into the dregs of her tea. "And he did so want a son. Well, better luck next time."

Next time? How could she contemplate going through all this, for a third time?

After that I never saw her cry again, though there was a strained look around her mouth sometimes, shadows in her eyes – but not when she thought anyone was looking at her. Tread softly, I told myself. Give it time.

Meanwhile, bringing the small house back into some semblance of order was better than doing nothing. There were servants – a native houseboy, and one for the garden, who worked when they were pushed, and escaped back to the location whenever possible. They were Barolongs, known respectively as Lemuel and Amos, since their native names were as unpronounceable as their melon-shaped smiles were infectious, even when they were being scolded. We set them to sweeping and polishing the floors, washing the windows, which they did in a lackadaisical fashion, obviously not seeing the point of it. Lyddie and I cleaned the photo-frames. I washed the lace curtains, we shared the cooking. After that, we had nothing to do but sit and talk, put another well-worn cylinder on the gramophone, or pay calls on other ladies, similarly placed. Lyddie despised needlework, and all her books had long since been read. She missed her piano, which had necessarily been left behind when they fled Bulawayo, along with most of her trousseau. What remained of those pretty dresses hung behind a curtain in her bedroom, their bright folds dimmed with the eternal dust that filtered everywhere, even into the food.

Dust and flies. Oh, how I hated those disgusting armies of flies, which had to be constantly swatted away from one's face! Even worse when they landed, torpid, on my damp skin, and had to be picked off.

"We'll have to see about you having riding lessons – you can't live here without riding. Everyone does," said Lyddie. "Then we can ride together as soon as Dr Smyth allows me to." She was dying to get once more on the beautiful mare which Lyall had given her on their arrival here, as an incentive to get better; a shrewd move, for riding had become her passion. I thought it was the enforced inactivity, in a nature as active as Lyddie's, that was contributing to her malaise more than anything.

"You're not making any plans to go home again just yet, are you, Hannah?" she asked me anxiously several times over the next few weeks, reminding me that I'd originally promised I would stay, not only for her confinement but at least for three or four months after the new baby was born – so there was no need for me to think of leaving just yet, was there?

I didn't hesitate. I told her I was in no hurry. "But if I'm to be here so long, I'd better find something to do. Other than painting pretty flowers on ostrich eggs." Which seemed to be a favourite occupation.

"Let's ask Sarah."

The Whiteleys were the people from Dewsbury whom Mrs Crowther had been delighted to hear were living in Mafeking. Frank, a man in a similar way of business to Lyall, had been elected the town's mayor, and Sarah's Tuesday At Homes I'd discovered to be one of the highlights of Mafeking society. She had proved herself a good friend to Lyddie, a cultured and charming woman with a great deal of energy and organising ability, and she immediately suggested a little teaching as an occupation for me. "There's a sad lack of anyone to do that – for the girls at any rate. In fact, there's no one at the moment."

The idea appealed to me. "I'm not trained for it, but maybe some of the younger ones – and what about the native children?"

She didn't exactly look horrified, but I belatedly realised this was not a permissible question. The population who had settled here were a diverse mixture of different races and occupations but, though they seemed to manage to exist together without much prejudice or class consciousness, there was little or no integration with the black people who lived in the stadt, apart from making use of them as servants, as everyone did. The white population kept themselves strictly to themselves: the Christians, Jews and Catholics; tradespeople who kept the town going; the army and the police and those who worked in the Bechuanaland administration; the railway engineers and the men who worked for the Telegraph Company, as well as neighbouring farmers and cattle ranchers who came in regularly to stock up with victuals. And the transients, footloose men on their way to and from Salisbury or Bulawayo in search of some new El Dorado. Also the people from Kimberley and Johannesburg who were not deterred by the stories of war in the north, and still wanted to be taken on hunting expeditions by men like Lyall.

Some of them were Dutch, new residents who, like Lyddie and Lyall, were refugees from their farms in Rhodesia. They rubbed along with the rest of the population, but where did their loyalties lie in those still continuing and dangerously escalating quarrels between Kruger and the British Government? Did they

support old Kruger's intransigent refusal to make any concessions in the matter of the Uitlanders? These were questions
which had temporarily assumed somewhat less importance in
view of the present emergency in Rhodesia, but ones that certainly weren't going to go away.

Messages came regularly from Lyall, up there over the border,
from whence, almost daily it seemed, came news of yet another
atrocity, or another miraculous escape. Lyddie held her head
high, determined not to let her worry show. She smiled and
agreed when everyone said they'd soon have the rebellious niggers by the tail, and order would be restored.

In a military centre such as Mafeking, horses, and everything
to do with them, were of paramount importance, and I knew I
should have to learn to ride. The task of teaching me fell to
Captain Osborne, who was still in Mafeking, kicking his heels, as
he put it, impatiently waiting for the arrival from England of
General Carrington's new chief of staff, who was to lead a serious campaign into Matabeleland and put an end to the rebellions
once and for all: such a task, as most people were beginning to
admit, was beyond the capabilities of the amateur fighters, willing and able as they were.

For my riding lessons, I was allotted a little mare I was assured
was as mild as milk, though with something as large and heavy as
a horse, that seemed to me to be a contradiction in terms.
However, I made some sort of progress, and became fond of my
staid old Marigold.

But much more than the actual riding, I came to love those
cool mornings and the pearly skies, before the punishing sun had
risen, when Captain Osborne and I rode out over the wide, open
terrain, where above the flowing grasses rose twisted old thorn-
thickets and the boulder-strewn slopes of the occasional kopje,
or little hill, which here and there interrupted the flatness of the
plain. We would ride up to its rounded top, from where we could
often see in the distance antelopes or herds of zebra, and sometimes giraffe, and the silver thread of the Malopo winding below,
the only promise of fertility in an arid and thirsty land. And I
increasingly enjoyed the company of Hugh Osborne. He was
very patient with my slowness, when I was sure he'd much

sooner be off at a stiff gallop over the stony plain.

I had to admit I was growing accustomed to the strangeness of living in this town on the veld and no longer found it quite so dismaying, though I sympathised with Lyddie and could not believe anyone would live permanently in Mafeking by choice, among the choking red dust and the eternal flies, and as I'd told Hugh, I certainly did not want to be here during the blazing summer, when the temperatures would soar. He gave me a rather curious look, which I couldn't, at that time, interpret.

"He's in love with you," Lyddie said.

"Well, I like him, too," I answered, trying not to blush.

"Like?" She looked hard at me. "You should marry him. He'd make an excellent husband, you know."

"Because of all those diamonds, you mean?"

"No, Hannah," she answered quietly. "Because he's true as steel."

That silenced me, for I knew she was right, though my feelings on the subject were very mixed. "The question doesn't arise," I said at last. "He hasn't asked me."

"He will." She gave an infuriatingly knowing smile.

At last came the day when General Carrington's new Chief Staff Officer arrived from England. A hearty fellow, experienced in campaigning both here and in India, Colonel Baden-Powell, or B-P as everyone seemed to call him, was a man whose optimism and enthusiasm were unquenchable, and who had no doubts whatever of his ability to succeed in putting down once and for all those savages across the border. And Hugh, in great spirits, remarking that their new commander was like a pint of champagne, rode off up country with him to mount his campaign, equally sure that it would be successful.

In the end, B-P's optimism was justified; by October, a peace treaty had been agreed, but when Hugh returned, as he did from time to time, he came back changed. This had turned out to be more than the usual border skirmishes or expeditions into the interior against the rebellious or cattle-thieving natives that he was used to: this had been blood and death on a grander scale. He had seen settlers, their wives and children, butchered atrociously, and watched his own men and brother officers die, not always killed by a clean bullet, but dying an agonising death, of gangrene or blood-poisoning, dysentery – or even torture. He'd seen families cut up into pieces. It would, however, take more than that to deter Hugh from doing his duty in the service of his country. Within days, he would be off again with the flying column B-P had commanded to clear the country of the remaining scattered bands of rebels. I saw him rarely but I remembered him every night in my prayers.

My estimated stay in Africa stretched to months, then nearly two years, during which Lyddie had another miscarriage and there arose the very real prospect of a bigger and very different conflict altogether: war with the Boers. Each passing month made the possibility less remote, and we knew that Mafeking, due to its strategic position on the border railway, would be in the front line. Kruger was making no secret that he was preparing for war, ready to call up his stand-by commando units and stockpiling arms and ammunition to an enormous extent, while from England had come Sir Alfred Milner, on a peace mission which no one realistically visualised as having any prospects of success after eighteen months of negotiations, since he had revealed himself as ardent an imperialist as Rhodes and as obdurate as Kruger in his obstinate refusal to compromise.

One evening, after a particularly gruellingly hot day, I was sitting in Lyddie's garden under the jacaranda, in the tender dusk that was so precious because it was so short, that hour between the heat of the day and the cold which would come when the fiery, brandy-coloured sunset was abruptly extinguished by the dark of the night. Within half an hour it would be too dark to read the letters we had received that day from Ned. He was eighteen now and had just left school.

'*Dear Hannah,*' mine began, '*I expect you are sweltering out there in the heat. I envy you. It rained cats and dogs for two days here, then turned to drizzle, which we've had to endure for a week. It's very dull here without Lyddie to tease me, and no one to have a good old chinwag with, as you and I used to, dear old girl. Bad luck about Lyddie. Ma says losing three babies is more than enough for any woman. She puts it down to the climate, and wishes Lyddie and*

Lyall would come home – which would mean you, too. Hooray!

'*Let me think of what news there is from here to regale you with. Well, since I declared my intention of not going up to Oxford, I've been given a month by Father and George to make the choice between putting my nose to the grindstone down at the mill or finding some other useful occupation. (Father's words, not mine.) Since no useful occupation has yet occurred to me, I'm making the most of my freedom and have just spent some time in London staying with a chap from school. He's quite decent – very well off – his people have a spiffing house and he has a very pretty sister, so a top-hole time was had by all. We saw some very decent cricket at Lords and some good rowing by the varsity crews at Henley regatta (perhaps I should have decided on Oxford, after all, if they would have had me). I won some money at Ascot – and lost some at Newmarket, and we went to see the new musical comedy,* The Belle of New York, *all the rage, full of pretty ladies and capital tunes that you can't get out of your head. But now Spenderford has gone up to Scotland to shoot grouse with some rich connections of his father, and I've had to come home back to Bridge End and decide what to do with the rest of my life, the prospect of which seems drearier than ever. Don't lecture me – I mean to put my mind to whatever I decide to do, though I'm not sure London was a good idea. It was very unsettling, though I dare say all that talk of junketing and high life must seem very trivial to you.*'

Not exactly the kind of life I'd once been determined to discover, perhaps, but one wider than the narrow, circumscribed life here. Suddenly, the trapped feeling – never very far away nowadays – was back. I swallowed and read on. '*The papers are full of the talk of war with the Boers. Most people think it's all bosh that we should go to war just because those Uitlanders want the vote. If it does come though, and we decide to give old Kruger a taste of his own medicine, I shall enlist (even Father must class the army as a useful occupation!) and then maybe I shall see you – and Lyddie, of course, though one would hope and pray the fighting wouldn't reach as far as Mafeking.*'

The letter brought Ned's laughing face vividly to mind. Dear Ned. I hated the notion of him fighting, maybe getting killed, but behind all his flippancy, I sensed he had grown up; such choices would be his to make. I looked up from the page at the parched red strip of earth that served as a garden, watched a column of ants march across it, opened the top buttons of my blouse and thought longingly of the damp days over the Pennines. I would even have welcomed at that moment those sharp cold winds which used to rack my lungs. During this heat, Lyddie and I had dispensed with petticoats altogether and only wore whatever underpinnings were absolutely necessary. The heat pressed down like a lid. The air was so still that when the sun went down you could hear the natives in the distant stadt singing above the crepitations of the night insects. As the darkness closed in, the birds had grown silent – strange but now familiar birds, some with long feathery tails and others black and white like magpies, only not; the stars were thick and brilliant as they never were at home.

Lyddie came hurrying out of the house. "It's Captain Osborne – Major, I should say now – and he wants to see you."

"Well, ask him to come out here, then. It's too hot indoors."

"He wants to talk to you privately."

"Oh." We looked at one another. During this last spell of leave Hugh had, as Lyddie put it, been living in my pocket, and though I wouldn't have phrased it in quite the same way, we had certainly seen a good deal of each other.

"Go on," she said.

My hand flew to fasten the buttons at my neck. "My hair! It needs combing. I look a fright."

"You look neat as a pin, as usual, and hurry up. He's in the parlour, champing at the bit because apparently he's had orders to be off again."

I couldn't go to my room from here without passing through the parlour, so I did my best to make myself presentable where I was, smoothing the damp tendrils of hair back from my face and tucking my blouse back into my waistband. It was the best I could do – at least the blue voile, despite its lack of starch due to the heat, was one of the most becoming things I had.

My heart hammering, I went into the parlour. Feeling suddenly very shy, I shut the door quietly and waited. He was looking out of the window, overlooking the dusty, now dark, road, his

hands clasped behind his back, and swung round as I came in.
Silhouetted against the darkened panes, he looked very large, his
broad-shouldered figure seeming to take up most of the space in
the tiny, shadowy room. For a moment or two, there was silence,
then he began to tell me that he would soon be taking his men
back up-country and might be away for several weeks, if not
months. Suddenly he stopped, we looked at each other in silence,
then at the same moment, we stepped towards each other.

Although I couldn't, with hand on heart, say it was entirely
unexpected, I hadn't realised until this moment just how very
fond I was of him. It was true that he had a rather guarded sense
of humour – though this was a minor point that I found quite
endearing – and I'd learned that he didn't care for me to voice my
opinions too strongly, but I admired him more than anyone I
knew. I liked his kindness and courtesy, his even temper and his
integrity. His manners, like his uniform, were impeccable.

So why was I hesitating, now that he'd asked me to marry
him?

"Don't tell me – there's someone else – in England." I could
feel him holding his breath.

"No one."

Sometimes, when the heat danced over at the boulder-strewn
kopje at the west end of the town it reminded me of the stony
road up to The Pack Horse, when Willie Dyson and I had taken
that last walk, in that lovely spring evening. I heard his voice
again, singing softly, 'When the fields are white with daisies…I'll
return.' I think I had known, even then, that I never would.

"I'm very relieved to hear that. As for me – well, there'll never
be anyone else for me, Hannah. I'm a dull sort of chap, the sort
who offers his heart only once," Hugh said, with that half-mock-
ing, self-deprecating smile of his that I found so attractive. "But
I dare say I can understand your reluctance to say yes immediately. Big decision, I appreciate, to make your home in a strange
country, and I know what you feel about Mafeking. Africa isn't
all like this, though – you haven't seen much of it yet. But if it's
social life you want," – he hesitated – "we could live in Jo'burg
or Cape Town – or even make our home in England if you
wished."

"What about your career?"

"What of it?" he asked quickly, after a slight pause. "These troubles won't go on for ever. And anyway, there are other ways of making a life."

His offer to marry me would bring me more than I had ever dreamed of. His share of his father's business had left him with enough money to do exactly as he wished. He could give me wealth, social position and a life of leisure, the opportunity to see the world. Love? Yes, I could be sure of that, too, no one would be more steadfast than Hugh. But it was another matter to ask him to renounce his true vocation. It was second nature to him: he had taken to the rigour and discipline of life in the border police like a duck to water. I knew that he also enjoyed the status of having his foot firmly planted on the ladder of authority, which he was confident of ascending, rung by rung. He had a natural air of command, and all the honourable attitudes of a true guardian of the peace.

How could I take that away from him?

Chapter Sixteen

We were married immediately, and very quietly, before he went away again. I wore the peacock silk dress I'd made over from Mrs Crowther's old one and, apart from Lyddie and Lyall, the only other guests were the Whiteleys and Major Thomas Douglas, Hugh's best friend in the regiment, and his mousy little wife. We moved into a small house of our own on the edge of the town, where I had a dovecote built, and in the garden I planted jasmine and yellow acacia for their dizzying perfume, and a jacaranda for its purple flowers and its shade. We settled into a life which was circumscribed by the times Hugh was away on duty and the few times he was at home. As a young bride, it was only natural that I should miss him when he was away, that there should be long periods of *ennui* in between, which I tried to combat by immersing myself in the social activity connected with the military, in friendship with other wives. I did a little teaching, and read a great deal – I could now afford to order and buy all the books I might ever want. I still had Lyddie.

And when Hugh came home, we were happy, although it surprised me how much time he still liked to spend with his fellow officers in the officers' mess at the Police Barracks, talking over their exploits until late at night. When he stayed at home he often repeated them to me. For the most part, I listened with interest, for I longed to be part of every aspect of his life, but occasionally, when I'd heard the story for the second, or perhaps the third time, I confess I had to stifle a yawn.

One morning about a year later, I bumped towards the Catholic school on my bicycle, which I did nearly every day now. Six nuns of the Order of the Sisters of Mercy, volunteers from their mother convent at Strabane in Northern Ireland, had come to Mafeking to establish a convent here. Being so few in number, they were glad of any help in their work of teaching and nursing. I wasn't a Roman Catholic, but then, neither were most of the pupils they had gathered for their little school. Nor was I qualified to teach. Still, I could show the girls how to sew, and help the younger ones with their sums and reading, and this was what

I did.

There was a dewy clarity to the air, a soft mist lay just above the ground after the rain which had drummed on the iron roof most of the night, and the ground smelled of slaked earth and new growth. Rain, bringing in its wake sweet new grass, was always welcome in this arid region, but although my umbrella was strapped across my handlebars, I hoped there wouldn't be another deluge while I was on my way to the school.

The parish priest was already at work on clearing the ground for the new convent, raising his pick-axe and bringing it down with a mighty thwack, striking sparks from the stony earth. His shirt stuck to his back as he levered up a rock, wary of uncovering nests of coiled snakes in the process as very often happened, none of which he would kill, however. A muscular man of tremendous enthusiasm, Father Ogle had rolled up his sleeves, proving he could heave up boulders and wield a spade or a crowbar with the best of them, setting a magnificent example to others, and early as it was this morning, around him milled a whole crowd of people anxious to help: other men were also digging, children were picking up stones and filling baskets with excavated earth, and Mr Harris from the general stores was supplying free lemonade.

Naturally, the nuns wanted their convent to be finished as soon as possible, but I feared they might be showing more optimism than was justified. The town had made a free gift of the site for the convent, which indeed they could well afford to do, for it was an unpromising piece of scrubland to put it at its best, which before anything else needed to have stubborn old thorn trees chopped down and their stumps grubbed out. The mudbrick walls would be rising as soon as the rock-hard ground could be levelled and boulders removed – not for nothing did the native name for the town, *Mafikeng*, mean 'the place of stones'. But the convent was altogether a far more ambitious project than any yet undertaken in Mafeking, destined to be the best yet, the only two-storeyed building in the town, in fact, and because of this, the builders were proceeding with extreme caution, not to mention slowness, however much Father Ogle bullied and cajoled. But this had dismayed the nuns not one whit.

"Will you look at how well it's coming on? It seems God has answered our prayers and our home will be finished sooner than we had dared to hope," said my friend, Sister Mary Columba, with her ever cheerful smile, joining me as I walked along to the school. She was a young, fresh faced and very pretty novice, totally unlike my admittedly vague notion of what a nun should be and, I think, a little unlike her own. She had a quick and puckish sense of humour; her face, rosily glowing with heat under the restricting coif, always bore a smile. Her voice was as soft as the rain falling from the skies of her native Donegal, though it was not so much what she said, as her silences, which fell upon her with disconcerting suddenness, whenever she remembered Mother Superior's caution that talking too much was an indulgence. But laughter and humour were never far away from her twinkling eyes.

She was happy at the prospect of the convent walls going up soon, with the gentle confidence that all would be well if their trust was put in God, and who could question her faith?

Indeed, I hoped for all their sakes that their faith would be rewarded.

In the event, it was opened early in the following year. Considering the difficulties, in record time.

The time I spent at the convent was something of a lifesaver for me, and not only because it filled in time that would otherwise have hung heavy on my hands. I had come to love those quiet, religious women who followed their own form of practical Christianity by teaching, nursing the sick and providing help wherever they could see it was needed to the people of Mafeking. I could not embrace their Catholic faith, but I believe I'd learned from them a composure I didn't have before, and to swallow my growing disappointment that life as the wife of a serving officer wasn't all it was cracked up to be. I'd learned the ability to hold my tongue, too, when I couldn't agree with the ingrained, stiff-necked and rigid code of discipline demanded of men like Hugh. I assisted in teaching the girls in the school and generally helped out as much as I could, often acting as a liaison between the nuns and the traders in the town. It was tiring work, especially in the hot season, but if the nuns could rise at three in the morning for prayer, work for a full day and then spend their evenings in contemplation and more prayer, I felt humbled enough to carry on.

One morning Hugh, back home after a long spell of duty, woke as I was getting ready to meet Sister Mary Columba at the convent. She had begun a routine of going down to the mission church in the native stadt, taking food and teaching the black children to read and write – and, incidentally, to be instructed in the Catholic faith. Braving the disapproval of many of the other ladies in the town, I had fallen into the habit of going with her, and while she ran the thread of her religion through everything she taught, I tried to instil some small idea that there was, out there, a wider world beyond Mafeking. The thirst for knowledge of some of these children amazed and delighted me. It was something with which I could sympathise.

I was taken aback by Hugh's disapproval when he learned where I was going. He was not against me having a useful occupation, something to fill in the time while he was away, and found nothing wrong with my teaching the girls at the convent, but when I told him what our plans were for that morning, he met my explanation with a look of frank disapproval, frowning and leaning back against the pillows, his arms folded behind his head. "I hope you're not getting any notions of treating the Kaffirs as equals, Hannah – that's just asking for trouble. You have to keep 'em under control, you know, or they'll soon have the upper hand. I thought you'd have learned that by now. Black's black and white's white, and they're not the same as us, however you look at it."

There were differences, I had to admit. Everyone knew that though they were childlike, amiable and willing to please, the blacks were also lazy, they told lies and they were cruel to their animals; they stole, and would promise anything to get themselves out of trouble. They were incapable of keeping time. But how could they ever learn to be otherwise if they were not educated? I asked.

This was not the time to argue the point, and neither of us said any more, but the exchange curiously disturbed me. I knew Hugh always treated the natives with the same courtesy as he treated everyone else – so how could he feel this way? I worried that he might be growing more imbued with the attitudes I encountered all too often in other officers. 'Give them an inch and they'll take a mile' was an expression one heard all too often. But to keep the black people of this land ignorant was surely as horrible a barbarity as using them as slaves and worse, as the Boers did.

We had been married for two years, during which I had learned several things. One was that marriage was not the grand passion, or even the meeting of soulmates which the silly, romantic girl I had been had once hoped for. Another was that my husband was a man who kept his life in separate compartments. Nor was he a demonstrative man. I knew in my heart that he would go to the ends of the earth for me if necessary and that should surely have been enough, but I longed for more, for some demonstration that I, and not that life he led when he was away from me, took first place. This was hard not to believe, when I saw how alive and interested he became when he was with his brother officers and their talk was all of the sporadic rebellions across the border, and what they were prepared to do in the face of the war with the Boers which was sure to come. But this was where my life had led me, and I reminded myself that regardless of everything else, we did love each other, if not passionately, at least truly.

"What's wrong with you lately, Hannah?" he asked now.

"I'm sorry, Hugh, perhaps I'm a little out of sorts. Maybe it's the weather."

I pretended not to see his disappointed look. There was plenty of time yet. I would not let the desire for a child dominate my life, as it did Lyddie's.

He was always kind and gentle. He rose and kissed me before I left, to show he had forgiven me.

As the storm clouds gathered and troops were moving into position on both sides, it became impossible to ignore the fact that war was on our doorstep. Food and other necessities of life were being stockpiled, and more and more of those who could leave Mafeking were taking the opportunity to do so, while refugees from other parts flocked in.

Lyall was worried about what would happen to his business in the event of hostilities, taking all the necessary preventive measures he could to conserve and protect his stock. To this end, he decided he needed to make a trip to inspect one of the ostrich farms, worked by two brothers out of England, who supplied him with feathers – for which England had a seemingly insatiable demand, not only for boas and hats and aigrettes for debutantes to wear in their hair, but also for feather dusters and as decorations to stick in vases. He reckoned he could make the trip in three days. Lyddie's eyes lit up. "Oh, do let me go with you – I'm sure I shall go quite mad if I don't get away from all this endless talk of war."

In the end he gave in, perhaps knowing how much she was in need of something to divert her thoughts from what was becoming an obsession with her and a great worry to him: her inability to have a child. I could understand how she, with all the abundant and robust good health that was part of her attraction, chafed against her inability to fulfil the quite normal function of carrying a baby to full term. On the other hand, she had been told that having another child might cost her her life. It was ironic that she had by now conceived three times, each of which had ended in failure, whereas I...I could not conceive at all.

Several more people joined us in the expedition, there being a general feeling there might not be another such chance for a very long time. With us was Roger Marriott, a young subaltern, and Caroline Douglas, the meek and silent wife of Hugh's friend, Major Thomas Douglas – only she was neither meek nor silent on this trip, I thought as I observed her laughing and teasing Roger. But the desert air had an exhilarating effect on all of us, as if it were charged with electricity, and we were all in gay spirits.

"Caroline Douglas? Must we, Lyall?" Lyddie had said, making a moue. "She's such a little goose." But we couldn't find any excuse to prevent her accompanying us, and Lyddie, with her usual good nature, made her feel welcome. But she was right, I thought: Caroline was a silly, vapid young woman, whose company was always a trial, and I was quite content to leave her to Lieutenant Marriott. Thomas was to have come with us too, but, like Hugh, he could not be spared from his duties at this time. Roger, I supposed, was not of enough importance for him to be forbidden two or three days' leave but, watching him with Caroline, I thought Lyddie hadn't shown much sense in inviting him along when she was to be there.

Like any small town, Mafeking was a place rife with gossip and rumour, petty quarrels and intrigues, and I was sure there was nothing much in the little scandal that was blowing up around Caroline and the young lieutenant, but having him accompany us on this trip was going to do nothing to lessen the gossip. Roger cut a handsome and dashing figure, and all the ladies were romantically in love with him. It was a surprise when he'd picked out Caroline for his special attentions, though it shouldn't have been; he liked a conquest. There was nothing more to it than a mild flirtation, I was sure, but Hugh took a different stance.

"She's making a fool of Tom – and the scandal could cost him his career if he doesn't watch out. She's going to ruin him, as well as Marriott, if she's not careful."

I knew that, unfair as it was, such scandals reflected as badly on the wretched husband as on the erring wife. He would be deemed incapable of controlling her, and it would be said that if he could let this happen in his private life, it was unlikely he would be able to control and keep the respect of the men under him.

"It's only a silly flirtation. They don't mean anything by it, either of them. He's just turned her head a bit, that's all. And you have to admit, Thomas isn't much fun." He was, in fact, the most solemn and silent man I'd ever met, very well thought of in the regiment, and his bravery was apparently legendary. It was often said that his men would follow him anywhere. But he never showed the faintest glimmer of humour. I didn't believe I'd seen him laugh, really laugh, once.

"She knew that when she married him," said Hugh, unforgiving. "That sort of thing simply isn't done. She should behave herself."

"And what about Roger Marriott?"

"Oh, he's incorrigible! But married ladies should know better than to allow him to take liberties."

"I suppose it's all Caroline's fault."

"Of course not. But she's older than him, and she shouldn't

encourage the young fool. It won't do his promotion prospects any good, mark my words. Tom might not say much but Marriott's already a marked man."

"That's one way of revenge, I suppose. What would you do in similar circumstances?"

"They'd never arise. You would never do such a thing."

He was a good man, my husband, I reminded myself, to be so utterly sure of me. But I suddenly wanted to shake him, to demand how he *knew*. Instead, I bit my lip and tried to make a joke of it. "Of course not. But then, I've never much liked Roger Marriott."

It took him a moment or two, but in the end his face broke into the diffident smile I had first fallen in love with.

On this trip, we ladies mostly travelled in the ox-wagon, with horses for riding when we felt we had had enough of the rough jolting, though neither mode of transport was comfortable. As for Lyddie...at the moment she was looking radiant, full of well being, and rode ahead with Lyall, astride her horse like a man. He often rode close to her, with his hand on her bridle. Seeing her like that, with the sun on her face and the dry, dusty wind blowing through her hair, one would have thought she hadn't a care in the world. She was magnificently attractive. I wondered, with a lurch of the heart, if she could possibly be starting yet another baby.

The road was little more than a track in the thick red sand and the carts lurched all over the place; the poor oxen were plagued all the way by tsetse flies. It was extremely hot in those shadeless wastes; the cold at night, when the sun went down and we set up tents, was extreme, but it was a great relief. On the way, gazelles, antelopes and zebra from the herds of game roaming the plains were shot as meat for the porters; for our own evening dinner, tables were set up near the camp fire, where we ate the meal that had been prepared for us – hares, and desert partridges, which tasted not so different from chicken or turkey, though not as tender.

There were moments of great drama, such as when we saw an awe-inspiring troop of elephants, silhouetted against the dying, fiery orange sky, processing majestically down to a watering hole at sunset. And more than once, we came across a pride of lions, like big cats snoozing in the sun, but this wasn't a hunting party, and they were left alone. One time we surprised a leopard, a solitary beast of such grace and beauty he took one's breath away. This time, one of our party took aim to shoot it, but its speed was such that he missed, at which I inwardly rejoiced. To kill it – or any animal – simply for its skin, or its tusks, seemed to me reprehensible; to kill it for sport was unforgivable. I said nothing, however. In view of Lyall's occupation, I'd long become accustomed to keeping such views to myself.

Ostriches, on the other hand, I found myself not able to love, given their appearance, which was unfair, but true – good looks give an unfair advantage to anyone, much less ostriches. "I see what you meant about Councillor Greenwood," I remarked to Lyddie on our arrival at Orchard Farm.

"Poor things. They can't help it, any more than he can."

They were such manifestly foolish birds, forever in a fluster about something, picking up and swallowing anything that lay around – to help with their digestion, we were told. Like our canary at home needed grit, I supposed – only the bigger the bird, the bigger the stones. "This old beggar," said Barty Fox, the younger of the brothers who ran the farm, pointing to one with a disagreeable expression and a mad, rolling eye, "he'll eat anything – chunks of metal, glass, anything. He'll chew through the fence to get out. The times we've had to chase him! Nothing'll keep him in. If he doesn't watch it, he'll be for the pot."

I laughed but hoped this didn't mean we were to have ostrich steaks for lunch, tender as I was assured they were.

Barty and his older brother had come out from Britain to run the farm, two young men of immense enthusiasm and determination. Robert, the elder, was married with two young children, but Barty was still a bachelor. Staying with them was their father, on a visit from England. Augustus Fox was a doctor who had recently lost his wife and he had brought with him on this visit his daughter, Louisa, a lively child of about thirteen, with glossy chestnut curly hair and sharp, observant eyes.

Dr Fox was an agreeable, imperturbable man who spent most of his days collecting insects and butterflies, drawing them and writing copious notes. He seemed quite unmoved by the talk of preparations for war, and refused to be panicked into cutting short his visit by making a hasty, and perhaps unnecessary, departure. His two sons were obviously worried that he could not, or would not, see the difficulties and danger of staying put, but Dr Fox only shrugged. "In the unlikely event that things do come to a fight, we shall be safe enough where we are. What is there out here to fight over?"

Barty laughed but Robert, who was of a more serious disposition, didn't appear to share the amusement. He was already talking of packing his wife and children off to Cape Town to stay with her sister, where they would be safer should the worst happen.

"A wise precaution," agreed Lyall, with a meaningful glance at his own wife. Lyddie simply smiled. It was an argument with which both she and I were becoming increasingly familiar. More and more men were sending their families away to safety; Sarah Whitely had already left with her two children and was even now on her way back to England, but Lyddie flatly refused to listen to any such suggestion, as did I. If there was to be trouble, my place was at Hugh's side, or as near to it as I could remain. Moreover, if war came, there would be useful work we could do, helping to nurse the sick and wounded.

"We can't shut our eyes to the inevitable. Give it another couple of months or so and we shall be at war, mark my words," said Robert, a sentiment which most of us by now were very used to hearing. "The only reason the burghers are waiting at all is for the rains; they can't go to war without grass for their horses."

"Possibly, but if I've understood the situation aright, that's precisely why hostilities can't last long," Dr Fox went on. "Won't they need to get back to their farms before the dry season comes?"

"That's true. They can't leave their farms for long – but I wouldn't be too sure about it being over soon," Lyall said, "Don't ever underestimate the stubbornness of a Boer."

The arguments didn't impress Dr Fox. He'd come prepared for a lengthy stay and wasn't going to be frightened off by any Dutch burgher. Things would turn out for the best, just wait and see. I admired the spirit with which it was said, but it seemed a somewhat Micawberish attitude to take, especially in view of the child who was with him. He was like one of the ostriches, burying its head in the sand when being chased, believing it couldn't be seen because it could not see.

The feverish air of expectation in Mafeking grew. Most people made a pretence of carrying on as though nothing unusual was happening, rather like dancing before Waterloo, though in reality, everyone was taking precautions for what must now come. Hugh was readying himself and his men, while Lyall spent much of his time serving on a committee to bring together as much as possible of the necessities of life to the town, in case supplies should be cut off for any length of time.

The probability of war approached certainty with the return of Baden-Powell as commander of the North West Frontier Forces, who made his headquarters in Mafeking and immediately set about erecting fortifications to enclose the town and as much commonage around it as was feasible. We, and especially the Baralong, were dependent on this for grazing cattle and growing crops. Within weeks the town proper and the native stadt had been surrounded by a ten-mile zigzag of earthworks and trenches, each connected by telephone, hedged by mines and ramparts made of sandbags and felled trees whose branches pointed outwards. By the end of September, the redoubtable colonel had also raised two regiments, horsed, equipped and trained, culled from crack cavalry regiments as well as from the border police. As one of the more experienced officers in border tactics, Hugh was by his side most of the time, advising on strategy, altogether quite in his element.

1909

The detective sergeant from Scotland Yard who had been sent by Crockett to Dr Lester Harvill in search of any information he might have about Mrs Hannah Smith chose an inopportune moment, just as the doctor was about to start a consulting session with a patient. He was rather curtly sent away, with the promise that Dr Harvill would do what he could about the matter when he had finished with his patients.

The request had, in fact, disturbed the doctor, who did not relish being questioned in any shape or form, being a person who stood on his dignity, and not one inclined to brook interference at the best of times. It was therefore not until the following day that he found himself willing to devote any time to the request – or what might indeed be an official demand. Perhaps he had no choice. Reluctantly, he telephoned Scotland Yard and agreed to a Chief Inspector Crockett coming to see him that evening for half an hour at his private nursing home in North London where he also lived and had his consulting rooms.

Well before Crockett was due to arrive, he armed himself with a cup of coffee and took himself off to his study. He drew the thick, dark green serge curtains against the autumn evening and refreshed the fire with more coal from the brass scuttle, switched on the electric desk lamp and then settled back and drew a bulky file containing a thick wad of notes towards him. By one of those strange coincidences which do exist in spite of all claims to the contrary, he was at that very time engaged in preparing a paper which he was to deliver to the Royal College of Physicians next month on the subject of post-traumatic retrograde amnesia.

He was a small, neatly made man of nondescript appearance, who would have passed unnoticed in any crowd. In his consulting rooms, however, or on the rostrum when delivering a paper, or especially when he lectured to his students, he seemed to gain stature because he always appeared so sure of what he said. If there were dissenters among his listeners who doubted whether he always knew what he was talking about, there were many more who hung on his words. He never raised his voice, yet managed to convey such authority that his pompous delivery carried conviction.

For a while he sat looking at the file, then pushed it aside and extracted from a drawer a now creased and yellowed report from an edition of the *Daily Bugle*, published the previous autumn, details from which he had incorporated in his notes and which he already knew by heart. Nonetheless, he read it carefully yet again, as if it might throw some hitherto unexpected light on the problem:

'Yesterday, 6th October, there occurred on Ludgate Hill an horrific accident, when a brewer's dray collided with a motor omnibus, with disastrous results. The omnibus was turned over on to its side and several passengers were injured, among them a young woman who now lies unconscious in a hospital bed with severe head injuries which might yet prove fatal, and a child who has as yet not been identified. In addition to this, four people have died, three of whom were riding on the open upper deck. The first of these was an unknown woman, who was thrown right out into the street and died immediately; the second a Mr Ernest Robson, a shipping clerk who was returning to his office with bills of lading he had been sent out to collect, and who suffered a severe heart attack and died within the hour. The third person to die was an innocent pedestrian, Mr Septimus French, a retired clergyman who was knocked off his feet by a rolling barrel and died under the thrashing feet of the unfortunate horses. Readers of this newspaper will also be greatly shocked to learn of the loss of a fine young man, later identified as Mr Harry Chetwynd, the son of Sir Henry Chetwynd, of Shropshire, who was thrown against the upper deck omnibus railing and broke his neck. Mr Chetwynd will be remembered by our readers chiefly for the vivid and well-informed despatches he sent to the *Bugle* from the various war fronts in South Africa during the late struggle with the Boers, and for the occasional articles he contributed since. He was, several times during the conflict, commended for acts of valour, quite outside his journalistic duties, and for his daring in getting his despatches through enemy lines. His death will be sadly mourned by all who knew him.

This needless loss of life was confined not only to human beings, for two of the magnificent Clydesdale horses drawing the dray also had to be destroyed. The whole affair was indeed altogether disgraceful, entirely occasioned by the drayman concerned being thoroughly inebriated while driving his heavy and potentially dangerous wagon without due care and attention, thus leading to losing control of his brakes on the downward slope.

When, demands this newspaper, will brewery companies learn to control the consumption of liquor by their employees during their working hours? It is not the first time such an accident has been recorded, though not, by the grace of God, with such an appalling loss of life. Thomas Watmough, the driver, admitted that it is the usual custom of draymen to partake of a free pint of the company's ale, offered at each public house when making their deliveries. Yesterday was warm and sunny, and no doubt the exertion of unloading beer kegs, coupled with the necessity of controlling the huge horses who pulled the heavy dray, made for thirsty work. Watmough, however, stated that he had only drunk his usual pint at each stop (though this was disputed by Miss Bessie Taffler, a barmaid interviewed by this newspaper, who is employed at The Three Blackbirds where he was due to make a delivery, and who stated that his 'usual pint' was more often than not two, or even three).'

Dr Harvill carefully refolded the newspaper, put it back in the drawer, took up his pen and reopened his file. For a little while longer he sat marshalling his thoughts before beginning to write:

Although I was not personally involved at the time, the case of the woman who was later identified as Mrs Smith was drawn to my attention shortly after she had regained consciousness, but not her memory. In the absence of any identification on her person (apart from a silver cross on a chain around her neck, with the words 'For Hannah, on her confirmation', engraved on the back) it was not possible to contact her relatives. Questions had apparently been raised as to whether she had been sitting next to Harry Chetwynd and might therefore have known him; Sir Henry Chetwynd, however, after having agreed to see her in the hospital when he went to identify the body of his son, denied any acquaintance with her. The lady had remained in a profound coma for nearly three weeks before regaining consciousness, and this was where I was called in, the head injuries she had suffered being related to my special field. Familiar as I am with cases of retrograde amnesia, I had never come across one exactly like hers before. She had no memory either of the accident, save for one fleeting recollection at the moment of impact between the omnibus and the brewer's dray, or of the time preceding it (which circumstance in itself is not, of course, an unusual occurrence). A more curious fact was that her memory lapse extended back for several years prior to the accident – and yet, she could remember her early life perfectly, in minute and exact detail. I suggested that the child on the omnibus might be brought to her, whom she would undoubtedly recognise if he were hers, and who would surely recognise his mother. But she refused, insisting that it would only further upset the little boy. She wore a wedding ring, but swore she had no child, and repeatedly said that they must look elsewhere for his mother. Despite this, the child, who was only two or three years old and could not, or would not, speak, was in fact taken to see her while she was sleeping, but when it was suggested to him that she might be his mother, the infant went into a paroxysm of screaming.

All enquiries failed to find anyone who might have connections with either the woman or the boy, who was eventually taken care of by some responsible woman the police found. The case interested me and I was about to arrange for 'Hannah' to be taken into my establishment, when suddenly she was claimed by a woman who said she was Hannah's maid, and from whom we learned that the patient's name was Mrs Hannah Smith. Since Mrs Smith's physical health had improved to an extent, there was no reason why she should not go home. We agreed that I should see her from time to time, and for a short while, this happened, but despite my counselling, her memory of what had happened in those lost years did not return, chiefly, I regret to say, through lack of co-operation on her part. Perhaps I did not gain her confidence enough. I think I may say with all due modesty that I am usually successful in obtaining the trust of my patients, and their willingness to accept my advice, but in this case, from the start, I was aware of a certain antipathy between us which I was not able to overcome.

Mrs Smith, as I now knew her, simply reiterated that she felt dead inside, and at first showed little or no curiosity as to what had brought her to that pass. For an intelligent woman such as she is, this seemed to me exceedingly strange. I felt sure that there was a husband and child somewhere, that there had been some great trauma or pain which had caused her subconscious to bury, but that somewhere locked inside her was the answer. I therefore endeavoured to persuade her to write the story of her life, or at any rate all that early part which she had no trouble in remembering, in an endeavour to stimulate a flow of further memories. I was particularly anxious for her to do this, as it would provide me with an opportunity to observe at first hand whether Dr Sigmund Freud's theories on the free association of ideas actually do hold water. Although she reluctantly agreed to my suggestions, she refused to let me see what she had written (a subconscious denial, of course) but it was not entirely unexpected that she eventually ceased her visits to me.

The doctor carefully blotted what he had written, read it through and capped his fountain pen, then sat with his hands steepled, thinking. Not long afterwards, Detective Inspector Crockett rang the doorbell.

When Crockett was shown in on the dot of eight and met the bland, expressionless features of the doctor, he knew at once that his mission was going to fail. He was invited to sit down, but almost immediately Harvill said, "The police already have all the records of this case. You must be aware that I am in no position to give you any more facts than you undoubtedly already possess."

"We have the details of the accident, of course. It's what happened to Mrs Smith afterwards that interests me."

"Ah...Well, here we come to the question of professional ethics. You must realise I cannot give details of Mrs Smith's medical history."

"I don't want the clinical details, doctor, I only want her address so that I can speak to her." Harvill did not reply. They stared at one another until Crockett asked, with disconcerting suddenness, "What was the name of Mrs Smith's maid – the one who took her home?"

Harvill, who was not often taken aback, blinked. "I'm afraid I have no idea. I did not see her personally and never heard her name mentioned."

Crockett's brows rose. "Her appearance didn't jog Mrs Smith's memory, then? Surely seeing her maid would have brought back the recent past?"

"Unfortunately, no, but that's hardly surprising – unless this woman had been her maid before the point at which Mrs Smith's memory stopped. But I wasn't there when the woman came to my nursing home, and on the few occasions I saw Mrs Smith here at my consulting rooms after she was discharged, she came alone."

Crockett felt the luxurious warmth of the quiet room, electrically lit, the thick carpet under his feet and the deeply cushioned chair in which he sat. He was aware of richly polished furniture, tall vases of out-of-season roses, a table in the corner where the flames from the fire winked on a cut glass jug of water, tumblers and a decanter with glowing amber contents. He didn't think Dr Harvill's fees would be cheap.

The doctor was saying, "All I can tell you is that the maid had been very anxious at the disappearance of her mistress – but for some reason made no enquiries until about three weeks later."

"I wonder why that was, doctor?"

Harvill shrugged.

"Was it perhaps because she was a foreigner, and didn't take the newspapers? If she had, she would surely have read about the accident before and known the woman was likely to be her mistress. It made all the headlines."

"Foreign?"

"We believe her name was Rosa Tartaryan. She was an Armenian."

"Armenian? Was?" Harvill seemed to have lost the ability to do anything but echo Crockett's words.

"Rosa Tartaryan is dead, doctor. She was murdered. I believe your Mrs Hannah Smith was her mistress. We need to speak to her and that's why I've come to see you."

Dr Harvill said nothing. His face was as bland as a rice pudding, and as pale. "I'm sorry to hear that," he said at last, "but I am unable to give you the information you want. Indeed, I cannot. As I said, Mrs Smith has not been to see me for some time.

She may have moved away, for all I know. She is no longer my patient." A black marble mantel clock chimed the second quarter, with a thin, silvery sound. Harvill glanced pointedly at it. Crockett had reached his allotted time. "And now, if that's all…"

"A moment longer, if you please, Dr Harvill. This child on the 'bus. Mrs Smith denied he was hers – in fact I understand she swore she'd never had a child. But she must have been physically examined when she was taken into the hospital after the accident and you, as a medical man, must know whether what she said was true or not."

"Inspector Crockett!" An indignant flush rose to the doctor's hairline. "You must know I cannot possibly answer that. I was not her medical adviser in that sense. I never examined her physically. And even had I done so, under no circumstances would I divulge what I know." He stretched out his arm and with a white, manicured hand, rang a brass bell on his desk.

Crockett had no alternative but to leave.

Since Dr Harvill had not been disposed to give Mrs Smith's address, perhaps the hospital might be persuaded, thought Crockett as he walked back along the discreet avenue where the nursing home was situated, cursing himself for having played the interview badly, and for letting Harvill get the better of him. One thing he could now do, however, was to send again to the Yorkshire Crowthers and ask if they knew anyone by the name of Hannah Smith, which might conceivably be the reason for Rosa Tartaryan having their address. It was another instance of clutching at straws, but if the dead woman had been of a blackmailing turn of mind, it was possible they might have been next on the list.

"Well, well! Sebastian, my dear – it isn't often we have the honour of seeing see you *chez nous*," said Sylvia.

As a welcome, it was scarcely warm, despite the fact that she was smiling and patting his hand. Two minutes, and he was already irritated with his sister and wishing he hadn't come – this after debating the wisdom of such a visit for so long, despite his instructions to himself as he'd made his way to the pretty but rather small house off Sloane Street, where she and Algy lived.

But he had resolved that he would not quarrel with her, no matter how she provoked him. It didn't really matter a jot what she thought, or said.

When he didn't respond to her little barb, she made a moue, then looked expectant, but he was not to be drawn, not just yet. He had brought messages from his grandmother which he must first deliver. He put a box of Sylvia's favourite rose creams on the white lacquered table and took a deep breath, bearing in mind what he and Louisa had agreed, that he must not ruin his chances. "I came as soon as I heard you were back from Biarritz."

Dusk was beginning to fall. He had found her leafing through the social gossip in the *London Mail*. The all-white room, relieved only by curtains patterned in a rather pallid pink and a curious shade of green, was strictly without knick-knacks, or even a family photograph or two. The sole ornamentation was afforded only by a few languid paintings of iris or lilies, and a high-shouldered pewter vase on the mantelpiece, with a knob of turquoise stuck to its middle, containing three peacock feathers. Neutrality was 'in' at the moment; nevertheless Sebastian thought this was going a bit too far.

On the other hand, Sylvia herself was looking very chic and ornamental, dressed with modish luxury in a Directoire-style tea gown of maroon shot silk, its olive-green lights accentuating the green of her long, cat-like eyes. She was always expensively dressed – Algy, Sebastian had to admit, was more than generous in that direction – and today she wore some very up-to-date silver jewellery, set with what he thought were bloodstones. With her white skin, her dark, attractively waved hair, and the uprightness of her little figure, she was extremely attractive. Small, dark, clever and amusing. Generally regarded as something of a beauty, though Sebastian was not sure about that; it all depended on her mood. And too thin, perhaps. Never trust a thin woman, Inky Winthrop was fond of saying, especially one whose clear profile showed a nose a little too sharp, a chin just a shade too determined. "I do have some news —" he began.

"You're going to be married!"

"No, Sylvia."

His irritation returned, he forgot how he had been going to

continue. Trying to get comfortable on an excessively upright chair with a long, straight back and no cushion, wanting any topic of conversation but that, he incautiously mentioned an item of news he had seen reported about her friend, Annie Besant.

"I hope you're not going to lecture me, Sebastian."

"Would I dare?"

She smiled. "Good. Because I'm not disposed to talk about her."

From this he gathered that Mrs Besant, like many another of Sylvia's enthusiasms, had been abandoned. He could not know for what reason, nor did he wish to know. He was only too relieved to find the unsuitable friendship was over. She was a woman, Mrs Besant, who, despite her good works, inspired and irritated in equal parts.

Sylvia had grown tired of waiting for him to come to the point. "I expect you've come to tell me about this new little idea of yours, then? But I must tell you, I've already heard, from Mama. I saw her yesterday. Monty gave us tea in Fortnums. These are some of their cakes. Do have one of these chocolate ones, they're divine."

This little idea! And there he had been working like a black for the last few weeks, throwing himself into learning the mundane practicalities of his new profession as Arthur Wagstaffe had advised, acquainting himself with drains and landfalls and damp courses with as much energy as he'd previously followed his other trivial pursuits. How right his prospective employer had been. Sebastian had never been naïve about how much there was to building even the simplest of houses – but there was much more to learn than he had ever imagined. But as a means to an end, he found it a better antidote to boredom than racing, chasing pretty girls or anything else, for that matter, had ever been.

"No thank you, no cake, I had rather a heavy lunch. I didn't know Mama was in Town, and – well, seeing that you've taken the wind out of my sails, what do you think? Were you surprised?"

"Utterly *bouleversée* – what else did you expect? But dear Seb, you don't usually do anything so out of character, do you? I do so hope you won't regret it."

"Is that what you said to Harry when he resigned his commission to become a journalist?"

He should not have said that, not even lightly. It was a Sylvia-sharp remark, unworthy. Though she tried to hide the grief she felt at the loss of Harry with a brittle sophistication, she was still raw at losing her twin. Her face closed every time his name was mentioned. But he had little time to regret his remark this time, for she came back immediately, with no sign of hurt and a sharp little dart of her own.

"A journalist? Hardly that, my dear boy. Not a professional one, at any rate. But Harry was always doing something out of character – that's what made him so interesting, wasn't it?"

He deserved that. Though he wasn't sure whether she had meant a joke or an insult. Like Harry, one never really knew with Sylvia. He hadn't ever, he now realised, thought of them as separate beings, but rather as a single, inseparable unit, Harry-and-Sylvia. And yet, Harry had kept from their sister the biggest secret of his life...

Or had he?

He looked across at her and found she was regarding him steadily over the rim of her delicate china teacup. "Well, since you haven't seen fit to go into politics, or something equally sensible, I can but say I hope you may find what you are going to do rewarding. We've never had an architect in the family before. Perhaps you'll turn out to be another Christopher Wren. Just imagine – Papa agreeing to it!"

"It's taken him nearly two months – though as he still believes it's a passing fancy, and that I'll come round in the end, he's decided he might as well let me have my head for the time being." Sebastian grimaced. He'd slowly come to accept that he had mistaken his father's silence over breakfast that morning at Belmonde for anger, and felt sure now that Sir Henry had in fact probably been too amazed to be angry. Indeed, no one had actually shown any opposition to what he proposed to do. Not even Sylvia, it seemed – though perhaps this was because their mother had paved the way and given her time to get used to the idea. Taking her lead from Sir Henry's surprising, if grudging, acquiescence, Adèle had accepted the inevitable with apparent good grace. Even Lady Emily, in her own way, had owned herself relieved to know that he had at last found something with which to occupy himself. It seemed that he had been envisaging demons where none were likely to exist. "While Father can't bring himself to say that he actually approves, he's at last come round to agreeing that it will certainly be better for me – *at present* – than doing nothing, as he puts it."

"And what does your little friend Louisa say?"

"I'm happy to say she heartily approves." He did not intend to get into a discussion about Louisa, and went on, "It's just that I'm not cut out for the sort of life Father still envisages for me, though I suppose I shall have to face it some day. In any case, as long as he's at Belmonde, I shall be surplus to requirements."

"But he won't always be there, will he? And then it'll be your turn to think about an heir."

"Please, Sylvia —" He put up a fending off hand. "Not now."

She lifted her shoulders. "So – what else is there to bring you out here to see me?"

"If you've been talking to Mama, I suppose you've already heard they've found the name of the woman who was murdered at Belmonde."

"Yes, some Armenian woman, I gather." She busied herself with the teacups. "How did they find out who she was, by the way?"

"Some of her friends reported to the police that she was missing, and she was identified from her clothing – and so on. Don't you find it all extremely odd? Why someone like that would be out at Belmonde? Apparently, her name was Rosa – Tartaryan, I believe it was, or something very like."

"Do you suppose she intended planting a bomb?" Sylvia gave a light laugh as she passed him his refilled cup.

"That's what we'd all like to know, wouldn't we? Perhaps we shall know soon, now that the police have something to go on."

A small silence fell on the room. His relief at hearing that the identity of the dead woman had at last been revealed had known no bounds. She was a stranger after all, not the woman he had feared she might have been. He broke the silence by saying abruptly, "I'm very glad she's been identified. I rather suspected she might be someone else." He paused, then went on, watching her carefully, "Sylvia, I'm aware it's a painful subject, but there's something I must know – about Harry."

She looked up quickly. Her catlike eyes glittered and instantly, the chilling suspicion which had begun to form in his mind was confirmed. Tread softly, he told himself. Here be dragons. "You know, don't you?"

"Oblige me by not looking so fierce, Sebastian. I know what?"

What a fool I've been, he thought. Ever to have even imagined that Sylvia wouldn't have known. Harry would have seen no need for secrecy, for not sharing any part of his life, however disreputable, with his twin. Even that secret he had confided to his brother in an unguarded moment – to be frank, when he was drunk – at a time when he, too, had been under pressure from the family to find a wife. "Let's not pretend, Sylvia. Of course you know."

"I haven't the least idea what you're talking about." She glanced at the little clock, busily ticking away on the mantelpiece. "Look, I have to go out now, and I still have to change. But it's been lovely seeing you. We don't see enough of each other, you and I."

"Sylvia. I think you know very well I'm talking about the woman Harry was keeping. Was she by any chance this Rosa Tartaryan?"

"An *Armenian*? I hardly think so." Her lip curled.

"Then who was it? I know there was someone – and I know Harry never kept secrets from you, of all people."

She turned her head from him and faced her own reflection in the looking glass, composed her face, and when she turned back she was smiling again. "Is that so reprehensible? Young men must be allowed to sow their wild oats, *après tout,* or where should we all be?"

"Please be serious. Where is she? Who is she? Where does she live?"

She eyed him narrowly for a moment, then shrugged her slim shoulders. Nevertheless, the glance she gave at the clock once more was rather desperate.

He went on. "Has no one thought we might have a responsibility towards this mistress of his? To see that she is being taken care of?"

She still said nothing, and her very silence hit him like a blow between the eyes. "Are you saying he *married* her? Good God. Was that why he resigned his commission in the regiment?" (Before he'd been compelled to do so under the strictly enforced rule that a Blues officer must not in any circumstances marry an 'actress'?)

"Married? *Married?* My dear, are you not being hopelessly naïve?"

She was very pale, with a spot of high colour on each cheekbone. She drew in a deep breath. After a moment, she spoke. "There is a son," she said abruptly. "And before you say anything else, there's something else you should know. The boy is – well, to put the best interpretation on it, he is – not quite right in the head. Sebastian, *mon cher,* the boy is an imbecile."

Chapter Eighteen

Crockett hadn't been able to rid himself of the idea that the name and address found in the Gladstone bag (which the Saroyan brothers had now positively identified as belonging to Rosa Tartaryan) was important to the investigation and the discovery of her killer. As a result of the brothers' visit, he had written hopefully once more to the Crowthers in Yorkshire – a shot in the dark, this, but one which had paid off, for one of the family now proposed to visit him. An early date and time were suggested, and promptly on time on the day specified, word was sent in to him as he sat in the busy CID office that a Mr Edward Crowther was there to see him. He asked for the visitor to be shown into an interviewing room and joined him there immediately.

"Ned Crowther," the tall, bronzed young man announced himself heartily, extending a large hand in answer to Crockett's greeting. "I'm very pleased to meet you, Chief Inspector."

"Please be seated, Mr Crowther. It's very good of you to come all this way."

"Not in the least. Only too glad to be of service. Came as soon as I could." He went on to say that he had only recently arrived home from South Africa, where he and his brother-in-law, Mr Lyall Armitage, ran an import and export company. "I came over to attend to the London end of our business, but when I've done that, I've made up my mind to cut my losses, and stay here for good. Fought out there in the Boer War," he went on to explain, "and when it was over, in ninety-two, I liked the country so much I decided to stay. Capital life out there, wonderful opportunities. I've no complaints, but the fact is, the climate don't suit my health – subject to bouts of malaria, you know. Weakens the constitution in the end. I've been told I should leave Africa. It's a blow, I'll admit, but the old country still has a lot to offer. As to this other business, I don't know if I'll be setting you up on a wild goose chase or not, but —"

"Mr Crowther, I regret we've had to trouble your family again – but if there's any information at all you can give, I assure you

I shall be in your debt," said Crockett with heartfelt truth.

"No trouble at all. In fact the help may be in the other direction. Our name and address in that murdered woman's bag – rum do, that, whichever way you look at it, ain't it?"

"True enough. And you've no idea how or why it might have been there?"

"If you hoped I'd be able to explain that, I'm sorry to disappoint you. But when my parents told me the story, I put certain facts together and came up with something which may help to put you on the right track." He paused, and then said, his pleasant face suddenly tight and anxious, "It's certain that this woman – the one who's been murdered – was a foreigner?"

"Yes. We're positive now that she was an Armenian, by the name of Rosa Tartaryan."

"Ah." He heaved a sigh of deep relief. "Well, that's it then. No connection with my family – not obviously so, that is. But as to the other name you gave us – the one you say this Rosa worked for, the one you want to trace. Well now, it came to me right away that you might have the answer to a mystery that's been troubling our family for some time. Long shot, I'll grant, but I suppose you're willing to try anything? I should be, in your shoes."

Crockett indicated that indeed he was.

"Well, it goes back a way, so if you'll bear with me? There was a young woman who was very close to us all, orphan daughter of friends of my family. Lived with us for many years. I was – we were all extremely fond of Hannah – she was like one of the family."

"Hannah – Smith?"

"No. Her name was Jackson. But she was certainly called Hannah. Hannah Mary Jackson." He smiled slightly, as if amused by some secret thought. "It was like this. My only sister, Lydia, married Lyall Armitage, the good fellow who's now my business partner, and went out to South Africa with him. Later Hannah went out to join her. It was only ever intended to be a

brief visit, but it was extended for one reason and another, and

"Where is she now?"

"Ah, that I wish we knew, Mr Crockett, upon my word I do. She returned to England – alone, I believe, but never went back to Bridge End. She wrote that for many reasons it was better she shouldn't return. What my mother thought it was, you see – m'brother George and his family had recently moved in with the parents. Sensible idea. Bridge End is a big house, built as a family dwelling, and it needs a big, growing family like George's to fill it. Plenty of room for them all, and the old folk delight in having their grandchildren around them – but my mother got the idea Hannah might not like the idea of sharing a house with George's wife. Capital woman, Nellie, cheerful and all that, great organiser – of things and people. But she and Hannah – chalk and cheese. Anyway, damned if we haven't heard a word from Hannah since then. Just the odd card at Christmas, and birthdays, saying she was well and hoped we all were. Not like Hannah, that, not a bit."

"Tell me. Where did she live, in South Africa?"

"In Mafeking. I suppose you've heard of Mafeking?"

"Who has not?" It was nearly seven years since the war with the Boers had ended, and nigh on a decade since the name of the small heroic frontier town on the South African veld had been on the lips of every man, woman and child in England, but who indeed could have forgotten it?

Crockett's thoughts were racing. It surely wasn't too much to believe that here at last were the connections he needed to confirm his suspicions. The woman who had worked for Hannah Smith had been murdered on the Chetwynd family estate. Harry Chetwynd had been a war correspondent in Mafeking at the same time as a woman called Hannah...Osborne as they might have to learn to call her. Both had been in the omnibus accident.

"I don't know how what you've told us is going to help, Mr Crowther, but I thank you for coming to us. Don't get your hopes up, but I think this Mrs Hannah Smith we've been trying to trace may possibly – just possibly, mind you – be the Hannah Osborne you're looking for. If you'll give me a few details about her last address and so on, I'd appreciate it."

"You won't get much out of that. Old George had a go for my

mother's sake – tried to trace her through the girls' old governess, a Miss Rhoda Rouncewell, who'd just returned from America and was teaching at a college in Surrey. Found poor Rouncey had died, and no trace of Hannah."

"We'll have to try some other way, then. We'd very much like to find her. Give me a few more details of Miss Rouncewell."

"I'd very much like to find my dear Hannah on my own account," Ned said quietly. "Understand what I mean?"

Sebastian, confounded by the information Sylvia had given him, discovered an urgent need to confer with Louisa, and that same afternoon, he drove his car to the Medical School where she was studying. His request to speak to her received a frosty reception from the dragon presiding over a desk in the front hall, who obviously saw the task of overseeing the hundred or so independently-minded young women in her charge as the cross she had to bear. "I'm sorry, Miss Fox is not in."

"Do you know when she's expected back?"

She was bound to know. He'd had it from Louisa that the students were required to sign in and out at stated times, but clearly, the lady was not going to budge an inch, even to this well mannered young man. "No," she stated, determined not to be thawed by a charming smile.

Sebastian could be equally stubborn. He was not about to give in so easily, either, and was settling down to pursue the matter to a satisfactory conclusion when a young woman in a fashionably cut coat and skirt and a rather fetching hat touched him on the shoulder. Ignoring the dragon's glare, she asked, "You're looking for Louisa? She's working on the wards, but she should be finishing any time now. I'm on my way to the hospital to take her place."

This modish young lady looked even less like his idea of an earnest medical student than Louisa did, but the truism that all bluestockings must be frights no longer seemed to apply. Some of the cleverest women around nowadays appeared determined to prove this. "Do you know where to find her?" she asked.

"I think so." The hospital to which she referred was the Royal Free, where the women medical students at the school here were allowed to gain their practical clinical instruction on the wards.

"But since you're going there too, may I not drive you?" he asked, indicating the Ascot which was drawn up to the kerb outside.

"Oh, I say, would you?" She had huge brown eyes and thick eyelashes which she could, and did, use to good effect, and a pretty, dimpled smile.

"Miss Winslow!"

"It's all right, Miss Madeley, this gentleman is a friend of my brother's." It was undoubtedly a wink Miss Winslow gave him, before flashing her dimples at the dragon, sauntering out and whisking herself into the Ascot with an aplomb that indicated she was no stranger to young men's motorcars.

She chattered non-stop from Hunter Street to the Grays Inn Road. By the time Sebastian stopped the engine, he had learned she was in her third year of study, how tremendously she admired the school's founder, Sophie Jex-Blake, that her father was an Irish landowner and she should have come out two seasons ago had she not nagged him into letting her study to become a doctor. "My mother isn't speaking to me over it. Too tedious. But learning to be a doctor is so much more fun," she said, flirting from under her eyelashes. Sebastian laughed. He was sure she would enjoy nothing better than to dance the night away.

A little later, climbing into the seat Miss Winslow had vacated, Louisa said, "Oh, Cynthia! Half the doctors in the hospital are in love with her – and she with them. She's the star of our year, you know. She'll walk away with all the honours, if she doesn't get herself put in prison too often. She chained herself to the railings at No. 10 last year – that was when her father realised there was no doing anything with her and gave up trying to persuade her to quit her studies and become a young lady. What are you doing here?"

"We have something to talk about. Let me take your books." They were in a satchel which she had slung over her shoulder. She wore a very short sealskin jacket, and he hoped its little rabbit fur collar made it warmer for the raw day than it appeared capable of doing. He thought she looked pale and as though she wasn't getting enough to eat, though this was unlikely; Louisa had a hearty appetite. She was probably working too hard. But the unaccustomed look of fragility brought out his protective instincts and he suggested they might find a teashop where they might have poached eggs on toast. Oh dear, she was very sorry, but she had arranged to meet someone else for tea. Yet another of her suffragette friends, he thought with a resigned sigh, registering that she sounded slightly evasive, for Louisa. But he thought it wiser to say nothing.

"Well then, let's talk here. Or would you rather drive around?"

"Let's stay where we are."

He reached behind the seat and pulled out a warm plaid rug which he draped over her knees. "The police have found the identity of the murdered woman, Louisa," he said abruptly. "She was an Armenian, by the name of Rosa Tartaryan."

"An Armenian? Oh." She digested this. "Does that mean she wasn't Harry's mistress, after all?"

"Probably. I've been speaking to Sylvia, and she didn't seem to think she was. But – that's not the least of it." The full story of his visit to his sister was soon related. He didn't feel this was the time for finesse, and told her plainly what it was he had learned.

She looked appalled. "Poor child," she said softly, "poor mother. Well, if Sylvia knows all this, she must know where they are to be found."

"She swears she doesn't, that Harry never told her anything more than the bare facts. I don't think I believe her, but I can't force her to tell. But if she's wrong, and this Rosa Tartaryan *was* his mistress – there's nothing to say she wasn't, just because she wasn't English – that means the child is alone now. Someone must be looking after him, but I do rather think that as a family we have a bounden duty to do something for him, especially if the boy is…defective in his mind."

"How like you, Seb." Her eyes were suspiciously bright as she touched his sleeve. And it was at that moment, when he saw her little gloved hand trembling very slightly against the smooth broadcloth of his overcoat, that he thought she might be willing to love him, too. But, though she answered his look with heightened colour, he nonetheless knew this wasn't the time. Not usually a man to miss an opportunity, he knew now that he must wait – but with rather more hope in his heart than heretofore.

"The police should know what happened to him, after the accident," she went on, "and we don't know what else they may have found out about Rosa Tartaryan, either."

"That's true." Sebastian considered. "I'll go and see Crockett tomorrow – though I doubt whether he'll tell me much. Struck me as a man who plays his cards very close to his chest."

"I've a better idea than that. You may sigh about my friends in the WSPU – (she *had* noticed, then) but one of them who I've become quite friendly with, Agnes Crawford, knows Crockett – in fact, she's probably going to marry him some day." Suddenly, she laughed. "She's been trying to get out of me – in the nicest possible way – whether I'm privy to any secrets about Belmonde, and thinks I haven't suspected, so I dare say it's my turn to probe now. I'll talk to her."

Crockett was in no doubt that the letters received by Sir Henry had been blackmail letters. From Rosa, who had needed money for the cause of Armenian liberation, to which she was deeply committed. Following that was the inescapable conclusion: like most blackmailers, she hadn't been able to resist increasing her demands, and had thereby provided the motive for her own murder. And what was she blackmailing Sir Henry about, if not something she'd learned through working as maid to Hannah Smith?

Since Ned Crowther's visit, his theories had moved on further. Assuming there had been a liaison between Sir Henry's son and Hannah Osborne – and there seemed no reason now to believe this wasn't so – and supposing the unclaimed child on the omnibus was a result of this – even supposing this, in what way had Rosa been using it as a motive for blackmailing the Chetwynds? Just another illegitimate child, fathered by one of the young bloods of society, was common enough. It would cause little stir – maybe a small scandal that would be soon hushed up and allowed to make no difference to the family concerned.

It was true that Dr Harvill's patient had denied ever having a child; but the little boy on the omnibus was only two or three years old, which meant he must have been born during those years which she had apparently lost. So completely as to forget the birth of her own child?

Harvill had indicated that he believed Hannah's memory loss was because subconsciously she did not want to remember some event which had made a deeply lasting, maybe painful, impression on her, and had possibly changed her life, preventing her from acknowledging the last few years. If they had been spent as the mistress of Harry Chetwynd, maybe the answer to the puzzle lay there.

It all came back to the child.

"Grayson," he said, approaching a constable. "You were one of those attending that Ludgate Hill omnibus collision, were you not?"

"Yes, sir. Won't forget it in a hurry."

"What happened to that little boy?"

"The one who belonged to the woman who was killed?"

"The one who was *believed* to have belonged to her." It had never made much sense to Crockett to have linked them together – a well dressed, well cared for child, and a poor woman from off the streets, who could very likely have barely have afforded the fare for the omnibus. But he understood that accepting they were together must have provided a convenient answer to the puzzle of why no one had ever come forward to claim the boy.

"Sarah Jenkins took him in, sir – you know, young Constable Jenkins's widow. She'd lost a baby of her own just before Jack died and was more than happy to take on the poor little mite, or he'd have been sent to an institution. Thinks the world of him, so my wife tells me."

"It can't be easy for her, a widow. She can't have much to go on with."

"Oh, as to that, there's been some help given. Remember the young toff as was killed in the same accident – Chetwynd? His family's seen to it that Sarah's all right. Good of them, no call to do that, after all, but well, what's it to folk like that, a few shillings here and there?"

"What indeed?" answered Crockett.

He went to his dinner in jubilant mood. Was his luck was turning at last? He didn't believe the Chetwynds had taken on the responsibility of an unknown child simply out of the goodness of their hearts. The fact that they'd done so indicated they knew a great deal more than they were prepared to admit at the time of the accident about the relationship of their son with the unidentified woman and the child. He came back to his desk, over-full with lamb chops and apple dumpling, determined to walk it off by legging it out to see Mrs Jenkins, but found a letter which had been forwarded from Meredith which, after he had read it, seemed to pose much more important questions.

Perhaps it hadn't been quite such a brilliant idea as he had at first thought, to have asked Agnes to gain the confidence of Louisa Fox – or to expect any results might come from it, but the inhabitants at Belmonde were turning out to be an interesting lot, right enough, and it suddenly seemed imperative that he should talk with her and find out if she had been able to find anything new about them.

The last time he'd seen her, he'd invited her to spend that evening at the theatre, with supper afterwards. They were both fond of an occasional night at the musical hall and Vesta Tilley, the male impersonator, was at present top of the bill at the Gaiety. Agnes had declined with some embarrassment, saying she'd already promised to attend a small sub-committee meeting which was to be held at the home of one of the WSPU members in a block of mansion flats near Queen Anne's Gate, which demanded her attendance and would not finish until about nine o'clock. Crockett damned the suffragettes. Committee meetings, sub-committees…if these women did ever get the vote they were demanding, they would at least be well set up to become members of Parliament, he thought sourly.

However, Queen Anne's Gate was well within walking distance of the Yard, and Crockett determined to catch her as she came out of the meeting. Nine o'clock found him stationed at some distance, where he could keep an eye out for her.

The night was chilly, there was a clammy mist rising from the river and seeping into the side streets, the hum of traffic beyond the quiet thoroughfare was deadened by the mist. It wasn't until ten minutes after Big Ben had struck the hour that the women began to come out of the door he was watching, mostly in twos and threes, disappearing into the shadows beyond the gas lamps, their footsteps receding hollowly. Then nothing. He shivered and turned up his collar, beginning to think he had misunderstood: it was only to be a small meeting, Agnes had said – perhaps the business had been over and done with before his arrival. He heard the mournful hoot of a tug from the river. Then he saw a graceful figure on the steps, her face almost obscured by a large hat and a fur collar drawn up to her chin, but unmistakably Agnes. She was with a smaller woman he thought might be Louisa Fox. At that moment, a motor-cab came phut-phutting out of the mist, and the two women rushed to the edge of the pavement and stood under a street lamp, signalling to him with their waving umbrellas. For a moment, it seemed as though it wasn't going to stop. London cabbies had learned to be wary of women – even innocent-looking women like these – out on the streets at night, unescorted. But fares were scarce on a night like this and at the last minute he jerked to a sudden halt. Crockett was already hurrying towards them, calling for them to wait, but the sound of the engine drowned his shouts, the women were too busy holding up their skirts as they got into the cab to see him and the driver was keeping an eye on them over his shoulder.

By the time the door had closed behind them and the cab was ready to move off, Crockett was running, and shouting, "Stop!" The cabbie knew a policeman when he saw one, even though he was so nattily dressed, and guessed the reason he was running. Rather than accelerating away, he turned round again to the women and snapped over his shoulder, "Come on, get out!"

"What? Did you not hear me? I asked you to take us to —" began Louisa.

"Out, I said! I don't want no trouble from the likes of you lot, brazen hussies! Get yourselves home where you belong, seeing to your husbands' suppers, never mind the bleedin' vote!"

Agnes was about to do as she was told, but Louisa, outraged, persisted. "How can we, if you won't take us home?"

"It's all right, Louisa," said her friend, opening the door and stepping on to the pavement. "It's only John Crockett."

"Out!" said the cabbie again, revving up his engine.

Suddenly, Louisa reached forward, and with a quick movement of both hands, dragged the cabbie's hat right down over his ears. Only then did she skip nimbly out of the motor, followed by a stream of abuse as the outraged driver tried to release his ears from his hat preparatory to jumping out after her. By then Crockett had reached them. He leaned over to bang on the glass and jerk his thumb to indicate the taxi should be off. The cabbie who had at last snatched off his hat, shook his fist at Crockett. Then, with his hand already on the door handle, he obviously thought the better of his intentions, and mouthing maledictions, finally drove off.

Crockett stood recovering his breath as the women, laughing helplessly, watched the rear view of the taxi disappear round the corner. "Well now, I'd like to have a little talk with you ladies, if that's all the same with you."

Agnes ceased laughing. "Here?" she demanded coldly. "We might have been half way home by now, if you hadn't interfered."

"Just a word or two —"

In truth, he hadn't the vaguest idea where he could have the sort of conversation he wanted with two respectable ladies, this time of night, in this weather. Not in a public house, that was for sure, though a bright fire and a drop of something to warm the cockles of the heart wouldn't have come amiss. He could think of nowhere else but his office. In desperation, he tried to make a joke of it. "Could I ask you two ladies to come along to the station with me and help with my enquiries?"

For a moment, he thought his quip had fallen on stony ground, then to his relief, they exchanged a glance and again

burst into giggles. It must have been a good meeting, he thought tetchily. "Oh, John," said Agnes, when she could. "That's a terrible joke."

"No joke. And it's not far."

Sebastian, almost more disconsolate than Crockett at not having been able to spend more time with Louisa, had gone home, eaten a sandwich and then worked until ten, when he gave it up. His meeting with Sylvia, despite Louisa's support afterwards, still oppressed him. Rather than wait for information which might or might not come from this friend of Louisa's, he wondered if he might go and see his mother.

It was late, and she was probably not in London, or still out if she was (it was still early for dances or after-theatre supper parties to have finished) but if he left it later, she might have gone to bed, and at any rate, walking to Jermyn Street would stop the eternal merry-go-round of his thoughts.

He turned off Piccadilly into the quiet street and there she was, a taxi waiting at the kerb, with Monty escorting her to the door. They were dressed for the opera, and stood there, as if in a scene on stage, spotlit by the gas lamp on the pavement, surrounded by the misty darkness of the silent street; she standing on the top step, he on the one below, so that their eyes were level. A train of soft blue flowed down the step from under her black velvet cloak. She was wearing diamonds in her hair and they glittered on her wrist as he held her hand – the same hand he had held so painfully in the stable yard – raised it tenderly to his lips and murmured something. Sebastian was too far away to hear what they said, but he saw his mother's other hand reach up to touch Monty's cheek gently, saw her smile; their eyes held as if nothing could break their gaze. Like Sylvia, her looks depended greatly on her mood, and tonight as she turned her face to Monty, her eyes brilliant in the lamplight, she looked incredibly beautiful. He almost fancied he could catch the faintest wave of her perfume, and was a small boy again, waiting for her to come and kiss him goodnight before she went out. The taxi-driver revved up his engine impatiently, breaking the spell. Still they looked, bewitched. Then Monty turned. The opera cloak swung from his shoulders, the light catching its red silk lining as he ran down the steps and into the taxi. His mother lingered to watch the cab disappear, then went indoors.

Sebastian stayed in the shadows, several things becoming clear to him at once.

* * *

Crockett couldn't imagine a drearier place than the CID office at Scotland Yard – but at least the gas mantles had been replaced and though they gave a bright, harsh light, and the gas fire popped irritatingly, it was warm – and, for the moment, empty. He fetched two chairs, thought about his whisky cache, but decided he had made enough tactical blunders with his beloved for one evening. He left them for a few minutes while he went to order some tea.

"Won't be long in coming," he told them when he returned, hitching himself on to his desk. "Successful meeting?"

"Never mind the meeting," said Agnes. "Just tell us what all this is about. I can think of better things to be doing than sitting here. Remember we have to get home yet, and if that little incident's anything to go by…"

"I'll see you get home safely. But for now – I have a little tale to tell you."

Louisa listened in perfect silence as he gave them the gist of the story as he now saw it, though she went quite pale when she heard of the money given to Sarah Jenkins. But it was when he came to the part about Ned Crowther that she sat up "Mafeking?"

"What is the matter, Miss Fox?"

"Osborne, did you say, Mr Crockett? Hannah Osborne?"

Augustus Fox, normally so easy going and amenable, could be stubborn in the way of such men when once they have made up their minds to do, or not to do, something. In the shock following his dear Ellen's death in late-age childbirth, his daughter Margaret, like the good girl she was, had competently picked up where her mother had so tragically left off and taken care of the new baby, Alice, without any discernible difference to the smooth running of the household; but for all of them the heart had been taken out of the family, the sunshine had gone from life.

Bereft of his dearest wife, Gus was totally at sea. He had always left the managing of the house, the children, every domestic detail, to Ellen, confident in the knowledge that she would keep things running like the smoothly oiled gears of one of the inventive bits of machinery he loved to tinker with. He never troubled himself with details, living life in the optimistic belief that things generally turned out well if you let them alone. Normally the most loving and approachable of fathers, after Ellen's death he had shut himself away with his grief and his guilt at having subjected his dearest wife to another dangerous pregnancy – and he, a doctor! – until at last he emerged with his own solution: in his youth, before he married, he had travelled adventurously and knew nothing better as a cure for melancholy. Always an impulsive man, he had conceived the notion of making the journey to South Africa to visit his boys, his eldest son Robert and his younger brother Barty, who had settled on the borders of British Bechuanaland and become ostrich farmers.

What folly, what could Gus be thinking of? cried the voices of reason. Did he not realise the dangers of travelling in a country existing at that moment in a state of high tension between the Boers and the British? Where war might break out at any time?

He pooh-poohed such cowardice. There was nothing to prevent his going. Of his two sons still in England, Joseph was doing well for himself in the Army, while the younger boy, William, was away at school. Just for a while, he did hesitate: if he went, the burden of keeping things running at home would fall on Margaret, but of course, she reacted to this exactly as he'd known she would.

"Do what you feel you must, Papa," she'd said calmly. Already five-and-twenty, born with an old head on her shoulders, she had inherited that wisdom from her mother which had always told her what Gus needed. "I'm quite capable of looking after the house and servants – and Louisa – and as for Baby…"

Even had her face not lit up as she cuddled the child to her, there was no need to ask how she felt about that. She adored little Alice with a fierceness that revealed she was making the most of an opportunity which might never come her way again. Eminently suitable though she was to make someone a good wife, there was already a spinster air about Margaret.

When the first shock of Gus's decision had subsided, another one took its place. To everyone's astonishment, there was young Louisa, begging and praying to be allowed to accompany her father, which was, of course, quite impossible – out of the question

– as everyone knew. It was not a sensible journey for even Gus to undertake in the circumstances, never mind encumbered with the responsibility of a child. Conditions out there were not suitable for children. What about her brother Robert's children on the ostrich farm? she demanded, they were only *babies*. That was entirely different, was the response, their parents had taken them there from necessity, when they themselves went out to make a new life. Yes, to live there permanently, Louisa retorted, so why should a mere visit be deemed out of the question for her?

It became a war of attrition. Anything from tantrums, tears, and requests to the Almighty in her nightly prayers. And a wounded, stricken look behind her eyes that made Gus blame himself for his selfishness in not sensing that her own desolation at her mother's death was as deep in its way as his own. He saw that Louisa, at thirteen, could not be expected to cope with the loss of her mother and also now, as she saw it, her father, too.

With a characteristic lack of regard for other people's opinions, he gave in and announced that she should go with him.

The journey that everyone predicted would be a fiasco, and might well have become so, turned out to be the most momentous adventure of Louisa's – and Gus's – life, and the one wherein she formed the decision she was to hold on to, in the face all difficulties, to study medicine, like her father. She had witnessed more suffering than most of her friends would ever see in a lifetime, and would never forget it.

1899

The child Louisa had found the ostrich farm nothing like she had expected it to be, but from the first she was as delighted with it as was her father. After expending all their savings on the purchase of an unpromising and dilapidated farm with a few dispirited ostrich penned into an enclosure, her brothers had first worked to increase the flock and make the business profitable again, then drilled more wells and made the land fruitful, planted trees and orchards around it and grew crops where no crops had ever grown before. As well as the ostriches, they raised a few cattle and Robert's wife Frances kept fowls and bees. By now Orchard Farm, as they renamed it, was well on the way to becoming a little Eden, a lush oasis of trees, fruit and flowers, where birds, small animals and butterflies abounded, set like a jewel in the echoing silences of the great plain that surrounded the farm.

Robert's children were too young for Louisa to play with but being of a naturally gregarious disposition it didn't take her long to find companions among the children of the workers on the farm. There was Tommy, a white boy of about her own age, son of the overseer Jock MacBean, a dour Scotsman who walked with a limp; and there was Tommy's black friend, who was called October and who was up to any kind of mischief which could be devised. Robert had immediately given Louisa a pony and Barty had taught her to ride and to look after it herself. Used to the company of boys, she spent hours galloping over the veld with her two new friends, who knew just how far to venture into the bush without danger. The farm was very isolated, except for the bushmen who wandered into the area from time to time.

For three months they had a blissful time. Gus, in his own way, had faced the fact that he must accept the loss of his wife, Ellen, coming to terms with her death for the first time. On the farm, he slipped back imperceptibly into his natural, easy-going self, content to do nothing more for the moment than blissfully collect moths and butterflies, drawing and preserving them for his scientific purposes, marvelling at the way the stony veld blossomed amazingly after the rain, and watching the copper-hued sunsets while sipping a sundowner.

All was not so rosy on the political front, where the situation was deteriorating by the day. Yet Gus, happy on the farm, kept putting off the decision to leave, while knowing he would sooner or later have to make up his mind and do so.

"You know you're more than welcome to stay as long as you wish, but don't leave it too late," advised Robert who, after much soul-searching, had some weeks before finally made up his mind and sent Frances and their two young children to stay at the Cape with her sister until such a time as he deemed it safe for her to return. "Think what it would mean to Louisa, if not your-self, if you were caught up in the middle of a war."

"In the unlikely event things do come to a head, don't you think we should be safe enough out here? In any case, they're saying it'll all be over by Christmas. The Boers won't have a chance against British army troops."

"If we can raise enough of them," replied Robert, who was cynical by now about the Home Government's response to the plight of its subjects out here. The Boers might be convinced that God was on their side, but the optimism (or the arrogance) of the politicians in London had persuaded them that Britain had the rest of the world with them, as well as God. They seemed astonished now to find that this was not so, and that the rest of the world was not being slow to condemn what was being viewed as the aggressive might of the British Empire pitted against the burghers of a small state.

"If that's so, rarely can aggressors have been so ill-prepared," Robert countered somewhat bitterly when he and Gus discussed this. It was undeniable that troops were being mustered from India and all parts of the British Empire, and support was com-ing readily from the Colonies, but even so, the numbers were niggardly compared with the force Kruger could raise. He had had a huge and formidable trained fighting force at his disposal for years in the form of well-organised, well-trained commando units, into which all burghers were liable to be called up for mil-itary service at a moment's notice. "A bunch of farmers! Our lads will soon have 'em by the tail," said Gus comfortably.

Robert sighed. It was easy to make fun of the Boer burghers, presented as they were in the newspapers: thickset men with beards and uncompromising hats, going to war in their farm clothes, with a Bible in one hand and the umbrella they always carried in the other; but Robert had a great respect for their staying power, their stubbornness. They were as hardy as their tough little horses. Moreover, every Boer had been trained from childhood to shoot straight and ride hard – they were used to the climate and they were as familiar with the terrain over which they'd be fighting as with the backs of their own hands. "Armitage was right when he said they won't give in easily," Robert said.

There was a pause, then he went on, "I have to tell you, Father, that as soon as we can get everything cleared up here, Barty and I are going to enlist as volunteers. We shall leave Jock MacBean in charge of the farm, pro tem. So I'm afraid —"

"Volunteer?" Gus was brought up short not only with the dismay of any parent when faced with the thought of their sons going into battle, but also because it had made him realise, as nothing else might have done, precisely how critical the situation was. Robert was quite right, of course; he was the sort of level-headed man who nearly always was, and though this was often irritating, Gus saw that he had been very remiss in tarrying here so long and perhaps, where Louisa was concerned, selfish. In Frances's absence, she had been allowed to run wild with the two farm boys, which to her was a life of perfect bliss. He knew she would ask nothing better than to stay here forever.

After this conversation with Robert, he watched her running across the paddock towards the house, with two of the farm dogs barking with hysterical joy and running circles around her, and realised he hadn't looked at her properly for weeks. She was like a little unkempt pony, invariably running about with her hair roughly tied back, or not at all. The sun had brought out a thick band of freckles across her nose. Like her mother, she was always going to be a little thing, but she was nearly fourteen and had grown these last few months to what was probably going to be her ultimate height. He realised suddenly that he hardly ever saw her in anything but riding breeches and shirt, such as the boys wore. When she did wear a dress it had become noticeably too short and too tight. She went bare-legged whenever possible. Margaret would have been ashamed of them both.

He was suddenly overcome with guilt. What was he doing, keeping her here and hiding himself away from life? Their sojourn in this beautiful spot had done its work, the spell of lotus-eating was over. They were both healed and ready to return to their old life.

But before any further move could be made, a calamity that no one could have foreseen occurred. Barty, a robust and vigorous young man who was never ill, had indeed escaped all of the usual childish ailments, fell sick with a tropical fever which within a few days had Gus despairing of his life. In this land of biting insects and water-borne infections no one could escape stomach upsets or unexplained agues for long. Malaria, bilharzia and typhoid were endemic – but this was different, a virulent disease unknown to Gus.

There could be nothing more harrowing than seeing a young man in the prime of his healthy young life brought down by an unexpected illness; here it was, his own son, and Gus was helpless. All his medical knowledge was brought to bear to save Barty, but he was not familiar with tropical diseases and without modern drugs, or the means of getting them, he knew he faced a difficult, if not impossible, task. A message was sent to the doctor in Mafeking, who arrived with a bag of potions but not much hope, and after he had heard what Gus had to say, and had examined the patient himself, he shook his head.

"God knows where he picked this up," said Gus wearily, "but my elder son informs me that one of the nomadic tribes arrived down by the creek a few weeks ago. Barty spoke to them while negotiating a place for them to set up their camp. I understand there was lately something of the same sort of epidemic amongst them."

Dr James spread his hands. "Then look no further for an explanation. These sort of fevers are endemic amongst the Kaffirs. You know how it is, they've built up a certain immunity over the years to diseases that kill us white men. They themselves can survive, but it's still possible for them to pass on the disease." He looked at the other man's blanched, weary face, and put a hand on his shoulder. "I'm sorry, old fellow – but I must warn you, you should prepare for the worst."

He and Louisa should have left Orchard Farm and been on their way home weeks ago – but Gus was very glad indeed now that they had not done so. He would be able to care for his son himself until he was well again. The days wore on, stretched into two weeks, but there was no question of their leaving. Barty lay, yellow and shivering one minute, consumed by heat and drenched in a cold sweat the next. He rambled and recognised no one. His big, strong frame grew skeletally thin overnight.

Gus was afraid of contagion and would allow no one but himself into the room where the sick boy lay but nursed him entirely alone. He doused himself with disinfectant whenever he emerged and hoped he would not pass on the disease. Louisa, frightened and miserable, crouched on the veranda while the heat pressed down like a lid, and watched the gathering banks of cumulus clouds, listened to the sounds from the sickroom and wondered whether it was ever likely to rain again.

One night Gus walked along the veranda and sat down on the step next to her. His hands reeked of carbolic as he clasped them over his knees. "Have you been praying, Louisa?"

"Yes," Louisa answered, looking down at her feet. "But it isn't doing much good, is it?"

"You must be very brave, my darling. Think only, God's will be done."

"Is Barty going to die?" It was the first time she had dared to voice this. Robert was unapproachable on the subject, and his wife Frances, to whom Louisa might have been able to talk and who would have given her motherly comfort, was hundreds of miles away. Gus had been too preoccupied and worried to bother him.

"Dearest child, we must be prepared," he said, drawing her to him.

She looked desperate. "Papa – October says his father knows the bushmen have a remedy that never fails – but Robert won't hear of using it, he says the Kaffirs might give him poison that would kill Barty. Won't you listen to what October says? We – we could at least try."

For a long time, Gus said nothing. His face was drawn and lined. He had aged ten years. He knew Barty was going to die.

"Please. Please, Papa."

He looked down at his daughter's clutching hand. He thought of October's father, a louche man who smoked an evil tobacco from a cow's horn, and his friend the witch doctor who could make people die simply by telling them they would do so. "Please, Papa."

"All right, child," he said at last. "Go fetch October, and we'll see what he has to say. But don't tell Robert." He need not tell Louisa, either, that he had no intention of administering to the patient whatever this cure might turn out to be.

Negotiations were conducted through one of the kitchen boys. Robert could never have been persuaded, even in the unlikely event of success, to part with cattle as a means of barter – which was all the bushmen were really interested in, money being of no account to them since you could not eat it when you were hungry – but Gus had a many-bladed penknife and a meerschaum pipe which they were persuaded to trade in exchange for the remedy. This thankfully turned out to be, not a potion of juice extracted from some unknown plant or root, and which may or may not have been mixed with urine or dung or some other unspeakable substance, but a bundle of herbs tied with grass and feathers which was to be hung around the patient's neck. It wouldn't do any good, thought Gus, but neither would it do any harm.

Barty that night grew worse. His life was ebbing away in a river of sweat, and Gus hung the fetish around his neck; he had ceased to be ashamed of himself for entertaining such barbaric methods. He might even, so great was his despair, have been prepared to administer to Barty one of the witch-doctor's potions, but about three o'clock, as he bent to wipe the sweat from his son's face once more, Barty opened his eyes and spoke. The fever had broken. Whether it had been the bundle of herbs and feathers, or whether the illness had taken its natural course, Gus neither knew nor cared to speculate. He threw himself into the armchair by the bed and within seconds was fast asleep.

* * *

It took Barty less than three weeks to regain any semblance to the healthy young man he had been before the fever hit him. He was very weak at first and had lost so much weight his clothes hung on him, but he had youth, strength and a splendid constitution to aid his recovery. Very soon he was eating enough for six and growing restless to be off with Robert to join the volunteers as news filtered through of the worsening political situation. Tales were reaching them of people deserting Johannesburg in thousands, grabbing every means they could of getting away – by trains packed to suffocation, by ox-wagon, or even by cattle-truck. These stories were so rife they could not be dismissed as mere rumour. Now that Barty was recovered and he and Robert were adamant to go and enlist, Gus knew it was time he and Louisa were off, too.

It was already dangerously late, but Robert calculated there was still time for his father to get a train south to Cape Town and from thence, a ship for Home. By the time they were packed up and ready to leave, however, Kruger's troops were massed on the border, ready to cross, and an ultimatum had been issued to the British to pull back their own troops within forty-eight hours. Failure to do so would be taken as a declaration of war by the British.

Nonetheless, the ox-cart was inspanned for Jock MacBean to take them to Mafeking, where there was still a chance of getting a train south. It was too late now to reverse their plans. Tommy and October, who had begged to go along for the ride, sat with Louisa on the tail-board and dangled their feet above the thick red dust of the track. It was suffocatingly hot and the dry winds soon covered them all with the gritty dust. Like all frontier towns at the beginning of a war, Mafeking as they entered was a seething mass of confusion. The little dorp in the middle of nowhere had opened its doors to anyone who needed sanctuary and the result was that it was bursting at the seams. Already overburdened with troops and militia, it was now further swollen with people clamouring for transport to the Cape and with those who had fled in from outlying farms, seeking refuge. The war was at last an established fact. Mafeking alone, up here in the far north of southern Africa, offered such safety and protection as was to be had, the town and its environs being now completely fortified owing to Colonel Baden-Powell's amazing organising ability.

The boys and Jock MacBean unloaded the Fox's possessions amid a throng of other ox-carts doing the same thing, and Jock, before turning the oxen round towards Orchard Farm thrust into Louisa's hands a bag of oranges and some honey cakes from his wife. She waved a sad goodbye to the boys until they were out of sight, then followed her brothers and her father into the station.

Robert came away from the booking office with two tickets, after being assured there would be seats available on the next train – which did not look at all likely in view of the milling crowds of tearful women and children on the platform, complete with baggage, accompanied by anxious husbands and fathers waiting to see them off to safety, but which optimistic statement they had no choice but to accept.

Although the brothers were worried about leaving Louisa and her father before seeing them off on the train, they were at last reluctantly persuaded to leave them at the station: Barty had been speaking to an acquaintance who advised them to enlist before the ranks were closed. Much as volunteers were needed, there were only so many who could be provisioned, armed and housed; already there were many freeloaders who were taking the opportunity to provide themselves with board and lodging, gratis. Whether it was true or not that the numbers were to be limited remained to be seen, his friend said, but it was as well to be aware of the possibility. It was quickly becoming a case of every man for himself in Mafeking – rumours were everywhere, of profiteering, unfulfilled promises of transport south, of spies in their midst.

The train was already hours late and showed no sign of arriving, and the station, hot as a furnace, had become a confused mass of tired, overheated humanity, fractious children and people endeavouring to find somewhere to rest while waiting. Gradually a sort of passive resignation descended; those who could, slept; those who couldn't sat on their luggage and stared into the distance. Hours and hours later, a huge explosion rocked the station. It was followed by a strange, eerie silence and then a hubbub of voices, shouting, screaming and crying; babies and children were pushed to safety under seats; some people attempted to leave the station, but most milled around not knowing what to do, terrified that the explosion, though it had seemingly been at some distance from the town, might signal an attack. Then, in the distance, came the sight of a train.

At last! A concerted outpouring of relief shivered through the crowds like wind passing through the dry grass of the veld. A ragged cheer went up. But as the groaning train steamed into the station, it was seen to be the same one which had left twelve hours ago, crammed with the women and children who had boarded it to travel south. As they poured out to add another dimension to the confusion on the platform, they brought with them the news that the Dutch had torn up two miles of the railway track to the south and cut the telegraph wires. And the explosion, the crowd was informed by loud hailer, had been to the north, out towards Ramathbalama, where the Boers had fired on a couple of dynamite trucks which had been sent out there, away from the town, for security reasons. The hole the explosion had made was forty feet deep.

It appeared that the last train had already left Mafeking. Either way.

For a space of time after this announcement, there was another, incredulous silence, and then all hell broke loose in a stampede for the exit. Several women in the crowd had hysterics, and a woman in late pregnancy fainted. She had been standing near to Gus and Louisa, and he automatically went to offer medical assistance while someone else went to find water. Kneeling beside the woman as she came round, jostled by the bewildered and frightened crowd, it was borne in upon him that the prospect of getting to Cape Town was not cheerful and the possibility of getting back to the farm, at least that day, and possibly for some time thereafter, was equally remote. Himself, he would be content to lay his head down on one of their bags and go to sleep and think about plans tomorrow, but he knew he must try to find some accommodation for Louisa. The child was looking pale, tired and not a little scared. "Come on, my darling, let's go and find somewhere to stay the night," he said gently, after the woman he was attending to had been taken away by friends.

Shouldering his way through the disordered crowds outside the station and in the town square, it rapidly became apparent to Gus that there wasn't much in Mafeking by way of hotels – two, in fact, of a sort, as far as he could ascertain – Riesle's, and Dixon's. The latter, he soon found, had been taken over as headquarters by the military, while Riesle's was packed to the eaves.

Night would soon make its rapid descent and beginning to feel more than a little desperate, he turned away, then bethought himself of Lyall Armitage. He hardly relished the possibility that his enquiry as to where he might find accommodation might be construed as throwing himself on the hospitality of one who was virtually a stranger; at the same time, he didn't feel he had the right to discount any help in the circumstances, if only for Louisa's sake. Going back into the hotel to enquire where Armitage might be found, advising Louisa to hold on to his coat-tails, since his hands were occupied with valises, while the straw basket containing their travelling necessities was strapped across his shoulder, he felt himself tapped on the arm.

"Excuse me, but – it's Dr Fox, isn't it? I saw you at the station, attending to Mrs Brightwell."

Gus found himself looking down at a small woman with dark hair and a sallow complexion. She smiled charmingly and held out her hand. "I believe we have met – my name is Osborne. Hannah Osborne."

"Of course, of course." Augustus belatedly recalled the woman who had visited the farm in company with the Armitages. "Augustus Fox. And you remember Louisa, my daughter."

"Indeed I do. You gave me a bookmark you had made out of ostrich leather, did you not, Louisa? I use it regularly." She smiled at the exhausted child, hot and dusty and clutching a netted bag of oranges. "Excuse me for intruding myself, Dr Fox, but after this catastrophe with the train, it occurred to me you might be having difficulty in finding somewhere to stay?"

"It occurs to *me* I might be doomed to failure, Mrs Osborne."

"Indeed you might. I fear there won't be a room to be had –

and Louisa looks quite done in, poor child."

"Oh, no, ma'am." Louisa was indignant. "I'm not in the least tired – only a little bit thirsty."

Mrs Osborne smiled kindly. "I believe somewhere might be found – at least until the railway line is mended and you can take the train to Cape Town...I presume that's where you were intended?"

"Yes," replied Gus with a sigh, facing this uncertain contingency with something like despair, and stroking the damp curls of bright hair back from his daughter's drooping but determined little face. "Where is it you are suggesting, ma'am?"

Her direct glance summed him up. "My own house has been given up to a family who are refugees from outside the town, otherwise you could have stayed there. But I believe they'll welcome you at the convent."

The convent building had already been earmarked by the military, ready to be turned into a field hospital, but at present its beds stood empty, ready and waiting for emergencies.

"A friend of Mrs Osborne's – and a doctor, too?" repeated the sister in charge of nursing, Sister Mary Evangelist, regarding Gus with a considering gleam in her eye. "Well, we have as yet, thanks be to God, no patients here. We are to share the accommodation and care of any casualties with the municipal hospital, for it's short they are with half their nursing staff fled south to join up with those ladies from England." A lifetime's discipline forbade her to elaborate on this last, but had she not been a nun, she would undoubtedly have sniffed. A buxom woman of Irish peasant stock who had been trained under Miss Nightingale at Scutari and observed scrupulous cleanliness and severity in looking after her patients, she regarded nursing as the highest form of service to God. It was clear she considered those nurses who had left as deserters, and the wealthy women she'd spoken of, those self-appointed ministering angels, who had arrived in South Africa (each with her own lady's maid) with the vowed intention of nursing the wounded, as naïve do-gooders. "A doctor, eh? Well, I dare say we might find you and your daughter a corner somewhere."

Her face softened as she took Louisa's hand. Within half an

hour, the child had been given something to eat and put to sleep in a cool, white bed, in a tiny room with a breeze blowing through the open window as night fell. Gus stood looking down at his sleeping daughter, wondering hopelessly how they were going to get out of this situation, before tip-toeing out to find Mrs Osborne and tell her that the question of accommodation had been settled. Giving his medical services was a small price for the nuns' goodness and one which he would be more than willing to pay, since it was looking more and more as though he and Louisa might be here in Mafeking for some time.

The nuns were obviously very fond of Hannah Osborne, who seemed to occupy a favoured position here in the convent. She was a small woman, with a quick way to her and rather clever dark eyes. A thoughtful woman, and somewhat sharp in her opinions, as he found when they talked over a simple meal provided for him by the nuns.

"What of your husband, Mrs Osborne? He's one of the militia, I recall."

"In the new commander's Protectorate Regiment now. He's so occupied, I scarcely see him. He tells me Mafeking is considered an obstacle in the way of enemy movements towards Bechuanaland and Rhodesia, and the Dutch, as you'll have gathered, are at the border and their General Kronje is bringing in heavy artillery to take the town. I'm afraid we shall be surrounded, Dr Fox."

"Help will soon arrive to rout them," said Gus, fervently hoping this must be so.

"Let us pray that it does. General Kronje is said to be one of Kruger's best generals. But let him do his worst. We, after all, have Colonel Baden-Powell."

He glanced at her and surprised a look of irony in her eyes. The name of the energetic commander seemed to be on everyone's lips and few were critical – his organisation was apparently outstanding, and even more so was his ability to jolly along the spirits of those crammed like herrings into an inadequate barrel.

"Look at it this way, Mrs Osborne. If the enemy does succeed in surrounding Mafeking, at least you'll have no more refugees like us able to get in. Which I'm sure will be a relief to all."

"We can scarcely close our doors. But at least two thousand blacks from other tribes have already poured in to camp along-side the Baralongs' kraal, and there may well be trouble among them. The various tribes don't always co-exist peacefully, you know."

"Will they not forget their differences and band together to defeat the common enemy?"

"Perhaps. More worrying is how are they all to be fed." She explained that the Barolong had their own cattle and crops, but as for the rest, they were nomadic tribes – and how would it be possible to get through the enemy lines to hunt and forage for food on the veld as they were accustomed to do? And when the rains came and the new grass grew outside the fortifications, how would any of them be able to drive their cattle out to graze on it? Above all was the vexed question as to whether to arm the natives or not. B-P, and indeed most of the military commanders – on both sides – were against it. This would be a different war altogether to any so far fought on South African soil – a white man's war, for neither side wished to invoke the assistance of the blacks, since that would mean arming them, and their huge num-bers were potentially dangerous, their allegiances questionable. Once armed, who knew that they might not turn against the men who had taken control of their land? Even the Baralong tribe were not averse to conflict; they had had longstanding grievances with the Boers, who had twice before overcome them.

She repeated what their old chief Lesoto had said: "They took our land and said it was theirs." He had added that he would very much like to meet the Boer who had once made his wife crawl towards him on hands and knees and then kicked her in the face.

AUGUST

I have read, as most people in the civilised world have now read, accounts of the siege of Mafeking, which subsequently became universally famed. Lest anyone be inclined to make light of the sufferings incurred by those beleaguered in the town, let me say here and now that this wasn't entirely due to the number of casualties (though a third of the total number of soldiers and civilians confined there was lost or cruelly injured by the time the siege ended, which was terrible enough) but perhaps even more by the constant fear and strain of being under almost incessant and random fire. No one who hasn't experienced this can begin to imagine what it can be like, day in, day out, never knowing when the next shell might come, or where it might land. As all the world is now aware, it was a time of hardship and privation and exceptional bravery, of incredibly stoical endurance, but it was that continual shelling and its awful consequences – the grief for the dead and wounded – which made the siege hardest to bear. By the end, every man, woman and child in Mafeking was indescribably weary, and for many of them their lives were ruined or their nerves in shreds. That we were desperately hungry goes without saying, though we whites were not quite on the brink of starvation: this was entirely due to men like Lyall and Frank Whiteley, by then the town's elected mayor, who were farsighted enough to foresee the possibility of our being cut off and had worked so unstintingly beforehand to lay in provisions. Even they could not have envisaged how desperately we should need them.

But my own, and Lyddie's, story is not entirely that of the tribulations endured during the siege – or only in so far as they affected us personally. I believe I may be forgiven if I feel that the shattering personal events which happened to us at that time began to seem of more importance than the capitulation or otherwise of the town to enemy forces. We are all, in the end, prisoners of circumstance, and victims of our own natures.

Chapter Twenty

It was all very well to say we could defeat the enemy with resource and ingenuity, but neither was any match for the lack of adequate means to defend ourselves. "Short of men, short of rifles, short of ammunition. When one looks at our armoury, it's pitiful – obsolete and pitiful." Hugh was indignant that no response to B-P's repeated requests for proper ordnance had yet been forthcoming, and he was afraid that, against the powerful long-range weapons the Dutch were known to possess, ours would prove sadly inadequate. All we had were obsolete single-loaders, in all no more than seven Maxim machine guns, a few ancient carbines of limited range and nowhere near enough Lee Enfield rifles to equip every man. Defending the town with such would be like facing an elephant herd with a catapult. "And as if that weren't enough, the gun carriages are in a shocking state, the fittings worn – and the fuses so old they've shrunk. There's nothing for it but to wedge them into the blessed shells with paper."

Hugh was now with the Protectorate Regiment, an elite corps formed mainly from the reinforcements the colonel had brought with him, led by the flower of the British aristocracy, with names like Cecil, Cavendish, Fitzclarence and the like. I saw even less of my husband than when he had been up north, patrolling the border. Occasionally, he would come home for a quick bath and a change of clothing, but as soon as he'd eaten the meal I'd so carefully cooked, he was off again, scarcely noticing what he'd eaten. His whole attention was focused on the job in hand, with no time or room for anything else. I knew well enough by now that this was the nature of the man I had married; I scarcely expected him to take time off simply to be with me, but my guilt at what seemed like my own disloyalty in hoping for this occasionally grew to be a presence that lived and breathed in the room beside us when we were together. I knew my decision to move in with Lyddie, giving my own house over to refugees, would not make any difference to him.

A few months previously, I had come across her looking over

the sad little layette Mrs Crowther had put together, and which I had brought with me when I came out. She was turning over the tiny hand-stitched garments, the knitted jackets and bootees, the linen caps, folding the lacy, crotcheted shawl and the long, beautifully embroidered gown in which all the Crowthers, including Lyddie herself, had been christened.

"Oh, Lyddie." How I wished she wouldn't torture herself like this – with what she must accept by now could never be.

She said nothing, but she looked across at me with a blinding smile, her eyes shining.

Again!

But this time, it was going to be all right. She knew it was. She felt so well, not even a trace of morning sickness. And indeed, she looked radiant. Her skin glowed as it used to in the damp British air, her hair took on its old shine and bounce, and the sunny optimism of her nature was once more to the fore. She could scarcely wait until January, when the baby would be born, and asserted confidently that the fighting would all be over by then, as if her present happy state endowed her with divine knowledge. She was, of course, advised to rest as much as possible. "I'm sure I shall become so fat and awkward, I shall feel disinclined to move much in any case," she assured Lyall comfortably, but even when the days became warmer and the baby grew inside her, she seemed to find it impossible to keep still. "But I promise I won't ride."

"I should hope not – but I would feel happier if you'd go somewhere safe – or better still, go back home."

But Lyddie was adamant that since Mafeking was where Lyall was, Mafeking was where she would stay. She was not being very wise, perhaps, but when has common sense ever had anything to do with love?

The war actually arrived quite literally for us with a bang – or series of bangs. We were awakened the very morning after Dr Fox and his daughter had been installed in the convent by what could only be the noise of gunfire echoing across the plain. The boy Amos ran in gabbling excitedly that the Boers had crossed the border and were approaching Mafeking, setting fire to every farm or native kraal they came across on the way: the gunfire we had heard was from our own troops firing on the enemy from an armoured train which was patrolling the line as far as it could get in both directions. That we were showing such spirit in fighting back was cheering news. Everyone assured everyone else that the Dutch would never take the town. For the moment, we might be effectively cut off from communications with the outside world, but never mind, pigeons had been sent off to Kimberley to inform them of our plight. In any case, help and support was expected any day. Colonel Plumer was patrolling the Limpopo with the Rhodesian Regiment and would soon march south with a flying column to meet reinforcements coming north.

I was working most of the time at the convent – running errands for the nuns, advising the girls to pray for victory, helping wherever they had need of help. There were no war casualties as yet, only the usual stream of patients with anything from minor accidents and illnesses, to fevers. The idea of myself self-lessly nursing the sick and wounded had very much appealed to me. I wasn't qualified, but I could soon learn. Mother Superior brought me up short by gently reminding me of St Theresa of Avila's words: *'We don't need any more saints here, but rather plenty of strong arms for scrubbing'*. She added that perhaps I'd be better employed in using any spare time helping Lyddie and a group of other women to roll bandages and stitch cartridge belts which were, like everything else, in short supply. Chastened, I swallowed my disappointment and did as I was bid.

"Can you ride a bicycle, Louisa?" I asked, finding the little girl all ready and waiting for me when I arrived at the convent the morning after she and her father had arrived, having promised to take her with me when I went down to the Chinese market garden to arrange for vegetables to be sent to the convent. These were to supplement the food we had been allotted for the many more mouths we now had to feed: women and children, crowded together in the tented laager, or camp, which the mayor had created to give them a measure of safety. Wagons had been drawn up as shelter and bombproof trenches erected around the tents. Swelling their numbers were those bitterly disappointed families who had been turned back when actually on their way to safety.

Louisa looked surprised that I needed to ask such a question.

"Oh yes, I can ride."

"Then we'll ask if you may borrow Sister Mary Columba's." This was a ramshackle old machine, and manifestly too big for such a small girl, but I was soon made aware that a trifle like that wouldn't defeat her, after a wobbly demonstration which seemed to satisfy the nuns. I could see they were very much taken with Louisa, even smiling indulgently at the breeches and cotton bush shirt she swore she'd been allowed to wear all the time at Orchard Farm. The poor child, when she arrived, had been stuffed like a sausage into a too tight frock that was in any case too warm for the day, and she was obviously more comfortable now. With her hair bundled up under a slouch hat, she could have been one of the boys of her own age who had been recruited as scouts to relay messages – and indeed, as we rode through the town, with the sporadic gunfire from the armoured train still continuing in the background, she watched them enviously as they pelted all over the place, hot, sweating and full of importance, furiously pedalling their bicycles between one command post and another.

"I'm going to ask if I can do that," she announced as we rode up through the shady avenue of peach trees that led up to the fields of vegetables cultivated by the pigtailed Chinese who owned the market garden. It was enclosed by a little orchard and kept watered by a conduit from the Malopo; a cool splash of water came from a little fountain in an enclosed courtyard they had built, where they gave us green tea to drink while negotiations went ahead for the extra supplies of potatoes and onions needed for the influx of people into the laager. The little yellow men drove a hard bargain while insisting that they were giving me a good price because it was on behalf of the nuns, but they gave Louisa a couple of luscious peaches to take away with her.

We had just set off back when we heard a sudden sharp burst of shelling, much nearer than that which had been going on intermittently all morning. It was so sudden and unexpected that for a moment we didn't realise that the noise of it had come from somewhere in the direction of the women's laager.

The convent, the Victoria hospital, and the women's laager, too, had indeed been hit, yet by a miracle no one was hurt. "Well, doesn't that just show!" exclaimed Sister Mary Columba. "If God hadn't wanted us to survive, He wouldn't have given us the brains to invent mud brick." It was the first indication we had that the construction of Mafeking's buildings would be a positive asset for which we should learn to be extremely grateful: when a shell hit a building, as it had hit the convent, as often as not it passed clean through the mud bricks and out at the other side.

Perhaps because we were in reality very afraid, everyone tried to appear nonchalant, those first days. We made fun of the damage that was done, and great play was made on the cowardice of the enemy for shelling the hospital and directing their fire on women and children. Mr Whale, the editor of our local newspaper, who was possessed of a sardonic wit and refused to be intimidated by mere Dutchmen, posted a casualty list outside his office: 'Killed, one hen; wounded, one yellow dog; smashed, one hotel window.'

But we were less inclined to laugh when the next day the Dutch seized the waterworks on the edge of the town and cut off the water supply. This could have spelt disaster and certain capitulation, had we not had many practical engineers in the town. Within hours, work had begun on drilling for water to supplement the tanks already in the town. The railway engineers trundled out machines for drilling and a great sigh of relief went up when, after the first well-shaft was sunk, only fifty feet below the hard, unforgiving rock upon which Mafeking stood, sweet, fresh water came gushing up. A second and a third had the same results. Whatever other privations we were likely to suffer, a shortage of water was unlikely to be one of them.

Scrubbing floors and stitching the stiff canvas for the cartridge belts, our fingers were soon very sore and raw. For once, I sympathised with Caroline Douglas when she moaned that she could no longer hold a needle. She was one of those women who had been on the train which had been turned back, and since the married quarters she and Thomas had occupied had now been taken by someone else, and the idea of sleeping in a tent in the women's laager brought on an attack of hysterics, the sisters had eventually found a tiny room in the convent where she could stay.

The more I saw of Caroline, the more I sympathised with her husband. Rather than being grateful to the nuns for their hospitality, she complained continually: she was not well, she couldn't eat the mealie porridge and the sausages at breakfast because the thought of it made her sick; she had blisters on her hands from stitching the cartridge belts; could she please have another blanket on her bed, for the nights were very cold?

"Dear Caroline, you'd better get used to the mealie porridge – and the horsemeat sausages – like the rest of us, or starve," Lyddie told her drily.

"Horsemeat? Oh, I never could!"

"You could, if you were hungry enough," I said, less kindly. "Try offering it up, like the nuns do."

We had already begun to eat a certain amount of horsemeat in lieu of beef and mutton. Grass was a commodity always in short supply in these parts and by now most of that within the enclosure had been nibbled down by the few cattle which had been allowed to be brought in; they would soon grow thin and become dry if they couldn't be driven out to seek sweet grass elsewhere. Horses, on the other hand, who also needed grass, we had more than a sufficiency of. Eating them killed two birds with one stone, though of course the very idea of eating horses was anathema to any Britisher. But those who were shot first tended to be sinewy old nags who'd had their day.

No wonder Thomas Douglas was always so unsmiling, I thought, listening to Caroline's complaints. The gossip about his wife and Roger Marriott had grown to such an extent that he must have been blind and deaf not to know of it – and I doubted whether he was the sort of man who would – or could – ignore such conduct in his wife. Perhaps that was why he had been glad of the excuse to pack her off to the Cape – and how mortified he must have been to see her back. I knew, from the languishing way she spoke of Marriott, that the affair was by no means over.

It was getting on for Christmas – and still relief didn't arrive. Intelligence reports circulated like wildfire; every day we had news of troops on their way but they never somehow got as far as Mafeking.

"Hugh, what are the Boers thinking of? They could surely have taken us by now. There are so many of them to our few that if they stormed us we'd surely have no chance."

"For the same reason that B-P isn't rushing out to attack them. They're obeying orders to avoid loss of their own men," replied Hugh, hollow-eyed from lack of sleep, unshaven since the beginning of the siege.

I put my arms around him and kissed him, and saw a flame leap in his eyes. Then he put me gently aside. "Not now, Hannah. The men are expecting me back."

An unspoken feeling was growing that we might perhaps not be able to last out as long as we had been told. We were being continually shelled now, a nerve-racking bombardment that made the nights as disturbed as the day. The Boers had a massive range of artillery with which they intended to make short work of our resistance; their general, Cronje, fearless and one of their most able commanders, evidently expecting to pulverise us into submission, was boasting he would wipe out every man, woman, child and beast in Mafeking. I began to believe this might not turn out to be an idle boast, or that we should be so worn down and short of sleep we should find capitulation the better option. Some hoped the Boers would get fed up and go away, but this unlikely prospect was one no one took seriously, especially after the arrival of an even bigger, long-range gun, a massive ninety-six pounder, so heavy it had to be pulled by sixteen oxen. It was positioned more than seven miles away, yet its range was such that the enormously heavy missiles had no difficulty in reaching the town. They made a terrible noise as they flew over our heads and burst, throwing great hot pieces of heavy metal for hundred of yards. A warning bell was rung in the town square when it was seen from the look-out tower to be loaded. If we were lucky, by the time the shell landed we had been able to take cover under upturned wagons or dugouts. But not everyone escaped. The injuries and mutilations inflicted by this big gun were horrific beyond words – arms and legs were regularly blown off and thrown into trees, on to roofs or far distant streets; it wasn't uncommon for insides and blood to be splattered everywhere. We became accustomed to treating children at the hospital for burns when they vied with each other, in spite of warnings, to find the biggest piece of shrapnel, and picked up pieces of still-hot metal as souvenirs.

The Boers didn't have it all their own way, though: daring raids on the enemy, sometimes with fixed bayonets, were ordered by B-P to clear out their advance positions. In one of these Roger Marriott was killed.

As retaliation, the nights were made hideous with smoke and flame as great shells came thundering through the dark, causing the doors and windows to rattle as they flew past. During the day, we learned to keep out of the streets as much as possible – or to run like billyo for shelter when a burst of machine gun fire rushed past our ears, sounding like the clattering wings of a plague of locusts. The silence when ambulances drove by and carts came past covered by blankets quickly became a fact of life.

The only respite we had was on Sundays, the day B-P decreed should be set aside for entertainments such as cricket matches, concerts, sales of work and competitions, as a morale-building antidote to the strain we all lived under, being the only day we were not troubled by the Boers. It was against their religion to kill on the Sabbath.

I watched Hugh's face grow older and thinner, the crease between his brows become permanent. We hadn't shared a bed since the siege began; when he could get home for a good night's rest, I slept on the sofa, so as not to disturb him by the restless sleep that had become habitual with me, though I doubt whether anything would have wakened him: as soon as his head touched the pillow, he slept as if pole-axed. I wished he would take a leaf from his admired commander's book: no one could accuse Baden-Powell of not being wholly absorbed in the struggle we were involved in, but at the same time, he understood the necessity of at least a pretence at living life normally, and the importance of keeping up morale. *Nil desperandum* was his repeatedly encouraging watchword. We shall beat Johnny Boer yet. Never let it be said that we Britishers didn't keep the flag flying. *Nil desperandum*.

Caroline Douglas took the news of Roger Marriott's death so badly it made me feel I'd maybe been too hard on her, in belittling their affair as simply a passing infatuation, or the determination of a spoiled young woman not to be thwarted in what she desired. We all mourned the loss of a gallant officer – for Roger had been brave, no doubt of that – but Caroline was inconsolable. "I wish it had been me," she said, time after time. "Perhaps it will be, soon," she would add, as another shell whizzed by. I was sorry for her, but to tell the truth, I couldn't help feeling she was enjoying the drama and, by the time several weeks had elapsed and she was showing no signs of even trying to overcome her grief, and had several times expressed the wish to follow Marriott to the grave, I was not the only one who lost patience with her.

"These bandages need to be rolled," Sister Evangelist told her crisply, handing her a pile of sheets torn into strips, "and they've been disinfected, so try not to weep all over them, my dear."

But Lyddie said generously, out of her own happiness, "Poor Caroline. We must all look after her."

Lyall had persuaded Mother Superior to let Lyddie stay in the convent for the last few weeks before her confinement, now that Dr Fox was in permanent residence there and would be on hand to keep an eye on her. Both he and Dr Smythe were cautiously optimistic, as the birth drew nearer, and there were no signs of her losing the child.

All hands were needed now to help with the nursing, and I was at last allowed to help as I wished in caring not only for the wounded, but the increasing numbers of sick children and others who were brought in suffering from malnutrition, dysentery and other problems associated with poor and inadequate food. Inevitably, this applied mostly to the children in the location. The tribes were not able to hunt for their usual food, the Dutch were shooting and stealing their cattle, mealie-meal was scarce and they did not have the money to buy other food, which had become far too expensive.

The boys acting as very useful message-carriers between one defence post and another undeniably had one of the most dangerous tasks, dodging bullets and flying shrapnel in the thick of an attack, but children were learning to grow up fast in Mafeking, and every person was needed to play their part, even

Louisa, who took food to her brothers in the trenches. The Cadets were formed into a well disciplined band, drilled and given a uniform like a junior army, and one of their number held the rank of sergeant. Louisa watched them, green with envy, and her father, seeing this, allowed her to help him. Soon she was never far from his side when he attended to the sick. Despite the horrific nature of the injuries inflicted by the shelling, she didn't faint at the sight of blood, or when she passed the dressings for an amputated limb, nor did she gag at the stench of a gangrened wound. She heard the screams of the wounded as they tore off their agonising bandages, and didn't flinch at the sight of mangled flesh. There were many who expressed the view that it was shocking for such a young girl to be allowed to witness such sights, but the patients loved her and Dr Fox calmly allowed her to continue. I, for one, believed he was right. Like many of the other children, Louisa had grown up overnight.

Chapter Twenty-One

No one could have failed to be aware of the rain that came down all that day just before Christmas, blotting out the light and making it difficult to hear what anyone was saying, but the mother of the sick little girl from the location, the nuns and I were too busy to pay it much attention at first. Emang was only one of several native children who had been brought in to the convent hospital with fever and dysentery. Several of them were very ill indeed, but she was the sickest of all. Sister Mary Columba and I took it in turns to sponge down the child's hot little body, while Mrs Mahelebe squatted by the end of her daughter's bed in dumb misery.

We had been thankful of the rain at first: at least it would cool the air and perhaps help us to get the fretful children's temperatures down a little. We went on doing what was necessary as the storm crashed over our heads, but we began to exchange worried glances as the rain grew into an absolute deluge and then came down in a positive cataract. An unheard-of panic seemed to be gripping the normally hushed and disciplined convent. Outside the wards, orderlies ran about like scalded cats, and as the afternoon wore on, brought news to us of the havoc wreaked by the storm: the hospital kitchen was under six feet of water; the dinner was spoiled; and the sisters' bombproof had been washed away, while the covered trenches in the women's laager were now nothing less than a subterranean canal.

"Carry on," ordered Sister Mary Evangelist calmly.

And so we did, and after a while, the rain abruptly ceased. Little Emang stopped thrashing about in her delirium and became very quiet. Sister Mary Columba held her hand until, a few minutes later, in the hush that at last succeeded the cloudburst, the child breathed her last. The sister laid Emang's hands across her breast, crossed herself and bowed her head. Then she spoke softly to the mother in her own language and the woman's keening began, soon taken up by the family who had been crouched outside on the veranda, waiting.

I left the ward, and walked round to the other side of the

building, where I stood in the unusual quietness, staring out into the still-dark afternoon. The deluge had at least brought a respite from the shelling, the Dutch presumably having their own disasters to look to, but the storm damage, and the steam now rising from the earth, had added an unreal dimension to the desolation already caused by the shelling of the compound. Tree branches scattered the ground; the tin roof of a little outhouse blown off by a shell, which had lain on the ground for days, now floated on its own little lake on the red mud that was now the path to the women's laager. A telegraph pole which had been hit lay on the ground like a wounded warrior.

Devastation and despair seemed to lie over everything. I felt overwhelmed by sadness. I suppose little Emang could have died at any time of such a fever, but she might have had a more sporting chance had she been better fed and well-nourished to begin with. How long could we go on like this?

"Mrs Osborne?"

Louisa was tapping my arm. "I can't find Mrs Armitage anywhere."

"Perhaps she's with Mrs Douglas."

"I can't find either of them. Nobody seems to have seen them for ages."

I looked round for the little Kaffir who ran errands for the nuns, and asked him if he'd seen either Lyddie or Caroline. He gave his wide smile and said, "They go see, missis." He pointed in the direction of the river.

I felt a sudden, inexplicable panic. I knew that as soon as the rain ceased people had flocked down to the river bank to marvel and see what the storm had done, as people will – but what on earth had possessed Lyddie to do likewise? She was so careful of her unborn baby that for the last few weeks she hadn't ventured out of the convent grounds, where she could easily dive for cover when the shelling started. With all that rain, the roads and paths would be traps for the unwary, and besides, the Dutch might take advantage of the confusion to start firing again at any time. My faith in Caroline as a protector was not great.

Louisa said in a frightened voice, "It's awful down by the river. The foot-drift's impassable and they say the stadt's flooded out."

For a moment, I stood paralysed, then flew for my bicycle. I grabbed it and began to pedal for all I was worth, followed by Louisa on the nuns' old boneshaker.

Darkness would arrive within an hour. But the boy hadn't said how long they'd been gone, so perhaps they were even now on their way back. All the same, I pedalled furiously and headed towards the river bank. Louisa valiantly kept up, and as we bumped through the streets without meeting them coming the other way, my worry and a premonition that something terrible had happened grew with every turn of the wheels. By this time, it had become apparent that the bicycles were worse than useless. With one accord, we dismounted and let them fall where they would, though it wasn't much better on foot.

The light was fading quickly, and as we neared the river, it seemed that the onlookers had abandoned their gaping. I heard the screams before I saw them, somewhere over by the Chinese garden. I lifted my skirts and ran as well as I could. Louisa, younger and unhampered by skirts, outstripped me, but not by much. I could hardly speak by the time we were near enough to see what looked like a struggle taking place on the river bank, two shapes outlined against the line of poplars on the far side, before they disappeared. When we reached the bank, they were nowhere to be seen.

It wasn't unusual for the river to flood during the rainy season, but today flash floods had swept the Malopo through its creek with a violence rarely seen before. The wide, slow-flowing river had become a rushing torrent of muddy, coffee-coloured water, simply tearing along, bringing with it chicken coops, dead fowls, cooking utensils, the carcase of a heifer, bathtubs.

At this point, the soft red earth of the steep, unevenly sloping bank was a mud slide about ten or twelve feet above the river. I couldn't see either of them, then I discerned one figure lying in a huddle on a sort of ledge or shelf a mere foot or two below the overhanging lip of the bank. Lyddie, thank God! She was making no sound and at first I thought she had lost consciousness, but then I saw her arm lift. I wanted to shout 'Don't move!' but dare not. The churned-up river racing below was a dangerous torrent. A corrugated iron roof was swept past as though it were a leaf and I knew if she fell in, she would be carried away just as surely as Caroline must have been…for I could see nothing of her.

Louisa seemed to know just what to do, and she and I together knelt and grabbed, first a handful of the shawl Lyddie had pinned around her shoulders, and then her arms. God knows how, but we managed to haul her up to safety. But then, just as we laid her on the grass and I was relieved of her weight, my feet slipped from under me. Unable to save myself, I tumbled helplessly down the bank and into the water. Had I not gone in feet first I should have followed Caroline. Even so, I was in up to my neck, right in the deep water of a *sluit*, one that led into the market garden, but hidden under the rushing water. Gasping for breath, bracing myself not to be knocked over by the tide of muddy water swirling around me, feeling the ugly suck and pull of it against my body, I suddenly saw strong hands were being extended towards me. Feeling as though my arms were being dragged from their sockets, I was eventually deposited on the grass beside Lyddie.

I wondered where they had all come from, what had brought them all there: the two Chinamen, several women from nearby houses and a few children. Then I remembered the screams. It seemed like hours since I'd heard them, but it could only have been minutes. "Lyddie?" I struggled to kneel over her where she was still lying on the ground, trying not to deluge her with water. "Are you all right?" I asked stupidly.

Her voice was the faintest whisper. "I shall be, directly. I only slipped."

One of the rescuers was a sensible woman with four children of her own whom I knew a little, and she took one glance at Lyddie and saw she must be attended to. "Mr Rowlands has a little cart. Best get him to take her home – I'll send one of my boys for the doctor."

"She's staying at the convent. There's a doctor there."

She nodded. "But you'll need attention too, otherwise you'll get pneumonia."

"Caroline —?" I began.

But Caroline had gone.

* * *

The sisters had Lyddie into bed within minutes. I was shivering in my wet clothes and they gave me some dry ones of a sort. My hair was in rat's tails but I was too exhausted to do anything but rub it roughly dry while Dr Fox examined Lyddie and advised that sleep would be the best medicine. There was no sign of the baby coming prematurely, so perhaps nothing more would come of this sorry adventure. Sister Mary Evangelist gave her some hot milk and I stayed with her and held her hand while she told me drowsily what had happened. Apparently Caroline had insisted that she would never sleep that night if she didn't get some fresh air; it had stopped raining and she said she was going to take a walk towards the swollen river and see if all they'd heard about the flood was true. Like me, Lyddie had never really believed she would carry out those histrionic threats of hers to follow her lover to the grave. Unlike me, she'd good-naturedly agreed to keep an eye on her, and decided she'd better agree to go with her.

"She was in such a strange mood, Hannah, I couldn't let her go alone. But I never thought that she meant —"

"She didn't, I'm sure...don't think of it. Try and sleep."

But she needed to talk before she could sleep. They had reached the river, she went on, and were peering down into the rushing water from the bank when Caroline began to talk wildly of how easy it would be, just to jump in and let herself be carried away. Lyddie had held on to her, desperately trying to talk her out of it, to pull her back, screaming for help, until somehow they both fell. "She wouldn't have done it, Hannah, when it came to it, I know she wouldn't. She was only trying to steady herself by holding on to me, and we both slipped. Such a silly accident."

Silly – and needless. Had Caroline ever meant to take her own life, or had it only been a gesture, a means of attracting attention? I had over the last few weeks become very tired of Caroline and the unnecessary drama she was making out of her situation. I felt ashamed of myself now. I should have had more sympathy, more compassion.

All the same, I could not imagine why Lyddie had agreed to that ridiculous request, especially knowing Caroline's state of mind, though she was not entirely rational either, these days. If this was what having a baby did to you, perhaps I was fortunate not to be having one.

Presently she fell quiet and her lids began to droop. "Don't worry about me, Hannah – or the baby," she whispered. "He has a charmed life." She fell asleep with a smile on her lips.

There was nothing I could do by staying at her bedside but I was not easily persuaded to leave her. I gave in only when Lyall arrived to take my place to sit grey and stone-faced by her side.

"I'll come back and see her tomorrow morning, first thing."

"God help you, Hannah dear," said Sister Mary Evangelist oddly.

I went to see Louisa before I went home. She had fallen into the deep, easy sleep of youth. I kissed her forehead, my gallant little friend, and she never even stirred. Our bicycles were still down by the market garden, but it didn't matter. I doubted whether I could have kept my balance, for my legs had been trembling uncontrollably ever since we had pulled Lyddie back from the brink of that fearful river. I walked homewards with dragging steps through the oddly silent streets, my footsteps echoing. The guns were still silent and the air smelt sweet. As I walked, my face was brushed by moths and night breezes.

With a part of my mind that was not still seeing those struggling figures on the bank, or feeling that filthy, rushing, sucking water around me, I noticed in a detached way how much damage the storm had done to the town which had already been looking very shabby and knocked about, its windows cracked and patched up with cardboard, tin roofs askew or missing altogether, piles of debris wherever a big shell had scored a direct hit. The lookout tower on top of Riesle's stood black against the sky, and through a line of poplars I saw the little red fort on the top of the kopje and I wondered if I should find Hugh at Lyddie's house when I arrived, for once snatching time off from military matters, as other men seemed able to do from time to time. I was not really surprised when I did not find him there. We were becoming virtual strangers.

The truth was, I had fallen out of love with my husband (or thought I had, which came to much the same thing). I had slowly come to realise that we had never, perhaps, spent enough time together to enable us to get to know each other. I saw now how different we were in our natures, how little we had in common, with few shared interests. He was a good man, none better, but the spark had gone from our marriage. There were black holes in our relationship, which we could only fill with superficialities. Wider issues were never discussed. But I tried not to think of it. These were black thoughts at the end of a black day.

Then as I walked up the short path to the house, I was halted in my tracks by – *music*. Not gramophone music, but a piece I didn't recognise, played on Lyddie's second-hand piano. A liquid outpouring of notes, as unlike her cheerful, energetic strumming of the popular songs of the day as anything could be. I was reminded of my first day in Mafeking, with Nellie Melba's glorious voice singing over the desert air. In its way this was even stranger. No one I knew played like this.

A stranger was sitting at the keyboard, his fingers moving effortlessly, caressingly, over the notes. Sitting in the circle of lamplight, he played with absorbed concentration, his eyes closed. I stood in the shadows, listening, and it was only the squeak of my boots as I shifted from one foot to another that broke his concentration. He stopped playing and stood up. "I say, I do beg your pardon. I must apologise for appropriating your piano – it's so long since I played, I couldn't resist…"

"Please don't apologise, it was exquisite. That piano's never been played like that before."

He laughed. "Oh, but you should hear my mother play Chopin, Mrs Armitage."

"I'm sorry…I'm not Mrs Armitage. Hannah Osborne."

"Oh, Lord. It's I who should be sorry, bursting like this and not introducing myself. I'm Harry Chetwynd." He smiled and held out his hand and I gave him mine. I saw him looking at my other hand, at my wedding ring.

He was a young man of medium height, with a thin, dark face, extremely good-looking, with winged eyebrows and a mouth that seemed used to smiling. I would have given anything if he hadn't been there at that particular moment. I wanted no one, least of all a stranger with whom I should have to make conversation.

He was looking at my hair, at my damp boots: they hadn't been able to find any others to fit me at the convent. "Mrs

Osborne, shouldn't you sit down? You look pretty well done up, if you'll forgive my saying so."

"I've just fallen in the sluit."

"The what?"

"Sluice, you would call it. By the river." I *was* done up, exhausted to my very bones, and not up to explaining further, and though I could sense his curiosity, he was too polite to ask for any. He was looking less than up to the mark himself. His bush jacket had evidently received a thorough soaking and dried on him, his boots seemed as wet as mine. He looked as drained and exhausted as I felt.

"You must be wondering what I'm doing here." He told me then that he was a war correspondent, of whom we already had several in the town. "I have an assignment to write something about the way you brave people are surviving in Mafeking. Mr Whale, editor of your local paper sent me to seek out Mr Armitage. The boy let me in, saying Missis would be back presently."

"You're very brave, coming into Mafeking. Everyone else wants to get out."

He laughed. "I dare say I can get out the same way I came in, if I want to." Which had been by way of the old post road from Vryburg, and through the enemy lines with the help of one of the native runners, and so through to the location and thence the town.

"Are you hungry?"

"I had some dried biltong last night. Wasn't bad, if you've the teeth of a tiger."

"You haven't tried our horsemeat sausages," I said, with a tired attempt to respond to his joke, mentally taking stock of what food there was. Amos might stretch the bully beef into something passable. He looked cheered by the prospect of something to eat, but then he said, unexpectedly, "Please – sit down and never mind the food. You've obviously had a bad day of it."

"A bad day? I – I think it's been the worst day of my whole life," I said shakily, having no intimation then that there was worse, much worse, to come.

He then did something quite extraordinary. He reached out a finger and gently pushed back from my face a lock of hair that had escaped the untidy knot into which I'd bundled it, an extraordinary liberty which in other circumstances would neither have been taken nor allowed. Why there was such intimacy between us, right from the start, was a mystery to me. We stood looking at one another – and as kindness will, his quite overwhelmed me. I couldn't help it, tears I hadn't shed all day filled my eyes. And it seemed quite natural that I should let this stranger, whom I had not known above five minutes, put his arms around me and press my head into his shoulder.

Afterwards, we were both embarrassed, and slightly shamefaced. I sat on the sofa and dried my eyes. "What about that food? I must tell Amos." I couldn't remember having eaten a thing all day myself, except for a barely palatable bowl of mealie porridge at lunch.

"Let me tell him —" he began, standing up, wincing as he did so. "It's all right, don't worry. Just twisted my knee getting in. Mistake to rest it. Should have kept it moving. I – I believe it's —" So saying, he turned deathly pale and grabbed on to the nearest thing, which happened to be the shawl covering the piano, and fell to the floor in a faint, still clutching the shawl, bringing down with him in a clatter the photos from the piano top.

His swoon was only momentary, though his colour was still bad, and as I knelt on the floor beside him, I saw that his knee was indeed swollen like a balloon over the top of his high laced boots. There was nothing I could do except help him up off the floor on to the sofa and give him some of Lyall's hoarded brandy before I roused Amos and sent him running for the doctor.

I was past tiredness now. It was all part of this terrible, terrible day.

When I reached the convent next morning, I went straight to Lyddie's room. She was lying on her back in the bed and the mound of her stomach was flat. Sister Mary Evangelist came in behind me and told me that the baby, a little boy, had been stillborn. Lyddie did not open her eyes, scarcely breathing as I stood by her bedside. I looked at her still, white face, and took her hand in mine. I did not need the nun to tell me she would not live.

* * *

And so it was, through the fortunes of war, that the Fox's and Harry Chetwynd, from a remote part of the English countryside, were brought together in this dusty little town on the South African veld.

"Bless my soul – Harry Chetwynd!"

"Dr Fox, by all that's wonderful!"

They came from the same village in Shropshire. They were near neighbours and friends of long standing. Even more amazing, Robert and Barty were here in Mafeking, too.

"So you left the regiment, then, young Harry?" asked Dr Fox.

"Yes, sir, twelve months ago. Didn't suit me, after all."

"Never thought it would, my boy."

"No, sir."

"Nothing wrong with what you're doing, telling the world what's happening to us here," said Dr Fox, "as long as you don't go knocking yourself up like this all the time – though there's nothing much wrong with the knee, either, that a bit of rest won't cure." He strapped up the joint and left it at that. Not so with Louisa, who came to see Harry first thing next day and exchanged hugs with him and so overwhelmed him with questions he held up his hand in defence. She wanted especially to know everything about their families – his brother Sebastian, still at school, and her elder sister and the baby left behind. Which was how I came to know what had brought father and daughter to Africa.

There was no privacy in the cramped rooms which Harry had been allotted to share with several other war correspondents, and Lyall told him he was welcome to use his house whenever he needed quiet to concentrate on his reports. It was empty enough during the day, for Lyall himself could not bear to be in the house now, and spent most of his time living with a rifle in his hands, crouched in a trench behind a rampart of sandbags. I suspected he was as much afraid as I was of the darkness left behind after Lyddie had died.

Harry took full advantage of the offer. If he wasn't at the house when I returned after finishing work at the convent, he would often arrive during the evening, his quick stride announcing his arrival, his hat immediately flung on to the nearest surface. So darkly handsome, and debonair despite the difficulties of keeping up appearances in the present circumstances, stirring the dark shadows with his magnetic personality.

We were too often alone. I knew it, and the thought of it spelled danger to me. But his presence brought in a breath of the outside world and re-awoke in me a longing for something I had long been suppressing. And he alone – perhaps because he knew nothing of my previous life – could lift my spirits when I felt depressed by the misery all around us and the sadness of being here, without Lyddie, so far from home and the people I loved. At first, I thought him flippant and often cynical, though his untailing good humour and his malicious asides still had the power to amuse me. I was not sure yet whether I liked or approved of him.

But Harry was a mass of contradictions. He was different; he questioned. He didn't believe everything we were told and didn't think that people back home should be told it, either. He let me see the despatches he contrived to have sent out by a native runner. I expected a hidden cynicism, but didn't find it. He said the truth must be told, though I wondered, as I read, whether such heresies would ever be published. The readers of the *Daily Bugle* would undoubtedly rather read more stories of the valour and praise of the gallant commander in Mafeking over their breakfast tables. Well, Harry was fair enough in giving praise where it was due – and much was due to Baden-Powell. But for his continual encouragement and cheerfulness, morale would have become non-existent as the circumstances of our penned-up, hazardous and yes, despite the danger, often monotonous life wore us down.

More than ever, Hugh allied himself to his leader. When the colonel was rallying the men in the trenches, or braving the enemy by showing himself on the redoubts, Hugh was never far away; he sat with him when he led a council of war; together they invented new gadgets, some schoolboy trick to fool the enemy, such as moving a searchlight devised from a biscuit tin from place to place so that it appeared we had dozens. The dapper, familiar figure of B-P in his wide brimmed hat with its four pinches in the crown and his cheery smile was seen everywhere, opening baby shows and sports days (designed to keep up morale), perching by the river bank in odd spare moments to make the most appealing and lively drawings in his sketchbook. And Hugh usually contrived to be in attendance somewhere, though he did not go so far as to do comic turns in the Sunday concerts, as Baden-Powell did.

"What a prince of good fellows!" said Harry, handing me a copy of his latest report, "Plucky chap, what's more. Nothing we British admire more than pluck. *Nil desperandum.*"

I couldn't help smiling, something I rarely did these days. The other railway towns of Ladysmith and Kimberley had also been besieged at the beginning of the war, but Kimberley had been relieved after four months and Ladysmith after five. Whereas we in Mafeking had become so accustomed to the non-arrival of relief which was reported a few days away and then never arrived, that we had almost ceased to believe it ever would – that we should all die here, trapped.

We had no news of our families in England, while they, one assumed, held their breath and prayed for us. I was very much afraid that Ned might have enlisted, and like his sister, have died far from his loved ones.

As supplies of everything dwindled, Harry became adept at winkling out anything that was scarce: even a bottle of French scent for me in a pretty, cut-glass bottle, for instance. Scent! A sweet breath of what now seemed a lost life. How on earth had he managed to get hold of it? Charm, I suppose. He wouldn't say. (When I opened it later, it had gone off, so someone had been hoarding it too long, but I kept the bottle.) I was shocked, however, when he brought things like corned beef, coffee and even tea, which had become scarce as gold dust. I should have refused them. Instead, to ease my conscience, I gave them to Amos and Lemuel, whose families were by now in dire straits as far as obtaining food went, far worse than we whites were: to put it bluntly, they were on the verge of starvation.

As the siege and the eternal, everlasting shelling dragged on into its fourth, fifth, sixth month, rescue did not come and we lived among constant noise, dust and confusion and danger, we whites were rationed to a pound of meal a week to make bread, no more than a spoonful or two of sugar, a cupful of coffee beans and half of tea. A tin of bully beef, and that was it, if you were honest. Many were not, and got their food by the back door. There was also something called 'sowens', a sort of meal made by grinding up grain husks, which you then sifted and blew away as much as you could of the chaff, to make gruel, but even with the most ingenious methods to make it palatable, it was sorry stuff. Nowhere was there any starch to be had, because it was now used to enrich and thicken soup. The sight of a horse carcase hanging from a tree waiting to be butchered became a common sight. Horsemeat sausages, when they were available, had begun to taste like a luxury.

"What's all this about not letting the natives share the rations?" Harry demanded, a snap in his eyes.

A good deal of brutality existed towards the blacks' condition. People shrugged and said the niggers were used to fending for themselves, they were expert cattle raiders, and they would eat anything that moved. I began to believe this when I saw one of the Fenji tribe kill one of the silent yellow dogs that abounded in the town by hitting it on the head with a stick. The smell of its roasting was perfectly sickening. Someone swore they had smelled roasting human flesh, too: how they knew it was human, I couldn't say, but there was no doubt of the Kaffirs' desperate situation. The men and women were gaunt as spectres, the children pot-bellied, their eyes protruding. It broke one's heart to see them begging for food and to have nothing to give them.

To be fair, Harry was not alone in his condemnation of the policy, even among the war correspondents. A good deal of moral pressure was building up to augment their rations. The mistake, Harry thought, had been to believe that this could ever have been simply a white man's war, which need not involve the native population. They had been expected at the onset of real trouble to decamp and leave the white man to it but they did – or could – not. They had been drawn in, willy-nilly, excluded from their traditional way of life, prevented from escaping the beleaguered town by the surrounding Boers, unable to graze their cattle, or having to watch them picked off or stolen by enemy raiders. They had no previously hoarded stores, as we had, and no other means of obtaining food was available to them.

"Well, it looks as though B-P will soon be relieved of part of the problem, if he has his way. His latest policy is to 'encourage' some of the blacks – several hundred women and children, I believe – to leave and find what food they can in the north."

"Yes, I've heard. With an offer of food for their journey – nine slaughtered horses."

"What a prospect," said Harry in his sardonic way. "Either be shot by the Boers when you try to leave, or stay here and die of starvation."

To give him his due, B-P believed the Boers would play the game and not shoot women and children. But the Boers were not British and had never heard of playing the game. The great exodus was driven back and the women shot if they did not obey.

"Ah well, *nil desperandum*," Harry said. This time we didn't laugh. By now, we could read each other's thoughts.

He had never again approached any moment of intimacy, after that tender gesture when he had pushed back my hair. But when our hands accidentally touched, or our eyes met, I thought of things that were not good for me to think.

What more is there to say?

Except that, just before the siege ended after seven long months, Harry Chetwynd and I inevitably became lovers. That Hugh came home unexpectedly one day and found us together. That he went out without a word and the next day, leading his men in a daring – and some said reckless – sortie against the Boer positions, was shot and killed, earning himself the Victoria Cross for his valour.

1909

SEPTEMBER

I never believed that I would write these words, but I must. I could never rid myself of the feeling that Dr Harvill was using me as an experiment, but now I have to say that I shall remain forever in his debt. The cloud under which I have lived for over a year has at last lifted.

Rosa watches me like a hawk. She tells me to be calm, and has brought me a tisane, *which she swears will soothe my nerves, but my fingers can hardly hold the pen steady enough to write. When I came to that part of this re-creation of my past, that point where Hugh was killed, and I faced what I had done – caused a true, honest and brave man to lose his life because of my faithlessness – that was when I knew I had come to the end of my journey of self-discovery, for that is what it has been. Memory did not come suddenly, with a blinding rush. First I would recall one thing, then another. Scenes, events and memories of people I had known piled themselves on top of one another in no sort of sequence. Only gradually did they begin to form some sort of order in my mind, until I no longer had to question each recollection. I had regained that basic human right – the right to a past.*

And the best – and the worst – of it was that it brought Ludovic back. Ludo.

While we in Mafeking waited for supply trains to bring us food, mourned our dead and wondered what the last seven months had accomplished in bringing the war to an end, England apparently went wild with people pouring into city centre streets to celebrate Mafeking's relief and honour the hero of the hour – Colonel Baden-Powell. Especially was this so in London – and of course, Yorkshire – where church bells rang and mill buzzers hooted not only in Dewsbury and Bridge End, but in Bradford and all over the West Riding in honour of their own heroes who had been caught up in the siege – and no doubt the townspeople crowded into the streets and the marketplaces there, too, to celebrate. Never mind that the war was still going on, Britain was in the grip of jingoism. Young men were still being urged to volunteer; to go out in the name of Queen and country, to be slaughtered or to die of fearful wounds, dysentery, enteric fever and gangrene.

I wished for nothing more, now, than to shake the dust of Africa from my feet. What I did not want to do was to go back to Bridge End, Willie Dyson and, above all, the Crowthers. How could I return without Lyddie? How could I return to them at all – those dear people who valued integrity above all else – as a grieving young widow, knowing how I had betrayed my marriage vows, and where it had led? But I had nowhere else to go.

Until I remembered the letters we had received from Rouncey before the siege, saying that she had returned to England from America and was now teaching young women students at the Royal Holloway College, at Egham Hill in Surrey. I wrote to her to ask if she had any suggestions as to how I might live, and she offered me a home.

On Hugh's death, I had been left with a considerable amount of money at my disposal, leaving me in no doubt that I need never be in want again for the rest of my life, but the thought of keeping that money filled me with so much revulsion and shame, I would not accept it. His family, who did not, of course, know the full story of his death, and my part in it, thought I was deranged when I agreed to take only what was necessary for my journey home. Maybe Rouncey would really be as glad to have me live with her as she said, and I felt that if I could act as her housekeeper (her own housekeeping skills being nil) my presence there need not be a burden.

"I didn't ask you to live with me to be my servant, Hannah, but as a companion. But if you feel you must do something to earn your keep, you may help me with the book I'm writing. It hasn't yet progressed very far beyond a huge accumulation of research documents, and they badly need sorting and classifying. What do you say to that?"

I wasn't sure whether I was qualified to do what she was asking, but I didn't dare to say so; nothing, in Rouncey's view, was ever beyond your grasp if you put your mind to it. Should I demur, I'd be faced with a brisk injunction to get my head down and buckle to, as I had so often been told to in the schoolroom. I smiled at the thought. Her energy and determination were already passing themsleves on to me and I began to feel that the prospect ahead might have something more to offer than a mere solution to the difficult situation in which I presently found myself. I discovered that her writing was concerned mostly with the rights of women; apart from gathering material for her book on the subject, she wrote leaflets for the Women's Social and Political Union, supporting their constant pressure to be given the vote. We lived together in her little house near the college for nearly three years, and I learned Mr Pitman's shorthand and how to work a typewriter to help with her voluminous correspondence.

"There's to be a WSPU meeting in Grosvenor Square next week. Shall we go, Hannah?" she asked one bitter, early December day. I looked at her doubtfully. She hadn't been well lately and still had a hacking cough; the weather was appalling. Snow had drifted in the lanes round the cottage, telegraph wires had come down, the post couldn't get through, but she would go. We had a slow, cold journey to London only to find the meeting cancelled. We stayed overnight with friends of hers, who were as worried as I was by her cough. The next day, by the time we had trudged the three miles from the station through a blizzard back to the cottage, it was evident she was very ill indeed; with pneumonia, as it turned out. When she died, three days later, I was bereft.

I had to leave the cottage because the owners wanted it for their son, who was getting married. Rouncey had left money to the WSPU and the rest, which amounted to nearly a hundred pounds, to me. It was enough to enable me to furnish a room I had found, and to provide me with a little cushion in case of need. With my typewriting skills I soon found a job in a firm which imported fans and Imari porcelain and lacquered goods from Japan. Twenty of us women sat in rows clattering away at our heavy, noisy machines all day long. It was hard, concentrated and extremely dull, repetitive work for which I was paid very little – and the noise, after the peacefulness of the cottage, was deafening. But I had my independence.

Three months later, on a lovely spring day, when I was standing in front of a flower seller, heart-stopped by a heavenly scented mimosa, which we had called acacia in Mafeking, and wondering whether I could afford to buy a bunch, I felt a hand on my shoulder. It was Harry Chetwynd.

I may be condemned as self-seeking by agreeing to live as his mistress in this pretty house he bought for me in St John's Wood, being grateful for whatever time he could spare to come to me. True, it was *a far cry from the shabby little room I rented, from the hard, ill-paid work at the office and the everlasting din of all those heavy machines – but I would not have done it had not my heart leaped at the sight and touch of him as I looked again into those laughing eyes.*

The attraction between us was very different from the sort of love which had existed between Hugh and myself – a love which, had I not been so foolish and wrong-headed as to fail to recognise it, would have outlasted life itself. I accepted from the start that Harry could not marry me. He was perfectly honest with me, but promised that even in the event of a convenient marriage being forced on him, it would make no difference to us. We existed for nothing but ourselves; it was only when Ludo was about to be born that the fly appeared in the ointment. By now, I had ceased to believe that I could ever bear a child, and when I found I was expecting one, my attitude changed. I did not want him or her to be born out of wedlock. I wanted Harry to be proud of us and for his family to meet and acknowledge us. Demanding this, I saw a side to Harry I did not like.

After Ludo was born, however, the three of us existed in a trinity of love – except that I could not get it out of my mind that Harry had a duty to tell his father, and his mother, that he had a son.

I sometimes think that there is something dark in me which presages death to all those I love – my parents; Lyddie; Hugh; Rouncey. My child. It was as the result of a quarrel over his refusal to do as I wished (though later lovingly made up), that Harry agreed to go on an outing 'to clear the air' as he put it. We would sit on the top of an omnibus and view London in the beautiful autumn weather, he said, and let the wind blow away all the dissensions that had been between us.

The last words I heard before I lost consciousness amid all the hideous confusion of the accident, as my hands were reaching out to find Ludo, were: "He's a goner."

Chapter Twenty-Two

All that Louisa Fox had told Crockett that night at Scotland Yard – about being in Mafeking at the time of the now famous siege; of having met both Hannah Osborne and Harry Chetwynd there; about having recently discovered that Harry had had a mistress and a child – all this had so far supported Crockett's own theories. Theories were one thing, however. Proof was another. And what he'd been told had given him no further pointers as to how he might find Mrs Osborne, who he was convinced would lead him to Rosa Tartaryan's murderer. And this was, after all, his paramount task, as he had been reminded by the Saroyans. The brothers were increasingly angry at the failure to discover her murderer. "I'm sorry, I know it's difficult for you, but we're doing all we can. For the moment, let's go over once more anything you can tell me about the time she was employed by Mrs Smith."

While they hadn't exactly approved of Rosa working as a servant to raise money for their funds, they hadn't quite disapproved. "She knew what she was doing, she was clever, my Rosa, very clever. Had she not been a woman, she would undoubtedly have been our leader," said Gevorg, without irony. But they still could recall nothing more of Mrs Smith than her name. They didn't even know how Rosa had come to hear of the vacant position.

Crockett had asked Louisa if she thought there had been an affair going on between Hannah Osborne and Harry Chetwynd in Mafeking.

"Nothing that I was aware of," she'd answered doubtfully, "I was barely fourteen after all, though one is always looking out for romance at that age, and Harry *was* very good-looking...but Mrs Osborne – well she was young, too, but she was a married woman. No, I'm sure there wasn't anything of that sort." Besides, she'd added after a moment or two, Mrs Osborne had been distraught when her husband had been killed in an engagement just before the end of the siege, for which he'd had received the highest decoration in the land, for bravery in the face of the enemy. He had been such a nice man, so kind and polite. No, they hadn't had any children.

But she added after a moment, looking very thoughtful, that perhaps Crockett should know that Sylvia Eustace-Bragge, Harry's twin sister, had known that after his return to England Harry had taken a mistress and had an illegitimate – and what was worse, retarded – child. Sylvia, however, did not know who this mistress was or where she lived. Crockett blew out his lips, disbelieving. Even Constable Grayson had known that the foster mother of the little boy on the 'bus was receiving money from the Chetwynds, and must have put two and two together. Farming out a bastard child was not an unusual happening, whatever circles you happened to move in.

Crockett thought he would somehow have to find the time to go and see Mrs Jenkins, the foster mother. Any opportunity to learn something wasn't to be missed. Unfortunately, however absorbing the Chetwynd affair might be to him, there were other pressing matters he had been obliged to deal with; even now, he couldn't put forward any justification for proposing he should put in further work on it, so any investigation had to be confined to odd times he was able to snatch. He had no desire to have his knuckles rapped for wasting constabulary time, but he thought he might fit in an hour that afternoon.

Sarah Jenkins lived in a neat little house on a decent street and was evidently in comfortable circumstances. There was snow in the air as Crockett knocked on her door, but the tidy living room into which she welcomed him was warm and snug, with a bright fire burning in a polished grate, and pervaded by a good, wholesome smell of baking. She was surprised but pleased to see him. "Nice to see you again, Mr Crockett, sit you down," she said, shooing off a marmalade cat curled on a cushion, brushing off stray cat hairs. The armchair certainly needed a cushion; it was horsehair, severe and upright, designed for a bigger man than Crockett, such as Jack Jenkins had been.

When Sarah had opened the door to his knock, a little, dark-haired boy of about three or four had been by her side, clutching her skirts as if afraid she would go away. Now he sat on the rag rug in front of the fire, playing with a pile of wooden bricks, taking not the slightest notice of anyone. "You'll have some tea?" asked Sarah.

"I wouldn't say no, Mrs Jenkins."

She went into the adjoining kitchen and the boy went with her. She came back with a tray spread with an embroidered cloth, on which were china tea things and an uncut cake, and he followed close on her heels. "Just made," she said, placing the tray on the tapestry cloth which covered the centre table. "Seed cake. It's not everybody likes it."

"Thank you, I'm very partial to the taste of caraway."

She cut him a generous slice, then seated herself in a plush-covered rocking chair on the opposite side of the hearth. Crockett, who wasn't used to children, placed a hand on the boy's shoulder, but quickly took it away when he felt him stiffen. "What's the lad's name, then?"

"I've named him Jack, after my husband – but he shakes his head and gets angry when I call him that, so it's usually chicken, or something. Isn't it, love?" She leaned forward and stroked the boy's dark hair. He was sitting on the floor again, absorbed in sharing his slice of cake with the cat, and made no response.

"Is it all right to talk?" Crockett asked.

"I reckon he hears and understands everything, when he wants to, which isn't always, so it might do some good in the end, who knows? Something he hears might some day make him want to talk." She was a simple woman, not particularly well educated, but she had a robust common sense and a kind and loving heart. He thought Agnes would have liked and approved of her.

"I'm sorry. I was under the impression there were difficulties with his – intelligence."

"Pardon me, Mr Crockett," she answered stiffly. "Pardon me, but whoever told you that is lying. The child's no idiot. He can read already, and make his letters. He can make pictures, too." She went to a drawer in the sideboard and fetched one of the lurid images the boy had made with his paint box. Thick slashes of red and black, a small dot in the centre, surrounded by what looked like thunderclouds. "Frightening, somehow." It was true he had never spoken, she said, but lately he had begun to utter a few, mostly unintelligible, words. Now and again she had surprised brief glimpses of a mischievous, boyish gleam in those dark brown eyes. Once or twice, he had even slipped a trusting little hand into hers – almost instantly withdrawn – but she believed he was 'coming round', as she put it.

"There's nothing wrong with him but that he's still missing his mother, poor lamb. Maybe he'll get over it in time, but he hasn't yet." She looked at Crockett with a sudden intake of breath. "Have you...you haven't found her?" He sensed in her a battle between hope and fear; between a desire for the child to be united with his real mother and the knowledge of the loss it would mean to her. Her love for the child won. "That would be a wonderful thing," she said generously, but couldn't prevent herself from adding, "Whoever she is, how could she not have claimed him by now?"

"I think she must believe him dead." Despite Harvill's assurances that Hannah's refusal to acknowledge the boy was due to a suppressed, unbearable memory, that was a conclusion Crockett himself thought more believable. He felt bound to add honestly, while knowing he was dealing Sarah a blow, "But I have hopes that may be remedied, before long."

She turned her head away for a moment so that he could not see her face. "Silly of me. I always knew it might happen, one day."

Crockett awkwardly patted her hand and wondered if she might take offence if he approached the subject of the allowance paid to her for looking after the child. She was the sort of woman who valued her independence, her ability to keep her head above water, despite not having a husband to provide for her. The room was comfortable, neat and clean as a new pin. Probably containing nothing that every other house in the street wouldn't possess, except perhaps the heavy mahogany sideboard that was of excellent quality, polished within an inch of its life, as was the small grandfather clock, and the harmonium in the corner. But she lived comfortably, without an occupation that would provide money for her and the boy.

The subject came up quite naturally, after she'd poured him another cup of tea, and served another slice of seed cake. "I was in service, used to be a nursemaid, before I married Jack, and I'm fond of children. I'd just lost my own baby and after Jack died, I was thinking of getting another position." A shadow of pain crossed her face, a double grief remembered and learned to live with. "Then I was asked to take in the little one here. Much as I wanted to, I'll admit I hesitated. I couldn't see how I could make ends meet, you see, but then, Lord bless us, if the lady didn't come and offer to help."

"Which lady was this?" He thought immediately of Lady Chetwynd, or even the grandmother, Lady Emily, but Sarah surprised him.

"Why, the sister of the young man who was killed, Mrs Eustace-Bragge. She said she was sorry for the child and offered to help from the goodness of her heart."

"Did she, by jingo? Was that the only reason, do you think?"

She looked at him directly. "Well, I have wondered. She didn't strike me as that sort – and I've known many an arrangement like this, when I was a nursemaid."

"I wonder why she, out of all the family, was chosen to sort out the business?"

"I doubt if anyone else at all knew about it, never mind the family. She talked a lot of high-flown rubbish about good works being of no value if everybody knew what you were doing – and by the amount she offered to pay me, I took it that meant I was to keep my mouth shut, if you see what I mean, Mr Crockett. I accepted the money, but I haven't spent it all. There's a tidy sum put by for the boy, when he needs it."

Chapter Twenty-Three

Sebastian's rooms in Albemarle Street, the usual bachelor quarters.

Half past four on this bitterly cold wintry afternoon found Crockett ringing the bell. In his mind, he had classed Sebastian as a young man-about-town, one of the leisured classes with no more thought in his head than the pursuit of his own pleasure, and was surprised to find him in shirt sleeves, working at a big drawing board set up in the centre of a large, well-furnished but unbelievably untidy room, architectural drawings pinned up all around the walls, books and papers strewn on every surface.

Sebastian saw his surprise and rather enjoyed it. He had been to see Wagstaffe and was still buoyed up with the rough sort of approval he had received on reporting to the architect about the studies he'd so far followed, along the lines suggested to him by the older man. He thought Wagstaffe was more impressed than he'd said by how willing Sebastian was showing himself, and by how much progress he had made since their last meeting, in preparation for the start of his new career.

"I'm soon to be a working man, Chief Inspector. Going in for architecture, what do you think of that?" Smiling, without waiting for answer, he asked, "What can I do for you?"

"You can give me your sister's address, for one thing, if you will. Where does she live?"

"Knightsbridge, but as a matter of fact, you're in luck, I'm expecting her any minute. I was just about to start clearing up." He looked round vaguely, thrusting his hands through his hair as he wondered where to start. "Women set such store by these things. Especially Sylvia. Do sit down."

In the absence of any seat devoid of books and papers and the scarcity of empty surfaces on which to remove them to, Crockett remained on his feet, contenting himself, while Sebastian shuffled papers around ineffectually, with examining the several very good pictures on the walls and the family photographs on the mantelpiece, one of which, in a silver frame, particularly caught his eye. It was of Lady Chetwynd, looking very elegant in lace and a huge, frilly hat, leaning on a parasol, beside a very young officer in the uniform of the Blues and Royals – the Royal Horse Guards. Presumably this was Harry Chetwynd, before he resigned his commission for a career that had ended up as dilettante journalism.

Finally abandoning any attempt at tidiness, Sebastian switched off the bright electric light over his drawing board, which left but one dim lamp burning in the corner. He drew together the thick, dark red serge curtains, cutting off all sound from the noisy street outside and enclosing the room with its low-burning fire in intimacy and warmth. He was about to turn on the overhead light when there was a knock on the door. "Here she is. Sylvia, my dear." He had to bend and dip his head under the sweeping brim of the hat skewered to his sister's piled-up hair in order to kiss her scented cheek.

Standing in the shadows, Crockett saw at once that she was very like her mother, but in a way somehow more sharply defined. Small and extremely slim, with a very upright carriage, she was wearing dark green: a beautifully cut coat and skirt relieved only by a touch of paler green in the ruffle of silk at her neck when she removed her fur. The same pale green also extravagantly trimmed her matching velour hat: an undoubtedly expensive ensemble which nevertheless drained her complexion, already naturally pale, he guessed, of all colour. There were dark, bruised-looking shadows under her eyes.

"What a mess!" she declared immediately, with sisterly candour, looking around her. "How can you live like this, Sebastian?"

"I don't, not all the time. I'm very busy just now and anyway, the merest thing out of place offends Knox's orderly Scottish soul and he cleans it up even before he brings me my tea in the morn- ing. I wish he wouldn't. I quite like living in squalor. Why don't you have a seat, Sylvia, take off your hat and I'll ring for some tea?" he added, sweeping a pile of papers to the floor from a bosomy Victorian velvet chair with a tapestry seat. "You don't look up to the mark, if I may say so."

"I – I haven't been sleeping too well. No tea, thank you." She put down her muff, drew off her elegant suede gloves, laid them on her lap and lifted her hands to remove the pins from her hat. Crockett cleared his throat and stepped forward from the shadows. She started.

"I'm sorry, Sylvia. Let me introduce Chief Inspector Crockett, the detective from Scotland Yard in charge of the Belmonde murder. My sister, Mrs Eustace-Bragge."

She immediately stood up again, looking very angry, ignoring Crockett's outstretched hand, and began to draw on her gloves once more. "You have got me here by a trick, Sebastian, and I won't have it. I shall not stay."

Sebastian forbore to remind her that it was she who had sent him a note asking to see him. The fact that she was prepared to visit him – here – meant she wished to keep their meeting secret, probably because she wanted to borrow money for reasons the often tight-fisted Algy mustn't know about – she had hinted as much when they spoke on the telephone. Which was rich. She must indeed be desperate if she was reduced to asking *him!* He said mildly, "Inspector Crockett has been here barely five minutes, and I wasn't expecting him."

"Please stay, Mrs Eustace-Bragge," Crockett intervened. "I should very much like a word with you, if you will spare me a few moments."

"Sylvia, Mr Crockett knows about the child."

There was no noticeable change in her expression. She looked Crockett up and down, taking in what he had previously thought to be one of his smartest suits, his high, stiff and spotless collar, his well groomed moustache and polished boots, then sat down again, abruptly. Resting her elbow on the chair arm, she shielded her eyes with one thin white hand, heavy with rings. A venerable old mantel clock, whose wheezy chime usually got on Sebastian's nerves, filled the awkward silence with the three-quarters.

"There doesn't seem much point," she said at last, "I can't tell you anything."

Crockett espied a stool in front of the drawing board and seized the opportunity to draw it forward and perch on it. Sebastian mended the low fire and then sat on the club fender.

"Perhaps not. But the accident when your brother was killed seems to have started off a disastrous chain of circumstances.

Why don't we begin there?"

"What's the use of bringing all that up again? The day that was the worst of my life. Unless you are a twin, you can never know what that feels like." Her face twisted with pain and she went on, almost as though speaking to herself, "I think sometimes we were like two sides of the same minted coin – he the bright, gleaming side, me the one which has tarnished and grown darker."

"Sylvia —" Sebastian protested, but Sylvia didn't appear to have heard.

"I can't tell you anything," she told Crockett again. "You must already have all the facts of the accident at your disposal."

"It's what happened afterwards that interests me. In particular, what happened to the little boy who was never claimed."

"Why do you assume I should know anything about him?"

"Since you pay Mrs Jenkins to look after him, I'm forced to that conclusion."

What little colour there was in her cheeks fled. Sebastian swung round to face her. "Is this true?"

Recovering herself, she shrugged. "They were talking of putting him into an institution. Since there was no one else to do it…" Her voice trailed off. "It was very little."

"Especially since you knew he was your brother's child."

Unaware of what she was doing, twisting her gloves together, she said reluctantly, "I – suspected he might be."

"Suspected?" Crockett pointed to the photograph.

She sighed. "All right, yes, I suppose I knew. He's the image of Harry."

"And the unidentified woman?" pressed Crockett. "I think you also knew she was your brother's mistress."

"I knew nothing about her."

"Not even her name, where she lived?"

"It wasn't a subject Harry and I were in the habit of discussing."

"Who took care of his things, his books and papers, when he died? I assume he must have left some indication behind."

When she still didn't reply, Sebastian said, "You were the one who cleared his rooms in Connaught Street and wouldn't let anyone else get a look in. Come on, Sylvia, there must have been *something*!"

Both sensed the struggle going on within her – the need to keep her own secrets against the necessity to tell the truth, since it was obvious now the truth was going to emerge sooner or later. Finally she looked up and said, with a sort of resignation, "There were some receipted bills and so on which had been sent to him at an address in St John's Wood. And documents which showed he'd arranged for money to be paid to her through the bank, until further notice, under the name of Mrs Hannah Smith."

Crockett fixed her with a steady look. "So you went there, found her maid and sent her to the hospital to confirm the patient was her mistress."

She looked at him strangely. After a moment she admitted, "Yes. That's how it was."

There followed a very long silence. At last, Crockett said, "But I'm afraid that couldn't be so. Rosa Tartaryan did not start working for Mrs Smith until the day she came out of hospital. After you had engaged her."

After one piercing glance at his sister, Sebastian sat motionless on the fender seat, his eyes turned from her as though he could not bear to look at her. The now blazing coals burned frostily, with an occasional hiss and burst of blue-green flame. The scent she was wearing, released in the warmth of the room, was sharp with a hint of citrus and undertones of musk. It reminded him of the scent he had fancied his mother had been wearing when he had seen her and Monty on the steps outside the house, and he felt as though he were being drawn into the web of lies in which his family seemed enmeshed.

"Supposing I did?" she said in a low voice at last. "It was the least I could do, to provide someone to look after her. That woman was in no position to look after herself."

"Perhaps you'd tell me why you engaged Rosa, in particular – a foreigner? Where did you get hold of her? And how did you explain the situation to her?"

"Get hold of her? Oh, some agency or other, I suppose. And I told her the truth, that Mrs Smith had been in a coma and had lost a large part of her memory. She understood and spoke English excellently. Enough," she added bitterly, "to drive a very hard bargain."

This set off another train of thought, which Crockett put to one side for the moment. "Which agency?" he asked.

"I don't remember. Oh yes, actually, it wasn't an agency, it was Monty who recommended her. Our uncle works in the Foreign Office and has connections with these refugee organisations. Those people are always glad of work, you know. He knew nothing of why I wanted Rosa, I simply asked if he knew of anyone discreet whom he could recommend as a sort of housekeeper. I assume he thought it was for myself. Monty never asks questions."

Yet when the murdered woman had turned out to be a foreigner, an Armenian, Monty Chetwynd had not spoken up. Crockett rubbed his nose. Had this been out of a desire to protect Sylvia, because he believed her in some way implicated in the murder? "Where were you, Mrs Eustace-Bragge, when Rosa Tartaryan was murdered?"

She raised one eyebrow and told him that she had never been out of London for the whole of September. She was on the organising committee for an important charity concert and had scarcely had a moment to herself. If he would tell her precisely the times he was interested in, she would certainly be able to find people who would corroborate it.

Sebastian, evidently still thinking of what had gone before, said suddenly, "Supposing Hannah Smith had recovered her memory? Which couldn't have been discounted. What did you propose to do about the boy then?"

"Well, of course we should have put her in touch with him," she said very quickly. "But there was a Dr Harvill looking after her, who thought it highly unlikely."

He looked at her very intensely. "I wonder," he said, "that it never occurred to her to wonder why there were children's clothes and toys and things at the house, if she believed she'd never had a child."

Sylvia was fiddling with her gloves again, wringing them together. The expensive suede was well on the way to being ruined. "Well, there weren't any. I saw that they were removed. There was no point in upsetting her further."

The wheezy old clock struck the hour. Sebastian buried his face in his hands. After a moment, he looked up. "Why did you do that, Sylvia? It was wrong, and cruel."

"Cruel? Had it not been for that woman, Harry would never have been riding on a public omnibus – and you dare to say I am cruel?"

Did she never have nightmares? Crockett wondered. Had she never thought that she might be causing pain and anguish to a woman she had never met – but one whom her brother had loved? He did not for a moment believe the reason she'd given for removing all traces of the child. All her actions seemed to him to have been motivated by unthinking jealousy – that her beloved twin had loved someone more than he loved her; even, perhaps, that his mistress had a child and Sylvia didn't...and perhaps by greed. He imagined her going to the St John's Wood house, rummaging through Hannah's personal possessions, perhaps even taking what she wanted. He could envisage her searching the house from top to bottom, avid for anything she might turn to her advantage, anything to add verisimilitude to the story she must concoct for Rosa to tell her supposed employer, which was where she had made her mistake. "Cruel or not, it was done for a reason," Crockett remarked. "The same reason you put Rosa there in order to keep an eye on Mrs Smith."

"How too ridiculous. Why should that have been necessary?"

"In case her memory returned, and she remembered things which were inconvenient for other people. Such as the fact that she did have a son, who was not only of a normal, sound mind, but also that he was legitimate. In other words, that your brother Harry had married Hannah Osborne. Was that why Rosa was blackmailing you?"

"What do you mean – of sound mind?" she asked, choosing to ignore what else he had said.

"There's nothing wrong with the boy. He's suffered a great shock, being involved in such a serious accident, waking up in hospital, injured, suddenly bereft of both parents. It robbed him of speech, but not intelligence."

* * *

Both accusations had been long shots, born of intuition, but intuition had not played him false: both had hit their mark. That, and the other things he had learned, gave Crockett much food for thought as he made his way back to his office. Once there, he telegraphed to Ned Crowther and received back a reply almost immediately to say that he could not be at Scotland Yard much before lunch time the following day, owing to the Sunday timetables. Crockett, who had been prepared to wait until Monday, smiled at this evidence of his impatience, but he was pleased. Now they could go to St John's Wood to see Hannah Smith the very next day. He was sure he had enough to go on now to persuade those upstairs to give him permission to take up the investigation officially again.

In the meantime, he made a decision to use the time before Crowther arrived to see Montague Chetwynd, at his home, since he did not expect him to be at the Foreign Office on Sunday. He was admitted, although he had made no appointment to see the MP, and was shown immediately into the study, where Chetwynd received him courteously, with a smile and a firm handshake. "What can I do for you, Chief Inspector?" he asked, reseating himself at the desk from which he had risen and indicating a chair opposite, a subtle move guaranteed to put any visitor at a disadvantage, noted Crockett.

Chetwynd had a formidable pile of papers in front of him, which he had evidently been working on, and was formally dressed, as if for a working day at the Foreign Office or in the House, in a suit which Crockett immediately appreciated as being tailored by one of the best tailors in London. His shirt and cuffs were as immaculate as his white, well-shaped hands. His discreet cravat was held in place by an onyx pin, and he wore a heavy, but not ostentatious gold signet ring. Clean-shaven, with his immaculately brushed fair hair, neatly parted and brushed, he looked as fresh and clean as a well-scrubbed schoolboy waiting to don his choir robes. But the light, sandy-lashed eyes were watchful.

He was known as a man of wit and intelligence, and one not without influence. It appeared, from what Crockett had been able to find out, that his career had so far had been distinguished in a moderate way. In his leisure time, he rode, shot and fished; he supported the arts, and he collected fine porcelain, evidence of which was displayed in various cabinets and on tables around the luxurious room. It was the room of a cultured man with taste and the money to indulge it. Long, embossed, dark blue velvet curtains at the windows, fine carpets and grey silk walls, against which hung gold-framed watercolours. The usual family photographs standing on various surfaces; and on the large walnut desk, from where he was sitting, Crockett could see, framed in exquisite enamels, the same photograph of Lady Chetwynd and her elder son which had been in Sebastian's room.

He came straight to the point, looking steadily at Chetwynd. "As you know, I'm working on the enquiry into the death of Rosa Tartaryan. I would be obliged if you could help me by telling me how and why you recommended her to Mrs Sylvia Eustace-Bragge as a housekeeper – which I believe may have led, indirectly, to her death."

Chetwynd looked startled. "Surely not!"

"I'm afraid so." He waited.

"Then I'm very sorry I ever did recommend her. And I'd be interested to know how you've come to draw that conclusion about the poor woman's death."

"If you can spare the time to listen, sir, I'll tell you." He watched the other man's face closely as the tale was told, not leaving anything out, even the fact of the child being fostered by Sarah Jenkins, and the boy's supposed low intelligence, but as Crockett had fully expected, the man's expression gave nothing away. It remained coolly interested, focused, but unreadable. Nor did he interrupt, until it came to the final revelation, that his nephew, Harry Chetwynd, had married his mistress, Hannah Osborne.

"Good God!" he said softly. "That'll put the cat among the pigeons, as far as Henry's concerned. Not," he added, registering Crockett's expression, "that my brother won't see the right thing done by the boy, or his mother; on the contrary. But he wouldn't like it to get out. Henry sets great store by the conventions." He paused. "The boy, of course, could never be allowed to become the heir. Not if he is not in full command of his senses."

"As I understand it, his intelligence is not in question. He merely needs time to recover from the shock and the loss of his parents."

Chetwynd steepled his fingers together. "This calls for some tact and negotiation. My brother is of a somewhat – volatile – personality. There's no telling what he might do if he were to hear of this in the wrong way. I'll tell him myself."

Keeping his steady gaze on Chetwynd's face, Crockett said, "Hardly necessary, sir. Rosa Tartaryan was blackmailing him over this very matter before she died."

Chetwynd's face was a study. Disbelief, coupled with something very like distaste, as if Crockett had made a social gaffe in speaking such ugly words in this exquisite room, crossed his face. "This is a very serious allegation – are you sure...?"

"I'm making no allegations, sir. Simply stating the facts. You only need to ask your brother yourself."

"Yes, yes, of course. I'm sorry for doubting you, Chief Inspector. It takes time to get accustomed to such an appalling idea."

Crockett inclined his head. "But I believe you haven't answered my original question, sir."

"Which was —? Ah, yes. Recommending Rosa. Well, you know, in my position, it pays to keep a finger in quite a number of pies. The Armenian Liberation Group, though not officially sanctioned, is one in which I – shall I say, take an interest? As a member of the public you understand, not in my official capacity. Anything I can do to help those poor, dispossessed people, I will do. An error of judgement in this case, it seems."

A true politician's answer. Crockett realised there was little to be gained in pressing him further and after thanking him for his time, made his departure.

When Crockett had left him, Monty stood looking out of the window into the bare winter garden: a paved and walled area he found rather more attractive in winter than in summer, without the roses and other plants cluttering its clean, formal lines, when the winter elegance of the trees could be better appreciated; as different from the excesses of his brother's gardens in

Shropshire as it was possible to be.

He was a good judge of men, and in Crockett's case, he had seen beyond the dandified figure with traces of Cockney in his voice to someone quick-witted and tenacious enough to upset the equilibrium. It was not often Montague Chetwynd regretted any decision he made, since they almost always involved careful thought, but this – the matter of Rosa Tartaryan – was the exception that proved the rule. He had a network of spies, and contacts with the louche underworld of foreign agents, all of which was necessary to keep a finger on the pulse of what was happening abroad. If it became known that he had put himself under an obligation – or had been doing favours to – the Balkan immigrant community, when European affairs were at such a highly volatile stage and certain delicate negotiations were in progress in which he was playing a major part, not only his judgement, but his loyalty, would be in question. This was not to be borne.

He had in the first place agreed to supply Sylvia – who had told him what now seemed to have been a little less than the truth about the affair – with someone discreet, not likely to gossip, because he thought it was, if only temporarily, an alternative to presenting Henry with the problem of an illegitimate grandchild. Henry was the sort of man who needed time to accustom himself to any unpleasant facts, and there was no knowing how he might react if faced with a situation to which he had to make an instant response. Monty had agreed to Sylvia's request, believing that things could be restored to the status quo without much difficulty, should the necessity arise…if the mother should recover her memory, in the face of all predictions to the contrary. He had foreseen that if such a thing were to happen she might well cause trouble now that Harry had died, but he had decided to deal with that problem if and when it arose. In the meantime, he had acknowledged that someone trustworthy was needed to keep an eye on the situation. It was instinctive to choose someone who, like himself, had habits of secrecy and discretion, and he had therefore provided Rosa. Clever, keeping her own counsel, but fanatical, it had turned out, over-zealous in the matter of finding funds for her cause. The whole thing had been the gravest mistake.

Sylvia had acted foolishly, precipitately, her only thought to get the boy out of the way, and her motives were muddled and suspect, influenced by her emotions. Monty sighed, but could not blame her, or not very much. He sometimes acted impulsively himself, a regrettable trait which he deplored and did his best to control – although the very nature of impulse was that one was only aware of it when it was too late. A fatal Chetwynd inheritance, perhaps.

He remembered as if it were yesterday the shock of that telephone call from Henry. A call from him always heralded trouble; he never quite trusted 'that damned instrument', convinced that it could not work without the assistance of human lungs, stretched to their utmost, and only used it under duress.

Sir Henry, too, was at that very moment thinking about that same conversation. Not surprisingly, since it had, in fact, recurred to him almost daily ever since he had made it, and on each occasion it worried him more.

He had seen, too late, that he should have sought Monty's advice right from the first. Monty had always been resourceful, knowing even as a boy how to get out of scrapes, but Henry had kept his troubles to himself, out of an inborn need for secrecy and a desire to keep such things within his own immediate family. It had come to the point, however, where it had gone beyond that. He'd known that he had to come out of the long grass and tell Monty everything, however disgraceful. He had telephoned his brother, determined to speak plainly and waste no words. "I've had some letters, from a woman."

"What sort of letters, Henry? What woman?"

"A damned woman who writes to say she works for someone who was Harry's mistress, that there's a child." The line had gone silent. "What? Monty? You there?"

He did not for a moment imagine that Monty's failure to reply was due to shock (few people in his experience, especially Monty, would find such a fact either surprising or difficult to accept, as long as it was discreetly covered up) and he repeated what he'd just said, raising his voice.

"All right, Henry, I heard you the first time. There's no need to panic. There have been by-blows before, without any bones broken."

"Panic? Not panicking at all. I simply want to know how to get this pesky female off my back before Adèle learns of it, or the woman makes it public as she threatens and —"

"Who is this letter-writer?"

"Some blasted foreigner. She says it's her mistress who needs the money, for herself and the child, but she's too proud to ask. So this woman is writing on her behalf."

"What did you say her name was?"

"I didn't. It's Tartaryan – God knows what nationality that is. T-A-R-T —"

"It's Armenian, as a matter of fact."

Monty's voice had sounded very odd and Henry's heart sank even further. Armenian? Good God, what the devil had Harry got himself involved with? Armenians in Henry's mind spelled anarchists, trouble-makers and Turks (as one assumed they must now be regarded), and the only good thing ever to come out of Turkey was their carpets. Henry did not relish the idea of a bastard grandson lurking in the background, but even less did he like the idea of one who was linked with infidels.

"This is very unfortunate, Henry."

"Unfortunate! It's a piece of damned impertinence!"

"Keep calm."

Henry breathed deeply. It was a warning he was accustomed to hearing. No one who was familiar with his dark temper liked to risk rousing it, and it must be evident, even over the cracklings and distortions of the telephone lines, that it was rising.

"You haven't by any chance done as she asks and given her anything?" Monty went on.

Foolishly, naïvely as he now saw, thinking he had been honourably discharging his responsibilities towards this woman Harry had got in the family way, he had indeed sent a remittance – though he wasn't about to confess the extent of it to Monty – hoping it would draw a line under the matter. He cleared his throat. "As a matter of fact, I – er – did send her a trifle —"

"Then you've been a bigger fool than usual. Did you imagine that would be an end of it?"

"She vowed she would ask for nothing more."

Monty laughed shortly. "That's all gammon, don't you believe it. Look here, it's better you see this woman face to face. Get her down to Belmonde."

"Why bring her down here? What's the point of that?"

"Meet her on your own ground, where you have the advantage."

"I dare say you're right," said Henry, after some cogitation, ready to agree to anything as long as it didn't involve him dressing up and going up to London. "But how the devil is that to be done?"

"We'll sort it out when we meet next weekend. But don't tell Sylvia."

"Sylvia? What has Sylvia to do with all this?"

"She'll only try to interfere," said Monty.

He had been left with the uneasy feeling that none of this had been the surprise to his brother that he'd imagined it would be – that Monty knew a good deal more about the affair than he was letting on.

And events had proved him right of course. How in Hades had it all got so out of hand?

DECEMBER

The very last thing on earth I expected when I opened the door was to see Ned Crowther standing on my doorstep. No longer the boy who'd laughed and joked and teased me in a brotherly way...he was a big, solid man now, with a tanned, humorous face and a slight limp. He had indeed fought in Africa against the Boers, but about all this, after my initial, overwhelming joy at meeting this dear friend, I was to learn later.

There was another man with him, a rakish-looking fellow in a check suit who turned out to be a policeman – a Detective Chief Inspector by the name of Crockett. I knew, as soon as I heard 'Scotland Yard', that he had come to give me news of Rosa, and I knew she must be dead, even before he told me that she had been murdered. It was two months since she disappeared and I had neither seen nor heard from her.

I had come downstairs for breakfast one morning in September, feeling alive and well for the first time in twelve months (not happy...how could I ever be happy again, knowing what I had so recently discovered? But yes, alive), and found Rosa gone. She had left no note. The weeks went by, and she still didn't return. I assumed she'd gone back to her friends but, secretive as she had been about her personal life, I had no idea how to get in touch with them. At last I accepted the fact that she had gone for good. But until that moment I had never thought she might be dead.

I can hardly bear the thought of yet another death of someone close to me, though I couldn't in all honesty say that I was fond of Rosa, nor she of me. But I had grown used to her, and she had looked after me when I needed someone. The detective asked me how long we had known each other, how had she come to work for me, and how had she discovered I was in hospital? I told him, as plainly as I could, the explanation sounding even less plausible than it did when it had been given to me, though I had no grounds then for not accepting it as the truth.

When I returned from that world of half-defined shadows in the hospital, they told me my name was Hannah; it was engraved on a crucifix around my neck. I said my father had given me the crucifix, and saw the smiles of relief that I had come round fully cognisant of everything. But soon, it was evident that all was not well.

I remembered my early life. I remembered being in the accident. But prior to that, a huge chunk of my life was missing. While I was still struggling and fighting to bring it back, a dark, sallow woman came to see me. To my knowledge I had never seen her before in my life, but she told me that her name was Rosa Tartaryan, and that I had engaged her in response to an advertisement I had inserted in a ladies' magazine, a few weeks before the accident. She explained why it had taken her so long to find me: apparently I had told her I should shortly be going away for a few days. When she returned from her day off and found me gone, she simply thought I had antic-ipated the journey and that she'd mistaken the length of time I had said I would be away. But as time went by she had become worried and started to make enquiries, which eventually led her to me.

She told me I lived alone, and brought me back to this house which she said belonged to me, and where I have been ever since. I had no reason then to doubt her. There were echoes and vibrations, as well as other sensations which I could not pin down or relate to anything, that spoke of home. I lived comfortably, with regular, gen-erous payments sent to me by the bank, from an annuity, under the name of Smith.

The months passed until, by doing as Dr Harvill suggested, I was at last able to remember those lost years. How many times since then have I thought it would have been better that they had remained for-gotten, since remembering has brought this almost unbearable agony. When the memory of my son – and of Harry – came back to me, I couldn't understand why Rosa had never mentioned either to me. When I pressed her, she reluctantly told me both had died in the accident and that she had decided, out of consideration for my state of mind and health, that it could only do me harm to talk of them. There was nothing of my child in the house, not a stitch of clothing, not even his beloved bear, or his hobby horse. She had removed every single thing which might remind me of him. I knew I should have to come to terms with the anguish of my darling Ludo being dead, and Harry too, but somehow, events did not quite add up. I admitted to myself that I didn't trust Rosa, that I'd never done so, ever since I first saw her in the hospital and heard the unlikely story that I'd engaged her before the accident. Why should I have done that? There was no need for any housekeeper here in this house. I was brought up by Mrs Crowther, a practical Yorkshirewoman, who taught me how to run a home, and this one here is small and easily cared for. I'd endured the rigours of a hard life in Mafeking and had never been averse to putting my hand to practical, even distasteful tasks. Clearly, Rosa was concealing the truth of my circumstances. I believe in the end she became aware that I was suspicious of her, and that was why she left.

Alone again, dependent only on myself, I forced myself to think about the accident. I could have no doubt that Harry and my child had indeed been killed on that fatal day, but I needed at least to know where they were buried, to mourn at their graves. Once my bodily strength was fully restored, I vowed I would obtain copies of the newspapers which had contained accounts of the accident. I would go to the hospital, the police.

There was something else I had to do, also. Search as I might throughout the house, I hadn't been able to find my marriage certificate. So I also needed to go the church where we were married, and see the entry in the parish register. I went there first. I learned that the old vicar was in retirement now in Wales, but I obtained a copy of the registration.

And last week I went to the hospital. They remembered me, of course, and reminded me how I had denied having a child, which had been the truth as far as I was concerned: had I not heard them say he was dead before I lost consciousness? I could see the starchy sister thought that the injuries I'd received had turned my brain when I asked to see the little boy who had been in the same accident, but just supposing, I thought, just supposing…? She said I must forget about him, that he was being well looked after. She was kind, but she was sure he couldn't possibly belong to me. Unless – unless, she said, my child had been – not quite right in the head.

Ludo, I thought. Ludo, with your impish, mischievous smile, your laughing eyes, so like Harry's, full of curiosity and sparkle. A child who nearly cost me my life when he was born, but whom I loved more than life itself. Such a bright little boy, full of childish chatter. Advanced for his two and a half years, who asked questions all day long, and learned so quickly. Did the concussion you suffered do more to you than the accident did to me? It had robbed me of my memory for a year – but you…

I could not, would not, believe that my beautiful little boy had been robbed permanently of that bright intelligence. Could Fate have been so cruel?

"Don't upset yourself, my dear," said Ned, as I finished my tale. "Your little boy's alive and quite well —"

"What?"

"— and is no more half-witted than I am – although," he added comically, trying to bring a smile to my stiff, shocked face, "maybe you think that's not saying very much, Hannah Mary, eh?"

A small boy is playing in the garden, attempting to master the art of rolling an iron hoop with a stick. He is not having much success, since the hoop is nearly as big as he is, but he tries again and again. Dressed roughly, but cleanly, a woollen scarf closed over his chest and fastened with a large safety pin in the back. He takes no notice as Inspector Crockett walks down the path and knocks on the door.

She watches from the shadows, willing her heart to resume something like a normal beat. Tiring of his game, he goes to perch on the edge of a low wall to begin peeling a left-over conker he has discovered in the grass, one leg tucked beneath him, one leg dangling, just as he had done so often in her dreams. He looks up and sees her watching him. Her heart stops. "Ludo." And this time he does not disappear.

He slides from the wall and runs towards her so quickly he almost trips and falls. Within seconds, he is in her arms.

"Mama, where have you been?" he asks chidingly.

Chapter Twenty-Four

At much the same time as Hannah was being reunited with her child, a different sort of scene was being enacted in a narrow white house in Leamington Spa, in the crescent where Dora Cashmore and her mother eked out winter lives of genteel poverty. Dusk was falling rapidly, and it was cold, but one had to be careful with coals and oil for the lamps, so there was neither a fire, nor sufficient light either to read, sew, or knit. Dora closed her lending-library book (the tales of Sherlock Holmes, which reading matter her mother considered far too highly coloured and over-exciting for ladies), blew her nose and sighed ostentatiously. She had a cold and was in one of her states – neither an unusual occurrence, but particularly annoying to her mother, who was much less docile and patient with her in private than she was in public.

Aspasia Cashmore was a formidable woman who could not forgive her daughter for failing to catch a husband, something she herself had been brought up from birth to believe was a woman's paramount duty. There was no getting away from the fact Dora was destined to be left, unclaimed, on the shelf, a fate simply too unthinkable for words. It wasn't as if she had never had a chance, woefully plain though she was. On the other hand, if marriage depended on beauty alone, the world would be far less populated than it was at present. One man, at least, had recognised this, and had been prepared to marry her. True, he had been a widower of some forty-four years who needed a mother for his children; he was rather fat and had some unprepossessing habits, but he was of unimpeachable character, being the well-respected vicar of a large parish, and he had not been short of money (inherited from the family manufacture of some unmentionable undergarments – but when one had reached Dora's age and was still a spinster, one couldn't afford to be too choosy). All she had to do was to make herself agreeable. Dora, however, could be tiresomely stubborn at times. She declared that nothing would induce her to marry a man who spoke with his mouth full, spraying one with soup or scrambled egg, and she stubbornly resisted the combined efforts of her mother and the array of formidable aunts whom Aspasia lined up for support. In the end the Reverend had lost patience and gone off and married a chit of a girl straight from the schoolroom, who had already given him another child.

Her mother, of course, knew very well on whom Dora's heart was set, and knew also how doomed, right from the start, had been such hopes. Foolish girl! It would never have occurred to anyone else but Dora – lumpy, unattractive Dora, with her permanent snuffles – that a handsome, sought-after young man like Sebastian Chetwynd might cast even a second glance at someone like her, unless there were money attached. He was always perfectly agreeable – such charming manners – but her unfortunate daughter should have had the sense to realise she had no chance – and perhaps she did, her mother thought, relenting, as Dora mopped her runny nose and sneezed again. Poor Dora. Winter here again already, and the house was so very cold and draughty in the long, dark months.

It would never do to let her see it, but Dora's mother, while impatient of her megrims, was really quite sorry for her. Mrs Cashmore knew what it was like to live in fear of becoming an old maid; moreover, she herself had once had more than a passing fancy for one of the Chetwynds, which had come to nothing, of course. After which, having reached twenty-nine without any other offers, she had been forced to marry beneath her, to give herself to a man in the civil service – a promising young man, it was true, but one who had inconsiderately died before that promise could be fulfilled, leaving her with insufficient means to live in the manner to which she thought she and her daughter were entitled. Their present penny-pinching existence was a matter of expediency, depending much on the hospitality of Adèle Chetwynd and her like. None of their other relatives, however, were as accommodating and generous as Adèle was in their rounds of visits, and for that reason, Mrs Cashmore felt she owed her at least a little allegiance – and now, here was Dora, snivelling and threatening to spoil everything by making these ridiculous claims...

"Fiddlesticks!" she said briskly. "You couldn't possibly have seen Monty Chetwynd's motorcar when we were returning from Cousin Agatha's. He didn't arrive at the Abbey until seven and it was a quarter to five when we got back."

"But I did see it. It was parked just inside the entrance to the bridle path that leads the back way down to the house. It was just under the trees but that yellow colour made it quite visible," Dora insisted. "One can hardly mistake it – it's an 18 h.p. Siddeley, with a long body," she went on, revealing such a hitherto unexpected knowledge of motorcars that Mrs Cashmore stared at her in undisguised amazement. "Oh, fancy, riding in one of those! Or even learning to drive —"

"Don't be a fool, Dora," said her mother, recovering herself before Dora should get entirely carried away. "I didn't see it." As if that settled the matter.

"Well, I did," Dora reiterated stubbornly. "It was right under the trees and I wouldn't have noticed it either if the sun hadn't made its first appearance that day and shone on it just as we came round the corner. I only caught a gleam, but it made me turn my head round to get a good look – and I'm quite *sure* I wasn't mistaken. He may have arrived at the house at six or seven, or whenever he was supposed to have done, but he was certainly in the vicinity before then."

"What," said her mother, recovering herself, "are you suggesting?"

"The police were very anxious to know exactly where everyone was from about four o'clock that afternoon, were they not? And if he wasn't motoring down from London, as he said, then he could have been at Belmonde, which he said he wasn't," she finished rather incoherently.

"Are you implying that Monty Chetwynd had something to do with this murder?" Mrs Cashmore's disbelief was immeasurable.

"Mama, I am not implying anything. It's up to the police to do that, and to find out what Mr Chetwynd meant by not telling the truth. If he is innocent, then he has nothing to fear."

"You read too many of those silly books, Dora."

But Mrs Cashmore was thinking of Monty, all those years ago, and the hopes she herself had entertained. And the way she had been treated, with much less kindness than Dora had been treated by Sebastian, simply through being ignored, or withered by a perfectly annihilating look from those light eyes.

"I am going to write," announced Dora with sudden determination, "to the man who was in charge – Inspector Meredith – and tell him what I saw."

For a moment the mother faced her daughter's implacability. Was there – could there be – the slightest element of revenge in Dora's intentions? Perhaps not, but it had sparked an idea of her own. "Oh no, Dora," she replied after a moment, smiling. At last, after all these years, was an opportunity to – well, she didn't quite like to say get her own back, but that was what she thought. "I think it's Monty Chetwynd we should write to."

And it was then that her daughter disconcerted Aspasia Cashmore even more than she had already done. "If you think I am going to be a party to blackmail, Mama, I assure you, you are quite mistaken."

What had meeting Hannah, after all, accomplished? Crockett asked himself, thoroughly disgruntled. Everything in the world, of course, from Hannah's point of view. Very little from his own, at least in terms of direct evidence. The mystery of Hannah Smith was solved but the bigger question – who had killed Rosa Tartaryan? – remained. And yet he felt a pricking in his thumbs that told him he was close on the heels of the murderer, all the more frustrating because the solution felt so tantalisingly to be just beyond his reach.

He viewed his list of suspects despondently. Two. That is, if you counted Jordan, against whom nothing could realistically be proven, or even suspected, who could scarcely have had any reason for killing Rosa Tartaryan, other than a brainstorm.

And the other…

Sir Henry was reputedly possessed by dark moods. He'd been out in the woods at the same time as Rosa. He had a motive of sorts – but was it enough, sufficient for him to think of committing murder? Probably not, in fact highly unlikely, if it was a mere question of bringing to light his son's illegitimate child. Crockett couldn't, however, discount the effect on him of the shame and disgrace brought on the family name if it were rumoured that they had tried to cover up their late son's indiscretions in the way they had – by denying knowledge of Hannah, by keeping mother and child apart. And now that the child was known to be legitimate, the censure would be greater. That Sir Henry himself had been involved in any such arrangements may not be true, but did that matter? Scandals had been generated by much less. No smoke without fire. It would be like manna from heaven to the society gossips. To a man like Sir Henry, who saw himself as a man of honour – and had evidently always acted that way, no matter how volatile his temper – disgrace in the eyes of the world would hurt him as nothing else could. And by extension, the same would apply to Adèle, his wife, and to his daughter, Sylvia: a ruined reputation was social suicide. Crockett thought he might very well have been persuaded to take the ultimate step.

But to accuse a man of murder, you had to have more than suspicions, and as yet there was nothing. No witnesses, nothing in the way of material evidence...no clues, except, perhaps, the doubtful silk scarf.

He chewed over the facts again and again, without getting any further. The medical evidence, for instance, showed that the body had lain for some time after death before being moved and put in the stream – and why that had been necessary seemed inexplicable. And in any case, where exactly had the murder been committed? Both house and grounds had been gone over and had revealed nothing, though the search had been necessarily superficial. Finding a bloodstain or two, a concealed weapon, would have been impossible in grounds so extensive, in a sprawling edifice like Belmonde Abbey.

Crockett rubbed his face. He wasn't easily cast down at any time, but his wasn't the sort of case he was used to. Give him the straightforward sort of villainy he had to deal with in the Smoke, something you could get your teeth into. There were undertones and nuances here he couldn't understand. Just thinking about them gave him a headache.

And then he received that extraordinary letter, forwarded by Meredith.

* * *

A feeling of melancholy premonition hung over Sebastian as he drove down to Belmonde. He should have been – *was*, he corrected, and smiled, despite his gloom – happier than ever before in his life, gloriously happy. The time was fast approaching when he would be taking up his new career, and Wagstaffe was more encouraging every time they met. The sense of euphoria this had brought had caused Sebastian to throw caution to the winds and ask Louisa to marry him. To his delighted astonishment she had accepted his proposal with joy. It was almost as if it were something she had been waiting for and had nearly ceased to expect…for she had had the problem of combining her future as a doctor with that of a wife already arranged and settled to her satisfaction in her mind. They would be married as soon as she was qualified and he was settled into his new life. He had telephoned to tell his family, and they had accepted the news with resignation, if not with unparalleled joy. They were, after all, very fond of Louisa. His grandmother had gone further – asked him to come down so that she could pass on her own ruby and diamond engagement ring for Louisa and discuss the transference of the sum she had intended to leave Sebastian on her death to his own bank account.

But despite this the cloud, somewhat bigger than a man's hand, which had settled on him since the revelations of what Sylvia had done to conceal Harry's mistress – and his son – would not lift. Sebastian couldn't endure to let matters stand at that. He had at last taken charge of his life and it had given him a new assurance. He had better clear the air by going down to Belmonde, and look sharp about it. He made hurried arrangements with Louisa and set off on the tedious trek, no light undertaking at any time. It had been a very cold and uncomfortable journey, despite his leather coat and his fur-lined boots. There was a thin covering of snow when he arrived.

As he passed the place where he had first seen the woman he now knew to have been Rosa Tartaryan, he was stirred by the same frisson of unease. His feeling then that she had been there because of Harry had turned out to be correct – only she'd been the wrong woman. All his ideas had been turned on their head. After the shocks about Sylvia delivered by Crockett that day in his rooms – the whole scene was burned forever into his memory; he could still smell Sylvia's perfume, see the flames curling round the coals in the fireplace – he had been further stunned when Crockett had told them of his suspicions regarding some letters Sir Henry had received. He could no more accept the inevitable conclusion, that his father – his father! – had murdered Rosa because of them – than Sylvia could. She had become almost hysterical at the very idea and swore she had acted entirely off her own initiative. It was true that Monty had helped her to find Rosa, but their father knew nothing of what she had done.

When Sebastian reached the house, he saw Monty's motorcar drawn up beside the front door. He hadn't known his uncle was to be here, and wasn't sure whether he welcomed it or not.

Adèle and Monty. Something he hadn't wanted to think about, over the last few days. He had always known his mother had for Monty a little *tendresse*, as Sylvia might have put it. But those few, speaking moments in the street, under the lamplight, had left him in little doubt that there was more to it – perhaps a great deal more – than that.

Then he remembered the little scene between them both in the stable yard, just after the body had been discovered, which had not left quite the same impression. And suddenly remembered something else, too. He put his hand into his pocket – the same tweed jacket he had been wearing that day. Yes, it was still there, the onyx cuff-link he had picked out of the ferns around the pool in the grotto. One of a pair, along with the matching cravat-pin, that Adèle had given Monty some time ago for Christmas. The same Christmas he had given her a Liberty scarf and a decadent-looking hair ornament in the shape of a naked woman with mermaid's tail and long, winding hair.

When Crockett saw the letter which had been sent to Meredith, he had to make an effort to recall who the Cashmores were. Of course. The women who had left Belmonde immediately after the murder, the ones the servants had recalled as that terrible old woman and her downtrodden daughter. The tone of the letter was, however, anything but downtrodden, though the idea of a spinster lady like Dora Cashmore knowing so much about motorcars was slightly comical. Meredith had with confidence declared that no other such vehicle as she had described was owned by anyone in the vicinity – but one as recognisable as that would surely have been seen and remarked on by someone, somewhere. He would make enquiries. Crockett's own enquiries quickly revealed that Monty Chetwynd did in fact own an 18 h.p. Siddeley, its coachwork painted yellow to order.

It was already dark, and viewed from outside, the scene through the drawing room window was like a tableau, caught by the camera obscura, the figures elegantly disposed in the pretty, delicately coloured room, lit by the golden light of the silk-shaded lamps. They were having tea. Monty leant with one elbow on the mantel, his teacup and saucer balanced in his other hand. Lady Emily sat stiffly upright in a chair by the brightly burning fire. His mother, presiding over the teacups, was graceful as a fashion plate in a soft wool midnight-blue dress, high-waisted, trimmed with a fall of ecru lace, with several ropes of pearls round her long, slender neck. Every inch the fashionable socialite, with her dark, sparkling eyes and that subtle smile with its hint of wilfulness. But when he entered the room, amid cries of surprise and welcome, he immediately detected signs of strain in her. Despite, or perhaps because of this, she still looked very beautiful.

She poured him a cup of tea and offered lemon, the rings sparkling on her fingers as they moved prettily amongst the china. Sebastian, who would rather have had brandy after his freezing journey down, nevertheless accepted the hot tea gratefully. Today there were crumpets, and buttered toast.

"Why did you not bring Louisa with you?" asked Lady Emily, prepared, now that the engagement, which she could do nothing to prevent – and perhaps didn't wish to, now – was a *fait accompli*. For once, she looked her age. Her hand actually trembled a little as she lifted her teacup, but she still smiled charmingly from under her royal fringe.

"Oh, she has lectures." His mother's eyebrows rose a little, but she smiled. Sebastian was pleased that there had been so little opposition from her. Louisa had always been a favourite, and he knew she had long ago accepted it had never, after all, been certain that Sebastian would do the sensible thing and marry well. If he could turn down such an attractive proposition as Violet Clerihugh, there was no hope for him.

Everything seemed the same. Tea and civilised conversation. A bright fire and comfortable chairs. Yet the very air breathed tension.

"Would you like me to play some Debussy?" asked Adèle, when the tea had been disposed of and removed. A little music was a ritual after tea, when everyone sat back for digestion and a little relaxation. Monty nodded, but Sebastian shrugged: he didn't care for impressionist music. "Try this prelude," she said, smiling at him. Her slender fingers moved across the keys and the precise, clear, yet haunting notes dropped like the first cold drops of a storm into the room.

Afterwards, in the silence, Sebastian cleared his throat and braced himself. "I came down on the spur of the moment," he began, "because something has happened which you will have to know about."

The wind was taken out of his sails when Monty said drily, "Dear boy, if you've come down to tell them about Sylvia's little indiscretion, you might have saved yourself a journey."

"Monty has told us everything," Adèle said, speaking rather fast, before Sebastian could get his breath back at that understatement, to say the least, of Sylvia's actions. "Who would have a daughter like Sylvia? Causing such trouble!"

Sebastian thought a good deal of it had been caused by Monty, too, in his abysmal choice of companion-housekeeper for Hannah, but a glance at his uncle's face, wearing that ironic, yet decidedly closed expression at the moment, forbade him to say so.

"If I were Algy," continued his mother, "I'd take her up to Scotland to that shooting box place he has there, where she can do no harm, and make her live on nothing but porridge." Adèle's conversation was often flippant, a cover for emotion. With a further touch of bravado, she added, "And now she's presented her father with a little heir – not hers of course. I wonder when we shall see him? Soon, I hope."

"I believe his mother is taking him up to Yorkshire to see – her family."

"*Yorkshire?*" But Adèle said no more, only made a little reprise of the last bars she had been playing on the piano.

Footsteps sounded outside. Sir Henry came in, followed by the unexpected appearance of Inspector Meredith, red-faced and stout in his navy blue uniform, and behind him the flashy London detective, cockily assured as usual. Adèle sat, still as a statue, her hands motionless.

"These gentlemen," said Sir Henry, "inform me they have more to say on the subject of that murder and wish to speak to us all."

"I thought everything about that had already been said," Monty drawled.

"Begging your pardon sir," said Crockett, "but much has happened since I was here last, concerning your family. Perhaps it needs explaining before we start."

Sebastian looked at his mother. "There's no need for that, Mr Crockett. My uncle here had already told them everything before I came."

"Then that should make my task easier."

"What task is that, Inspector?" asked Monty.

"The task of, shall we say, unmasking the killer of Rosa Tartaryan."

A silence you could cut with a knife followed his words. It seemed to Sebastian that the thin, shivery notes of the Debussy prelude still splintered the air.

"Please sit down, gentlemen," Adèle said, recovering herself, "and tell us how we can help, though I don't see how we can. The woman was a blackmailer, you know, and blackmailers might expect to come to a bad end." For some reason, her transatlantic vowels were suddenly more apparent.

"Whatever she was, she is dead, and deserves your pity, Lady Chetwynd." She had the grace to look ashamed, coloured very slightly and looked down at her hands. "My business here is to find out how she was murdered and who did it."

There was a certainty and a confidence about Crockett that silenced further comment.

"How do you propose to do that?" asked Sir Henry at last.

"Supposing we forget the statements you all made earlier," he answered agreeably, "and work on a supposition I've put together. Nothing laid down in tablets of stone, you understand, just a hypothesis." He clasped a leg around his other knee, an awkward posture he apparently felt quite comfortable with. "Let's start with the supposition, Mr Chetwynd," he went on, addressing Monty, "that you arrived at Belmonde much earlier than you did – several hours earlier, perhaps. That you left your motor car under the trees just off the road, where the ride begins that leads into the woods, and then walked to the house and entered unannounced. Where Rosa Tartaryan – and you, Sir Henry, were waiting, and also —"

Sir Henry began to bluster, but Monty signalled him to be silent. His own eyes, watchful as a cat's, never wavered.

"— and also, Lady Chetwynd."

Sebastian stared at his mother. She had grown quite white. "What makes you say my mother was involved in anything like this?"

"Oh," Crockett said "The matter of a scarf, found near the body."

"I lost it," Adèle said, "days before, when I was out walking in the woods."

"Is that so? Well, never mind that for the moment. Where was I? Oh yes, Rosa. She was a young woman of strong character, you know, and she lived and worked for the liberation of her country. It's a well-known fact that the Armenian exiles here are always short of money for their cause, and Rosa's commitment to her beliefs was so strong she was prepared to do anything to get hold of some. How and why she was blackmailing you, Sir Henry, is no longer any concern of mine. Only that she was – and that it may have proved the motive for her death."

"Never have I heard anything so preposterous!" blustered Henry.

"We shall see." Crockett smiled, still master of the situation, and enjoying it, but his voice hardened as he went on. "The medical reports state that Rosa had suffered an injury to the side of her head, but the cause of her death was manual strangulation. After she died, she was left where she was for some hours, before being removed to where she was found, in the stream by the bothy. I suggest she died in this house, that she was brought here purposely to meet her death. I believe it was planned. Did you not kill her, Sir Henry, because she was becoming outrageous in her demands, and then with your brother's help, carry her to the stream and dump her there like so much rubbish?"

"I did not kill her for that or any other reason," Sir Henry said, his face congested, his dark brows drawn together. "Yes, I will admit that I foolishly paid money to her, thinking that would hush up the matter of my son's illegitimate child. I did not know the full circumstances then, but I was prepared to do what I could to support both mother and child. As it is, now, I shall acknowledge him as my heir, and be proud to do so."

"Well said, Sir Henry. But the fact remains that someone killed Rosa. Deliberately put their hands around her throat and strangled the life out of her."

"No!" said Adèle, in a voice which, though low, was heard by everyone, "It wasn't like that at all!" Her face had grown ashen. Her breath came fast and shallow. "It was an accident."

Sebastian went to her, knelt and took her hands. "Mother."

"Adèle!" At the same time as Sebastian spoke, the warning came simultaneously from Sir Henry and his brother. Her husky voice trembled with the force of her emotions, but she was not to be stopped. "She came as you said, Inspector – she was brought here with false promises – an offer to help her with enough real money to ensure she would keep silent..."

"Be silent yourself, Adèle, or you may be sorry," said Monty. Henry looked beside himself. Lady Emily's face had gone as grey as her hair.

"I *will* tell them, Monty. I will. There's to be an end to it. I don't want to live a life founded on lies any longer."

"Very well," he said. "I can't stop you. But let us not get carried away. Let's take it calmly, what?" He patted his pockets for his cigarette case and not finding it, walked stiffly to the credence table by the door and took a Turkish cigarette from the silver box there. He held up the box to Adèle, who waved it away, before lighting his own cigarette and drawing deeply on it. The smoke went down the wrong way. He began to cough and could hardly give up. "Excuse me…a glass of water," he gasped, and hurried from the room.

It was Meredith, hitherto silent in the background, concentrating on following where the story was leading, who was the first to realise what had happened. He reached out for the door, and was clutching the knob when the door was pulled sharply to from the other side and it slipped from his grasp. He wrenched the door open again and rushed after Monty into the hall.

But Monty was faster, and fitter – and moreover knew where he was headed. Meredith, confronted in the big hall with corridors and doors leading he knew not where, came to a baffled halt.

Sebastian was propelled by instinct. The instant Monty left the room, knowing the French window was kept locked in the winter, he went for the side window. The sash was stiff, but he used the heels of his hands, and it shot open. He climbed easily out on to the sill and dropped down on to the soft earth below. He sprinted diagonally across the parterre at the front of the house towards the wing where the business room was.

The gun-room, through the door behind his father's desk, was locked from the other side. "Monty!" he shouted, rattling the knob.

There was no answer. With rising panic, he shouted and rattled again, put his shoulder to the door, but it wouldn't give. He could hear sounds of movement in the room beyond… And then, finally, the single shot. And after that, silence.

Chapter Twenty-Five

Crockett, back at Scotland Yard, looking through the statements made by Sir Henry Chetwynd and his wife prior to writing up his report, thought the solution to Rosa's murder had, after all, been simple enough.

Sir Henry's statement was laboured and short to the point of brusqueness, Adèle's a more longer exposition of what she'd first, haltingly, told him, as soon as she was able after the first shock of her brother-in-law's death.

She had affirmed that Monty had indeed arrived at Belmonde some hours before his admission to the house by Blythe. He had left his motorcar hidden under the trees and walked along to the house, letting himself into what they called the fernery, a gloomy little corner wedged in between two wings of the house, where she was waiting. Henry had been keeping watch for Rosa Tartaryan from the business room window, in order to intercept her before she could announce herself at the door, ready to bring her into the fernery by its front entrance. After they arrived, both doors of the windowless room were locked – which was fortunate, because while they were there someone who later turned out to be Blythe had made strenuous efforts to open the notoriously badly-fitting door (which he had, in fact, had repaired the following day).

Rosa had been brought down to Belmonde on the pretext of meeting Sir Henry and coming to some arrangement regarding Hannah and her child. But it was evident from the first that she had been lying about acting for her mistress, Lady Chetwynd had said contemptuously. Monty accused her of wanting the money for herself, and told her she would not get another penny from them.

"She went for him like a little cat. She would have scratched his eyes out had he not taken hold of her. It was only a little shake. But when he let go, she fell and hit her head on the basin. She was hanging over the water and seemed to have fainted, and I said, 'Splash her with water, that'll bring her round.' He took hold of her, he had his back to me, and then…then he turned round and said, 'She's dead.'"

"Dipped her head in the water – but put her too far in, don't you see?" said Sir Henry flatly. "She drowned."

"Let me tell you she didn't drown," Crockett had said, "she was dead before she was ever pushed into the water – and not from the wound she got on her head when she fell, but because that 'little shake' your brother gave her – with his hands around her throat – had already killed her."

Henry had rested his eyes on his wife with a look Crockett could not fathom. "Oh, my dear God," she said.

"Well, we weren't to know that, Adèle," said her husband. He turned to face Crockett. "All I thought of was getting her out of the house. It was Monty who suggested we put her in the stream, to make it look as though she'd fallen in and drowned there. Medical people can tell how somebody died, can't they? We couldn't carry her to the stream in daylight, so we left her where she was with the doors locked, and waited to do that until about midnight."

Crockett thought about how the case might be presented.

Chetwynd had taken care to conceal the true time of his arrival at Belmonde – did this mean he anticipated the murder? Probably not. The statements of Lady Chetwynd and her husband, when put together, rang true enough to confirm that it was not premeditated. That it *was* murder, however, was clear enough in Crockett's own mind. All the same, he thought Monty might have got away with a plea of manslaughter. A little distortion of the true facts by the two witnesses, combined with his otherwise unblemished reputation; his knowledge of the law and how to get round it, and Chetwynd would not have hanged. But it would certainly have put an end to his career. He had preferred to take the way out which he had done, and by an impulsive and unnecessary action, defeated the gallows, rather than face a trial where all the dirty washing would have been brought out for public inspection.

The statements of Sir Henry and his wife supported one another. They had been the only witnesses to the crime. But there was nothing to say the statements had provided the whole truth. Collusion was a word which had crept into Crockett's mind and stayed there. Collusion between Sylvia and her uncle, between Sir Henry and Monty in enticing Rosa to Belmond, in getting the body to the place where it was found. Something had passed between husband and wife when they were describing the murder. He thought of the indomitable will he had sensed in her. He thought of those strong, piano-playing fingers. He thought of the confession she had been about to make which Monty had prevented by what he had done. Perhaps Monty's action had not been as cowardly as might have been supposed. Perhaps, in the end, he had been a hero.

But only Sir Henry Chetwynd would ever be able to prove otherwise, and he would never tell.

Crockett finished his report and put it aside. He had in a way been deprived of his quarry, but that was a disappointment he had to swallow. He was going to see Agnes tonight, take her to the theatre and to supper afterwards. He would have the little pearl and garnet ring in his pocket, and this time he wasn't going to take no for an answer. She at least wasn't going to be allowed to slip through his fingers.

"But my dears," said Lady Emily, taking charge of the situation as usual, "your mother has done the best thing by going home to her father in America for a while. Taking Sylvia with her, what's more. Sylvia can be of an ungovernable and headstrong disposition if she doesn't have her own way, and it's a pity they haven't got on better – they need to be together for a while. And when they come home, everyone will have forgotten."

"Not everyone," said Sebastian. "What about us?"

"We shall not forget, my dear, how could we? But we must not permit our lives to be ruined by what has happened. Remember why your mother wanted it all brought out into the open? A family life founded on lies – that is what she said, did she not? – is a life not worth living. Monty..." Her voice almost broke, her shoulders sagged, just a little. Then she pulled herself together and sat up straight, looking wonderfully regal in her pearl choker. "Monty did what he had to. There will be gossip, a great deal of talk as to why he – did what he did, but he saved the family from so much worse than that."

She met Sebastian's eyes. She had known about Monty and his

mother. He put his hand in his pocket and felt the cuff-link. He hadn't handed it over to Crockett; he hadn't thought it would prove anything, but it didn't matter now.

I did not imagine there would ever be such joy again for me. When Dr Harvill suggested that my long memory lapse was in fact a retreat from reality, a refusal to accept painful truths, I didn't want to believe him, but I think now he was right. I feel free, at last.

We are to go to Yorkshire for a while. I shall meet Lyddie's mother and father again, and perhaps they'll forgive me for my lack of courage in refusing to see them before now. Ned says there is no perhaps about it, and in my heart I believe what he says. I am not yet quite as confident as I was before, and I'm coming to realise I can rely more and more on his judgement.

I have not yet found the courage to meet Harry's family, other than Sebastian – and Louisa, who is the only one who remembers the grief and terror of Mafeking.

Harry's father, especially, wishes to meet Ludo. He has written me a short, and on the face of it curt, letter, but Sebastian laughed and said one must learn to read between the lines of anything his father writes or says, and that he is more than ready to welcome Ludo with open arms. Sebastian, relieved now of the burden of being the heir to the Belmonde title and estate, welcomes the idea even more, but I view the prospect with not a little alarm. Whatever happens, though, I will not let him be taken from me.

Meanwhile, there is Bridge End again. It's spring, and the forsythias will be in bloom.